Capriccio: A Novel

2nd edition

A tale of Literary Lovers for Lovers of Literature

Based on a True Story

Dina Davis

Shortlisted for the NT Chief Minister's Best Fiction Award 2020

© Dina Davis 2019

Dina Davis asserts the moral right to be identified as the author of
'Capriccio: A Novel - A tale of Literary Lovers for Lovers of Literature'.

Cover design and typeset by Green Avenue Design.

Author Photo by Bella Davis

2nd Edition
Hardback ISBN: 978-0-6485587-0-5
Paperback ISBN: 978-0-6487566-7-5

Published by Cilento Publishing, Sydney Australia.

First published 2018
IngramSpark Edition ISBN: 978-0-6482398-8-8
Amazon Edition ISBN: 978-0-6482398-9-5
Amazon Kindle ISBN: 978-0-6483932-0-7

Dedicated to the memory of
Lucy Anne Lieberman, 1993 — 2009

Disclaimer

While the main text of *Capriccio: A Novel* is entirely a work of fiction, this second edition contains supplementary non-fiction material in the form of a Prelude, Coda, Appendices and Bibliography.

However, the characters, dialogue, and interactions between the characters in the novel itself, are entirely the products of the author's imagination.

❋

PRELUDE

Who was the real Assia Gutmann Wevill? Was she a temptress, seducer of husbands, sensation-seeker, or a woman much maligned, hated even, for her unusual beauty, her strange accent, her airs and graces – in short, because of her otherness?

In today's age of the 'MeToo' movement, it is unthinkable that a woman who'd been subject to abuse, emotional and social, would be shunned, ignored, and even blamed for the suicide of her rival in love, Sylvia Plath.

In the many biographies of Ted Hughes and Sylvia Plath, a brief chapter, or sometimes only a paragraph, is devoted to this "other woman" – evidence in itself of the contempt in which she was held by the literati. Unlike the other famous protagonists in this notorious love triangle, Assia has largely been written out of history.

Only one writer, Australia's poet Peter Porter, acknowledges that Assia was 'natural and straightforward, with wit, charm and generosity – never in [my] eyes the *femme fatale*.' (The Guardian, 28 October 2006).

Ted Hughes's sequence of poems about Assia, *Capriccio*, have inspired this story, and given the book its title. Extensive research has contributed to *Capriccio: A Novel*, while it is entirely a work of fiction.

❖

Winter End, Hertfordshire

To see again and no more

The black northern pond,

Its autumn spent

Its eye burning with crippled cedar wings

And four black feet deep with

Summer's rotting rooks,

Like Thomas Head's and my time's

Unlamented, springless, past.

– Assia Gutmann Wevill

Quoted with permission of Celia Chaikin

❋

Contents

'The bird flies itself to the hunter....
but who's the hunter, and who's the bird in this case?'

Fyodor Dostoevsky, The Double.

CHAPTER 1

Tel Aviv, 1936 — 1943

To Esther, everything in this new place seems the wrong way around. Even the writing runs from right to left, and books start from the back instead of the front. There's a feeling of the desert encroaching on the edge of this bourgeoning city, where the Arab markets flourish next to European restaurants. Sand seeps into the streets, into the cracks of the newly laid concrete footpaths.

In Tel Aviv, young Esther doesn't fit in straight away. Some say she and her younger sister, Hannah, are not of the faith, because their mother is a Gentile. The fact that Esther's father, Yacov is a Russian Jew counts for nothing according to the Orthodoxy. In Palestine being Jewish means acceptance, whereas in Germany it is a death sentence.

By the time she's eight, Esther is speaking Hebrew almost fluently, although she has difficulty writing and reading its spidery letters sprawling across the page backwards. Because Palestine is under British rule, the sisters have to learn English for three hours a week, although the language of instruction is Hebrew. Esther soon adds English to her German, Italian and Hebrew.

The family lives in Balfour Street, named after a British politician. Their mother, Trudi, likes the sound of the street's name, its clean English consonants. The cosmopolitan atmosphere of the city soothes Trudi's homesickness.

'Come, girls, we'll go for ice cream at the beach,' Trudi says to her daughters, shortly after their arrival in Tel Aviv. 'The sun is shining, so perhaps we'll go for a dip in the ocean.' The two girls scream with excitement, and run to get their swimming costumes.

'Mutti, can I wear that new skirt over my costume?' says Esther, preening herself in front of the wardrobe mirror in their little flat.

Trudi laughs. 'You're much too young to be worrying about your looks, child; wait another ten years, and we'll see. Now be a good girl and put on your beach dress, like Hannah.'

'No, I won't! I want to wear my new blue skirt, the one with lace at the bottom.' Esther stamps her foot, threatening a tantrum.

Her mother sighs, and decides to give in this time. Her elder daughter is proving a challenge, and such disobedience must be checked. Still, she reflects, she's turning into a beauty, so perhaps she'll get away with her wild nature.

Trudi, Esther and Hannah set off for the beachfront, where cafés of every nationality are starting to spring up. 'Look, Mutti, this one has gelato, like in Pisa,' cries Esther. Having got her own way with the frilly skirt, she expects to do the same in the choice of café.

But Trudi is already guiding the children to a *kaffeehaus*, which proclaims in big German letters that it serves real coffee, with strudel or *kugelhopf*. Esther's eyes go to the cake counter with its strudel and cheesecake, and the gelato is forgotten.

❀

Yacov loses no time in setting up his practice as an orthopaedic specialist. His patients are mostly fervent Zionists, often non-religious, who've come with their hopes and dreams, as well as the strength in their bodies, to create this new homeland. Because he speaks Yiddish, many of the older generation flock to him, their backs aching from clearing the land or building new houses. His surgery, held in the front rooms of their spacious apartment, is always full. Soon the family's fortunes improve.

For Trudi life here is not always easy. Non-Jewish Germans are viewed with distrust. There is always the danger that the British, now at war with Germany, could arrest Trudi and her daughters. Esther's mother becomes increasingly unhappy in Palestine, feeling always a foreigner in a hostile land.

❀

In the school playground, Esther and her new friend Rivke share lunch, and stories.

'After we left Berlin, we went to Italy first, to a place called Pisa,' Esther tells Rivke. 'I made a special friend and she taught me words in Italian. Her name was Aurora, and I cried when we had to leave. She was my best friend then, but now you are.'

Rivke is quiet for a moment, before she answers in her native German. 'I had a best friend in Munich, called Lotte, but she got taken away by the soldiers, with my Aunty Leah and my *Zaida* — my grand-papa. Some kind friends helped us escape, after Mutti gave them all her money and jewellery. We had to hide and pretend we had different names. But you - how did you get away?'

'It was the middle of the night. I was so scared! We could only take two suitcases onto the train. Hannah screamed when she couldn't take Bruno the Bear. He was much too big, you see, so I gave her my furry rabbit, instead. On the train we both hid under the seat when we heard the soldiers' boots outside our carriage.'

'You were so lucky, Esther, to get away in time,' Rivke says. 'At our house, two policemen wearing big boots, and with that crooked cross on their coats, banged on our door one night. I was practicing the piano while Mama was in the kitchen. Papa and my brother Stefan were playing chess. The soldiers broke down our door. One of them knocked the chessboard to the floor. All the pieces rolled everywhere. I couldn't believe what was happening; I felt terrified, but all I could think of was getting down on the floor to pick all those chess pieces up.'

Rivke's blue eyes fill with tears. 'One policeman grabbed Papa and twisted his arms behind his back, while the first one kicked poor Papa down here,' she points to her groin. 'Mutti was screaming for them to let him go, so one of them hit her on the face. The worst was when they stood over Stefan and shouted at him to pull down his trousers, or else they'd shoot him, and all of us as well. Poor Stefan went very red, but he didn't cry. When the soldiers saw he was circumcised,' Rivke looks away, her face reddening, 'they laughed, and said, "You're coming with your traitor father, you filthy little Jewboy." Then the soldiers hit Papa and Stefan and took them away. Mutti and I ran to our friends, and they hid us for weeks till we managed to escape. I cry for Papa and Stefan every night.'

Esther is silent. She throws her arms around Rivke. 'You can share my Papa, only you must call him Vati,' she whispers into her friend's ear. Her heart swells with pity.

❈

Yacov is a little in love with his Esther, his first-born, and determined that she and her sister will have the best opportunities money can buy. With her pale creamy skin, delicate features and luminous grey eyes, Esther is becoming a beauty. Yacov wants her to have a top-notch education. At twelve, Esther is enrolled in a private British-run school where only the King's English is taught and spoken. Already Esther aspires to the dignity and *sang-froid* of the English.

Esther loves learning British history and English literature. Hannah chooses to stay at the more religious Hebrew-speaking school, whereas Esther studies Shakespeare, Dickens and the great English poets. Literature becomes her favourite subject, and she impresses her teachers by memorizing and reciting passages from Keats, Wordsworth and Tennyson. Forever after, Esther will speak English with the cut-glass accent of the upper classes, charmingly tinged with her early German and Italian. Her unique accent becomes one of her beauties.

Somehow Esther usually gets what she wants. By age fifteen, she is one of the most popular girls in the British school. All the girls wear short tailored navy skirts with pale pink blouses and dark lisle stockings. Some look dumpy or gawky in this outfit, depending on whether they are short or tall. Esther makes it look like a sample from a Paris fashion house.

At Mendel's the butcher's, Trudi learns a way to get special treatment, and the best cuts of meat. One day she takes her eldest daughter with her. Mendel, a big florid-faced man, leans over the counter and pinches Esther's creamy cheek. '*Du bist sehr schön* — you are very pretty,' he says. He gives Trudi her veal steaks, pounded extra thin for her famous *wiener schnitzel*, at a reduced price.

Esther shrinks from Mendel, especially when he tries to kiss her on the cheek with his wet lips. *Danke schön*, says Trudi. Mendel forgives her for speaking German instead of Hebrew or Yiddish; others in the community don't.

Although disgusted by the butcher's attentions, Esther goes along with the charade for her mother's sake. Soon Mendel wants more than a sloppy peck on the cheek. Esther recoils, her face screwed up in disgust, which excites Mendel even more. She instinctively knows this is part of a game, which she's learning fast, and wills herself into feeling nothing at the touch of his greasy fat fingers. She will draw on this way of numbing her feelings throughout her life.

❧

When Esther is sixteen, she is shocked to find her father weeping at the breakfast table; she's never seen her father cry before. Yacov is reading *Ha'aretz*, Tel Aviv's daily newspaper.

'Come here, *schönele*,' he says, stretching out his arm to draw her to his side. 'Look at this — this hideous photo. You see what those *momzas* are doing to our people?' Now she is shocked; she'd only ever heard her father use that rude word *momza*, which meant something like 'bastards', when he was very angry, and didn't know she was listening.

Yacov is pointing at a full-page spread, a black and white photograph splayed over the newspaper. At first all Esther sees is grainy newsprint, the tiny black and white dots gradually dissolving in front of her eyes into vague shapes. She catches her breath when the shapes become distinct, and she sees contorted bodies, cadaverous in death. There seem to be hundreds of them, naked and skeletal, piled on top of each other like meat at the butcher's, only with less care. Esther is sickened; she doesn't want to look, and turns her head away.

'You must never forget this,' Yacov tells her, staring at the picture with angry, tear-filled eyes. 'If we hadn't left Germany when we did, you and I, Mutti and Hannah, we would all have been starved, tortured, and murdered, just like in this picture. Never forget, *liebling*, these are your people.'

Esther says nothing, putting her arms around Yacov's neck to comfort him. But in her heart she feels bitter. *These corpses are not my people. I want nothing to do with them.*

❈

CHAPTER 2

Tel Aviv, 1943 - 1949

Rivke is a year below Esther in the new school. Unlike Esther, she does not take to the indoctrination into all things British, refusing to speak English unless the teacher insists. Their childhood friendship has evolved into a more distant one. One day the girls walk home together, and Esther decides it's time for Rivke to meet the family.

'Rivke, if you want to be my true friend, will you do anything I tell you to?'

'Anything,' says Rivke breathlessly.

'Well then, listen to me. You can come inside and meet my parents so they know who you are. I'm not allowed to go out on my own at night, but if they think I'm with you, they'll let me go. Understand?'

Rivke nods, speechless, staring adoringly into Esther's eyes.

'Come inside and we can talk to my parents. Mutti knows your mother; that's why you ended up at Miss Tabitha's, because our mothers talked about how excellent the school is. If we're lucky enough to be allowed, we could go to that tea-dance at the Pavilion tonight.'

Inside, Trudi has afternoon tea of homemade Berliner cakes and orangeade ready for her girls, who are always starving after school. Hannah has already taken a big bite out of the sugary cake, and says nothing, her mouth too full for speech.

'Mutti, is it all right if I stay over at Rivke's place tonight? We have a big essay on Shakespeare, and Rivke's got the 'Complete Works' at her house.'

'Couldn't you both stay here and study together? I'm making schnitzels for dinner. You're welcome to stay, Rivke.'

'Yes, please stay, I can show you my horse pictures,' says tomboy Hannah.

'But Mutti, I told you,' Esther says urgently, ignoring her little sister, 'Rivke has all the books we need at her place, and her mama's invited me to have dinner there.'

'Ach, very well. As long as Lotte doesn't mind. And you must help, Esther, even if it's just to lay the table. You know how hard it is for poor Lotte, all on her own. Make sure you pack all your school things for tomorrow.'

Hannah begins to cry. 'Why do you let Essie go to Rivke's? Make them stay here, and we can all play together. Please, Mutti,' she sobs.

'There, there, shoosh little one,' soothes Trudi, 'I have a special treat for you after dinner tonight. We'll read the next chapter of your story-book together, and we can have some *sachertorte* for an extra treat.' She puts her arms around Hannah's plump shoulders. 'Rivke, will you and my Esther take the school bus in the morning?'

Esther gives Rivke a quick kick under the table. Rivke jumps, and says, 'Oh — yes, we'll get the bus together in the morning, Frau Goldberg.'

Trudi, appeased by the 'Frau', smiles at Rivke. 'That's all right, then. And why you don't call me Aunt Trudi? After all, we've known each other such a long time.'

Esther charms Rivke's mother, Lotte Feldmann, entertaining her with fanciful tales, most of which are fabrications, of a grand life back in Berlin. 'We lived in a big three storey house, and had a cook, and a maid. My mother visited the beauty parlour every day, and often we went to the Opera House to see the latest performance. It was always so splendid!' Esther warms to her theme.

'Really, dear?' says Frau Feldmann, 'So you must find life here in Palestine rather dull.'

'Yes, indeed,' Esther replies. 'I do miss the operas and the concerts back in Berlin.'

Lotte Feldmann reflects what a precocious little Miss this friend of Rivke was turning into, and wondered, not for the first time, if she'd done the right thing by letting her Rivke attend the private British school. She worried that Esther, with her airs and graces, might lead her innocent daughter astray.

'Thank you for a sumptuous dinner, Aunt Lotte. May we be excused? We have so much homework to do.'

'Of course, my dear. Off you both go. Don't stay up too late; remember you've got school in the morning. Esther, have you everything you need? I see you remembered to bring your sports bag. Just ask me, if you need to borrow anything.'

In Rivke's bedroom, Esther throws off her school clothes to reveal a short strapless dress underneath her uniform. It's made of cream satin and fringed with coffee-coloured lace. A few silver sequins decorate the bodice. She pulls a shawl of gold silk, lavishly fringed, from her sports bag.

'Where — where did you get that dress? And that adorable shawl?' gasps Rivke, her eyes wide with admiration.

'It's one of Mutti's petticoats,' Esther replies. 'I sewed the sequins on myself.'

'Really? But — but where are you going, dressed up like that?'

'You mean where are *we* going. I told you — the tea dance at the Pavilion. All the British soldiers will be there. It'll be fun, you'll see. You can wear that blue taffeta skirt, the one you got for your birthday. Now, have you got a necklace or a choker I could borrow? Don't look so scared.'

Rivke goes to her dressing table, and opens the top drawer to reveal a tray full of baubles. Esther rummages through them. She pulls out a black velvet choker with a brilliant green brooch pinned to it.

'I'll take this, thanks; it'll look good with my eyes. Now, can we sneak out the back way?'

'But — but it's Mutti 's favourite brooch.' Rivke's voice is small and shaky. 'She'll be angry if she finds it missing.'

'Don't worry, silly,' Esther gives Rivke a quick kiss. 'I promise I'll give it back; it's only a loan, don't you see? Come on, let's go! We can creep down the back stairs. Oh, and put pillows in your bed so your mother thinks we're safely asleep.'

❀

The next day the whole school is called to Assembly, and Miss Tabitha announces in her sternest voice:

'Last night two of our girls were seen at a dance, at the British Servicemen's Pavilion. May I remind all of you that you are under age, and that this reflects very badly on the school? When I find the girls in question, they will be suspended immediately. That applies to any of you who take it into your head to break our school rules. Is that understood? Discretion and dignity, ladies, that is our motto.'

Everyone stares at Esther, and Rivke starts to cry, giving the game away.

❀

As the war in Europe draws to an end, British soldiers are sent to Palestine, to help keep the peace. Palestine is now under British rule. The citizens of Tel Aviv are encouraged to make the soldiers welcome, and even to open their homes to them.

Trudi wastes no time in inviting these eligible young men home. One of them accepts an invitation to the Goldberg home for high tea on a Sunday afternoon.

'Come in, *bitte*,' Trudi effuses, remembering that while her British guests are here, she must not speak German. 'Here my daughters are, they speak the English good. This one my Esther, this my Hannah. Yacov!' She calls for her husband, who is hiding in his study.

Esther comes forward, extending her hand and smiling. She is wearing a freshly ironed dress of white broderie anglaise. Her dark hair is tied back with a pink satin ribbon. The effect is modest and virginal, but the body underneath the dress is that of a young woman.

'How do you do,' says Esther in her upper crust English. 'You are most welcome. May I offer you and your friend some tea and some of Mama's *apfelkuchen*?'

Impressed, the young soldier nods assent. 'Thank you. I'm Sergeant Marshall, but please call me Charles.' He stares at Esther as he speaks, and she smiles prettily.

The family and guests sit at a round table laid with a spotless embroidered cloth, and Trudi's best silver and china. The table's laden with cucumber sandwiches (at Esther's insistence), bowls of nuts, and Trudi's famous *apfelkuchen*. Hannah, shy at twelve years old, holds back, and barely opens her mouth except to put food in it. Yacov finally appears, looks at the visitor over his spectacles, and utters a gruff 'hello'. He notices the soldier looking at Esther, and glares at him.

Esther is cautiously interested in Charles, and confides later to Hannah that he reminds her of Clark Gable, her favourite movie star. She sees herself as a young, glamorous Hedy Lamarr, to whom she does bear a striking resemblance. In his smart uniform Charles looks very different to the sturdy open-shirted boys at the sedate school dances, held once a month under the watchful eyes of teachers and parents. Esther is not attracted to her clammy-handed dance partners, whom she considers uncouth. Nevertheless she displays enough interest to excite these boys, who flock to her.

Yacov is suspicious of his wife's ruse in inviting these British soldiers to her home. He knows she's not above using her prized eldest daughter to help the family get out of Palestine. Trudi wants only the best for her daughters, and should either of them happen to fall in love with a handsome English gentleman, why then, they might marry and be whisked off to England, where the whole family could follow.

And so the dutiful daughter embarks on a flirtation with the handsome sergeant. Her task is almost done before it starts; he is already head over heels in love with her. She protects her virtue, while seducing him with stolen kisses during romantic walks on the beach. It's a little like those earlier times in the butcher's shop, only this time there is more at stake than an extra lamb chop. This time the prize will be a passport to Britain.

❖

CHAPTER 3

The Atlantic, August 1957

Esther had been watching the boy for some time. She was reclining in a striped deckchair, well wrapped in a fleecy blanket against the brisk wind. Oblivious to the pitch and toss of the big ocean liner, she breathed in the sea air, letting the wind whip her dark hair about her face. The book she'd been reading lay open on her lap.

The *SS Strathair* was a newly fitted-out vessel, her hull a brilliant white against the black ocean. Apart from the lone figure leaning on the railing, the wind-swept deck was deserted. Usually at this time of day there would be other passengers lolling in the deckchairs, enjoying the sea breezes, sipping hot beef tea, served by a white-suited waiter.

'We must be the only ones on this boat who aren't sea-sick this morning.' Esther's voice echoed through the surging of the ocean. The young man turned around, surprised out of his reverie, and smiled vaguely in her direction. He said nothing, merely nodding his agreement. He'd been staring into the indigo depths of the ever-moving sea below, as if lost in thought.

'There was hardly anyone at breakfast this morning, did you notice? Even the purser looked a bit green around the gills. At least you and I have our sea legs. D'you think the weather's going to get worse?'

He hesitated for a moment, seeming to struggle for words. 'I hope not, for everyone's sake. Rough weather doesn't worry me, though, except for the wind. I rather like being tossed about.'

'So do I. It's exciting, like being on a roller coaster at the fair without all the noise and fuss. I'm Esther, by the way '

'Oh — and — I'm — I'm Tony.' Even from her distance, Esther could see him blushing.

He looks like a poet, she thought. His face was half-hidden by his coat collar, which he'd turned up against the salt-laden wind. When he looked towards her, she saw a sensitive face, with regular features and deep-set eyes. *Like that handsome film star, Gary Cooper, only younger.*

'Getting a bit blowy out here,' the young man said at last, turning his eyes back to the ocean. 'I'll see you later perhaps.'

Esther said nothing in reply, merely waved and nodded as she watched the boy's progress. He weaved his way along the deck, steadying himself against the railing as the ship rolled. *I wonder where he's from, and why he seems to be travelling all alone? There's something rather attractive about him, although he's so very young. He looks innocent and gentle, so unlike Charles. I'm sure I could coax him out of his shell.*

Tony recognized the lively face, its grey eyes alight, gazing at him with frank interest. She was the same striking woman he'd noticed in the dining room, in the company of a tall man with a military bearing. *Way out of my league*, he thought, as he made his way back to his cabin, where his books awaited him.

❦

Esther felt an affinity with the sea, its everlasting motion, sometimes gentle, sometimes more violent. It seemed to echo her own rapidly changing moods, the volatile energy deep within her.

The ship pitched and tossed from port to starboard, rolling with the rising waves. Earlier that morning she saw a teenage girl standing unsteadily at the ship's railing. Suddenly the girl put her hand to her mouth, and lurched forward, gagging. Out of her mouth there spewed a greenish-yellow fountain, falling in an arc into the sea below. The girl's companion, an older woman, stayed solicitously by her side.

Esther watched with interest, fighting her natural revulsion, as the lady companion led the girl, pale and shaking, towards their cabin. *I've seen so much worse*, she thought, *helping my father in the surgery back home. Thank goodness I have an iron constitution, not like that poor young thing.*

❦

By that evening the sea had settled to a calmer swell, and there were only a few empty chairs at the second sitting in the dining room. Esther noticed the young man she'd met that morning, sitting alone at a table in the corner. As he bent his head over his book, a lock of fine silky hair, the colour of golden sand, fell over his forehead. He looked up as if he felt her gaze, and their eyes met.

'Charles, dear,'Esther said to her husband, who was chatting to the elderly lady on his left, 'could we invite that poor young man to join us? He looks so lonely, sitting there all by himself — and,' she added in a whisper, 'it would be so nice to have some *young* company for a change.'

'Very well, if you're so bored with my company,' Charles replied. There was an edge to his voice, and Esther knew he wasn't joking.

'Don't be so silly, I didn't mean that at all, you know I didn't. Only …I do feel rather sorry for him. I'd ask him myself, only … won't you be a dear, and invite him?'

Charles somewhat mollified by the endearment, didn't answer, but rose stiffly to his feet, saying to the assembled company at their table:

'Do you mind if we ask the young man all on his lonesome over in the corner to join us? My wife here has a habit of adopting stray dogs, she's excessively tender-hearted; to her credit, I suppose.'

The others responded with a few polite murmurs and a general air of acquiescence. Charles ambled over to the table in the corner.

'Sorry to interrupt your reading, young sir. I'm Charles Marshall, at your service. My wife and I would like you to join our table.'

The young man coloured slightly, and got to his feet, still clutching his book.

'I'd be delighted,' he replied, his voice soft, with a Canadian accent. He walked over with Charles to the large round table.

'Good evening' he said quietly. 'Pleased to meet you.'

A ring of faces looked up at him. The diners were waiting for an introduction.

'I'm Tony…' he mumbled. He added a surname too softly to be understood.

'This is my wife, Esther.' Charles turned towards her, and put a proprietorial arm over her shoulder. Tony nodded, trying to avoid Esther's eyes, knowing without looking, that they were fixed on his.

'Actually, we've already met,' Esther said lightly.

'Is that so? You never mentioned it, my dear.' Charles frowned, then chuckled. 'But then, we all have our secrets, eh what?' There were a few titters and nodding of heads.

Charles introduced the other passengers at his table one by one.

'This is Mrs Blomberg, and her companion, Miss Campbell,' he said, indicating a heavily made-up woman on his left, wearing large diamond earrings and a matching necklet, and the plump fair-haired young girl next to her. Esther recognised the girl who'd been seasick that morning, and was surprised to realise she was companion, not charge, of the older woman.

'And may I introduce our young honeymooners, Margaret and Arnold Onslow, who we'll excuse from our canasta game after dinner; I'll wager they have more pleasurable ways to spend their evenings.'

A small frisson rippled round the table. Margaret Onslow bent her blushing head, and Arnold scowled behind his polite nod to Tony.

'So — what takes you to England, young man?' Charles asked, after Tony was seated in the only vacant chair. It happened to be directly opposite Esther. She felt Tony look at her properly for the first time, and met his gaze with an equally frank one. She opened to him, with relief, feeling at last that here was someone she could talk to. Tony did not take his eyes off her.

Charles's question still hung in the air. Tony answered as if in a dream. 'I'm on my way to take up a scholarship at Cambridge.'

'Really? In what discipline, may I ask?'

'English Literature.' Tony replied.

'I knew it!' cried Esther, loudly enough to turn heads. 'I felt sure you were a man of letters.' Esther's voice was rich and deep, its polished vowels suggesting an expensive private school education. Her upper-crust British accent cut across murmured conversations at nearby tables.

The diners looked up from their bowls of soup for a moment, then went back to plying their spoons.

'May I see your book?' Esther went on, ignoring her husband's baleful stare.

Tony felt his face grow hot as he handed the book to her across the table. Taking it, she allowed her hand to brush Tony's lightly.

'Wordsworth — he's one of my favourite English poets. We studied him back in Tel Aviv, where I went to school. Such lovely verses — we called him the nature poet. I've always loved those lines: "I wandered lonely as a cloud that floats on high o'er vales and hills." Do you know, I always thought the word was "wondered", you know, with an "o" rather than an "a", so I had the wrong meaning entirely, or at least not the meaning the poet intended.'

Tony found his voice at last. 'I thought the same at first, and couldn't quite make sense of that verse. English can be a confusing language.'

'Especially for me, as it wasn't my first. German's my mother tongue; I can speak Hebrew too, and some Italian, so sometimes forget what language I'm speaking. From your accent I guess you're from Canada?'

'Indeed. But I was actually born in Japan.'

'Really? How exotic! And a coincidence too —we've been living in Canada for the past six years. Now that Charles has a new appointment in the Economics Department at London University, we're on our way there. I simply can't wait to see those daffodils.' Her voice dropped to a conspiratorial tone, shutting the others out.

'Tell me, do you write poetry yourself?'

A fine fragrance wafted from Esther, of flowers and spices, as exotic as her dark beauty. Tony breathed the scent in, transported.

'I — I scribble a bit, mostly poetry, so I suppose I could call myself a poet,' Tony replied. 'Wordsworth is one of my inspirations, as well as Keats and Shelley. It's strange, isn't it, how we make these poems our talismans.'

'Yes, they're my favourites too. Not forgetting the great Lord Byron, you know? "Roll on, thou deep and dark blue Ocean, — roll!" Those lines were going through my head, when we were on deck this morning.'

Esther lost awareness of those around her. It was as if the two of them were enclosed in their own private space. She was intensely focused, not only in their conversation, but on the man himself.

'Do you think I could see some of your poems, next time we're on deck together?'

Tony felt his face grow hot. He could barely manage a nod. Was this stunning woman actually flirting with him? A married woman, at that. No, surely she was merely being polite.

Esther was dimly aware that Charles was seething, although he presented a calm demeanour to the other passengers. *Damn him, why can't he ever leave me be.* She felt even more determined to pursue her interest in this beautiful boy.

Noticing that Tony was aware of Charles's displeasure, she felt a flutter of panic. She was determined to keep Tony talking, wanting to keep him there.

Charles had turned his attention to the gentleman on his left, and was carrying on a conversation, or rather a lecture, about the state of world politics. The others at the table were eating dessert, and seemed oblivious to Esther's rudeness in ignoring them.

The orchestra was tuning up for a waltz. Turning to the bejewelled woman on his right, Charles invited her to dance. She was not unattractive, and her sequined gown glittered as they moved sedately around the dance floor to the strains of Strauss. Esther pretended to ignore the couple as she listened intently to Tony, who was so engrossed by his love of poetry, he lost his awkward shyness.

An elderly man with silver hair and an elegant moustache approached the table, making a beeline for Esther.

'Excuse me for interrupting. May I have the honour of this dance?' Esther cast a rueful look at Tony, and without smiling, rose to her feet. It would look odd to Charles if she refused the gentleman's offer.

'Actually,' Tony said, standing up suddenly, 'I have some letters to write. It's been good to meet you all. Please excuse me.' He took his leave, bowing slightly. A moment later he was gone.

❋

Back in their cabin, Esther avoided looking at Charles. She could sense his anger seething under the surface, waiting for the moment to erupt. They hadn't stayed for the canasta game. She knew that was a bad sign.

Keeping her voice light, she said, 'Darling, you were so gallant tonight, entertaining Mrs Blomberg. I'm glad you asked her to dance; she must feel lonely without a husband.'

Charles said nothing, glaring at her. She tried a lighter tone.

'Dearest, I'm always happy to share you, as long as it's with some woman who's advanced in years and has several chins.'

'I notice you lost no time encouraging that effeminate young dandy's attentions. Wouldn't be surprised if he bats for the other side, so to speak,' Charles said. 'You don't seem to realize how it must look to everyone. You made a fool of yourself tonight, and of me as well. I'm heartily sick of your flirting so outrageously with every stray man in your line of vision. And what did you mean, you've spoken to that boy already?'

'For heavens sake, Charles, don't tell me you're jealous of me having an innocent conversation about poetry. Who else amongst this tiresome company can I talk to? If you must know, I simply exchanged pleasantries with Tony about us not being seasick, while we were both on deck this morning.'

'I've told you before, your behaviour in company is not only damned rude, it's simply unacceptable. How do you think it makes me look? I'm sick of you making eyes at every man in the room.'

'That's not true, it's they who stare at me — how can I help it? Anyway, I can't take any more of your stupid jealousy. I'll talk to whoever I like. You act as if you own me! Why can't you leave me alone, with your incessant complaints? I hate you!'

❋

CHAPTER 4

The Rose Estate, London, 1961

'Part-furnished apartment in convenient location. Please contact Mr or Mrs L. Wilde at 6 Eliot Court, The Rose Estate.' Esther was reading aloud from the Real Estate notices. She and Tony were spending a lazy morning in bed, still savouring the novelty of being married, and looking for a home they could afford. The extravagance of the little hotel in the middle of London meant baked beans for dinner too often.

The last few years had not been kind to Esther; there was the constant need for subterfuge while she was meeting Tony at every opportunity, and then the long dragged out divorce from Charles. He'd made sure to humiliate her, naming her a cheat and liar in court, and making sure her name was in the newspaper as "the guilty party" to the marriage breakdown. The bitterness and frustration of those years made her union with Tony all the more precious. At last she'd met a man she could truly love; he was gentle, tender, and loved the very same pleasures, physical and intellectual, as did she. The five years between them, making her the elder, only enhanced her contentment.

Tony, snuggled next to Esther under a patchwork quilt, turned and planted a light kiss on Esther's forehead. 'Hang on, show me that ad again,' he said. 'Yes, I thought so. Mr and Mrs L. Wilde. L for Laurence.' His face lit up. 'Surely that couldn't be *the* Larry Wilde?'

'Who, darling?'

'You know — Larry Wilde, the poet everyone's talking about. Just had his first collection published. It's powerful stuff — you'd love it. Nature poetry, mostly, yet quite different to your Keats or Wordsworth.'

'Could be anyone, darling, it's such a common name.'

Tony reached over Esther, picked up the black receiver from the bedside table, and dialled the number.

'We're interested in your ad for tenants,' Tony's voice shook a little. 'When would it be convenient to inspect the flat?' He listened, and said in a firmer voice, 'Three o'clock this afternoon? Perfect. Yes, that sounds good. We'll see you then.'

Esther felt lazy and contented, after a night of lovemaking, and her favourite Sunday morning breakfast in bed: a half grapefruit sprinkled with sugar, accompanied by one or two slices of thick buttery toast with lashings of orange marmalade. And tea, brewed in the silver pot she'd brought with her from house to house. *How delightfully English*, she thought with satisfaction, still enjoying the novelty of being a newcomer to this land.

'I've a feeling it's him,' Tony said. 'When I was at the meeting of The Group last Friday — you know, that rather elite bunch of writers in London — Nathaniel mentioned that Larry Wilde lives near Regent's Park, not far from the Rose Estate. He hardly ever turns up for meetings, but he's a presence there just the same. This looks like we're meant to take the flat, don't you think?'

'You're such a romantic, sweetheart. It's one of the things I love about you. Only one of them, mind you.' She turned to him, drawn by the closeness of his body, and caressed him to an answering arousal. *Sunday morning, how I love it*, she purred to herself.

❧

Some time later, Esther was bathed and dressed, her straight dark hair brushed to brilliance, her large grey eyes subtly enhanced by a touch of dark mascara. The mirror showed a slim, striking woman, wearing a simple grey suit with a jacket nipped at the waist. She'd chosen her outfit with care, anxious to make a good impression.

'Should we take a taxi there, d'you think? What time did she say to come?' When Tony didn't answer, Esther encircled him with her arms, where he sat at his makeshift desk in the corner of their one room. He sighed, and rested his pen.

'What? Oh, about three this afternoon, she said. We can take a bus; there's one goes from near here to The Rose Estate, and then it's just a short walk from there.'

'The Rose Estate! I've always wanted to live around there; it's so pretty, and there are lots of artists and writers around. I begged Charles to find us a place there, but...' Esther stopped, remembering how Tony hated hearing about her first husband, not wanting to start a fight after their lovely, lazy morning.

Esther sighed, and turned back to her dressing table. Which earrings would go with her outfit, the filigree hoops from Tel Aviv, or the burnished silver drops from Burma? In the end she clipped on the small emerald studs from Pisa, to match her eyes, which sometimes turned from grey to green.

❖

Esther and Tony arrived at No.6 Eliot Court promptly at three. The two-decker red 74 bus had taken them almost to the door. Both stood for a moment, looking up at the tall narrow Georgian building, shaded by plane trees. At the ornate art deco entrance, Tony lifted the brass knocker. They heard slow footsteps descending stairs within. A tall young woman, wearing a loose smock over her checked skirt, opened the front door. She had an open face with a welcoming smile.

'Hi, I'm Grace. You must be Mr and Mrs Buchanan?' Her hand was warm and slightly chafed when it grasped Esther's.

'Call me Tony. And this is my wife, Esther.' Tony extended his hand.

Mrs Wilde's grasp was firm. She greeted them with a friendliness they'd not often encountered in this big, impersonal city. Her touch sent a small shiver through Esther. She noticed that the woman's smock was creased and slightly stained, and felt a stab of pity.

Grace led Tony and Esther up the narrow stairs, flight after flight, until they reached the flat on the top floor. She stood awkwardly in the narrow entrance hall, saying, 'Larry will be out in a minute.' At the mention of Larry's name, Tony gave Esther a slight nudge. *It's him,* his silent signal said.

Esther entered first, in a cloud of Dior perfume. The tiny sitting room was filled with books, some piled on makeshift shelves made of two broad planks supported by a brick at either end, others stacked on the floor, or threatening to topple from the arms of the large upholstered chair. Esther was conscious of her smart outfit, next to the rather dowdy, but handsome woman who'd led them both into the small room. *Have I overdressed?* she thought, with a flutter of panic.

She looked up to see a tall man standing by the bookshelves. His face seemed enormous, its rough-hewn features sparking another strange twinge of fear within her. He had a shock of dark brown hair falling over his forehead, almost obscuring his deep-set hazel eyes. His great height filled the room, making it seem even smaller. He was dressed carelessly, in shabby brown corduroy trousers and an old-looking green pullover worn thin at the elbows. Without looking at them directly, he said, 'Just a minute — I'll just get some chairs from the kitchen.' His voice was deep and resonant, with the trace of a North Country accent.

'Darling, this is Mr and Mrs Buchanan — Tony and Esther – they're here to look at the flat.' Grace gave her husband a meaningful look. *Make a good impression — they might be our new tenants,* it said.

'Er — how do you do — I'm Larry. Excuse the mess here, or try to look beyond it, if you will.' The effort of being polite appeared to exhaust him. Esther waited for the appreciative glance she normally received. Unlike most men, this one seemed not to notice her. There was a mere nod in her direction.

'Forgive me, ' Tony said, 'are you *the* Larry Wilde? I've heard mention of the name at a gathering I've been to once or twice, calls itself *The Group.*'

'Indeed I am. Yes, I know *The Group*, mostly good friends of mine. I was at Cambridge with a few of them. Can't get to their meetings all that often, since our daughter was born, but I contribute from time to time.' Larry seemed to relax, and looked at Tony with a new interest.

'But this is a wonderful coincidence.' Tony's voice was high with excitement. 'I must say I'm mightily impressed by your poems; we all are. It's an honour to finally meet the man himself.'

'I assume you write too? What sort of stuff?' said Larry. He looked keenly at Tony.

'Oh, I guess you'd call it confessional poetry. I write under Athony Wells, by the way.'

'Ah, now I know who you are. I liked that piece of yours, 'The Whale Meeting', in the latest Penguin anthology. 'Somewhat in the style of Robert Lowell. ' Larry said. Tony flushed with pleasure.

'Lowell! He's one of my very favourite poets, in fact I had him as a tutor once.' Grace addressed Tony, her face alight.

'Really?' said Tony, as if seeing Grace for the first time. Esther was silent, feeling rather left out of the literary name-dropping. She was piqued that Larry hadn't yet glanced her way. From somewhere close by, she heard a whimper.

'That's our daughter, Fleur,' Grace's face softened. 'I've just put her down for her nap. She'll settle soon.'

The four of them sat rather stiffly on ill-assorted chairs in the flat's cramped sitting room, so close that their knees were almost touching. The two men continued to talk poetry. Grace and Esther were finding it difficult to talk over the men. Looking more closely at Grace, Esther saw a strong-faced, vivacious young woman, her tawny hair pulled back from her face into a chignon, her brown eyes alight with interest. There was a swelling under her smock.

'I see you've noticed,' said Grace, looking down at her hardly perceptible bump. Esther quickly glanced away. 'Yes, there's another one on the way. You can see why we need to move — but this place is a perfect size for a couple such as yourselves.'

'Well, we do like this area, and the convenience of having a small place to look after,' said Esther, 'and I love The Rose Estate, even the name has a certain charm.' Esther's perfectly elocuted vowels contrasted sharply with Grace's broad Boston accent, and Tony's softer Canadian one.

Tony broke in, 'Look, we're both really keen to move out of our hotel, it's somewhat beyond our means at the moment, you see. We're both working as copywriters, and I scribble poetry on the side. I can assure you we'll be good tenants.'

'Yes, I'm quite sure you will. We have another year on the lease,' said Grace, 'so we need someone to take it over from us. This place is on the small side, but we're only leaving because — well, as I said, I'm expecting again, and with little Fleur growing out of her cot, we simply need more space. I guess you two don't have children yet?'

Esther was taken aback by Grace's words; she thought they verged on rudeness. She drew a deep breath before replying.

'Oh no, not yet; we're too busy with our careers to think of complicating our lives with extra responsibilities. Besides, one needs money to raise a family, and right now we're poor as church mice.' Esther's words seemed to strike the right note with Grace.

'We're prepared to drop the rent a little for the right tenants,' Grace said, 'and frankly, you two seem just perfect.'

Esther was aware of the two men deep in conversation. Larry, leaning against the mantelpiece, was showing Tony a book, which the two were poring over. He'd still hardly looked at her. Who was this man, and why was he ignoring her?

Grace stood up suddenly. 'Come, I'll show you the rest of the flat, 'only let's keep our voices down — Fleur's just gone to sleep, and I don't want to wake her.'

As Esther stood to follow Grace, the doorbell rang. Larry and Grace looked at each other. Grace spoke first, sounding annoyed.

'It's probably the man who phoned earlier, wanting to see the place too. I guess he could look at it at the same time.'

'Wait,' Tony looked at Esther. 'What do you think, darling? We'll have to make a decision straight away.' Esther was amazed at this sudden assertiveness; Tony usually left major decisions to her.

'I'll just go downstairs and let this chap in, while you two make up your minds,' said Larry, going towards the door.

'Do you remember,' Esther whispered to Tony, 'that little hotel where we used to meet, whenever I could get away, all those years ago? It was right near here, in Regent's Park. Wouldn't it be romantic to live near there again?'

'More importantly, darling, at least we can afford it.'

Grace went into the kitchen to prepare tea. Esther, following her, noticed she'd taken her hair down, and it hung down to her shoulders, thick and shiny.

'I like the feel of this place, and it's in a perfect location for us,' she said. 'We'd need to see the other rooms first, though.'

'Let's talk about it over tea.' Grace was laying some mis-matched cups and saucers on the tiny table.

In the distance Esther thought she heard the roar of a lion. Grace laughed at her bemused expression. 'Yes, it really is a lion. That's coming from the zoo — we're a stone's throw away from Regent's Park.'

They were interrupted by Larry, ushering in a middle-aged man in a business suit. His tie seemed to be choking him, his neck swelling below his florid face. After a hurried greeting, the three potential tenants followed Grace down the hallway to the small kitchen, which contained a shiny new refrigerator, a stove and sink, and a square table pushed up against the window. Esther noticed that the cupboards above the sink had been freshly painted white, as had the walls throughout, as if to give the illusion of more space.

Across a small hallway there was a bedroom, which was completely filled by a double bed and a small white cot, in which a small child was sleeping. They peeped in. Grace whispered,

'Ssh, I don't want her to wake yet.'

Esther, uncomfortable with the intimate surroundings, stepped back from the sight of the little girl curled sweetly asleep in the white wooden cot. Behind them, the other prospective tenant coughed impatiently.

The only other room was the bathroom at the end of the hall, which had a large claw-footed bath taking up most of the space. The flat was all perfectly clean and bright, although cluttered with furniture.

The gentleman in the suit, having completed his inspection during which he tapped on walls, and turned on taps, took his chequebook from his breast pocket.

'I'll take it. Here's the first month's rent.' His voice, brusque and clipped, matched his three-piece suit. He quickly wrote out a cheque and thrust it at Larry. 'My address and phone number's on the back. Let me know when I can move in.' With that, he was gone, leaving all four looking at each other in astonishment.

'We were about to tell you that this place is perfect for us, and we're ready to take over the lease,' Tony said, 'but I guess it's too late now.' His voice shook slightly with disappointment.

Esther felt flustered, and murmured, 'What a shame, this flat's exactly what we wanted. It's charming.' She was already planning to remove the oilcloth-covered table, and to put a plush velvet sofa in the sitting room instead of those ugly chairs.

Larry stood up. Esther noticed his head almost hit the ceiling. 'And you two seem the ideal tenants. We have no obligation to that man, rude fellow that he is, even though he's left a cheque. If you both really want to take over the lease, I'll make up some story — tell him we've changed our minds — and the flat's yours.' Ceremoniously, he held up the cheque between thumb and forefinger, and after a nod of approval from Grace, tore it in two. He shook Tony by the hand.

'Really? We can take over the lease?'

'We writers look after each other, Tony. We'd rather you keep up the tradition.'

'Let's celebrate with a cup of tea.' Grace sounded jubilant. 'I've made my special cornflour and molasses cookies. Come, we'll sit in the kitchen, that's if we can squeeze around the table.' Grace poured tea, amid a general air of relief.

Tony's eyes were bright with excitement. 'Wherever do you find space to write?' he asked Larry, as they stood in the entrance hall.

'Right here,' said Larry, with a short laugh. 'I put up a card table — it just fits the old Olivetti and a few papers. No one can get in or out the front door when I'm writing.'

'Thank you so much, for letting us have the flat, and for the tea.' Esther felt an urge to reciprocate. 'Why don't you both come to supper next week, so we can talk over the arrangements?'

'We'd love to,' said Grace. 'You don't mind if we bring little Fleur with us, do you?'

'Of course not, we'd love to meet her,' Esther said, smiling.

Grace leaned forward and hugged Esther. The spontaneous gesture took Esther by surprise, and she instinctively pulled back a little.

Larry said nothing, staring into his tea.

❈

CHAPTER 5

Chalk Farm, Saturday, May 1962

Slipping a diaphanous orange chemise over her head, Esther was pleased with the way it complemented her ankle-length skirt with its swirly pattern in yellow, reds and orange. Bending over, she smoothed her sheer nylon stockings, straightening the seams, and slipped dainty red suede court shoes on first one foot, then the other.

'Isn't that outfit rather impractical for a weekend in the country?' Tony asked. 'It'll be muddy out there in Devon, you know.'

'I don't intend to spend time outside anyway, darling,' Esther said, clipping on the byzantine earrings, which matched the gold and green filigree necklace around her neck. She used a kohl stick to draw a fine black line along her lower lid, defining her eyes. She thickened her already dark lashes with black mascara, moistening the tip of the tiny brush with her saliva, watching Tony's gaze reflected behind her own image in the mirror above the dressing table.

'Do me up, darling, will you?' she said, turning her back to Tony, and lifting her silky dark hair from her neck with both hands. Tony sighed. When would his wife ever grow up? He imagined the country house where the Wildes lived, where the rich soil would stick to one's shoes, and the trip to the outside loo would be through brambles and cow pats.

❀

Larry welcomed Esther and Tony at the rusted wrought iron gate at the entrance to Chalk Farm. Esther said nothing, beyond a murmured response to Larry's greeting. She was uncomfortably aware of the contrast between herself in her bold finery, and Grace in her housedress and apron.

'Come in, and please take no notice of our mess. It's just great to see you both; we adore having visitors to Chalk Farm, now that spring has finally come. Come and have the grand tour of the house,' she said to Esther, ' while we leave the men to inspect the garden.'

She led Esther by the hand into the front hallway, where they stopped to admire an antique hallstand.

'We spotted this in the village. Isn't it just perfect? And we got it for a song. I just love the turned legs, and the curve of the mirror. It's kind of speckled, I know, but Larry says he can fix that.'

Esther smiled and nodded. She disliked anything old and dull, and reminiscent of the past. Besides, the hallway was cavernous and cold despite the warm spring day outside. There was a slight smell of damp. She shivered. Grace led her down the dim passage to the living room. It was crowded with furniture, dominated by the well-stocked bookshelves on three sides of the room. The fourth wall had French doors leading to the garden, hung with velvet curtains in a rich red colour.

'How colourful you've made this room. It's quite exotic — such lovely, rich hues,' Esther heard herself gushing. Privately, she was thinking how garish it all looked, with those lurid red curtains right to the floor. The whole effect struck her as rather like a Spanish bordello.

'Red wasn't my first choice at all. But something happened the other day that kind of dictated the décor. Larry dragged in a rabbit, freshly killed, still bleeding.

'So — you dyed all the curtains blood colour?'

'Oh no, I knew there was no chance of getting the colour right, and anyway the process is too messy. I went out that very day and bought reams of that red. Now I quite like the colour, and I've painted the bedroom walls red, too. It reminds me of back home. Where I come from bright shades are popular; it seems to me the English have a fetish for blandness.'

Esther was warming to Grace. *She's like me, an outsider in this country.* And maybe a little crazy too, choosing such a florid colour scheme. She smiled at her hostess, and followed her upstairs.

'That flat of ours was much too tiny once Fleur came along, but it's a perfect size for you two. Larry and I just knew you were the right people to take over our lease.'

They stopped in the doorway of the main bedroom. Esther hung back a little, feeling she was invading an intimate space. 'I do hope we're all going to be great friends. Tony admires Larry enormously, you know. His own poetry is inspired by Larry's, he says.'

'We do have that in common, both of us married to poets. Actually, I write poetry myself — that's when I'm not typing up Larry's work. Lately there's so little time, even for that. It's just that since moving to Chalk Farm I've been in thrall to domesticity. In fact I've just taken up tapestry. I've been looking everywhere for one particular design, the one with the roses and ribbons, but it's so hard to find it here in the village.'

'I can help you there. I saw a lovely pattern in last week's Women's Pages in the *Sunday Times*. It's called Rose Bouquet.'

'That's the very one! I could send to London for it.'

'You'll do no such thing! I can easily get it from Harrods in my lunch-hour on Monday. But be warned, tapestry is seriously addictive.'

The two women, one fair skinned, large-boned, and still with that bland soft look of the new mother, the other dramatically dark, perfumed and exotically dressed, went downstairs together as if they were already old friends.

The round dining table was set with a brightly patterned cloth, crystal glasses, and shining silver cutlery. There was French wine gleaming red in its elegant glass bottle, and pink pansies, freshly picked from the garden, nodded their heads in a pottery vase set in the middle of the table. The first course, an entrée of smoked salmon and dill, with finely sliced rye bread, was served on white china plates already laid in each place.

'Do sit down, everyone, and let's eat.' Grace's words sounded awkwardly formal. She'd removed her apron, and twisted her hair into a chignon, revealing her high cheekbones. Her face was handsome rather than classically beautiful, Esther thought. She noticed a tiny scar at Grace's hairline, almost hidden by her thick fringe.

'Larry, darling, will you pour the wine? None for me, I'm afraid,' Grace said, without looking at her husband. She turned to Esther and said, 'Why don't you sit here, next to Tony.' She whispered 'I'm feeding Tim myself, and — you know, much as I love a glass of wine, it's not good for the baby. '

Esther nodded, and felt her face grow hot when she found herself sitting opposite Larry, who was filling Tony's glass to the brim. Tony was talking animatedly to Larry across the table, telling him about the time he and Esther had lived in Burma, and how he'd loved the life and the people there. She was aware that Larry still hadn't looked properly at her, and felt a twinge of chagrin.

A child's cry sounded through the wall, cutting through their murmurs of conversation.

'Excuse me a minute,' Grace said, 'while I tuck Fleur in. I gave her dinner early tonight, but she was too excited about your visit to go off to sleep.'

'So — Mrs Buchanan — Esther — tell me, are you from these parts?' Larry was at last looking straight at Esther, his deep-set eyes alight.

'My father's Russian originally, but moved to Germany for his medical studies. I was born in Berlin.'

'Ah — so you're German, then. How did you manage, during the war?'

'Oh, we escaped Germany just in time. My father's Jewish, you know. But please, let's not talk about the war.'

Esther's face flushed again when she sensed Larry looking at her. Avoiding his gaze, she turned her attention to Grace.

'It all smells delicious, and you've gone to far too much trouble. I hope you'll let me cook for you, one day.' She was still conscious of Larry's eyes on her, making her skin prickle with excitement, and hoped Grace hadn't noticed. 'Is the little one asleep?' Esther continued, steadying her voice. She sensed a sudden stillness in the room.

'I got Fleur to sleep at last, but don't be surprised if Timothy wakes any minute,' Grace replied, her voice sounding cooler. A lusty cry resounded from the nursery. 'Excuse me, won't you — I must go feed the baby,' and she stood up abruptly, leaving the other three shifting uncomfortably in their chairs.

Larry leant over and refilled their glasses. Esther hoped no one noticed his hand lightly brush hers, as he poured the ruby wine for her.

❀

CHAPTER 6

Chalk Farm, Sunday, May 1962

Sunday at Chalk Farm dawned with intimations of the coming summer. Esther woke to a warm breeze wafting through the half-open window of the downstairs guest room. She had slept badly, tossing and turning all night beside the peacefully sleeping Tony. Turning over onto her side, she found herself looking into bright brown eyes which were staring solemnly back at her. A little hand pulled at her nightgown. Fleur was standing so close that Esther could feel the child's breath on her face.

'Come see our chickies? Get eggs for my Daddy?'

Cringing from the thought of plodding through mud in her night-clothes and flimsy shoes, Esther yawned, and tried to smile.

'Sweetie, that's a lovely idea, but can I do it a little later? After I'm dressed, I'd love to come with you to see the chickens.'

Fleur stared curiously at Esther. She showed no signs of moving, but stood patiently by the bed. Esther found the similarity between mother and child unnerving. With a sigh, she swung her legs over the edge of the bed, slipped her feet into her only shoes, regretting they were suede, and reached for Tony's light overcoat. Pulling it close over her nightgown, she held out her hand to Fleur.

'Let's go see your chickens. Will you take me there, sweetie?' She glanced at Tony in the bed, and saw with relief that the sheet covered his nakedness. Hand in hand, the woman and the girl tiptoed from the room, into the chilly hall, and out through the French doors.

Once outside, Esther breathed in the fragrant air of late spring, revelling in the fresh smell of dew-kissed grass. She tilted her face towards the gentle warmth of the sun, and decided that life in the country might have its compensations after all. Unbidden, her thoughts turned to Larry, and she suddenly remembered her strange dream that had made her cry out in the night. It had been about a giant fish, and somehow, all through it, she had felt a connection to him.

Little Fleur and Esther walked along a well-trodden path, its pavers old and cracked. Stopping outside the wire-enclosed chicken coop, the little girl pointed.

'Look! — There's Fluff. That's Bruno and that's Bianca. Bruno's brown. He's a boy. Bianca's white 'cos her name means white. Fluff's mine, we got her from a teenie chickie. Daddy let me name her. Open the gate!'

'Not yet, dear. I think we should wait for your Daddy to come and feed them.' Esther drew the line at walking through food scraps and chicken feed, to say nothing of the smelly droppings everywhere. 'Let's go inside and help your Mummy with breakfast.' She was tiring now, and realised she had no idea how to talk to children, although this little girl spoke so well for one so young.

'No — we bring eggs for my Daddy,' remonstrated Fleur.

Esther pushed open the wire gate of the chicken coop.

'You go and find some eggs. I'll wait out here for you.'

Fleur hesitated at first, then toddled on her little legs through the gate. She disappeared momentarily inside a little shed, and emerged smiling, carrying three brown eggs, which she put into the pocket of her pinafore. Esther's heart softened at the sight of the child's glowing face.

Inside the big kitchen, Esther found Larry turning strips of bacon in a heavy-bottomed frying pan. It smelled tantalising, and somehow forbidden; she remembered how her grandparents would never allow bacon, ham or pork in their house. Larry looked dishevelled, his thick hair still ruffled from sleep, and his creased shirtsleeves rolled to the elbow. Esther's eyes were drawn to his large hands, as they performed their domestic task with quiet precision.

'Good morning,' she said cheerfully, moving to stand beside him. 'Can I help?' Larry didn't answer immediately, but continued pushing the bacon around the pan. After a moment's silence, he said, in a deep formal voice, 'I trust you both spent a comfortable night.' He moved the pan from the range. Esther waited for Larry to turn towards her, but he resolutely kept his back to her. She knew, without looking at him, that they were on the brink of something exciting, and shameful. She moved away, so that she could catch her breath.

'Yes, very comfortable, thank you,' she said in her husky morning voice, 'except that I had the strangest dream last night. In it, I was back in Tel Aviv, floating free in the ocean. There in the water swam a giant fish, a pike I think it was. Then the strangest thing happened. As the fish swam closer to where I was treading water, it looked at me with its great golden eye. In its pupil, I saw reflected a human foetus. I heard myself cry out, and I woke in tears.'

Larry turned from the stove, and stared at Esther, taking in her heart-shaped face, and her grey eyes returning his gaze.

Esther became aware of someone in the doorway. Grace was standing there, holding baby Timothy. Her green chenille gown was pulled roughly around her waist, and her eyes were shadowed with sleep.

'What an amazing dream,' Grace said. Her voice shook a little. 'I can't imagine what it could mean, unless you were thinking of Larry's poem? You must know it; it's called "The Fish Pond". Surely you must have read it?'

'To be honest, I haven't read much of Larry's poetry yet.'

Grace said nothing at first. She stared unsmiling at her guest. Larry had put a pot of coffee on to brew. He placed a steaming cup of black coffee in front of Grace. She pushed it away from the baby's fluttering hands, pouting.

'Isn't there any milk?'

'Straight from the cow, just for you. Harry's already been with a pail this morning,' Larry said. His hand was shaking slightly as he placed the frothing jug on the table. Esther saw he avoided looking at her, and wondered if Grace had noticed. All three felt a change in the air around them.

Holding baby Timothy close, as if for protection, Grace hurried off to feed him, and to dress herself.

Larry turned at last to face Esther, who'd stood from her seat to fetch the plates. 'Now let me tell you my dream,' he said. 'In it I saw a woman bathed in sunlight, standing by a pool shadowed by giant oak trees. She was gazing down into the water at a swarm of golden fish. Her dark hair fell over her face, half hiding it. Somehow I knew that woman was you.' Larry stood before her, and bending his head, grazed her lips with his. Esther pulled away sharply. 'You know what's happening to us, don't you?' He spoke in a low voice.

Esther stood quite still, her heart pounding. The hairs on her neck bristled, as a tremor of shock went through her. She could either pretend she felt nothing, or follow where her heart was leading. But it was her head that made her say,

'Yes, we're cooking breakfast in your kitchen, on this perfect spring morning. Your wife has asked us to peel potatoes, and my husband's about to come and join us any moment.'

As if on cue, Tony entered the kitchen to find Larry and Esther standing awkwardly opposite each other. Esther immediately walked over to the sink and plunged her hands with their scarlet nails into the sink full of water, where potatoes were soaking. Finding a small paring knife nearby, she automatically began peeling a potato. Tony yawned and stretched, uttered a sleepy 'Good morning,' and sniffed the air appreciatively. 'Do I smell bacon?'

'You do indeed,' said Larry. 'Would you like one egg or two? Freshly laid this morning, by the way. Fleur took Esther on a tour of the chicken coop this morning.'

'So that's where you were, while I was still in the arms of Morpheus,' said Tony, moving over to Esther and kissing her lightly on the cheek. 'Must be the country air — never slept so well in my life.'

The three of them sat down at the big oak table. Outside the apple trees were in full bloom, and they could see crowds of daffodils nodding their golden heads.

'What a magnificent place you have here, Larry.' Tony spoke with forced jollity. 'I imagine it's a perfect place to write?'

'On those rare occasions I get the chance,' Larry replied tersely. 'It's Grace who writes in the mornings, while I look after the children till lunchtime. There's a lot to do here — we have three acres, you know.'

Larry busied himself at the stove, cracking more eggs to join the bacon in the pan. He was obviously practiced at this everyday task. Fleur's little feet came pattering down the stairs, as she and her mother came down to join the others for breakfast. Larry doled the food out onto the waiting plates, and put a small dish of fried bread on the bunny plate in Fleur's place.

Fleur, her hair done on either side of her head in two golden bunches, immediately went over to Esther.

'We play farms now? Look, horse, cows, and chickens too, same like ours.' The little girl was holding a cardboard box, containing small plastic animals, and all the accoutrements of a miniature farm, including fake green grass and thin brown fence railings.

Esther smiled, and murmured, 'Later, dear.' Her heart was still pounding; she felt sure the others could hear it. Her mind was whirling with the exchange of dreams between herself and Larry, and what it could all mean.

Grace poured more strong coffee for herself, and gestured to her guests to do the same. Her face was a mask.

'I'm feeling utterly exhausted this morning. If you don't mind, it would be best if you could leave after lunch. Larry'll drive you to the station.' She spoke without hesitation, as if she'd rehearsed this little speech. The missile didn't miss its mark. Tony looked visibly shocked, while Esther quickly covered her displeasure with a shrug.

During lunch, a cold collation supplemented by Esther's potato salad, the men kept up a strained dialogue on Whitman, Lowell, and Eliot, while the two women said little. Fleur stopped grizzling, and chattered away, as she played with her toys on the rag rug woven by her mother.

After the meal Grace flatly refused Esther's offer to wash up, saying, 'Really, that's not necessary. Please leave the dishes. They can wait until

I've put the babies down for their afternoon naps, and after I've had a rest myself.'

A pall had fallen over the gathering. Only the baby, held in his mother's arms, gave a crooked smile to anyone who looked his way. Tony and Esther said their goodbyes. Tony's was subdued, but Esther thanked Grace effusively, and bent down to kiss little Fleur, smoothing the child's hair. Esther, Tony and Larry piled into the old Austin, and drove down the bumpy country road to Exeter station, with Larry at the wheel. The tension in the car was palpable. For a long moment, not a word was spoken.

❀

CHAPTER 7

Chalk Farm to London, June 1962

The tapestry kit arrived at Chalk Farm a month after the Buchanans' visit. It had an unusual design of deep pink roses, intertwined with tendrils of heart-shaped leaves. Along with the pattern itself, Esther had included threads of silvery grey and soft green, the colours Grace said she'd been unable to find. The design and its colours would go well with the hearts and flowers Grace had painted on various objects in the country house. Cupboards, chair backs, and even doorframes, were decorated with tiny bright green leaves, red hearts and pink roses, all meticulously drawn.

Esther's gift was accompanied by a warm note of thanks for the weekend, with the hope that they would meet again soon. *Any time either of you need a place to stay in London,* she wrote, *our home is your home (literally). We love living in the flat that was yours, and you're both welcome to come and visit, any time. And be careful, if you're anything like me, you'll find tapestry seriously addictive.*

As the days grew longer, Grace sensed a change in Larry, a lack of gentleness, and a distance on the rare occasions that they made love. In the long summer evenings, Grace sat bent over her *gros point*, working on the tapestry Esther had sent, while she and Larry listened to a play or concert on the BBC. All seemed calm and peaceful, but underneath the coziness, there was a sense of unease. The Buchanans' visit had excited them both.

Larry couldn't stop seeing the image of the dark haired woman in her flame orange silks, gazing at him across the dinner table. From that night she'd filled his dreams, awakening the old lust in him. He saw her as a magnificent tiger, waiting to pounce — or to be pounced upon. The sense of danger she'd brought into his humdrum domestic life aroused a hunger for adventure he'd not felt since before Fleur and Timothy were born. The hunter in him recognised something both predatory and vulnerable in Esther; *but who is the hunter, who the prey?*

Since the birth of Timothy he'd lost the sharpness of his desire for Grace, going through the motions of lovemaking without real passion. The night after Esther and Tony's visit, he turned again to Grace, making rough love, substituting his wife's body for that of the fantasised one of Esther's. Grace sensed his absence from her, and suffered for it. The memory of the green-eyed woman in her silks and perfume, who'd sat opposite him at their table on that night in May, drove him to an explosive climax.

On a warm morning in June, Larry was up early. 'I've lined up two sessions with the BBC today,' he told Grace. 'Not sure how long it'll take, or when I'll be back.' He kissed Grace, just missing her lips, and picking up little Fleur, enfolded her in a great bear hug. 'Look after your mother,' he whispered in her tiny ear.

On the train from Exeter to London, Larry's thoughts turned to Grace. She seemed to him to be revelling in the messiness of motherhood. *She need never know of this little peccadillo. It may even breathe new life into our marriage.* He thought again of the lines he'd written to Richard: '*One should dynamite one's life every ten years, even if it means blasting apart the whole careful edifice of home and children.*' He had not mentioned Esther. He remembered the thrill of those early morning hunting expeditions with Richard, on the moors of Yorkshire. It would kill him to live in the prison of domesticity forever.

Larry knew all he needed was a change, a release, that was all; nothing permanent, for permanency itself was anathema to him in his present mood. Richard, far away in Australia, had made no comment on his brother's confession, being used to his frequent outbursts of frustration. Thinking again of Esther, of her silky blue-black hair framing the delicately featured face, and of her scent, a subtle female fragrance underneath the musky perfume, he felt the old excitement bringing him back to life. He heard again her low voice, its ultra British accent not quite hiding the guttural tones of her native German.

In London, Larry's senses were aroused by the sultry June air, with its smells of sun-warmed pavements mixed with the detritus of the city's gutters and back alleys. At the BBC, he delivered the first episode of poetry readings, helped by the adrenalin surging through his blood. He had two hours to fill between recordings. Usually he would have looked up his friend Luke from their poetry group, and had a beery lunch in their favourite pub, the Shakespeare. Today, he jumped into a waiting taxi.

'Prentiss & Son, please,' he directed the cabbie, having memorised the address of Esther's Ad Agency. He arrived just before midday, knowing only that he had to see her again. Even if Esther had only been playing with him, he was aroused by the excitement of the chase.

In the streamlined foyer of Esther's office, Larry felt like a boy again, escaping the bounds of hearth and home.

'I'd like to see Mrs Buchanan. Please tell her Mr Wilde is here,' he told the receptionist, who was sitting behind a sleek oval desk. The sign at the front of her desk said "Lily Bloom". Larry couldn't help an inward smile at the poetic synchronicity of her name. Nor could he help his eyes scanning her curvaceous body, his senses sharp and seeking.

'By all means, Sir, I'll tell Mrs Buchanan you're here. Was she expecting you?'

'I believe not — that is, she may well be,' he said, feeling as confused as a schoolboy on his first date.

'Very well, Sir, I'll see if she's free.' Lily trotted away on her black patent high heels.

In the foyer Larry was waiting, composing what he would say to Esther. Lily returned alone, interrupting his thoughts. 'Mrs Buchanan's in a meeting, sir, and will be occupied all afternoon. Would you care to leave a message?'

Playing hard to get. I like that. Larry smiled to himself as he tore a page from his notebook, scribbled two lines on it, and folded the page in half. He handed the paper to Lily. 'Give this to her, tell her no answer's required.' He had the same feeling that he used to have when putting a juicy bit of bait on the end of his hook.

Before Larry could take his leave, Lily said, blushing prettily, 'Excuse me for asking, Sir, but are you the Mr Wilde who's just won that poetry prize? I forget what they call it now. I saw all about it in the paper, with your picture there and all.'

'The same,' Larry said curtly, secretly gratified by her recognition. It did nothing to quieten his impatience. He turned on his heel, and left the Agency. Fate would either complete the course he had set in motion, or else he might be proven wrong about Esther's intentions. He walked off his frustration, striding the three miles back to his second appointment at the BBC.

❀

Lily gave Larry's note to Esther, and blurted, 'Oh, but the gentleman's so good-looking, Mrs Buchanan. Did you know he's a famous poet? He's been written up in *The Times*. I'd give anything to go out with him, but I don't think it's me he's interested in,' she winked at Esther as she hurried out.

Alone at last, Esther was looking again at the handwritten note. She read the jagged black letters:

I have come to see you, despite all marriages.

She'd seen that writing before, in the book of poetry, which Larry had lent Tony. What had she been playing at, flirting so shamelessly with Larry in the kitchen of Chalk Farm? She'd never really been serious. Esther felt a stab of real fear, and with it, a frisson of excitement. *I'd never come between Larry and that poor wife of his, and what about the children? And I can't bear to hurt Tony. He knows how much I love him. Would it really matter, if I were to have a secret fling?*

Soon after Larry left, Rivke, Esther's old friend from Tel Aviv, dropped in to the Agency. Their friendship had survived the long separation while Esther had lived in Canada, and grown stronger over the years. Esther heard her familiar voice, heavily accented still in spite of her years in England; unlike Esther, Rivke had never strived to sound more English than the English.

'Send Miss Feldmann straight in, please, Lily,' Esther said into the intercom on her desk. Rivke, with her Israeli candour, was the ideal confidante. She'd surely help to solve this dilemma.

Rivke's smile was as innocent and eager as when she'd been a child. Her wide blue eyes still looked surprised. They hugged each other, Esther feeling enveloped in warmth, and the earthy smell that instantly signalled the feeling of home.

'How about we have lunch, darlink?' Rivke, as usual, was short and to the point.

'Yes, let's, I've got so much to tell you,' said Esther. The two women left Esther's office arm in arm, and headed for their favourite bistro.

'What should I do?' Esther asked Rivke, over steaming plates of spaghetti bolognese. Flustered, she showed Rivke Larry's note. 'This came right out of the blue, I had no idea he … Rivke, I'm not ready for this. I wasn't prepared to see him today. I had to pretend I was in a meeting. Anyway, look at this boring dress — they call it the shirtmaker here, and it does nothing for my figure. Such a dull colour, this new taupe, and don't you think the cut of the skirt makes my *tuchus* look big?' She swirled around, sticking her bottom out. In spite of the mischievous gesture, Esther felt suddenly miserable, hating the stiffness of the dress material, constraining her body.

'Don't be *meshugge*, darlink. You must be crazy — whatever you wear makes you look like some fashion plate. For goodnezz sake, your bottom, it is beautiful, and also sexy. But my Essie, do not see this Wilde man again. He is married man, with two young children also. You must think of your Tony. He so much adores you. Essie, *liebling*, please do not hurt Tony. For such a husband what wouldn't I give?'

'Yes, you're right, Rivke, I must be crazy. I know you're right. I just can't think straight, and you must know I adore Tony. God, Rivke, I'm so mixed up — what should I do?' As she spoke the words, Esther was composing an answer to Larry's letter. 'But Rivke — fancy a famous poet chasing after someone like me? Remember how we used to flirt with the soldiers at the tea dances in Tel Aviv?'

'*Ja*, and all the trouble you got us into. I say again, you are crazy. I tell you, don't do it. Think of how people will say bad things about you, a married woman. Why do you need this?'

'Look darling, it's only a game. He's a handsome, interesting man, and I think he must like me. Why shouldn't I have some fun? I'd never let it get serious, you know that. He probably just wants some excitement, and so do I. And anyway, Tony's been so passive lately. He needs a bit of shaking up.'

'You frighten me, Essie, with this bad talk. You'll get in trouble like before, and where's Vati, your dear father, to rescue you? Grow up and don't rockaboat as the English say.'

'It's "rock the boat", Rivke darling. When will you learn proper English? Listen, you will keep all this quiet, won't you? It must be our secret. If you promise not to tell anyone, I promise not to do anything silly.' She paid the bill, adding a generous tip, and sent Rivke on her way with a big hug. Rivke turned back to look at Esther's disappearing figure, and shook her head, a worry line creasing her freckled forehead.

❦

Leaning back in her soft leather chair, Esther tried to banish Larry's note from her mind. *I have come to see you, despite all marriages.* Over and over, she saw the words as if they were etched on her brain. She shook her head. She had work to do, something she could control. The cachet of being part of the advertising world suited her yearning for glamour perfectly, and the art of fabrication with words satisfied some of her creative energy.

Gazing out of her office window, her eye fell on the tiny garden in the little courtyard below. She saw that the freshly mown grass was still glistening from a recent shower of rain. Perfect. She slipped her manicure scissors into her handbag, which held her pack of Embassy cigarettes, and the gold lighter Tony had given her.

'I'm just stepping outside for a moment, won't be long,' Esther called to Lily, as she exited the foyer into the lift. An idea was forming in her mind, a way to answer a poet, without words.

Downstairs in the small garden, Esther lit a cigarette, inhaling the acrid smoke deeply. With her tiny scissors, she snipped a single blade of grass. *Why not? It's only a game,* she thought, and knew she could amuse Tony later, with the joke of how she'd teased the great poet with a faintly phallic symbol. Gestures, she knew, could be more persuasive than words. Larry could either take her message as an invitation, or as a hint to leave well enough alone. To send a blade of grass, and no word, seemed to her the height of sophistication.

Back at her desk again, she opened her secret top drawer, extracted a tiny scent bottle, and dipped the tip of the single, perfect shoot into her signature 'Dior' perfume. She folded the stiff green blade of grass inside a sheet of white unlined paper, and slid the package into an envelope with the Agency's scrolled initials 'CPV' embossed on its reverse side. She hand-wrote the address in her best bold script: *Mr Laurence J Wilde, care of the BBC, London.* Carefully, Esther slipped the folded sheet into the envelope. For better or for worse, Larry had her answer.

❁

CHAPTER 8

London, June 1962

Looking at her name scrawled on the envelope, *Mrs A. Buchanan, Head Copywriter, c/-CPV Ltd.*, Esther felt a jolt of excitement. The postmark on the envelope was from Woodberry, the village nearest to the Wildes' country home. Slitting the letter open, trying to stop her hands shaking, Esther found two blades of grass folded inside a blank sheet of paper. She imagined Larry plucking the fresh shoots from the lawn of Chalk Farm that morning. His message was unmistakable. Two shoots to her one. Larry had accepted her challenge, picked up the gauntlet she'd thrown. The unknown was drawing her towards its secrets, and she knew she could only go forward. *So, he's playing my game*, she thought, as a shiver went through her. *Mein Gott, what have I started now?*

Through the blur of panic, Esther saw that the white sheet of paper was not blank. She made out a fragment of writing. It was a draft of a poem, but she could pick out only a few words: 'your absence' 'Sunlight'; the rest was scribbled over. As she looked more closely she noticed a date and initial, in bolder writing, at the bottom of the page.

3rd July? L.

It looked to be scribbled almost as an afterthought. *Is this supposed to be his way of making a date with me? Does he think I'm going to jump to his tune? The arrogance! Forget it …* Esther crumpled Larry's note, first carefully extracting the shiny blades of grass and putting them into the vase on her desk, which always contained a few fresh blooms. Today they were pansies, deep orange and gold.

Her thoughts wandered back to that day almost a year ago, when Tony and she had answered the ad for taking over the lease of a flat in The Rose Estate. Fate had led them into the lives of Larry and Grace, she told herself. She remembered that Larry had hardly looked at her, that day, and felt again her chagrin at his diffidence.

The new cream phone on her desk rang. 'Yes, Lily,' she said into the receiver.

'Mrs Buchanan, there's a Mr Wall who wants to discuss a new contract with you.'

Mr Wall? She had no client with that name.

'Put him through please, Lily,' she said.

'Did you get my note?' It was unmistakably Larry's voice on the line. Its deep timbre sent a shiver through her.

There was a moment's silence while she steadied her heart.

'What note?' She would hardly dignify that scribble as a note. She waited, holding her breath.

'Esther — I need to see you, even if it's just for a drink. So — is next Thursday about three o'clock a suitable time for me to call? I have an hour or so between appointments in London that day.'

Esther thought quickly. Was she being 'fitted in' between his more important appointments? Pride urged her to refuse, if only to play for time. After another pause, she heard herself say, almost as if another voice was speaking, 'Yes, I suppose I could get away around three, just for a short time.'

She heard his deep sigh. 'Good', in his deep voice, followed by silence. To break it Esther said, 'But why Mr Wall?'

Larry chuckled, 'Oh, it's my pseudonym. I'm the fly on the wall, wherever you are, don't you see?' She put down the phone, feeling a frisson of fear.

❀

In Lyon's teashop the following Thursday, they found a quiet table in the corner. Esther sank into the booth against the leather seat, and felt the tension leave her body. She was glad the light was dim, and there was hardly anyone else in the teashop. Larry sat adjacent to her, his knee almost touching hers. She moved away slightly. They ordered a pot of tea (lemon for Esther, milk for Larry). Neither wanted anything to eat.

'Well, this isn't exactly what I had in mind,' Larry said. His hand, when it touched hers, was warm, and seemed to vibrate with coiled energy. She let it rest on her delicate white fingers, their perfect oval nails polished ruby. 'At least we can talk freely here. I want to know everything about you, Esther, in every way. Tell me everything — your childhood, your family, your travels. But not your loves, I don't want to hear any of that.'

Esther hardly heard his words, so mesmerized was she by the music of his voice, and the movement of his mouth. It was wide and generous, yet she imagined a cruel twist to it. She held herself in, and away from him.

She told him about Berlin, and the terrifying train journey escaping the jack-booted Nazis, and her school in Italy, and her best friend there. She told him about growing up in Palestine, and the schoolgirl scrapes she'd got herself into. She told him her parents and sister lived in Canada, where her first marriage had taken her. She told him about her father, who was once doctor to the Bolshoi Ballet in Tel Aviv, and about her travels with Tony in Burma.

She didn't tell him about her first failed marriage, her forced escape from Tel Aviv; it had already disappeared from her mind. Her disastrous marriage to Charles was nothing like the serious and loving union she and Tony had. Perhaps she and he were more like brother and sister, twin souls maybe. Was that why she was here with Larry, allowing him to flirt with her?

'My family and close friends in Palestine called me Essie, but no one ever does in England.'

'Not even Tony?' Larry asked.

'Not even Tony.' She was silent for a few moments, wondering why Larry would mention her husband, after begging her not to tell him of her past loves. His next question made her wonder — did he ever really mean what he said?'

'How did you two meet?' asked Larry.

'Oh, it was a shipboard romance.' Esther wondered if she'd mistaken Larry's intentions. Maybe his interest in her was purely academic. But she brushed the thought away, and went on, 'you know, being on the ocean, in a way it frees one to follow one's heart. And mine led me towards Tony. I think it was because he's a poet. Oh… I didn't mean…'

Esther coloured, but Larry simply smiled slightly. He seemed to drink in every word. She loved the way he listened intently, holding her in his sights as if she were a precious bird, which might fly away at any moment.

'What a life you've led. No wonder I'm drawn to you, not only to your beauty,' he touched her cheek, 'but to the richness of your spirit. It's as if I can be transported to those places, as if you're taking me there. My own life feels like a prison. It's nothing but cows and babies. But tell me — why do you not have children yourself then?' Larry's faint Yorkshire brogue thickened when he relaxed. He was sitting very close to her. She was aware of a sharp animal scent.

'I told you, I have so much else in my life. I don't want to be a slave to anyone, not like …' she cut herself off just in time.

'I know what you mean.' Larry's mouth became a straight line, and he looked away. 'You can see what it's done to us, her and me, and how my writing's suffered.'

She heard only the word 'us' and felt a stab of jealousy. Why was he bothering with her, then? As if reading her thoughts, Larry went on:

'I can't tolerate that stultifying life any more. As soon as I saw you, Esther, I knew you could bring about the change I need. Right from that first day when you came to see the flat, you transported me to — how can I put it — a world of elegance and beauty. How I've longed to meet someone like you…'

'Someone like me? Oh, I can find you any number of women who'd fit the bill,' she said, offended that he thought of her as a type, one of a category sent to save him from whatever it was he was escaping.

'No — that's not what I meant,' he said quietly, leaning closer towards her. 'You make me so confused, I can't even think straight. I want you so much, Esther, you must know that. I feel drunk when I'm near you. He kissed her lips softly, as if it were the most natural thing in the world.

She didn't return the kiss, neither did she pull away. She felt intoxicated; the taste of his mouth on her lips was like wine. With an effort she said,

'And what about your wife? Grace? Everyone says you two are the dream couple.'

Larry gave a short laugh. 'Nay, we were once, but for months now we've been going through a bad patch. Ever since the boy was born, it's not been the same. The energy's changed. I can tell she cares only for the children.'

'Larry, please. I'm flattered, but I've no wish to come between you and your family. Besides, I'm fond of Grace. I was hoping she and I could become friends.'

He seemed not to hear her, but pulled her closer and this time kissed her more deeply. She felt his tongue pressing against hers, and a warmth rising from her groin. She twisted away, and looked around the tearoom, her face flushed. Fortunately the place was almost empty, but for an elderly couple sipping tea at a central table. They had their backs to Larry and Esther. Smoke from the man's cigarette wafted over to them. Esther craved one of her own.

Smoothing her ruffled hair, she straightened her shoulders, and looking straight at Larry, said, 'I love Tony. He's a dear to me, and I could never hurt him.'

'I see. Well then, he's a lucky fellow. So what are you doing here, taking tea here with me, in the afternoon, and allowing your lovely self to be kissed by a strange man?'

Blushing, she said, 'I really don't know. I never meant this to happen.'

'Oh yes, you did. The way you looked at me that night, your eyes so bright, in your silks and perfume, you meant it all right. Surely you recognised that we're kindred spirits. Why, even our dreams told us so. As soon as you told me your dream of the great golden fish — so like my own dream — I knew we were destined to be together. We are the same, you and I. We need adventure, change, excitement. And our Others need never know.'

Esther's mind clouded, as she let his words, impossible words, wash over her. She pushed her half-drunk tea away. 'I have to go. It's almost five, and I need to get back to the office.'

'Please, don't go. At least tell me that we can meet again. I come to London again ten days from now. Let me see you, take you to lunch, anything.'

'I can't possibly. It's too dangerous, and I'm sorry it's gone this far.'

'I beg you to think about it. I'll wait for your answer.'

The door of the tearoom opened, letting in a blast of warm city air. Two young girls, their skirts above their knees, their lacquered hair piled up on their heads, came in, giggling. Esther saw Larry's eyes go straight to the girls' pretty bare legs, and felt the rise of irritation.

'Thank you for the tea,' she said stiffly, rising to her feet, and reaching for her handbag. Larry threw a few shillings on the table, and followed Esther out into the street. There, in front of the few passing pedestrians, he drew her into him, his lips seeking hers. She longed to kiss him, but stopped herself. Without another word, she turned and walked away.

Outside again, she could hardly bear her conflicted feelings of excitement and trepidation. *This is unthinkable; it's a game that's gone too far.* Yet her body belied her, quivering with something like joy.

❖

CHAPTER 9

Lansdowne Hotel, London, July 1962

Esther stepped out of her office, into the busy London street. It was Friday, the day she and Larry had arranged to meet. All week she'd dreamed of how it would be: romantic, secret, mysterious.

There was a smell of summer in the London air, warm and spicy. All around her she saw young girls, their eyes kohl-rimmed, their lipstick pale. Their straight skirts seemed to be getting shorter every day; some were even above the knee. The gloom of the post-war years had lifted. Even the young men looked smart, with their stovepipe trousers and pointed winkle-picker shoes, their hair slick with brilliantine.

The spectacle interested Esther, who remained impervious to the fashion of the day, preferring her well-cut suits, or the full skirts covering her hips, which she thought were too wide. She thought the new look was quite ugly, and determined never to succumb to fashion unless it enhanced her figure. Today she'd chosen a light floral skirt, which flared around her bare legs in the light summer breeze. She teamed it with a white blouse, its pearl buttons done up almost to the neck. The soft cotton fabric felt smooth against her skin. It was a classic outfit, modest except for the fact that the third button of her blouse strained, revealing a glimpse of cleavage.

The secret kisses she'd exchanged with Larry, in the darkness of the smoky London pub, held the promise of forbidden pleasures. Later she castigated herself, *how could I do this to Tony?* It was as if Larry had cast her under a powerful spell, dispelling thoughts of right and wrong. Despite her love for Tony, she found it impossible to deny the demands of her body. *After today, I'll be free of him, and this madness will end.*

She was walking to their appointed meeting place, well away from the Agency, when she felt her elbow gripped by a large firm hand. A

voice sounded in her ear. She thrilled to its timbre, the depth of it reso-
nating within her.

'At last,' she heard. She looked up to see Larry's face gazing down at
her. He kissed her full on the mouth, right there in broad daylight. She
felt her body respond with an immediacy that shocked her. Without
speaking further, they walked the two blocks towards the small hotel
Larry had chosen. It was hidden away in the back streets, he'd told her,
safe from prying eyes. His assurance of secrecy added to Esther's trembling excitement. Her knees felt weak.

An image of Tony came to her without warning, and a wave of guilt
engulfed her.

'Wait a moment,' Esther said. She stopped outside a phone booth
on the corner, its bright red paint scratched, black graffiti scrawled over
the glass-panelled door. 'I need to make a call.' Fishing in her purse for
coins, she stepped inside the protective box of the booth. The smells of
urine and stale tobacco both excited and repelled her. She slipped the
two pennies into the slot, and dialled the number of Tony's office. The
coins fell with a clang.

'Chambers and Company, can I help you?' How could the receptionist's voice sound so calm, so normal, as if this were an ordinary day?

'I'd like to speak to Tony Buchanan, please. It's Mrs Buchanan here.'

'He's right here, ma'am.' Was there mockery in the light young
voice? Was Tony perhaps standing right behind the young receptionist who'd picked up the phone? Had he been flirting with her? Esther
wanted her vision to be true, to assuage the pang she felt as soon as she
heard Tony's voice.

'I may be late home tonight, darling,' she said into the black mouthpiece, trying not to inhale the foul breath of the last caller. 'An important
client's taking me out for drinks, and after that we might go on to dinner
with the boss, if all goes well. Wish me luck.' There was a pause while
she listened impatiently, conscious of Larry waiting outside, and feeling
the pull towards him through the wood and glass of the phone box.

'No, don't wait up, Tony dear, I've no idea when I'll be home.' She spoke quickly, anxious to get the call over with. There was another long pause. She heard a tap on the glass, and turned to see Larry's hand raised to it, and his eyebrows raised. 'I'll be all right. No, don't worry, I'll catch a cab.' Distracted, she half-listened to his response.

'Good idea, join them for dinner. No need to wait up. Bye, darling.' She replaced the receiver with a sigh.

Stepping outside into the summer evening, she turned to Larry. 'I don't think I can go through with it,' she said. 'I can't do this to Tony. You don't know him.'

He turned her roughly to him, and kissed her with such ferocity, it shook her.

'When I wrote, *in spite of all marriages*, I meant it.' Thoughts of Tony evaporated

The hotel Larry led her to was hidden away in a back street, anonymous and silent. Esther's skin tingled wherever he touched her. *So he's made all the necessary arrangements; he means this to happen*. She was on a trajectory, impossible to stop.

Inside the dark foyer, smelling of stale cigarettes and boiled cabbage, Larry pulled out a wad of pound notes, peeled off two, and handed them to the receptionist, a balding gentleman wearing a vest with a Fair Isle pattern. *Probably knitted by his wife, waiting at home for him*, Esther thought, waves of guilt returning.

The man hardly looked up from his *Times* crossword as he swept the cash into a drawer, and pushed the hotel register towards Larry. Glancing down, Esther noticed the date, *Friday 13th July*, and a shiver went through her. She tried convincing herself that black Friday, as she'd heard it called in England, was just a silly superstition, and that surely the date might just as well bring good luck as bad.

Every now and then the hotel proprietor licked the tip of his lead pencil in an almost lewd gesture. Esther kept her eyes firmly on the intricate pattern of his vest, ignoring the smirk she sensed on the man's face, while Larry wrote their names as 'Mr and Mrs Wall', with a flourish.

'Here you are, then, Mr Wall, Room 69,' the man said with a wink to Larry, handing him the key. He cast a look at Esther, a look of knowing contempt, which chilled her.

A rickety old lift took them to the third floor. With the big brass key Larry opened the door to a small room. In the dim light, Esther saw a wooden wardrobe, its door ajar, and a double bed covered in a green chenille spread. There was no other furniture in the small room.

'Here we are at last, Mrs Wall,'he said, turning the lock on the inside of the door with careful deliberation. His voice set Esther a-shiver again. She didn't care about the shabbiness of the room or its musty smell, feeling only the craving of her body. Underneath her filmy skirt, she wore French lace scanties. They were pale pink and wide-legged, called 'scanties' by the cheeky London girls. These she'd chosen with great care, along with a very expensive nightgown in ivory silk. If this was to be her first and only betrayal of her marriage vows to Tony, it might as well be romantic, a one-off lapse that no one would ever know about, but that could be stored away in her mind as a special memory.

Reaching down into her bag, she pulled out her toilet sachet containing her dutch cap, and groped for the silky nightdress. The feel of its smooth slippery material excited her again. Yet she felt a quiver of fear, of his unknown body. She turned to Larry, waiting for his embrace. Instead he pushed her roughly onto the bed, and threw his body on top of her. Her body stiffened against him, as she pushed him off, whispering,

'Not yet, darling — I need to be ready for you.' She reached her arms up for an embrace, but Larry was already hard and pulsating. He bore down on her, forcing her legs apart with rough hands.

'No!' She pushed him away with all her strength, her hands clawing at his chest. He forced himself hard inside her, his eyes bulging and unfocused. She felt herself tighten around him, as if to shut him out. His rank animal stink both aroused and repelled her, but the pain inside her clenched body dispelled all desire. She tried to ward him off as she cried out. Her resistance drove him on, and he thrust harder until she thought her body would split. At last, with a great roar, he burst inside her.

Immediately he rolled off her and his viscous emission leaked out of her torn body. Her blood mixed with his hot semen, staining the bedspread. She reached for something to wipe away the sticky mess from her thighs. A metallic stink filled the room. On the bed, her hands found the pretty nightgown she'd bought, with romantic notions of tender lovemaking. She bit her lip to stop the tears. Larry said nothing, lying on his side, turned away from her.

To break the silence, she said, 'We've made a frightful mess of the bed.' Larry grunted in answer. She mopped herself with what was left of the bloodied scanties. Was this the exciting sex she'd read about, but never experienced before? Where was the romantic poet of the last few weeks, the gentle touches, and the sensuous kisses?

Words of anger and disgust stuck in her throat. She didn't know if his violent thrusting was the measure of his passion for her, or in fact a brutal rape. No man had ever been so rough with her body, but perhaps, she wondered in confusion, no man had ever felt such animal lust for her.

Larry stayed turned on his side, sweating profusely and breathing heavily. She imagined his body as a carcass, and a smell like raw flesh assaulted her. Suddenly she was back in the butcher's shop in Tel Aviv, being fondled by fleshy hands. Her eyes filled with tears and humiliation at the memory of it. And now this. When he turned to her at last, she saw he was crying. She forced herself to speak calmly.

'You've ruined my clothes. What on earth am I going to wear, to get out of this hell-hole?'

'My God, can you ever forgive me? What have we done?'

'We?' she said, in shock. 'How could you? You're an animal, a monster. And you've torn me. Look at the blood on the bedspread. *Schweinhund*! Just get me out of here, for God's sake.' The guttural sounds of her native German broke through the cut-glass accent.

'You drove me to this, Esther. I went crazy for you, with the force of my wanting. It's as Blake wrote: *The cistern contains, the fountain overflows.* The great poet knew what he was talking about.'

'You're quoting poetry at me? At a time like this?'

'Forgive me,' he said, his hand reaching out to stroke her face. 'I never, ever, meant to do you any harm. Please, Esther, let me make it up to you. I'll buy you a new blouse, and I'll take you to the best hotel in London. I'll do anything if you'll just forget what happened. I promise you, it'll never be like this again.' He kissed her softly on her mouth, and on her eyes, kissing away her tears.

'No, it won't, because there'll never be a next time,' she said, reaching for the thin white towel. She raised herself from the soiled bed and crept down the dingy hallway to the bathroom.

Once inside, she locked the door and ran hot water into the bathtub, slowly peeling off her torn blouse. She splashed her face with cold water, and looked at herself in the mirror. Her eyes looked huge, their pupils dilated, and her cheeks were pale. Otherwise her face was unchanged. Why didn't she look ravaged, ruined? Pain and violence had frozen any response, except her need to protect herself. Yet even in the midst of her distress, she knew she was possessed by this man.

She lowered her aching body into the warmth of the water and washed the blood from her thighs as best she could. There were no bruises, only a raw tenderness inside her. Closing her eyes, she felt the shock and pain slowly subside. Her mind was in chaos. *There can be no future in this, she told herself. I must never see him again.* She dried herself as best she could, noticing a smear of blood on the white towel.. She couldn't find the new lace scanties, so left herself bare, relieved to have no friction added to her soreness. The champagne-coloured petticoat would cover her enough for decency. She fastened the remaining buttons of her blouse with trembling fingers. Its collar was torn where Larry had ripped it.

Tiptoeing back into the hotel room, Esther avoided looking at the tousled bed. Larry was asleep on top of the stained coverlet. It had fallen to the floor, discarded like a bride's wedding gown. The room had a rank smell, of sweat and semen. *He smells like a butcher*, she thought, fighting her revulsion.

Her shoes were splayed apart from each other on the carpet in a lewd gesture of abandonment, their spiked heels pointing in opposite directions. She pulled Larry's suit jacket over her torn blouse. Hesitating for a moment she glanced at the bed, and quietly walked from the room, carrying her shoes and handbag. The door closed behind her with a click of finality.

❀

CHAPTER 10

Eliot Court, London, July 1962

The taxi dropped Esther a few doors from the flat in Eliot Court. She felt obscurely ashamed, as if the taxi driver would think her a common prostitute. Tony would be in bed asleep by now. She crept quietly up the stairs, anxious to sink into the warm safety of his arms, to be comforted by his familiar smell.

Walking into the living room she saw at once that Tony was asleep on the couch. The dear man must have sat up waiting for her, although she'd told him not to. He was still wearing his street clothes. But something about him didn't look right. His head was at an awkward angle, and his face was deathly pale. As she kneeled down in front of him she saw a glint of silver on the floor. It was the carved hunting knife from Burma, lying under his slack open hand. She took the hand and pressed it, and shook his shoulder. There was no response.

'Tony, darling, wake up.'

She shook him again, but he lay as slack as a dead fish. A sour smell came from his half open mouth as a trickle of saliva dribbled down his chin. She saw an empty pill bottle on the floor. It was labelled 'Seconal', a drug she took occasionally to get to sleep. Panic flooded her body, rising to her throat. She felt she would vomit. Crawling on her knees to the phone on the corner table, she swallowed her nausea and grabbed the receiver to dial the emergency number.

'I need an ambulance immediately,' she screamed into the phone. In a steadier voice she gave the address and begged them to hurry.

Tony was breathing heavily, and his face had a grey pallor, when she returned to his side. 'Don't die, Tony, please, please don't die, it's all my fault, I didn't want it to happen, I couldn't help it, he practically raped me. Stay with me, please don't leave me,' she babbled, until at last there was a loud knock on the door. She rushed to open it. Two young ambulance officers stood there holding a hospital stretcher between them. The taller of the two went quickly to Tony, felt his pulse, and shook his head.

'He's on the way out, Miss; we've got to get him to Emergency quick smart. You take his legs, Jim,' he said to his offsider. In a trice they had Tony's limp body on the stretcher.

'I'm coming with him,' said Esther, automatically grabbing the empty pill bottle and the knife, along with her handbag, which still held evidence of her own night's disaster.

In the ambulance Esther held Tony's hand. Believing he couldn't hear or see her, she blurted out the whole story to his inert body, telling him how a one-night stand had turned into a rape, how Larry was a vicious animal, how she would never betray Tony again. She felt the relief of confession as she willed Tony not to die.

They drove at high speed, sirens blaring, into the emergency entrance of Guy's Hospital. Two orderlies came out and expertly transferred Tony's body to a hospital gurney. Esther followed, aware of her nakedness under her skirt, as if it could betray her.

'He's pretty far gone. What did he take?' asked the white-coated intern who hurried to Tony's side. Esther wordlessly gave him the empty Seconal bottle.

'We're going to pump his stomach. You'll have to wait outside. You realise this could be a police matter,' the young doctor said to Esther.

In the waiting room, Esther came as close to praying as she'd ever been. A few random Hebrew phrases suddenly surfaced, *sh'ma y'israél, adonai elohenu'*, prayers she'd heard her father chant when he got the news of his parents' murder in Auschwitz. She whispered the words over and over again. This must be her punishment, she knew, for playing such a dangerous game, for giving in to her fantasy. It had turned out so very differently to the dream of a secret romance with Larry, a fantasy that had been obsessing her for weeks. Now she would tell the world what he was really like.

Some hours later, a different doctor emerged from the swinging doors to the ward.

'Are you this man's relative?' he said to Esther.

'I'm his wife. Please tell me — will he be all right?'

'He's out of danger — for now. It was close, and he'll need careful observation. Has he ever tried something like this before?'

'No, never. Please, Doctor, let me take him home — it's all a misunderstanding. I'll make sure nothing like this happens again.'

'Not so fast, young lady. You'll need to come with me and fill in some papers.'

'But please — can't I see him first?' Esther looked into the doctor's eyes, widening her own in the way she knew few could resist. Under his bushy eyebrows, his expression was kind, in spite of his obvious exhaustion. He was an older man, but not too old to be immune to Esther's beauty, made more vivid by her wing of blue-black hair falling across her pale face.

'Well ... just for a minute. Actually, perhaps you could be of some help. The challenge now is to keep the patient conscious by stimulating him to wakefulness. We need someone to walk him and to keep him constantly on his feet. Could you take over from the nurse for a while? We have so many other patients and we're short-staffed.'

'By all means, Doctor. I'll do anything to save my husband. Thank you, thank you.' Esther leaned over and planted a light kiss on his stubbly cheek. He recoiled, embarrassed, saying gruffly, 'Follow me.'

In the ward, Esther saw Tony, thin and grey-faced, being dragged along by a young nurse. She was trying to get him to walk, but his feet barely brushed the ground. Esther went up to them, and took Tony's other arm.

'I'll take him now; you can go about your business.' Esther spoke brusquely, dismissing the nurse as if she were a bothersome fly. It piqued her wifely pride to see Tony with another woman, even in these circumstances.

Together Tony and Esther began their ghastly promenade, his eyes glassy and unfocused, hers brimming now with long held back tears. Slowly Tony's feet began to connect more firmly to the shiny linoleum beneath them. To keep him awake, and believing him barely conscious, Esther talked to him softly. She told him again the story of how she'd been ravished, as usual embellishing the truth in the telling. She described congress between herself and Larry a vicious attack, far more vicious than it actually was. Often, under stress, her imagination ran away with her.

By Sunday night Tony had recovered enough to leave the hospital, with a warning that he must be carefully monitored over the next few days. Esther and he took a taxi back to Eliot Court. They went straight to bed, and Esther, regardless of her healing wounds, made tender love to him. Later Tony remembered the stories she'd told him while he was coming back to life, and wondered whether he'd had an elaborate dream.

'What's happened? Were you really with Wilde on Friday?' he asked her as they lay together, his arm cradling her head.

'Yes — I was. He forced himself on me. It was frightening, yet I couldn't stop him. Please, please, understand. It's you I love. You must never doubt that.'

'What are you saying? How could you let him touch you? For God's sake, Esther, tell me it's not true.'

'Darling, darling, I'm so sorry, believe me. He — he was like an animal — '

'So — the great poet's a hypocrite after all. Parading himself as a devoted family man, a martyr to home and hearth. Did he spare a thought for Grace, and remember his two children?'

Esther forced calm into her voice. It was too late now to take back the words she should never have spoken.

'He says he feels stifled in the marriage, and that Grace is moody, and hard to live with. You saw the way she behaved that weekend. She's insanely jealous, too, in assuming Larry was lusting after me that weekend. It was just an innocent flirtation, on my part anyway. You must know that, darling. I never wanted it to go any further. If only I could undo the past, what happened with Larry, I would.'

'So the great poet plays at happy families while he rapes another man's wife. Thinks he has artistic license to break every law of common decency.'

'Darling, please believe me. It was just a silly infatuation, one that went too far. I only care about you, and our life together. I couldn't bear to lose you. How could you have done anything so dangerous? It's over now, and you must promise me you'll never do anything so foolish again.'

'It's you who must promise me never to see that bastard again.'

'Dearest Tony, I'll do anything to make up for this. To think I almost lost you! You must get well again, and we have to put this behind us.' She embraced him tenderly, feeling the sweat still on his skin, noticing his breath still bore the foul stench of vomit. Her heart was wrung with pity, and unbearable guilt.

To herself she thought, *I need to see this through. How else can I rid myself of the hold Larry has over me? I'm in thrall to that man, trapped in a dream that must end.* She could never lie to Tony, or make false promises to him. 'Sshh,' she whispered, stroking his face, as she held him to her.

❋

CHAPTER 11

London, August 1962

At work, Esther cautioned Lily to screen all her calls, and to put through only those from bona fide clients. She pushed thoughts of Larry away, but at night he came to her in her dreams, sometimes violently, sometimes gently. In spite of his roughness with her in the hotel, or perhaps because of it, she woke from these dreams pulsating with desire, which she lavished on Tony lying so innocently beside her.

Larry never did call during the next few empty weeks, weeks that seemed to Esther like time not fully lived. His silence served to fan the flame of her secret longing. She heard his voice in her dreams, and felt again the touch of his hand on her arm. Every day she found herself wishing for some sign from him, perhaps a note containing another cryptic message, reminiscent of the blade of grass he'd sent that day so many weeks ago.

'Lily, I know I've asked you not to put any calls through — but — are you quite sure there's been no call from Mr Wall today?'

Lily rolled her eyes. 'If you don't mind my saying so, Mrs Buchanan, we all know who this Mr Wall really is, and that he's a married man.'

Esther was always entertaining the office with tales of her exploits, imaginary or real, and usually much exaggerated. Doing so kept her fantasy alive. Nevertheless she was infuriated by Lily's arched eyebrows and knowing look.

'I just need to know if he's trying to get in touch, for my own peace of mind. You will tell me if there's a call, won't you? I don't mean you to put him through to me, I'd just like to know, that's all.'

'Of course, Mrs Buchanan.' Lily stifled a giggle.

❀

As the office's senior copywriter, Esther had strict deadlines, and usually met them conscientiously. Lately, however, she found it almost impossible to concentrate. Unusually for her, she'd been a day or two late with their biggest client, the Lux account. Because her work for the Agency was so brilliant, her boss forgave her — this time.

The next day, Lily had to leave the office early. Esther had forgotten to switch her calls through to her colleague Jim, who, like the rest of the office, had been well informed of her secret admirer. When the phone on her desk rang, she picked it up unthinkingly.

'Mr Wall here. I'd like to speak to Mrs Buchanan.'

Esther froze as soon as she heard the deep tones of a familiar voice. She started to hang up, but shock made her say, 'It's — it's me.' The silence on the other end was a warning. *Hang up now.*

'Essie — may I call you Essie? — I'm going crazy for a sight of you. Tell me quickly you'll meet me again. Grace is going shopping with her mother tomorrow. You can ring me at Chalk Farm in the afternoon; I'll be alone except for the children.' A pause while she drew breath. 'Sorry, someone's coming. I have to go.' And he hung up.

That night, Esther lay sleepless beside Tony. Confusion and guilt fought with desire. In the days following Tony's suicide attempt, Esther was the very model of wifely propriety. She cosseted her husband as a mother does a sickly child. Always she made sure to be home from the office before him.

Should she ring Larry tomorrow, as he'd asked her to? Maybe she could finally put an end to this madness. Yes, she'd tell him there was no way she could meet him alone, ever again. She finally fell asleep with the relief of having made a decision, which would keep her safe, and true to Tony.

The next day, Lily took her lunch in the office, leaving Esther no opportunity to ring Larry secretly. He'd told her Grace and Eva would be out shopping while he was minding the children, but hadn't said exactly what time they'd be home. At last, after Lily left for the day at 4.30pm precisely, Esther knew she must make the call. She must free herself from the net of danger, always coming closer. But her courage was waning.

Esther's love of mischief kicked in again. *I know, I'll play him at his own game. I can be Mr Wall too. Easy to change my voice, to sound like a man — just in case someone else answers.* She had to extricate herself from the dangerous adventure she'd embarked on with her blade of grass. *Let this be an end to it,* she thought, even as her body was urging her in the opposite direction whenever she thought of Larry. She picked up the phone, and dialled the number for Chalk Farm.

❉

CHAPTER 12

Chalk Farm, August 1962

When Grace's mother, Eva, arrived from America, Grace showed her a rosy picture of her marriage: their joy in their children, their work together on Larry's literary career, and the many improvements they'd made to the old house. She didn't share her doubts, didn't talk about the explosive silences between herself and Larry, the chill of the rooms even when the sun shone, the ticking of clocks after the children were asleep.

Eva had met Larry once before, at her daughter's wedding to him in London four years ago. She was the only guest, except for a couple of witnesses provided by the celebrant. She shared her daughter's pride in Larry, the upcoming poet, winner of literary prizes. Now, four years later, Eva sensed a change in the chemistry between her daughter and son-in-law. She noticed that Larry rarely picked up baby Timothy. *Nose out of joint,* she reflected, *like so many men when they have to compete with another male, even if it's his own baby son.*

Grace and Eva decided to go shopping in nearby Exeter, leaving Larry in charge of the children. Timothy would be having his morning nap, and Fleur could help Larry in the garden, picking daffodils to sell at the markets. Grace felt light at heart at the prospect of a few hours freedom from domesticity.

Both women were in a frivolous mood as they toured the select few boutiques in Exeter. Thanks to her mother's generosity, Grace acquired a full black skirt, and a blue cashmere jumper. The outfit would be perfect for her next trip to London in ten days time, when she was to give a reading for the BBC. Eva bought herself a paisley-patterned scarf in swirls of maroon and navy, woven from the local wool. Not forgetting Larry, Grace found a fine cotton shirt in his size, and a tie to match.

'Larry needs some decent clothes for his trips to his publisher in London. It doesn't do to look like a poor struggling poet these days, Mother.'

Eva insisted on treating Grace to lunch at the best hotel in Exeter, to celebrate their purchases. Excited about her new clothes, and almost dizzy in her liberation, Grace agreed to have a glass of their best red wine even though she was breast-feeding.

'A little tipple won't hurt Tim,' said Eva, 'and might even help his colic.'

As they drove home after lunch, Grace said, 'Mother, I've never been so happy in my life.' Tears shone in her eyes as she spoke, wishing her words to be true. 'I have a beautiful home, two adorable children, a wonderful husband, and at last the chance to write as I've always wanted to. Larry and I share so much, more than in most marriages.'

'I'm so happy for you, dear,' said Eva, 'after all our little troubles of the past. I just knew you'd come through, and make us all proud. '

Grace shuddered at her mother's mention of her 'little troubles.' She remembered the white hospital bed, and felt again the cold wet pads being pressed to her temples. How could her mother, any mother, allow her child to have electro-convulsive therapy? She fell silent for the rest of the short drive back to Chalk Farm. Eva too was silent, thinking of the struggle she'd had as a single mother, when Grace had had her breakdown. Now all that was behind her, thank God.

When Grace and Eva arrived home, a little the merrier from the wine, the house seemed eerily empty and cold. Larry must have been upstairs. Tim had woken and the two children were in the playpen, the baby rolling around on his tummy, and little Fleur intent on building a house from coloured wooden blocks.

'Mummy!' Fleur squealed with delight when she saw Grace. She stood up and shook the bars of her playpen, knocking the carefully built edifice over. Tim gurgled and laughed, reaching for the tumbling blocks.

As Grace was about to lift Fleur from the playpen, the phone rang. It had a shrill, piercing sound in the cold air. Grace walked quickly across the room to where the black phone hung on the wall. Eva scooped up Fleur, who cried and reached out her arms to her mother.

Grace plucked up the receiver on the fourth ring. Eva, watching, saw her daughter's face turn pale. She listened for a long moment. As if it were a red-hot poker, she let the receiver drop from her hand.

'Larry,' she called shrilly 'It's for you!' She ran from the room.

Larry came bounding downstairs two at a time, almost stumbling on the last step. He grabbed the dangling phone. 'Yes, this is Mr Wilde. No, we don't require any subscriptions to your paper thanks very much. And please, Mr Wall, don't ring here again.'

Grace, wild-eyed, walked back into the room. With one great wrench, she tore the dangling phone from its socket. The cord twisted and turned like a dying snake, with its head an ugly black mouthpiece.

'It was her!' Grace screamed. 'I'd know that voice anywhere, with its fake Kensington accent. She's a German, Mother, like you and Daddy, but she pretends to be a high-born English woman. A German whore, that's all she is, plastered in makeup, and boasting of her abortions. Thought she could fool me into thinking it was a man on the phone. "Mr Wall here, can I speak to Mr Wilde, if you please?" It was her ultra Oxford English that gave her away.' Grace burst into tears. Eva was too busy covering her granddaughter's ears to intervene. *I knew this perfect marriage was too good to be true*, she thought. *I could feel all along there was something wrong.*

Larry rushed upstairs, away from his wife's diatribe. Grace ran after him, sobbing hysterically. Eva heard their bedroom door close with a bang. She tried to soothe Fleur, who'd started to cry, her breath coming in shuddering gulps. The little girl wriggled out of her grandmother's arms and ran to the stairs after her mother. Eva grabbed her, and sat her on the couch.

Timothy was starting to whimper. Eva sat him on her knee and, as Fleur's sobs subsided, all three huddled close together on the red velvet couch. A book of fairy tales was lying on the arm of the chair. Eva picked it up, and in a singsong voice, began to read the tale of 'Sleeping Beauty.' It had been Grace's favourite when she was a little girl.

Almost an hour passed. The baby was crying now, nuzzling in Eva's blouse for the comforting breast, to no avail. Fleur had cried herself to sleep. Eva gently disengaging the little girl from her lap, and laid her on the sofa. She slowly climbed the stairs, holding the squirming Tim, and tiptoed to the closed door of the master bedroom. She knocked softly.

'Come in,' Grace's voice sounded rough, as if she'd been sobbing. Eva pushed the door open. To her embarrassment, she saw Larry and Grace in bed, under the covers but fully clothed. Larry appeared to be asleep, his back turned away from Grace.

'Tim's hungry, Grace. Can you take him?' Eva held the squalling infant out to her daughter. Sitting up in the tousled bed, Grace reached her arms out for the baby, and unbuttoning her blouse, put him to her engorged breast. Both mother and baby relaxed instantly. Tim sucked away with all his might, making little grunts of satisfaction, and Grace, red-eyed, sighed deeply.

'Mother, I'm so sorry about all this. I'll explain everything when the children are in bed. Can you help me get the tea? We'll talk later.'

Walking slowly back downstairs, Eva felt the first flush of anger towards her daughter. She hadn't come all the way from the States, only to be caught in the middle of an angry row. Grace was over-reacting, as usual, and as her mother she would have to do what she could to restore normality. Sighing in resignation, Eva headed for the kitchen to find something for Fleur's tea.

❖

CHAPTER 13

Chalk Farm, August 1962

After Eva had finally settled both children, grumbling to herself all the while, Grace came downstairs and slumped on the sofa beside her mother.

'What am I going to do, Mother? I can't live with Larry another minute. I've told him to go. Go to his whore with her sickening perfume and fancy clothes. Let him come back for his things — what's left of them — when I'm not here.'

Grace was twisting her hands together, her knuckles turning white.

'Grace dear, do try not to overreact. Think of the children. You're just as likely to drive Larry into this woman's arms. How could you make a good man like that leave? It was a phone call, that's all. Let it blow over, dear, that's my advice.'

Grace sprang up, wild-eyed and shaking. Her eyes were blazing dangerously. She paced the floor, her fists clenched.

'How could you say such a thing, Mother? To think I ever trusted him. He's betrayed me with that bitch, she of the abortions and lies. If you could've heard her, and seen her making great eyes at Larry, after I gave her a bed under my own roof, and fed her, and her fool of a husband.'

'Grace, listen to me. It was probably just a silly prank. Sometimes we have to let our men have their bit of fun. After all, Larry's been a good husband. Look how he helps you with the children. Your father never did that for me.'

'What would you know about him? He told me that hussy tried to seduce him. He even has the gall to lie, that he hasn't succumbed to her — yet. You should see that whore, Mother. Trying to fool me with her hateful tapestry. She's an abomination, with her painted face and empty womb. I saw the way they looked at each other, at my own table.'

Eva stood up and tried to put her arms around her daughter, who shook her off violently.

'Calm yourself, dear. You mustn't let those nerves of yours get the better of you. Poor little Fleur and Timothy don't want a mother who isn't coping. Believe me, I had my own bad times when you and Robert were little, but I never let you two see me crying.'

'You! You! Always about You! Oh yes, Mother, you're a saint, or a martyr more like it. Who was it who threw me into hospital when all I wanted was to die? And stood by while they clamped those wet pads to my temples to shock the life out of me?'

A nerve jumped on Grace's cheek, and she put her hand up to touch the faint scar on her forehead, as if to touch the memory. Her eyes shone with a febrile glitter.

Eva backed away from Grace, and held on to the back of a chair.

'But Grace — it was for your own good — how can you say those things to me? After all I've been through on your account? You're not well, dear. Why don't you fix yourself up, go into town? I think you should see that nice doctor, the one that came when you had the 'flu. I'll look after the children.'

Grace's face contorted in fury. She rushed from the living room into the study. Eva heard the sound of heavy objects being thrown against the wall, and paper being ripped. She feared the children would wake up, and went upstairs to close the door to their bedroom.

When Eva came downstairs again, the light outside was just fading. Grace staggered from the study holding a large cardboard box overflowing with books and papers. She carried her burden through the French doors and into the garden. The circle of stones where they'd lit the fire for Guy Fawkes' Night was still there.

Before Eva could stop her, Grace threw the pile of books into the circle, and tossed a burning match to the papers. First a small flame, then a full-blown fire flared up, with a hiss and crackle. It quickly became a conflagration. Grace danced around the fire chanting incomprehensible words, *mani mani om gehenna* over and over, in a low, rhythmic voice.

To Eva the fire looked like a funeral pyre, the death of so much labour, so many memories. Shaking with fear and anger, she ran into the scullery to fetch water. By the time she struggled outside with a full bucket in each hand, the blaze was furious, but controlled within the circle. She heard her daughter's voice again, chanting in that strange tongue.

Visions of Grace's dreadful adolescent outbursts came back to Eva, as she watched her daughter's body jerking and out of control. *She's having another of her episodes*, she thought, numb with despair. *How could I have ever entrusted her to Larry, after all the work and expensive treatment I've given her?*

As Eva gazed mesmerised at the flames, she saw the edge of an envelope uncurl, and on it, her own hand. *She's burning my letters*, she thought dully. Transfixed in horror, she tried to lift the heavy bucket of water. She urged her arms to hurl the water into the flames, dousing the furious fire. But her body refused to obey, as she stayed, a helpless observer, rooted to the spot.

With a wild gesture, Grace threw the thick manuscript of her new novel, the one that was to be a present for Larry, into the flames.

'No!' Eva shrieked, her voice piercing above the roaring of the fire. 'It's your book, Grace, all that work! You can't do this'! She moved forward at last, reaching desperately towards the flame already licking at the edges of Grace's manuscript. Helplessly, Eva watched the pages blacken and curl.

'It's all right, Mother, it's worthless, full of lies about two people who loved each other once. But that's all over now.' Grace's voice was flat. She went inside again, and came out with the small red book of Shakespeare's sonnets; it was the same one Eva had seen her daughter give Larry as a wedding gift. Her face incandescent with fury, Grace tore the flyleaf that bore her loving inscription from the book, and hurled it, followed by the whole volume, into the flames. Eva stood there, silent and helpless, and watched her daughter consign to the fire all that had meant love, work and hope. The flames surged for a moment, then died down.

❧

They'll surely work it out, and I'm better off out of here while they do, Eva thought. *If I stay here at Chalk Farm I'll just be the dogsbody. God, after all we've been through, why should my Grace have to suffer like this? That man has a lot to answer for.*

'Grace, I was considering moving out for a while. Who knows when that man of yours will come to his senses? Perhaps it'd be better if I'm not here when he comes back, and come back he will, believe me, with his tail between his legs. When he does, Grace, perhaps you should try to forgive him. He's been such a help with the children, after all.'

'Never, Mother! If you only knew what we used to have between us — all ruined now. Love can never come here ever again. I hate him! He's become such a *little* man. I don't need him, and nor do the children.'

'But my dear, how will you manage? I can only stay a few more days, get the nursery teas, help you with the baby, but I've a job to get back to at home, as you well know. Dear, you're not thinking straight. I can see you're not well. I want you to see that nice Dr Coplin in London.'

❧

When Larry arrived back a few days later, Chalk Farm was a changed place. The very air smelled different. It reeked of misery as if nothing was in its right place. The bitter smell of fire lingered in the air, adding to the feeling of dislocation.

Eva moved towards her son-in-law, ready to hear his abject apologies, and almost prepared to forgive him. Larry, far from being chastened, pushed past Eva with a stony face.

Fleur ran to Larry the moment he walked through the door.

'Daddy!' she squealed in delight, as he swung her up in his arms. 'Tim's got a new tooth, it's sharp and he bit me. Come and see.' Larry's grim expression melted for a moment, but he put the child down without speaking, and headed for the study.

Eva hurried to take Fleur outside. She braced herself for what was coming. There was an ominous silence, broken by a great roar coming from the study. Outside, Eva stiffened and put her hands over her granddaughter's ears.

'You bitch, what've you done with my Shakespeare? And where's the manuscript I left on my desk? My God — thirty new poems at least, and the play I've been working on for months.'

Grace appeared in the doorway. She was still wearing her stained dressing gown. '

'Please, please, tell me they're safe somewhere. Have you hidden them? Where the hell are they?'

'I burnt them,' she said, her face expressionless.

'You what? No, you couldn't have — they were my only copies, years of work I can never get back. The poems weren't even typed up. Surely you wouldn't do such a crazy thing? I don't believe you. For God's sake, tell me you're joking.'

'Sure, I'm joking, just like when I burned all Mother's letters, and yours too. And the funniest thing of all: I've got rid of my own manuscript, the one I've been writing since last Christmas, about a great love between two poets. It's gone up in flames.'

Larry sank down heavily on the chair at his desk, his head in his hands. 'You gave me that Shakespeare,' he said softly, 'before Fleur was born. I carried it with me everywhere.'

'Well, it's gone now, and I want you gone too. Get out. Go back to your Jezebel, tell her about my little joke. Will she laugh, do you think? Or maybe she'd be afraid to ruin her image, and forget to look like a tragic refugee. Does she think she's the only one in this world whose family had to leave Germany?' Grace turned her back on the study, and flung herself on the sofa.

Fleur burst out crying. Eva tried to comfort her, but the little girl shook her grandmother off, and ran to her father. She wrapped her arms round his trouser leg while he threw the few remaining papers from his desk into the suitcase. Gently, he detached Fleur from his leg. Picking up his case, he threw a bundle of pound notes onto the desk.

'Make sure the children have everything they need,' he told Eva. 'I'll leave the car here, and get a cab to the station.' And he was gone, leaving Fleur wailing behind him.

❀

CHAPTER 14

Eliot Court, London, August 1962

In London Larry sought out his friend Luke, a member of The Group, the company of writers who met monthly in London. Although he rarely came to the weekly meetings, Larry was the unofficial leader of the Group. Like nearly all this élite circle of poets, Luke admired Larry's poetry. He'd once offered his bachelor pad 'if ever you need a place to doss down when you're in London.' Now Larry had taken him up on the offer, and was sleeping on the lumpy sofa in Luke's untidy living room.

He set to work immediately, to redeem the devastating loss of his work, by replicating as many of his lost poems as he could remember. But it was hopeless. He thought with regret of the afternoons at Chalk Farm when he'd slaved over those poems, after he'd spent the whole morning caring for the children, so that Grace could write. How she must hate him, to have burnt everything, even the precious Shakespeare. It had been a talisman of their early love, and in destroying it Grace had killed something in him.

On his first night in London, trying to put the loss of his work behind him, Larry went out and bought three bottles of the best champagne. His liberation from what had become the hell of his old life was something to be celebrated. And there was only one person with whom he wanted to share the immensity of his release. It was nearly dark by the time he knocked on the door of his old apartment in Eliot Court.

It opened immediately. Esther stood in the doorway, her eyes wide with apprehension.

'Oh — it's you. What are you doing here?' She said, keeping her voice as steady as she could.

'Let's just say it's my birthday, and I felt nostalgic for the old place,' Larry's eyes were darting past Esther, searching into the room behind her.

'If it's Tony you're looking for, he's gone out, probably to the pub again for all I know. Look, this is insane. You're the last person he'd want to see. How could you come here, after what's happened?'

'I'm leaving Grace,' Larry said, moving towards her. She instinctively backed away, her heart thudding like a trapped animal's. He put the bottles down on the sideboard.

She stared at him. 'My God, Larry. But — but why? What about the children? I — I don't understand …'

'Understand this. I've come to be with you, in spite of all marriages.'

The old fire rose in her, and in a second Esther was in his arms. They kissed with an urgency that shook Esther. This time she didn't pull away.

'Tell me you'll meet me tomorrow, at The Lamb, after work.' He spoke rapidly knowing Tony could be back at any minute.

Esther's heart was beating wildly. She shook her head, and stepped away from Larry. Nothing would make her hurt Tony again.

'Please, please, go, and take your champagne with you.'

❉

Esther spent the following weeks trying to be good. She lavished love on Tony, cosseting him with little treats, even missing work to spend the day together, seeing a movie and cooking his favourite food. But within herself, she felt flat, as if she were playing a role.

One night, arriving home dutifully on the dot of six, she found Tony waiting for her with a Campari on ice, their favourite summer drink, and a telegram that had arrived from Canada. She tore open the envelope.

'It's Mother.' There was alarm in her voice, which shook a little. 'She's having more treatment for the cancer, and needs me there. Darling, can you spare me for a few weeks? I've got loads of leave saved at work, and it's about time I took it. Besides, it might be good for us both, to have a break from all this.' She meant from the constant threat of Larry, hanging over them.

'Of course you must go, if your mother needs you. You're right, after these ghastly last weeks we could both do with a break. I don't mean from each other, though, but from this whole ridiculous situation. This thing with Larry — it's like a tropical plant gone crazy, choking us.'

'I told you, dearest, compared to you, Larry means nothing to me. The whole sorry saga is all a dreadful mistake. Things just got out of hand, that's all. For me to leave the scene now might be just what we all need. But darling, promise me you'll be all right?'

'Come here,' Tony said, and pulled her to him. He stroked her face, looked into her eyes, and saw nothing but candour there. 'We love each other in a way that has nothing to do with that bastard. We need to give each other space when we need it, and there's never been a better time. Besides, we have our trip to Germany to look forward to.' He kissed her lightly on the lips, a kiss that felt foreign to her, its delicacy a feather's touch compared to Larry's hot urgent probing.

She drew away, and went immediately to the ivory-coloured telephone on the little table in the corner, drink in hand. She dialled the airline and proceeded to book herself on a flight to Vancouver on the following Monday. It was settled.

Back at work the next day, Esther felt released, knowing she'd soon be out of Larry's orbit. She set about efficiently, contacting clients and arranging for the other senior copywriter to handle their accounts for the next few weeks. Just the thought of escape gave impetus to her creativity, and new designs for slogans flew off the page. She took great pride in knowing she was indispensable to the company for her originality and skill.

Just as Esther was about to step out for lunch, her phone rang. She instantly froze on hearing a familiar deep voice. Its timbre sent the old thrill through her, and in spite of herself, her body softened in response. The colours in her office grew brighter, as she drew a deep breath.

'I tried to contact you, but that harridan you have working with you keeps saying you're in meetings.'

She paused before answering. Lily had been obedient to a fault, blocking Larry's calls. She couldn't help a frisson of pleasure. *So he's been thinking about me, after all.*

'Are you there? Essie, don't hang up, tell me you're still there.'

'I'm here.' She spoke evenly and politely. She knew she should hang up, yet the spell of his voice stopped her. 'I've been extremely busy at work, so couldn't take personal calls. In any case, I'm taking leave for a few weeks.'

'Good. Because that could fit in with a plan I have for us. Come away with me, Esther. I have to be with you again, wherever and however we can. My marriage is over, so you need have no worries on that score.'

'Well, mine certainly isn't. I'm surprised you'd even suggest such a thing, after the scare I've had with Tony,' said Esther, recovering some of her spirit. 'In any case, I've already booked my flight to Canada, to see my mother. She's gravely ill.'

There was a pause on the line. She imagined she could hear him thinking of how to persuade her, and smiled. *As if she'd jump to his tune!*

'When are you leaving?' he said, after a pause.

'On Monday, straight after this weekend. And I've no fixed date of return, it will all depend how Mutti is. I've loads of leave owing to me from work.' Talking to Larry about work and her family made her feel safe, and separate from him.

'Well then, you must come with me — to Spain. I know a place there where no one could find us. Please, Essie. I've been going crazy for you these last weeks. We owe this to each other, to see this thing through. No one need know — Grace thinks I'm in Ireland, and surely you can cut short your family visit to Canada. It's perfect.'

Esther felt her whole body grow hot, then immediately cold. How dare he presume she would drop everything just to be with him? She was shaking with rage, yet couldn't put down the receiver. 'I am going to visit my sick mother, and to see my sister and father after an absence of two years. How can you expect me to abandon them?'

'Sweetness, just think about it. Please. We need to get away from the stares and jibes of London's vicious gossips. Give them any morsel, and they'll make a meal of it. Spain's the place where you and I can be free from all this. You can let me know; write to me at the BBC when you've decided.' He hung up without saying goodbye.

❧

CHAPTER 15

Vancouver, September 1962

Esther had no intention of joining Larry in Spain, and thought the idea impossibly crazy as she kissed Tony goodbye at Heathrow Airport.

Once in Vancouver, the old loneliness and anger rose up. She found her mother tolerably well after her treatment, and the doctors said the prognosis looked good. In fact Trudi was back to her old self, demanding from Esther what she could not give: undivided attention, undying loyalty.

Trudi had always looked to her elder daughter to work her magic, and get the family back to its lost high standing. Surely, she prayed, a face like Esther's would be their fortune, even now after her two marriages had failed to deliver the wealthy son-in-law who was supposed to rescue the Goldbergs from obscurity. The British serviceman who'd been their hope for escape from Palestine had been a disaster, or else, assumed Trudi, Esther had let him slip through her fingers. That was her daughter all over, Trudi thought. Still, she felt proud of Esther, for her strength as well as her beauty.

Esther had never felt at home in Canada, the country that had adopted her family. Added to her feeling of alienation there, she was seized with a longing for escape. She thought constantly of Larry and his crazy offer. She tried her best to put it out of her mind, and to distract herself by re-connecting with her family.

While Esther was being a dutiful daughter to Yacov and Trudi, she could not resist some sisterly intimacies with Hannah. She told her younger sister that she was being courted by an important poet, a celebrated genius who would be world famous, and that one day she would marry him. In the bedroom they shared, Esther regaled Hannah with highly embroidered tales of her London lover.

'He took me to a hotel — a really posh one — because it was the first time we'd ever made love. I'd bought a slinky new nightgown just for the occasion, and I expected it would all be so romantic. Oh, Hannah, it was terrifying! He was so rough with me, he tore my best blouse, and I never even got to wear the nightie. Later he cried and said sorry. I felt so wretched, and then — poor Tony — but that's another story. You see, it was only a silly flirtation at first, but it went too far. Darling, promise me you'll never get yourself into such a situation. I do worry about you, you know.'

Hannah listened wide-eyed to her sister's confession. 'Essie, you're so brave! I could never do anything like that, it's much too dangerous. How could you let that man touch you? Tell me — did he hurt you?'

Esther was careful to keep from her sister the more sordid details of her congress with Larry. She could never describe it as lovemaking, but she no longer called it rape. She knew her words would excite and alarm her still innocent sister.

'If you saw him, Hannah, you'd understand. He's so handsome, very tall and well built. He has a strong-featured face, with a mouth that can be both cruel and kind. And his hands are so elegant, the hands of a poet.' Esther's voice trailed off and she looked dreamily into the distance, imagining Larry's hands on her face, his lips on hers.

Hannah stared at her glamorous sister in awe. 'But what about Tony?' she whispered in the dark of their bedroom, 'Don't you still love him?'

'*Ach, liebling,* that's the whole trouble. I still love him, but it's a different love entirely to what I feel for Larry. You see, I've discovered it's quite possible to love two men at the same time, but in different ways. Tony's my rock, the one I feel safe with, yet there's no excitement there — you know, that shivery feeling inside you. Don't you sometimes feel it?'

'Well — don't tell Mutti this — there's this boy who works with me in the ski shop, and the way he looks at me - well, you know, I guess he likes me. I want to talk to him, but Vati and Mutti would be shocked if I went out with a boy like that; you know what they're like.'

'You're old enough now to follow your heart, darling. I always have.' *Yes, and look where it's got me.* 'Now, next time you see this young man — what did you say his name is? — This is what will work.' Esther proceeded to share her secrets of seduction with her sister, titillating her, while Hannah giggled with excitement and shame.

When the note arrived, forwarded from her London office, Esther had all but given up hope of hearing from Larry. She felt faint with excitement, and couldn't resist showing it to Hannah.

There's a flight leaving Vancouver for Barcelona every Tuesday. I'll be waiting for you, whichever Tuesday.

Hannah stared at her, aghast. 'Surely you won't answer him? Essie, not after what he did to you. Besides, he has a wife already, and children. What about them?'

'Can't you see, darling? He's left his family, and I'm sure it's because he wants to be with me. That first time — well, he just wanted me so badly. I've forgiven him now. You know I would never leave Tony — but — what's the harm? No one need ever know, that is if you promise absolutely never, ever, to tell.'

Hannah flushed, suddenly angry. 'So — what are you going to do? You can't just leave us so suddenly. This isn't one of your games. What about Mutti? Vati will be so furious, and I — I'll miss you.' She burst into tears.

'Sweetie, listen to me. You have to understand. I'm trying not to hurt anybody, while I work this thing out. I may never get another chance. Mutti's just fine, but you can tell I'm starting to get on her nerves. And Vati always wants only what's best for me. I'll just say I've received a letter from work — which is the absolute truth — and I'm needed back urgently. It's only a small white lie. Besides, it'll only be for a little while. I'll be back before you know it.'

'And what about Tony?' Hannah choked through her sobs. 'How can you deceive him like that? Won't he find out?'

'Not if you do as I say, and swear on our mother's life that you won't breathe a word of this to anyone. Now listen: I'm going to write three letters to Tony, which you must send from here, so they'll be postmarked from Canada. You'll post the first one next Monday, the day I plan to leave, and the other two at weekly intervals. I'll tell Mutti and Vati that I've had to go finalise a lucrative deal for the Agency. It'll make them proud of me, you'll see. Lily will cover for me there, if there are any phone calls. Besides, I should only be away for a week or two.'

'But how can you go to him now, Essie? What if — you know — he hurts you again like you say he did that first time?' Hannah began to cry again, her tears running unchecked down her soft round cheeks. She got out of bed, and leaned over to hug her sister, as if to hold her safe.

Esther stroked her sister's shaking shoulders, and said dreamily, 'Yes, he will hurt me, I know, but not in that way. I can't help it, darling, it's a *fait accompli*; I have to do this. Perhaps only then, I'll be free of him.'

❀

CHAPTER 16

Spain, October 1962

'I'm in heaven.' Esther stretched bare brown arms above her head. She turned over to look at Larry, supine on the sand beside her. Spain was all she had imagined it to be and more: the southern light painting the ancient buildings gold, the crooked cobbled streets, the bustling markets with their makeshift stalls, selling plump glistening olives from huge vats, the trays of salty sardines. She loved the people, the old women in their colourful headscarves and white aprons, the young men with their smooth oiled bodies, and dark Raphaelite faces. Here it was as if she was no outsider, but one with the people, her foreignness no longer apparent. Even the language soon came easily to her, with her flair for other tongues, and she would mingle with the crowds at the daily markets like a native of this little village by the sea.

Now at last she was lying on the warm sand of the little beach at Benidorm. Larry was stroking her bare midriff with the lightest touch, until she could hardly bear the quaking as her whole body responded, and she raised her mouth to his. She felt his answering arousal, and wanted him to take her then and there, but he pulled away from her.

'Not now.' He sat up abruptly, turning away from her, and rose to walk to the water. In a moment he'd plunged under a wave, and was lost to her. Her body cried with its longing as she lay there, still as a statue.

Later, in their whitewashed room he laid her on the soft cotton sheet, and with his tongue explored her open body. The smells and tastes of the market in the square below mingled with their sweet saltiness as she opened to him. She felt a surge, and a tremble, as he touched the quick of her. She heard herself cry out as the spasms jerked through her body. And then he was inside her, thrusting as she convulsed tightly around him, until he too cried out with one last juddering burst.

❖

During one of their forays at the market, Esther spied a small, red book, its leather cover only slightly worn by the hot sun of Spain. She picked it up curiously. It was the Oxford edition of Shakespeare's sonnets, identical to the one Larry had once shown her, and a replica of the one Grace had destroyed. He'd almost wept when he told her of its loss. She bought it immediately, hardly bothering to barter for it.

After their lovemaking, Esther rose from the tousled bed and tiptoed over to the window of their little *pensión*. She went to her big brightly coloured bag with its spoils from her morning foray to the market. Remembering the book she'd bought, she took it out and turned the first page cautiously. Inside its leather covers, the volume was in near-perfect condition. The flyleaf was blank. While Larry still lay in his post-coital daze, Esther found her calligraphy pen and wrote on the blank page: '*To my dearest Larry, who has brought me to life. May this book stay as whole as our love. Yours forever, Esther.*'

❖

Larry's thoughts were torturing him, as he lay pretending to sleep. How could he have taken Esther to Benidorm, of all places? To the site of his and Grace's honeymoon, where his new wife had cried like a baby, a lost child in this strange and threatening place? He must have been crazy to come here again with Esther, she who had 'sniffed them out' and destroyed their marriage. But had she? True, she had got into his bloodstream with her strange beauty, like that of a rare animal in the wild. He'd fallen dangerously in love with her, or maybe in lust. Wasn't it also his lust for life after the stifling few years with Grace in Devon that had propelled him towards her? Somehow Esther was bound up with that surge towards the light. She was his temptress, who made him forget the bonds of family, farm, and duty. He knew only that he desired her helplessly, to the point where he could even hurt those he truly loved.

For all his obsession with Esther, nothing and no one would ever break his bond with Grace. He and the mother of his children were joined forever, like the twin stars Gemini, their horoscopes always parallel.

After the cloak-and-dagger existence he'd been living in London, bedding down on the cold floors of his friends' flats, he craved freedom, space and warmth. Grace had hated Spain. It had been the first disappointment of his marriage. To see Esther so at one with the place, her gypsy soul, revelling in its Mediterranean light, mingling with the people like a native, gave him a guilty pleasure. It was as if he'd corrected a wrong done to him long ago.

Warm air caressed them, as they lay together on the unmade bed. Their lovemaking had been long and passionate. Esther was naked except for the gold locket around her neck, glittering against her smooth skin. Larry traced a line down her neck and between her breasts, lifting the gold chain.

'Tell me, Essie, why do you never take it off?' he said lazily.

How she loved him calling her that. Esther began to talk, in a soft dreamy voice. Larry rolled onto his back, and listened without interrupting.

❀

'I was only six when Mutti and Vati give me this locket. See - it has my initials engraved on the outside. Inside it, there are two tiny photos, on one side my father, on the other, my mother. Look here,' she opened the locket wide. There was Trudi, looking ethereal, faintly smiling, her lush hair piled high above her delicate face. Yacov's portrait was done in sepia, his sensual features sober for the photographer.

'Vati told me I must wear the locket always, that it would keep me safe. He's always been proud of me, even if I give him no reason. Then and there, I determined to make him proud, so that he would never be disappointed in me.

'My parents wanted to send me to the élite private school, but they couldn't afford it right away, not until I went to secondary school. Vati often treated his poorer patients for nothing, even though our family was struggling, like most people in Germany. So they had no choice but to send me to the free municipal *Schule Erste*, which was only a walk away.

'Mutti took me to the Berlin Emporium, one of the only shops still trading, where Vati set up an account. She always bought our clothes one size larger than necessary. "You'll grow into it in no time, *liebchen*," she'd say. It was her way of economising, so that Hannah and I would get more wear out of our clothes. Everything always felt loose and baggy on me; I suppose that's why now I like my clothes to be well cut, and to fit perfectly. I can still remember the letter we got from the *Schule*, with all the items listed:

- one navy blue tunic, belted
- three white blouses with detachable collars
- four pairs white ankle socks
- one navy blue jacket or pullover

'I imagined lots of other children my age getting new clothes too. I expected to look just like them when I started school, because Mutti told me that's what the word "uniform" meant: everyone the same as each other. What I didn't know then was that the uniform wasn't compulsory.

'I remember getting the creaky old lift up to the third floor of the Emporium, where you could smell new clothes, freshly ironed — I still love that smell. The shop assistant looked crossly at Mutti when she asks them to put everything on credit for the Goldberg account, and called the supervisor. "*Natürlich, Fraülein Goldberg*," the supervisor said; he was most likely one of the patients Vati was treating for nothing. "My regards to *Herr Doktor*." We went home with everything on the list.

'I heard my parents talking in Yiddish, when they didn't want me and Hannah to understand. The thing is, I did understand, the gist of it anyway. Yiddish is much like German, you know. Mutti and Vati used to talk about the *gelt* and the *tsuris* –that meant money, and trouble.

'On that first day at *Shule Erste*, I saw straight away that most of the girls were bigger than me. Most of them had blonde hair and blue eyes, good little Aryan *mädchen*. And there was me, with my jet black hair, a dead giveaway. The girls wore faded floral dresses. Not a uniform in sight. There I was, all dressed up in my smart navy-blue tunic, ironed white shirt, and shiny black laced up shoes. I wanted to run away.

'At playtime a group of boys and girls surrounded me, chanting, "Brown eyes pickle pies!" You can see my eyes are greeny-grey, not brown, but that made no difference. I saw my friend Hansel, who lived in our street, staring at me. I smiled at him, called his name, but he pretended not to hear me. *Du bist Judin*, his eyes say. All I wanted was to be exactly like the others. How I wished to have fair hair and blue eyes like them.

'A big brawny boy pushed me down to the ground. Another boy held me down. I could smell his breath; it stank of raw onion. The other children started to kick and punch me. Even while my body was being pummelled, I worried that my brand new uniform would get ruined from the dust. The gravel scratched my bare legs, and ants crawled all over me. I felt my belt being ripped off.'

'This is a shocking story, Essie. I had no idea how you must have suffered,' Larry said, refilling their glasses with Spanish rosé, and handing one to Esther.

Esther warmed to her theme, embellishing the story as was her wont. She loved to entertain, and she knew she had Larry in her thrall. This time, however, she didn't need to employ the exaggeration for which she was famous.

'I held my breath so as not to cry with each punch and kick. I remember the children's pasty faces and lank sandy hair, and most of all their blue eyes, full of hatred. Their mouths snarled, "Dirty Jew, dirty Jew … your father's a dirty Jew."

'I knew my father wasn't dirty. Every morning I watched him through the half-closed door of the bathroom, putting lots of white fluffy froth on his face with a little brush, as he smoothed a razor over his cheeks and chin. He always smelled fresh and sweet, of a mixture of soap and the faint aroma of tobacco, when he kissed me goodbye. So what did they mean by "dirty Jew"? How was Vati different from other fathers? In the evenings, he used to draw for me, beautiful delicate images of the fairies and witches, princes and princesses, from the stories we'd read together. Perhaps Jewish meant being good at drawing, I thought, or wearing clean socks and new shoes to school when the other children were barefoot. Or having tiny egg sandwiches cut in neat squares in a little box, while the others had brown bread with jam, or strong-smelling *würst* wrapped in newspaper. I knew that day, and I've always known, that Jewish meant being different in a bad way.

'A big fair girl broke through the scrum and pulled the two big boys off me. She had two thick yellow plaits, and her eyes bulged their blueness. The girl's name was Gretchen, Gretchen Braun I think. She stood so close to me, that I could smell her sweat. The other bullies stood back, watching their leader.

"My Mum says that you and your folk killed Jesus," she taunted. I struggled to stand up.

'Gretchen reached inside my blouse and pulled at my locket. I tried to grab it back. There was a fierce tug, until I felt the fine gold chain break. A great cheer went up from the group of bullies, as she held my locket up high, like a trophy she'd just won.

'Do you know, Larry, I felt relieved to lose that locket, as if one of my differences were being taken away. I knew Mutti might cry, and Vati might be angry, but I didn't care. *"Now you'll be sorry, Jew girl,"* Gretchen yelled at me as she walked off, waving the locket above her head to show the others. I remember so clearly how it glinted in the sun. The mob followed her, chanting *"Brown eyes, pickle pies, blue eyes beauty. Your father's a dirty Jew."* I was left standing alone in the middle of the playground. Purple bruises formed on my legs, and my cheek was bleeding. But I held my chin high, and bit my lip to stop the tears. I had my pride, even as a child.

'A voice, a long way above my head, said, "Where's your lunch? Go and eat it like the others, before the bell goes. What's wrong? Lost our tongue, have we? My word, don't we look a sight." Fraülein Weiss stood over me. Her hair was always rolled in a thick yellow sausage around her head, and she wore bright red lipstick. Her eyes seemed to drill into me, no doubt taking in my scratches and bruises, and my beltless uniform. "You people all think yourselves better than us decent folk," she said. "Now, go and wash yourself and go and get your lunchbox, like the others."

'There was a crowd around Gretchen on the other side of the playground, circling her and her trophy. Fraülein Weiss walked over to the group, which dispersed like a flock of birds. Out came their parcels of bread wrapped in newspaper. I can still smell rancid meat whenever I remember that day. It made me feel sick, and still does. I ran to the washrooms, leaned over the foul white bowl of the toilet, and let the hot vomit spill. My nose filled with its stench, and my ears rang with the sound of my retching. It was horrible. Ever since, I've had a horror of throwing up.

'When the bell rang, calling us back to class, I ignored it. I ran over to the big iron gate, but it was locked. There was no other way out of that schoolyard, other than to jump over the high fence, or somehow squeeze into the back lane full of stinking rubbish. I pushed through the weeds and old newspapers smeared with excrement. There was another smaller gate at the other end of the lane. Locked too. I had no choice but to go back to the classroom, and creep to my desk in the back row.

"So — I see our new little rich girl has decided to join us." Fraülein's voice sounded harsh, but I feared only my mother's disappointment when she saw the new clothes, not yet paid for, dirty and torn. When school was at last over, mothers and big sisters, some with their hair in curlers wrapped in scarves, came to take their children home. Mutti walked across the playground, smiling at me, carrying baby Hannah high on her hip. As soon as she saw the state I was in, she ran towards me, calling, "*Liebchen*, what happened? Did you fall? Where's your belt?"

'Once we got home — I still hadn't cried, mind you — Mutti opened my new leather satchel and the tin lunchbox, to find my lunch uneaten, the egg sandwiches still in their waxed paper. Then she undressed me, gently touching the darkening bruises. I can still see her sad face, the tears in her eyes. She would have smelled the vomit on my breath. When she realised my neck was bare, the precious locket gone, she cried out, "Your locket, did you lose it? Your father had to borrow so much for it. Tell me, *bubele*, what happened?"

'I gave it to my friend. Her name's Gretchen. She wanted my locket so 1 gave it to her. Mutti, is it true we killed Jesus?'

'What? No, *schönele*. That's wicked, ignorant talk. But your locket, Essie, surely you didn't give it. Someone must have stolen it. Tomorrow your father and I will go with you to the school. We'll get it back for you.'

'I screamed at Mutti, 'No, no, I don't want you to, please Mutti!' I didn't cry until Vati came home. I ran to him and buried my face in his jacket. I can still remember his warm, comforting smell. He picked me up, soothing me until my sobs stopped, and I told him the whole story.'

Esther stops speaking, and sits up suddenly, as if waking from a dream. Larry listens intently, his face still. There's silence in the little whitewashed room, except for the blind at the window gently tapping against the frame.

'My poor Esther,' he says. 'What a dreadful thing to happen to a child. I see now why you always put on airs, trying to be more English than the English. Sweetling, you don't have to try so hard any more. You're perfect as your true self, without the veneer.'

Esther is staring into space like one in a trance, seeing again Gretchen's plaits swinging above her. 'I've never told anyone the whole story, not even Tony.' She looks at Larry as if seeing him for the first time. 'I know now that I'm bound to you, after this.'

Larry squeezes her hand. 'What happened to the locket? Is this the same one?'

'Wait. Well, the very next day, I remember sitting with my father and mother in Fraülein Weiss's office. "Herr Goldberg," she said, "I can't be responsible for every squabble in the playground. Your daughter must learn to stand up for herself. If you'll forgive me for saying so, spoiling her with trinkets isn't going to help her in this school. Even if she tells me who took the necklace, I can't do a thing about it."

"In that case I'll be contacting the police and reporting this as theft, with you and the school liable. You might remember, Fraülein Weiss, that Herr Schmidt, the local chief of police, and his family, are my regular patients."

"Do as you wish," Fraülein replies, "but I must remind you of our new Government's policy, Herr Goldberg, which Herr Schmidt will surely follow. You and your kind are not wanted here."

"You dare to speak to me like this? What sort of a school is this? My daughter is too good for this place. And you can call me *Doktor* Goldberg. I'll be reporting this to the authorities," Vati was white with fury.

'Fraülein's face went red. "I haven't the time to argue with you. Now if you'll excuse me, I have an assembly in five minutes."

"Excuse you? You see my child beaten and robbed and do nothing? You know what Hitler's doing to our people? Is the evil here too? We're leaving. Come away from this place.'

'So the Nazis were spreading their evil even to the children.' Larry strokes her arm, leans over, and kisses her eyes and mouth.

'Vati, Mutti, Hannah and I went to the *kaffeehaus* and ordered *apfelstrüdel* with lots of cream. It was supposed to be a treat, but nothing could take away the sick feeling in my tummy. The waitress told Vati they'd run out of cream. Yet the people at the table opposite were eating pancakes with lashings of cream on top. At that moment I understood how much everyone in Berlin hated us.

'Soon after, no patients come to Vati's surgery any more, not even his most loyal ones. There was a sign, *Jude*, in big white letters on our front door. Jewish students everywhere were being expelled. Worse things were happening out in the street. I remember seeing our neighbour, an old religious man called Herr Goldstein, on his knees while two policemen kicked him and ripped his *yarmulka* off his white head. One of them took out a knife, grabbed his long beard, and cut it off right up to his chin. They walked away laughing.

'That night I heard my parents talking, my father's voice angry, my mother's tearful. The next day Vati announced that we were going on a long holiday. I was allowed to pack my two most favourite things. Hannah cried when she wasn't allowed to bring her special teddy, which was almost as big as her. We boarded a train for Italy, with only one small suitcase each.'

Esther stops talking, and lies back on the pillows, stretching her arms above her head. The locket, its clasp open just a slit, swings between her breasts. Larry lifts it from her neck and gently holds it between his fingers.

'And this locket? You didn't tell me. Is it the same one?'

'Oh, I forgot to finish the story. Vati did go to see Herr Schmidt at the Police Station. You see, he'd treated him, and also his elderly mother, for nothing, although they could well afford to pay him. So when Vati told him what had happened, *Polizist* Schmidt went to Herr Braun's house and demanded Gretchen give the locket back. No one was ever charged. So yes, this is the very same locket, although I've long since realised not even this can protect me. There's still such evil in the world.' Esther opens the locket, her eyes moist, and gazes at the tiny portraits of her mother and father inside it. Larry leans over her, takes her hands in his, and gently kisses her again. 'My poor, brave, love. If you'll let me, I'll protect you, always.' He covers her with his body, and she feels the solid warmth of him, melting her willing flesh.

❖

CHAPTER 17

Eliot Court, London, November 1962

'It's so good to be home — Canada was quite boring a lot of the time.' In her cosy bedroom, Esther felt safe again. Tony watched as his wife unpacked skirts, frocks, and lingerie, which she folded or hung in their walnut-fronted wardrobe. Her new lingerie could easily be explained as an impulse purchase; other than these, her luggage bore no trace of her time in Spain.

'I've never seen those before,' Tony said, as Esther lifted from her suitcase a rose-coloured camisole, and a matching pair of lacy French scanties. 'I can't wait to see you in them. They remind me how much I've missed you — in all sorts of ways.'

'Really? It's only been six weeks or so. But I'll make it up to you, sweetheart.' She felt a pang of guilt, aware that it was over a month since she and Tony had made love. 'At least you had your new poems to take your mind off things, while I was stuck in Vancouver, with the same old family problems. As soon as I knew Mutti was all right without me, I felt it was safe to leave. Oh, and it was wonderful to see Hannah again, and to share our news of the last two years. And Vati — he's as crazy and funny as ever. I do so wish you could meet him again one day.'

'Of course I will. Next time we'll go to Canada together, make it a second honeymoon.' Tony held her close, inhaling her familiar musky scent. 'You know I'd never stand between you and your family. Only — there's one thing still worrying at me, keeping me awake at night. The thing with Larry. Is it over? '

Esther drew away from Tony's embrace. She felt the gross lie between them, pushing them apart. *I can't hurt him*, she thought, *but nor can I keep protecting him with lies.*

'The truth is, I don't really know. I hardly gave him a thought while I was away. I told you, the stupid affair started as a silly dalliance, a flirtation if you like. You know me, darling, I'm always looking for adventure, but I'd never let anything jeopardise our marriage. The thing with Larry — it was nothing compared to what you and I have together.'

Touching Tony's face, its smoothness so different to Larry's rough skin, she said, 'I feel safe with you. You make the world stop spinning so fast; when I'm with you, everything slips back into its right place. Come — let's have a drink to celebrate my coming home.' She leaned her head on Tony's shoulder, as they walked from the tiny bedroom, the same room in which Larry and Grace had slept before they'd moved to Chalk Farm.

The living room was brighter and more welcoming than it had been when Grace showed it to them, just before Tony and Esther took over the lease. The worn carpet, an indeterminate shade of green, was concealed by a scattering of small Persian rugs woven in colours of olive, maroon, and gold. Esther had combed the second-hand furniture shops near The Rose Estate, and found two wing chairs in rich green velvet, which she placed either side of the little fireplace. A bookshelf belonging to the Wildes stood beside the hearth, containing mostly classics, and several copies of the new Penguin poetry books, which featured some of Larry's poems as well as a few of Tony's.

'Oh — I almost forgot.' Esther said, settling into one of the velvet chairs. The glowing green fabric set off her green eyes, a fact of which she was well aware, and which played no small part in her choice of décor. 'I bought you a gift in Vancouver; hopefully you haven't already got this one. His poetry reminds me of yours, somehow.'

Tony took the small parcel she offered him and unwrapped it slowly. 'Yevtushenko! Darling, how did you know I wanted this? He's a new voice amongst poets, been on my list for weeks. I very nearly bought this very book the other day. You see, we're twin souls; you always know what's in my mind. Thank you, dearest.'

Esther felt a twinge of guilt, remembering that she'd bought the book on returning to London, after Larry had told her about this new, exciting Russian poet, a reminder to them both of Esther's heritage.

'Well, he's Russian, after all, so how could I resist?' she replied, slowly sipping the sweet white wine, which Tony had poured for her. 'By the way, did you get my last two letters?'

'I received one from you today, dated three weeks ago. I thought that rather strange for airmail, although I guess the Canadian mail can be a bit erratic. You know, I feel like I know your father already, the way you write about him. I see now where you must get your sense of adventure. What did he think of my latest poem?'

Esther played for time before answering, silently cursing Hannah for her delay in posting the letters she'd entrusted to her. The silly girl must have forgotten, or got her dates mixed up. She always was such a dreamy, absent-minded child.

'Oh darling, I can't remember what Vati said just now — that was weeks ago. I loved the poem — show it to me again, after dinner? But first, I'm dying for a bath.'

'Why don't you run one while I start making dinner?'

'Good idea — thanks, darling. Must admit I'm feeling exhausted, a bath will be lovely.'

As she ran warm water into the old claw-footed bath, Esther was grateful for the wall separating her from Tony. She wanted to be alone with her thoughts. She remembered the taste of shiny black olives she'd eaten in Benidorm, at the little café by the sea, where she and Larry would sit and have aperitifs every sundown. The taste of him was in her mouth again. She tried to stem the flood of desire, but was helpless with the force of it.

Fragrant steam wafted from rose-scented salts. Almost dozing, she felt herself somehow changed. Her breasts suddenly felt heavier. Their nipples tingled to her touch almost painfully, and her belly felt tender. *Probably my monthlies coming on*, she thought drowsily.

❖

'Dinner's almost ready! Let's have that drink first,' Tony's voice cut sharply across her reverie. Esther stepped unsteadily from the cooling water and wrapped herself in a thick white bathrobe. In the kitchen she put together a tray carrying biscuits, a wedge of cheddar, and a few cornichons.

'Can't find any olives in the pantry,' she called to Tony. 'I developed a taste for them while I was away.' She bit her tongue for letting slip something that might give her away.

'What, olives in Canada? Couldn't get them for love nor money, when I was there.'

She quickly changed the subject. 'You know, I'm not sure I'm ready to revisit my past, so soon after Canada. It's going to bring back all sorts of memories, not all of them happy. Could we not postpone Germany? I'm afraid sometimes, of going back there to find the old prejudices have never changed.'

'Come on, darling. We booked this trip ages ago, and at the time you were all for it. Look, this is the perfect time to go, it's the end of summer, there'll be hardly any tourists, perfect. Don't you want to see how the country's changed? The war's well and truly over, after all, and the people have been shamed for what was done under Hitler. Give yourself time to come down to earth, and you'll feel more like it.

❀

CHAPTER 18

Berlin, late November 1962

Esther tried to quell her memories of hiding from heavy-booted soldiers in the carriage of the train, taking her family away from danger. The war was over now, she told herself, and there were no more Nazis. Some of the worst perpetrators had been caught, and they'd hung Eichmann only that year.

Tony had put so much time into arranging this holiday, their first together for over a year. In West Berlin they were to meet up with an old friend they'd known during their time in Burma, a colleague of Tony's. They'd booked a tour of the wine country, and Esther wanted to see Beethoven's house in Bonn. She was excited and nervous to visit the country of her birth after so many years, and to be able to speak her mother tongue. Coming from Berlin, Esther spoke *Hochdeutsch*, the language of upper class Berliners.

Esther knew that her Jewish grandparents, aunt and cousins had been murdered by the Nazis. The day her father had received the news was burned into her memory like an ugly scar. She could still hear him reciting the *Kaddish*, the mourner's prayer, for his dead parents. Apart from witnessing her father's terrible grief, she felt strangely distant from the atrocities being reported almost daily in the British news broadcasts and newspapers. Some said these reports were exaggerated, and that the stories of death camps and mass murder were beyond belief. It was easier to think like this, to deny the horrors, which the latest newsreels were only too graphically portraying, than to realise she too would have been fuel for the gas ovens if the Goldberg family hadn't left Germany in time.

Germany was greatly changed since the long ago days of her childhood. The towns reeked of poverty and defeat, and the villagers appeared mute and suspicious. Only the year before, a huge wall had been erected in Berlin, dividing the city into East and West. Her mother's family still lived in the more liberal West. Esther had no plans to visit them; she suspected they may have condoned Hitler's regime, even though their daughter had married a Jew.

She remembered being in a *kaffehaus* as a child, being refused cream with her cake, because she was Jewish. These days, in the *kaffeehausen*, nobody got cream with their cakes; there was privation everywhere.

Soon after their arrival, Esther and Tony travelled by coach to the countryside, where Tony had planned a hiking trip. The forest in late autumn was still beautiful; russet and gold leaves quivered, and fell from the great pine trees, standing tall and straight like sentinels. After picnicking in the shaded woods on dark pumpernickel bread, and cream cheese with paprika, their walk had slowed. It was getting dark, and both of them were weary.

Towards nightfall they reached a pretty little township, straight out of *Hansel and Gretel.* According to their map, the village was called Boppard, and was an ancient town rich with history. Tony was fascinated, but Esther felt afraid, being surrounded by the dark forests of her childhood. It was as if she'd returned to the world of *Grimm's Fairy Tales*, which used to terrify her when she was little. Her body craved rest. She imagined sinking into clean white sheets under an eiderdown filled with soft goose feathers.

'Let's stay here tonight, darling. I'm worn out, and that little *gasthaus* we passed just now looks so welcoming. Not nearly as dilapidated as some of the houses here. I remember those little inns, like our bed-and-breakfast cottages in England. Vati and Mutti used to take me and Hannah to little *gasthausen* just like this one, in the summer holidays. The innkeepers were always so friendly and welcoming — before everything changed here, that is, when we were never welcome anywhere.'

'Well, as long as they've got room for us,' Tony said anxiously. ' Otherwise, we could take a late train to Berlin. I'm sure there's a coach from here which would get us to the station in time.' He stopped in the narrow cobbled street to rummage in his rucksack for the maps and timetables he carried with him.

'Please, darling, I'm exhausted. And it's getting late. Anyway, why wouldn't they have room for us? After all, I'm the real thing, a native-born German, and you could pass for pure Aryan — is that what they call being 'one of them' now? With your fair hair and good looks, like a true Adonis, who could resist you? '

They entered the inn, its peaked roof and flowered entrance look-ing just like the original gingerbread house of Esther's childhood stories. In the wood panelled foyer, she admired the old-fashioned furniture and pretty landscapes on the wall.

'*Guten abend, mein Herr,*' said the proprietor, a short stocky man with round spectacles. He continued to speak in German, while looking closely at them both. Tony looked to Esther to translate.

'He says welcome, he is pleased we have found this place which has the highest reputation for cleanliness and comfort. He's sure he can accommodate us. Would we mind waiting, while he talks to his wife first?'

As Esther was translating, the innkeeper's eyes never left her face. Something in their expression made her skin crawl.

She and Tony waited in the foyer. There was nowhere to sit in the small space and in her weariness, Esther leaned against Tony. He put his arm around her tenderly. 'Wonder what the hold-up is,' he whis-pered smoothing the velvety dark hair from her forehead. His hand felt cool against her clammy skin, and for a moment Esther let go of her misgivings.

After waiting in silence for what seemed an interminable time, they heard footsteps on the stairway. Two sets. The innkeeper led the way down, followed by a rotund woman wearing a floral dirndl, her hair hidden under a matching scarf. There was a starched white apron tied around her expansive girth.

'*Hier ist meine Frau.*' The host gestured towards his wife. He stood back so that her body shielded him. The woman's eyes glittered, boring into Esther. There was a moment's uncomfortable silence. Esther felt the hairs on the back of her neck prickling, and a cold shiver passed over her. The innkeeper's wife began to speak rapidly in German, addressing Tony. Esther's face grew paler as she listened.

'But — but — this is crazy. She says, "Unfortunately, Sir, but my husband is mistaken. We have no room available tonight." '

'For heaven's sake, ask her why? What's the reason? This place is as quiet as the grave — looks like there are no guests here at all.'

'Probably not. But can't you see? She probably suspects something. Maybe she can tell I'm part-Jewish, and she thinks the war's still on.'

'Don't be silly, Esther, how on earth could she tell?'

The woman watched and waited, her thick arms folded across her capacious bosom. Her husband stood behind her, pretending to busy himself with the big open ledger on the counter.

'You'd be surprised, darling.' Esther said. 'They can sniff us out. Don't worry, I'll pretend that I'm a *bona fide* German. That might put her nasty mind at rest.'

Esther turned to the woman, her eyes blazing with anger. *'Aber meine gute Frau, ich bin Berliner* — but my good woman, I'm from Berlin,' she said in her most polished *Hochdeutsch*.

'Nein, du bist eine schmutzige Judin, du bist nicht willkommen hierin,' and with that the woman turned away, leaving Tony and Esther standing open-mouthed.

'She says I'm a dirty Jewess, and we are not welcome here,' Esther said slowly. 'She's using the familiar *'du'* to show her contempt.' *After all,* thought Esther, *there's no point denying I'm Jewish, and why should I?* Esther spoke in a low voice to Tony. 'Clearly my father's race is still hated here.'

The memory of that first day at school in Berlin flooded Esther's mind. She heard again the taunts of the children: "*Brown eyes, pickle pies. Your father's a dirty Jew.* "

Tony turned to her, his face ablaze with anger. 'These people are crazy, sweetheart. They're furious, because they lost the war, and they have to blame somebody. Anything, but take responsibility for failure themselves. You can sense it everywhere, the air of defeat, and underneath the old hatred's still lurking. It's pathetic. Let's get out of this place; it reeks of pure evil. Tell them we wouldn't stay here if it were the last place on earth.'

Esther stood her ground. Glaring at the woman, she translated word for word what Tony had said, and saw the woman's mouth curl in contempt. With her head held high, Esther walked out on Tony's arm, with a sarcastic '*Vielen Danke* — many thanks.'

❉

After this, Esther felt suspicious of everyone she met. My differences will never go away, she thought bitterly. Little did that woman know I'm good enough to be the mistress of one of England's greatest poets. But I'll never be the same as the English with their cool polite talk and their easy manners.

Wherever she and Tony went, Esther delighted in speaking her perfect German, and eating again the *apfelkuchen* and *kugelhopf* of her childhood. They had taken a room in a West Berlin hotel, near the Tiergarten. One night, having a late supper, the bitter coffee tasted like ashes in her mouth. She pushed the cup away.

'Darling, could I have some hot chocolate, or maybe a lemon tea, instead of this coffee? It tastes like dishwater.'

As he raised his hand to summon the waiter, she said, 'On second thoughts, I'll not have anything. Do you mind if I go upstairs to lie down?'

'Of course not. Are you sure you're OK? You look a bit pale.'

'I'm just tired from the train. It jolted me around too much.'

Esther rose abruptly and took the key he handed her. Once inside the hotel room, she unhooked her skirt and released the tight waistband with a sigh. Too tired to wash, she slipped out of her underwear, noticing again that the smear of blood had still not appeared. She lay down wearily on the brocade-covered bed. She shot bolt upright. *Gott im Himmel*, I couldn't be — surely not. She felt the same wave of panic that had heralded her earlier, unwanted pregnancies. True, she and Larry had been less than careful during Tony's absence, but Esther judged the 'safe' days in her cycle, by the *mittelschmerz*, the sharp pain in her abdomen which signalled her ovulation. These were the days to avoid. Once or twice her usual precautions were abandoned in the urgency of the moment. Later she'd douched in the little private bathroom, and believed herself protected.

What if she really were pregnant? How could she explain this to Tony? Impossible for him to believe this could be his child, when they'd made rather desultory love only once, five days ago, just before leaving for Germany. Her head felt hot with the horror of it.

Even now, with so many signs, she could not believe that her body had betrayed her. She felt calm and stolid instead of anxious and tense, as she usually did before her menses. Memories of Larry and their love-making, sometimes rough, at other times gentle, aroused her. Perhaps, she fantasised, she'd conceived his child against all odds. It would be a gift, a message from the fates, that their union was inevitable. At the same time, she felt the old terror at the thought of cells multiplying inside her.

At breakfast in the hotel dining room next morning, Tony was again solicitous. Esther looked pale, and he noticed a fine film of sweat on her brow. She'd pushed her plate of *würst* and eggs away with a grimace of distaste.

'Are you all right, dearest?' Tony said, his eyes wide with concern.

'I'm just a bit shaky in the stomach still, after the flight. You'd think I'd be a seasoned traveller after all the journeys I've taken in my life. Don't worry, dear one, it will pass.' Esther swallowed down hard on her nausea. Tony must never suspect anything. After all, he still had no idea she'd been to Spain with Larry, and she'd make sure he never would. The time would come for decisions later, when her pregnancy became obvious. She pushed all thoughts of the future away.

❊

CHAPTER 19

Chalk Farm, December 1962

Larry made the long drive from London to Devon in an old Vauxhall, borrowed from a friend who was overseas, and whose flat he was occupying. All the way his head was full of confusion, and a feeling of unreality. How had he been sucked into this madness? Instead of freedom, he felt trapped by this powerful pull towards Esther. It was as if his will were suspended, and he was helpless to resist her,

He had half thought of a rapprochement between himself and Grace, in spite of being aware of her rage against him. It was mostly the separation from Fleur, who'd been his constant companion since her birth, which tore at his heart.

As soon as he walked in the door of the cottage, little Fleur ran to him, shouting with joy. 'Daddy, Daddy, me go with you?' He swept her up and held her close, as near to tears as he'd ever been in front of his daughter.

Grace came slowly downstairs with baby Tim. Larry was shocked at how much weight she'd lost. She had a raw-boned look, as if her skin were stretched too tightly over her skeleton. She looked at him unsmiling.

'So you're back. Just as well, I need some money to pay a mother's help. Daphne has found me a girl from the village, who'll come and look after the children every morning while I write — or try to write.'

Tim wriggled out of Grace's embrace, holding out his chubby arms to his father. Larry ignored him. He'd never taken to the boy, finding his maleness a subtle threat. He kept his hands busy, fishing in his pockets in search of something.

'Here,' he said, handing a chequebook to Grace. 'I've signed over the whole account to you. I won't be drawing on it myself; I've made other arrangements. It's for you and the children while I'm not here. I came to tell you I've taken a bedsit in Charing Cross. Here's the address, in case you need to find me.' Larry put Fleur down tenderly. 'Go and play outside, sweetheart. Daddy will be there soon.' Fleur ran off into the sunny garden.

'You're finally abandoning us? You think money can make up for what you've done? Oh You! You and your painted whore, both of you faithless and arrogant. What is it about her? Is it the sex? Tell me — is the Jewess good in bed? '

'It's nothing to do with that. Esther's a diversion, that's all. She comes with no strings. She was just the catalyst, the force that I needed to dynamite my life. You must understand, I can't stay suffocated, stulti-fied here. You were right to tell me to go.'

Grace's eyes filled with angry tears. 'So go! Leave us again, leave me alone like you did in Ireland. You're such a *little* man, after all. That witch has shrunk you down to a manikin. She'll eat you up like a black widow spider with her prey.'

'Grace, listen to me. You must understand that I need complete freedom to write. Remember what D.H. Lawrence said about the cre-ative life, following one's instincts? It's what you and I lived by, once. Remember the life we had before the children came? The life we both talked about, Lawrence's unfettered existence? We need to give each other that space, so that our writing can live again.'

'How nice for you to have space. What about my space, for my writing? Tell me, why can't you have that Lawrentian life here? With me and the children?'

'One day we will, perhaps, when we've both moved on. Just now, it's impossible. I'm on a new path, and I have to follow it. It's nothing to do with any other woman.'

'So you're just going to walk away from Fleur and Tim, as if they're so much excess baggage? You think your money could make up for destroying their lives, and mine?'. They were facing each other, Grace's face frozen in anger, Larry's eyes still red. She turned from him, and walked towards the kitchen, not caring whether he followed.

They stood and stared at each other. 'It's killing me,' Larry said, 'not to be with Fleur. You know I'll be back, often, to see them.'

'Oh, really? I'll see about that. Don't think you can just waltz in here any time you like. Get out, go back to your filthy whore, with her painted face and crazy eyes.'

'Enough!' Larry bellowed. He went into the garden to say goodbye to Fleur. He found her playing by herself, arranging pebbles in a pattern. Sweeping her up in his arms, he kissed her face, and whispered, 'Daddy will be back soon, sweetheart.'

Grabbing his hastily packed bag, he slipped away without a backward glance, like Adam leaving the Garden of Eden. The sound of Fleur's loud crying pierced his heart.

❁

A few weeks after her return, from Germany, Esther met Larry in their favourite pub, The Lamb. It was always dim and smoky, and filled with London's literati..

'It was shocking,' she told him, widening pale grey eyes. 'The old witch was a rabid anti-Semite. It was as if she could sniff out the Jewishness in me. And what was most shocking is that nothing's changed in Germany. I could feel people's eyes on me, with their hatred of anyone not 'Aryan', you know, blonde and blue-eyed.'

'Come on, Sweetling, you must've imagined it. The old bag was jealous of your loveliness, that was all. Those people can't see true beauty, blinded as they must've been by all that Nazi propaganda. Try to forget the whole thing, and be proud of your heritage. It's one of the many things I love about you, your many-blooded beauty.'

'How can I ever forget it? I'll never go back there.'

'Too bad. After all, it's the country of your birth. You may feel differently one day. Now, for some good news. I've found a place to rent, here in London. A place of my own at last. It's only a one-bedder, but has good light, and I know I'll be able to write there.'

'Darling, that's wonderful. A place of our own. When can I come and see it?'

'It's not going to be 'our' place, Esther. As I said, it's for me to have a place to live and write, instead of having to sleep on friends' floors or their lumpy sofas. It would spoil things for us to live together. And you're still with Tony. It wouldn't do at all. No, let's lie low.'

'Can't for much longer, my love. I have some exciting news too. I'm pregnant.' Shaking a little, she reached for his hand.

Larry went still, and dropped her hand. His face turned to stone; his mouth, smiling a moment before, drew a grim line. There was an awful silence.

'You can't be. You told me you don't want children. And — you told me you were taking — you know — precautions.'

'Oh, darling, even the best precautions can go wrong. Haven't you noticed anything different about me? Why do you think I'm drinking orange juice instead of wine? Larry — do you understand what I'm saying? I'm having your child.'

'How can you be sure?'

'I saw my doctor this morning. He's confirmed what I already knew, have known since before Germany

Larry stared at her with an expression of horror. 'If this is true, it surely must be Tony's. Unless you've tricked me.'

'Don't be ridiculous, darling. I told you, it's yours. According to the dates, it happened in Spain. I haven't slept with Tony since before he went to Canada. He and I often go for months without — you know — and besides, I just know it's yours.'

'For God's sake, how am I supposed to believe that? What do you take me for, Esther? Tony's your husband, you live with him. Look, you know perfectly well I have my own two children, who are more than enough for me. Why d'you think I left Chalk Farm? I'm only just getting free of domesticity at last. I couldn't deal with another child.'

Esther drew back from him, and spoke only when she trusted her voice not to shake.

'Nobody's asking you to 'deal with it' as you put it. This will be my child, and yours too, but I'll take all the responsibility. I'm not asking you for anything, except to be happy for us. And to want this child. It's a gift, given to us by Fate, the same Fate you always say governs our lives. Well, if your precious stars have lined themselves up to make this come about, who are we to argue with them? Why can't you see, this is the sign we were waiting for?'

She began to weep noiselessly, her tears coursing unchecked down her cheeks.

'Essie, control yourself. Listen to me.' Larry lowered his voice, although the pub was near empty. 'We have each other, our special closeness, our life together that defies common convention. Don't let this spoil it. And I can't bear to think of your body torn apart, your beauty coarsened. Just consider what it could do to you, to us, if you had a child. No, you must do with this one as you've done with the others.' He spoke quietly, firmly, looking fixedly at her.

'But this is different. The child is already part of us. You'll see — it will be a new life for us both.' With an effort, Esther stopped crying and leaned towards him, seeking his embrace. He held himself away.

'Come on, Esther. You've been pregnant before, and got rid of it before. Surely you're not thinking of going ahead with this? Look, there's still time if you act soon.'

Esther felt the familiar nausea rising. The panelled walls of the pub seemed to buckle and melt around her. She pushed her orange juice away. The very sight of it turned her stomach.

'Larry, I want this child. This is different to every other time, because it's yours, part of you inside me, and' — covering her mouth, she rose and ran to the lavatory. She reached the basin just in time to let the hot vomit spill. Splashing her face with water, she rinsed away the vomit, as her tears mingled with the cold water on her cheeks. When she returned to the dimly lit saloon, their booth was empty.

Sitting on the crowded tube on her way home to Tony, Esther was powerless to stop her tears. Passengers averted their eyes at the sight of this beautiful woman crying silently, as if she were unaware of her surroundings. On the short walk home from the station, she collected herself, and prepared to face her husband.

Tony had guessed weeks ago that Esther was pregnant, knowing his wife's body as intimately as he did. While they were in Germany he'd recognised the early signs: her tiredness, and her aversion to coffee. Just like the last time, which had ended so sadly. Hope and happiness filled him. When his wife came in the door he attributed her flushed face and red-rimmed eyes to her condition.

'Darling, come and sit down, you look all in. You can tell me now, what I've suspected for weeks. The sickness, the dizzy spells you had while we were away, does it all mean what I think it does?'

'I was going to tell you as soon as I was sure — but yes, it's true. I'm pregnant. I saw a doctor only this morning.' She sank back in the easy chair and closed her eyes.

'Thank God. It's what I've been secretly hoping for, ever since we lost the baby last year. I want us to have this child. Sweetheart, I know how much your career means to you. If you want to keep working, I'll stay home and take care of the baby.'

Esther was silent, reflecting on how to tell Tony that this child might not be his. Suppressing her natural impulse towards confession, she melted into his arms. She kissed her husband, tears of gratitude in her eyes.

It seemed to Esther as if Tony had read her thoughts, and was accepting the situation.

'Your child is my child. It's part of you, and you're still my wife, whatever else has happened. If this is true, we've been blessed. Our son will carry on my name, and we'll be a real family at last. I'll always look after you both'

'What makes you think it's going to be a boy, you foolish man?'

❖

In her new state of contentment, Esther found it all too easy to accept Tony's promise of support. She was convinced that somehow everything would work out; nature would take its course. Although it was the coldest winter England had known for over thirty years, Esther felt an inner warmth, an invulnerability to frost and snow. Her pale skin glowed golden, and there was a radiance about her that seemed to her a magic circle of safety. For the first time in her life, she felt a strong sense of protection toward another being.

❀

CHAPTER 20

London, January 1963

Esther decided to keep working at the Agency until six weeks before her due date. She had found an excellent doctor through the wife of one of the poets in The Group. Dr Coplin had assured her it would be safe to work up to seven months gestation, which would bring her to May or early June, depending on whether the baby was early or late. At the thought of Larry's child inside her, happiness flooded her mind and heart.

Esther knew she was invaluable to the Agency, with her consummate skill as a wordsmith, and her connections to the London literati. As Mrs Buchanan, she could project the image of a respectable married woman in the bloom of early pregnancy, and her dignity would be intact. If some whispered behind their hands, she hoped it would only add to her aura of intrigue and mystery.

One day early in the New Year, Audrey and Esther met for lunch. Esther's face glowed under the fur-fringed hood of her blue velvet cloak.

'Dr Coplin's so kind and understanding. I think I'm even falling for him a little myself,' Esther joked, over their bowls of steaming minestrone. 'Tell me, how did you discover him?'

'Oh, darling, all our crowd goes to him. He doesn't just deliver babies, you know. He's good for all sorts of women's ailments, even the blues. I went to him myself once, just for a check-up. Apparently the medical world's working on this amazing new drug, a pill that is guaranteed to stop one getting pregnant. Imagine, no more messy diaphragms and douches.'

'Too late for me, I'm afraid, darling,' Esther laughed. Both women took another spoonful of the rich soup. Esther said: 'When you say "all our crowd" would that include Larry's wife, Grace?'

'Oh yes, now I come to think of it, it was she who recommended him in the first place. Why? Surely you're not worried about Dr Coplin having treated her in the past? He's a highly ethical specialist, you know; I'm sure he'd never breach patient confidentiality.'

'It's just that I've heard Grace's back in London; thank goodness we've moved to Highgate Fields, well away from The Rose Estate, so there's little chance I'll bump into her in the streets or shops. The last thing I'd want is to come face to face in Dr Coplin's waiting room. Larry says it would kill her to see me in this condition.'

'Surely he exaggerates, Esther. Anyway, that's all past history, isn't it? Aren't you back with your husband?'

'Yes, but it's still all so raw, and Grace hates me so much, Audrey. Don't ask me how I know; let's just say I saw something I shouldn't have, a poem she left lying around. I think I'll have to find another doctor.'

'Don't be silly, my dear. We're all over the drama now, and Grace's obviously moving on in her life. Apparently she turned up at the PEN annual soirée the other night, done up to the nines, according to reports I've heard. She's an intelligent woman, you know. Writes a bit herself, I believe.'

'Can I ask you something? You've known the poetry crowd for years. Do you think Larry still loves Grace?'

'I believe he must — look at how much they have in common: their writing, his poetry. Apparently she even used to organise his manuscripts for publication. To say nothing of the children they have between them — two, isn't it? It's so complicated when children are involved. Anyway, I wouldn't be at all surprised if Larry and Grace got back together before too long. Men are so fickle, darling. You should play your cards right, Esther, and look after Tony. You wouldn't want to lose him, would you?'

Esther put down her spoon and pushed her bowl away. 'I think you should mind your own business, Audrey, and let others live their own lives.' Gathering her cloak around her thickening body, she rose with as much dignity as her condition would allow, and took a handful of pound notes from her matching velvet purse.

'That should cover lunch, including the tip,' she said, as she walked off, leaving Audrey open-mouthed, spoon halfway to her lips.

Typical of the woman, Audrey thought, when she'd recovered her equanimity. *She's even more outspoken with those hormones surging through her. Wonder if all Israelis are as rude as her? Chutzpa, they call it.*

❀

London was enveloped in soft white snow. Esther and Tony were spending the New Year quietly at home together. Larry was still in Yorkshire, visiting his family. Tony had accepted an invitation for the first soirée of the New Year from Ben, Audrey's husband.

Esther was tortured by the thought that Grace was in Yorkshire with Larry. Perhaps she'd taken the children to see their grandparents for Christmas, and been persuaded to stay on. Maybe Grace had forgiven him, had realised that Fleur and Timothy needed their father, and had succumbed to family pressure. She knew, with a sick feeling, that Larry could easily be swayed — hadn't she proved it?

Trying to put those haunting thoughts out of her head, she determined to show no weakness to these literati. They were as capable of malicious gossip as a Greek chorus, or the village fishwives.

❀

'Happy New Year! Come in out of the cold, you two.' Audrey welcomed them warmly at her front door, despite her tiff with Esther over lunch the previous week. Tony and Esther returned the greeting while removing their heavy outdoor coats and galoshes. Esther was again wearing her fur-trimmed cloak, as if cast in the title role of Anna Karenina. Snowflakes sparkled on the dark velvet hood, and on her escaping strands of blue-black hair.

Inside there was the usual crowd, most of them poets and their wives. It was one of the few occasions that spouses were included in The Group. The wives tended to band together, as if for solidarity. Esther drifted over to join the women.

'Well, there's one couple conspicuous by their absence,' said Jane, an inveterate gossip. 'The Wildes were here with bells on, last January, as I remember. It was just before Grace had their second child; she was huge. Sad what's happened to them, don't you think?' She addressed no one in particular. Everyone steadfastly refused to look at Esther, which made her feel the focus of attention.

Holding her head high, and smoothing the soft grey wool of her dress over her rounded stomach, she said brightly, 'Well, Tony and I spent a cosy day at home in front of a roaring fire on Christmas Day, very happy to avoid the tiresome trappings of a family dinner.'

It was as if Esther had never spoken. The women ignored her comment.

'I heard the Wildes have gone to Yorkshire — that's where Larry's from, you know, and his parents still live there. He's really a country boy, after all. Must have been frightfully cold way up there. No wonder he left that backwater for civilization in London. Grace would've taken the children to Larry's family, I expect.' said Jane.

'So it looks like there might be a reconciliation? This is the perfect time to make a new start, New Year resolutions and all that. Although how she could take him back, I really don't know. If it were me, I couldn't forgive such betrayal.'

Esther felt her cheeks burning. She sat very still, determined not to give these gossips the satisfaction of seeing her discomfort. *They're jealous, these pathetic women, with their narrow little lives*, she thought. But curiosity held her captive.

Audrey came over to join the women's contingent, offering a plate of homemade savouries. She'd overheard the last part of the conversation, and felt disgusted on her friend's behalf. Besides, as a consummate hostess, it shamed Audrey to see Esther as the butt of malice.

'As a matter of fact, you're all wrong. Larry went to Yorkshire alone. Esther, darling, come and meet my cousin from Zürich, and practice your German. You two should have lots in common.' Ignoring Jane and the other women, Audrey whisked Esther away from their staring eyes and whispering tongues.

Esther whispered 'thank you' to her hostess, who led her to the other side of the room. The aforementioned cousin was an elegant gentleman in his sixties, wearing a well-cut suit and smoking a gold-tipped Sobranie cigarette. He snapped open a silver cigarette case with a flourish, and offered one to Esther. She took it gratefully, forgetting Dr Coplin's injunctions against smoking in pregnancy, and accepted a light from his matching silver lighter. He reminded Esther of her father, with his urbane ways and kind eyes. She felt a pang of nostalgia for Yacov.

'Herr Gustav Schmidt, at your service,' the gentleman said in heavily accented English. 'You are the wife of that brilliant young poet, Buchanan, I believe? I've been reading the new Penguin Poets, and I see he's in illustrious company, being published alongside the likes of Larry Wilde.' Herr Schmidt glanced at Tony standing by the bookshelves in conversation with Ben. Before Esther could answer, Herr Schmidt pressed Esther's hand, and said, 'He is a very lucky man indeed.'

❖

CHAPTER 21

Charing Cross, London, January 1963

The small bedsit was barely furnished, with a table under the window, which served as his desk, a comfortable chair, and bookshelves, which had been thrown out in the street. Larry had knocked them together and sanded the old paint off, and they housed the dozen or so books he couldn't live without.

Larry insisted that Esther visit strictly by arrangement, an order that Esther defiantly ignored. Reluctantly, he'd given her a key, worn down by her insistence. They often made love on the single bed he'd borrowed from a friend, as long she agreed to leave afterwards. The erotic force Esther aroused in Larry was as irresistible as ever. He'd even come to terms with the idea of her having this child, provided there were no extra demands on him.

Still, he could never be sure the child was really his. Wasn't she still living with Tony, to all appearances the perfect wife? She rarely talked about her pregnancy, but her body was perceptibly changing. Her swollen breasts with their darkened nipples excited him, in spite of what they portended.

One evening, a few weeks after he'd moved in, there was a soft knock on his door. When he opened it, there stood Grace, resplendent in a dark blue evening gown made of shot silk. Her hair was piled into a coiled coronet, and her long silver earrings shimmered, quivering slightly in the cold night air. Larry's heart lurched with pity at the sight of her wide brown eyes outlined with black kohl, and her lashes thick with mascara. Her painted lips, red as blood, were like a wound slashed against the unearthly whiteness of her skin.

Larry gasped and took a step back, as if she were a ghost. He was frightened by the gauntness of her frame. Her eyes had a febrile glitter, and under them dark shadows of exhaustion looked like faint bruises.

What if Esther suddenly appears? Larry's stomach lurched in panic. *Damn the woman, if she'd just let me know.* He stepped forward and ushered Grace inside. He stretched out his arms to embrace her, but she pushed him away and strode past him, looking wildly around the room.

'Why — Grace. You — you look amazing. Don't look at this mess. I've only just moved in. Please - sit down, tell me why you're here.'

'I just wanted to see the hovel you live in, to know how low the father of my children has sunk. And to ask you to leave London. I can't live in this city while you're here.'

'Grace — don't let's start. Can't we at least be civil to each other?'

'Civil? Is that what you call it? Forget it — I don't need anything from you any more. I'm on my way to a party tonight, with all the literary luminaries — Eliot, Spender, Porter, you know. I was afraid you'd be invited too, but after all, why should that worry me? I'm my own woman now. Who knows, I might meet someone there tonight, just like the time I first met you at the student party. Remember? I bit your cheek till the blood ran. God, I was so drunk that night. Did you hear my interview with the BBC?' She was babbling, her voice high and shrill.

'I did hear it — how can you think I'd miss that? And Grace, those poems — they're incredible — you've found your true voice. Perhaps it was me holding you back, like a big black cloak you could hide under. But now — these poems will make your name. I always knew you had it in you.'

Grace burst into tears, her raucous sobs echoing in the dingy room. Rivulets of kohl and mascara, mixed with her tears, gave her the look of a grimy-faced child. Larry stepped forward, and put his arms around his wife's shaking shoulders.

She softened into his chest for a second, then drew back, looking into his eyes. 'Tell me we can be together again — that this is all a nightmare, and we're phantoms in our own dreams. Tell me we'll sit together amongst the daffodils next summer, and watch our children grow.'

Her words were broken, almost incoherent. As he saw her over made-up face melt into red splotches and black streaks, his heart was wrung with pity. She cried like a little girl, and he saw Fleur in her face, and wept himself.

'Grace. Listen to me. It's you I love. I must've been crazy last summer, bewitched somehow. We could work things out, live our lives in a new way. Think of it. By next summer we could be together, with our children back in Devon. In summer, yes — the laburnum will be in bloom, and we'll be different, we'll start afresh.'

Something snapped inside Grace, and she fell forward into Larry's arms, weeping silently. They stood locked together for a long moment. She lifted her face to his, and saw his eyes too were wet.

She stared at him and pulled away.

'No, we've gone too far for that. You — you were my jailer back then, when I thought you would free me, from my mother, from myself.' She stepped away from him, and again looked wildly around the half-furnished room. Her eyes fell on a familiar red-covered book on his desk. It looked exactly like the Oxford Shakespeare she had given him, with such love in her heart, when they were courting. But — how could it be? Hadn't she destroyed it, torn the flyleaf out and burnt the book, in that nightmare of a summer? Her own mother had been witness to the deed. That Shakespeare didn't, couldn't, exist any more. She must be hallucinating. Unless? Her eyes wide with surprise, she picked up the slim leather volume in disbelief. It was a miracle, a sign; the book had come back to them. She smoothed the leather cover, slightly worn with age.

'Why? How is this possible? Perhaps everything, your leaving, the barren witch, the fire, was only a terrible dream. As if that German bitch placed an evil spell on us the night they came to dinner. And now I'm awake, and this precious book is real.'

With trembling fingers Grace turned the first page, tenderly, reverently. Before Larry could stop her, Grace saw the flyleaf and caught sight of its inscription:

To my dearest Larry, who has brought me to life. May this book stay
as whole as our love.
Yours forever, Esther.

As if it had burnt her fingers, Grace dropped the book with a single cry, like the plaintive call of a great bird. She turned to Larry, her face aflame.

'You've deserted your children, left our marriage — for what? Life with a barren witch?'

At that moment they heard slow heavy steps coming up the stairs, and a woman's voice, deep and guttural, calling, 'I've brought you a surprise, darling!' Larry froze in horror. How he hated Esther at that moment.

Grace knew that voice, the same one that had snaked down the phone line that dreadful day last summer, announcing the beginning of the end. And the same voice that had sweetly offered her a tapestry, which now lay unfinished in a drawer of her old life. Why had she not burnt it, along with the Shakespeare? She flinched, and made to leave. But it was too late.

They heard a key turning in the lock, and Esther, her face flushed with the effort of climbing, stepped inside. The two women stared at each other. For Grace, one look at Esther's face, smooth and contented, and her swollen breasts, was enough. As if she'd been shot, Grace recoiled, and ran from the room. The silence was loud in Esther's ears. For a moment she had a mad urge to laugh. She stared at Larry, horrified, her hand over her mouth.

'Why didn't you tell her about the baby before? You promised me you would.'

Larry sat heavily into the chair by the desk, and sank his head into his hands. Esther stood in the middle of the barely furnished room, staring at the door through which Grace had fled.

'Why? Why didn't I tell her? Because I knew it would kill her, that's why.'

'Oh Larry, surely not. Can't we be civilised about all this? She was bound to find out soon, it's all over London. The old days of shame and secrecy are over. Isn't it better for her to know the truth?'

'The truth? What truth? That you insist on keeping this child, claim it as mine, while still living in apparent connubial bliss with your saint of a husband? Deceiving him, deceiving me? Rubbing salt into the fresh wounds we've both inflicted on Grace?'

'Darling, don't be so dramatic. Judging by the way Grace was dressed tonight, she's obviously moving on. After all, this child will be a half brother or half sister to Fleur and Tim. Grace and I are sensible women, and I hope one day we'll be friends.'

Larry's face darkened, his lips compressed into a thin line. 'Friends? You clearly don't know her at all. This new shock could tip her over the edge. Grace is extremely fragile, as well I know from looking after her for these last six years. Don't talk to me about her moving on, Esther.' Standing abruptly, he added, 'I'm in no mood for company tonight. It's best you leave now.'

'So you don't want your surprise then?' Esther's heart was breaking, as she moved towards the bed. She masked her pain with a smile, as her years of subterfuge had taught her. With a flourish, she took a small book from her bag. 'It's a first edition of Yeats. I found it in that little bookshop, on the way here. It's the exact one you've been searching for.'

Larry slowly lifted his head and glanced towards Esther. He saw again the image of a magnificent jaguar, like an animal ready to pounce. For a long moment, he held her silver eyes in his gaze.

'If you want it, come and get it,' Esther said, holding the book above her head, and leaning back as she lifted her wide skirt just enough to reveal a glimpse of creamy white thigh above her grey stockings.

Larry rose from his chair and moved towards her.

❧

CHAPTER 22

Cambridge Crescent, London, February 1963

Rubbing her hands together, desperate for warmth, Grace rose from the bed she shared with her children and dragged a blanket from the empty cot nearby, to drape over her shoulders. It took a supreme effort of will to shuffle to the little table under the bedroom window that served as a desk. She opened her journal with stiff aching fingers, and reached for her fountain pen.

The water's frozen in the pipes, and the blood's frozen in my veins. My hands are stiff and blue with cold as I write this. It's the worst winter London has known in over thirty years. Thirty years, my age last birthday, and what have I to show for it? A failed marriage, a few poems, and a mediocre novel. At least I didn't publish it under my own name. Mother would be mortified if she knew that monster was based on her.

There's nothing left. Only the children — my two roses. They'll surely be better off without me. How it breaks my heart to see them, both asleep now, thank God, curled up into their little balls in the bed we needs must share, just to keep warm.

I'm seizing these precious moments to write, before they wake. As the temperature drops so the words, bitter words, are pouring out of me on these dark mornings. I've a feeling these new poems are the ones that will make my name, and make Mother proud of me.

There was just enough light to see the loose page with the draft of her last poem, its many crossed-out lines and scribbled notes rebuking her. With a sigh, Grace crossed out the old working title for her collection, *The Rival*, and replaced it with *A Birthday Present*. It was an ironic title, reflecting her bitterness at the end of her fairy-tale marriage. The birthday gift she wrote of was release, an end to her pain. Like her other poems, this one sang with the force of her burgeoning creativity. The words were wrung out of her in these early mornings, when she woke to the blackness, after the effects of her sedative had worn off.

These hours before dawn, while the children were still mercifully asleep, were hers alone. It was as if she needed to fill the gaping wound of Larry's absence with these new, angry, savage poems. She would dedicate her manuscript to Fleur and Timothy.

When they last spoke on the phone, only a few days ago, Grace had almost believed that she and Larry would be together again. He'd talked of a holiday together, not Ireland this time, but maybe France, Brittany by the sea. Grace felt her stomach flip at the thought of it. She quenched the joy inside her. *He'll betray me again, this is all talk, how could I ever trust him again?*

Since that call, Grace's depression had deepened. The new tablets prescribed by Dr Coplin hadn't helped. In fact, if anything her spirits had sunk further, and the voices in her head were becoming incessant.

It was almost six now, yet still dark outside. She switched on the reading lamp; it shone its yellow light on the black ring binder on her writing table. Stretching and shivering at the same time, she closed her eyes to fight the blackness that always engulfed her on waking, drawing her in and down, deeper than sleep. *Let me die,* the voice in her head whispered again. There was no stopping it.

As the weak light filtered into the bedroom, a chesty cough from the bed interrupted Grace's writing. She laid down her pen, and rose stiffly. Little Timothy was coughing in his sleep, his cheeks pale, and snot blocking his tiny nostrils. At least the worst of the fever had gone, leaving both children weak and irritable. Ammonia fumes from the baby's urine-soaked nappy struck her nostrils, and she turned to fetch a clean one from the diminishing pile beside the bed.

Fleur as usual sat straight up, wide awake and ready for the new day. Ignoring her baby brother stirring beside her, she lifted her arms to Grace.

'Mummy, will Daddy come and take us to the zoo today?'

'Not today, my darling,' Grace said, hugging her daughter and burying her face in the child's soft hair. 'It's still snowing outside. We'll read stories together and you can help me make pancakes for breakfast. And tomorrow, a new nanny's coming to help Mummy, won't that be good?'

She forced her voice up higher, striving for a semblance of cheerfulness, for Fleur's sake. But inside, her heart was hollow; there was no room for hope any more. *Let me die,* the voice echoed once more. She closed her mind to it, as she'd done again, and again. Only the children mattered.

Fleur, once out of bed, and seemingly oblivious to the cold, ran to the toy box and started undressing her favourite doll, mimicking Grace's actions as she changed, Timothy. The little girl sang a tuneless song to her dolly, punctuated with the occasional chesty cough.

'He smells,' Fleur whined, holding her nose as Grace peeled Tim's nappy off. She put the sodden cloth in the large metal bin. With limited water for washing, the bin was filling up, and the stench was becoming overpowering. It mingled in Grace's nostrils with that of her own unwashed body, its female smells sickening her.

She looked at the laundry basket in the bedroom, overflowing with the children's clothes, and thought of the dishes piling up in the sink downstairs. Not only was there no hot water, a bare trickle of icy water was struggling through the frozen pipes. She'd used what little water she'd salvaged in a bucket, to wash the children. Now, when the bucket was near to empty, she kept a damp flannel close at hand to wipe sticky faces and fingers

Thank goodness I thought to fill the kettle and pots with water yesterday. I can warm the kitchen up by lighting the stove. At least they haven't cut the gas off yet. And again she heard the voice in her head: *Let me die,* as she saw her body perfected, still, at peace at last.

'Mummy, I'm hungry.' Fleur pulled at Grace's dressing gown. Shaking herself out of the blackness with a huge effort, she lifted Fleur to her and kissed her forehead, cheeks and nose. 'Then let's get Tim and you dressed, and we'll go downstairs to make those pancakes.'

At the stove, Fleur pulled up a kitchen chair and climbed up to stand alongside her mother. Their heads were almost at the same level.

The little girl watched as Grace broke an egg into a glass bowl, then, with great concentration, passed her mother another from the open carton. As the beaters broke the yolks and whites into a golden froth, Fleur put her little hand on her mother's, feeling the vibration linking the two of them. Suddenly the satisfying sound of the whirring beaters stopped.

'Mummy, why you crying?' the child asked, gazing wide-eyed as Grace stopped mid-beat, a long string of half-mixed egg hanging from the metal beaters. She made no sound, but her face was contorted. Fleur took the handle from Grace's loosening hand and tried to turn the twin beaters in the gluey mixture, her eyes firmly averted from her mother's face.

As Fleur began to wind the handle, the bowl tipped and in a second the floor was awash with sticky yellow fluid. Grace came back to herself and let out a howl. To Fleur it sounded like the wolves in the nearby zoo in the dead of night. Hearing his mother's broken voice, Timothy joined in from his baby seat, setting up a wail of sheer misery.

Grace scooped up Timothy and held him close to her breasts, months ago emptied of life-giving milk. She inhaled the scent of his scalp, still baby-sweet despite the lack of baths. The mess of beaten egg lay congealing on the floor. She stared at it blankly.

'Mummy, Mummy, eggs gone. Me put them back in?' Fleur began to sob now, at the loss of her breakfast, and the noise of her brother's wailing. 'I w-want p-p-pancakes.'

'Come, love, I have a much better treat for you.' With her free hand, Grace reached up to the top shelf of the pantry where some Christmas treats were still hidden. She found a packet of mince pies almost forgotten since December, but well preserved by the icy weather. 'Let's go curl up on the sofa, and Mummy will read stories to you both, while we eat our treats. Go pick your favourite book, Fleurkin, while I make up Tim's bottle.'

Fleur stopped crying. She ran to the bookshelves in the sparsely furnished lounge room. Climbing on to the plump cushions of the old brocade sofa, she arranged four picture books in a pile. Snuffling a little, she waited for her mother and brother to join her.

❈

Grace and the children were incarcerated together the whole day, prisoners in their own home. The snow had stopped falling and was banked up almost to the sills of the downstairs windows. Grace wrapped her arms around her body, feeling her ribs sharp through the flannel of her gown, and gazed at the whiteness outside. Even if she'd had the strength to go out, there was no way she could navigate the pram through those frozen streets. The baby carriage stood empty and sad at the bottom of the stairs, annoying the downstairs tenant, who regularly complained about it blocking his passageway.

There was no question of driving to the library either, or a museum, or anywhere else warm, where they could escape the freezing flat. Grace's car, a gift from Larry, had stalled with the icy weather last Friday night, that fateful night she'd at last had the courage to visit him in his flat. She'd left it parked in the street, covered in sleet.

Only last weekend, Grace and the children had sheltered in the cosy warmth of the Steinmann's welcoming home, filled with good nourishing food, children's laughter, and music from Michael's gramophone. They'd been good friends to Grace over the years, always including her in their family rituals. Grace and Jennifer had met at a playgroup for their toddlers, and had immediately formed a bond.

The white-clothed table was a circle of light in Grace's darkness. The candles and the challah bread on Friday night, as the family gathered around the table, spoke to Grace of all she'd lost, and all that would never be hers.

Later that same night, Jennifer heard Grace sobbing in her sleep. She and Michael begged her to stay till Monday, but Grace declined, saying she was fine, and needed to get back for the new nanny. All the way home, in the back of Michael's old London cab, Grace wept, until he stopped the car and tried to comfort her.

'I'll be all right, I j-just have to go home,' she said, stifling harsh sobs

❀

All three of them were still recovering from colds and coughs, the children's noses still runny. They huddled together all day under eiderdowns for warmth, while Grace read story after story, and the children curled into her body, listening to their mother's voice.

'Mummy, will Daddy come tomorrow?' whined Fleur, her blocked nose making her words thick.

'Tomorrow's Monday, Fleurkin, your daddy might be busy. But he's sure to come soon to see you and Tim. He loves you both so much.'

Fleur's eyes filled with tears, and her lip trembled. Grace felt her soul dissolve, and wept without sound. She lifted Tim who'd fallen asleep on the couch, and nuzzled his neck softly as she carried him upstairs, where she laid him gently in his cot. Fleur followed, still crying, clutching her favourite rabbit, its ears limp and wet where she'd chewed them. It was her way of getting to sleep.

'Come my darling, let's sing our special song for sleep time.'

Softly, so as not to wake Tim, Grace sang the first notes, and soon Fleur's husky voice joined in:

You are my sunshine, my only sunshine

You make me happy, when skies are grey...

Lifting Fleur in her arms, Grace held her close. 'You're a big girl now, almost three. You'll always look after your brother, won't you?' There was no answer as Fleur closed her eyes, hugging her rabbit. She tucked in both children with infinite tenderness.

❀

Grace sat shrouded in blankets at her makeshift desk in the white bedroom, a small two-bar electric radiator the only light, besides her reading lamp. A swathe of blood-red corduroy velvet lay limply in the corner. She would never make those curtains from the material Larry had brought her from Chalk Farm. It was too late. She would write the letter tonight, after she put the children down. Yes, she'd write to the witch who'd stolen her husband, and who dared to claim the baby she carried was his. It was the ultimate treachery. And it warranted the ultimate punishment. The bitch. She'd show her, she'd wipe the smile off that beautiful, evil, face.

Grace took out her notepaper. Ever alert for any sound from the children, at last sleeping fitfully in the nursery, she began to write:

To the witch who stole my husband,

I cannot bear to write your name; its very sound is a hiss from the tongue of a serpent. You snaked your way into our lives and destroyed all that was once wholesome and fertile, and changed my husband from a god to a devil. Here is the gift you have wished for, freeing him to be yours. But rest assured, he will never love you, or your bastard child, as he's loved me and our children. With this act I curse you forever. I will always be between you, watching and waiting. The day will come when you and yours will join me in hell.

She folded the letter with precision, and inserted it into a matching envelope. She was using her best cream letter set, a Christmas gift from her mother. No sense in saving it now.

As the effects of the pills Dr Coplin had prescribed began to wear off, Grace felt herself succumbing to the voice, embracing it. *Let me die, and this time get it right.* Lines from her own poems flooded her mind, intertwined with images of her one-legged father, and Larry in his black suit, his face covered in bee-stings. *Mother will be pleased with me; I've succeeded at last. This time, I'll do it exceptionally well.*

The only address she knew for Esther was Larry's flat in Charing Cross, set among bookshops and brothels. How appropriate, she thought, as she wrote the street number, and stuck down the flap of thick cream envelope. The glue tasted bitter in her mouth. I'll get the nanny to post this when she comes this morning. But where are my stamps? She looked frantically in her pocket book hanging over the back of the chair. It was empty, except for Larry's last cheque, which she'd been unable to cash in the last frozen weeks.

Still in her old blue dressing gown, Grace shrugged off the blankets, and tiptoed to the cots. The children were sleeping peacefully at last. Fleur had flung back her eiderdown, one little leg in its pyjamas exposed to the cold. Covering her tenderly, Grace stooped and kissed her daughter gently on the forehead, relieved that it was at last dry and cool. Tim was sleeping with his bottom in the air, his perpetual sleeping pose. He still held the shred of a burst red balloon in his small fist. As she gently spread the thick blue blanket over his tiny body, her heart almost burst with love and loss.

Closing the nursery door with a soft click, Grace picked up her letter and change purse from the desk, and crept downstairs. She knocked firmly on Mr Stanford's door. There was no answer. She knocked again, more loudly. After what seemed an eternity standing in the cold passageway, the door to the downstairs flat opened, and out poked the head of Mr Stanford. He wore a tasseled nightcap over his sparse white hair.

'For heaven's sake, young lady, what do you think you're doing in the middle of the night, knocking me up like this? Do you realise it's well after midnight? There'd better be a good explanation for this. Is there a fire, or a robbery?'

'Oh no, Mr Stanford, everything's just fine. I just need a stamp, that's all, and I've run out. I can pay you straight away if you have one, and then the new nanny can post this for me in the morning. You see, she's starting tomorrow. Oh, and that's the other thing — could you be sure to let her in, just in case I don't hear her?'

Grumbling, the old man shuffled off and returned in a few minutes with a single stamp, to find Grace standing still as a statue, her eyes wide and staring at something only she could see. He noticed her hair hung long and matted, a sharp animal smell coming from it. In spite of himself, he felt pity for the poor woman. *Always knew she was crazy,* he thought.

'Here you are, then, and don't bother me again for such a trivial matter. No, you can pay me later.' He waved away the florin from Grace's outstretched hand.

'No, please, you must take this now, I want nothing on my conscience.'

'Oh, all right then, and for heaven's sake, when are you going to move that pram of yours? It's a damned nuisance,' he called after Grace's retreating back.

Downstairs again, Grace acted quickly. *Hurry. There is no time to lose*, the voice whispered. Taking a thick roll of masking tape from the packing box, still in the corner after their move here only weeks ago, she taped around the windows and door frame of the kitchen. Then she took some unwashed towels from the laundry basket, and dipped them into the bucket of stagnant water she'd been forced to use to wash the children. Rolling the towels into sausage shapes, she stuffed the space under the doors to the landing and the sitting room. Robot-like, she went upstairs to the bedrooms, carrying a tray with a cup of milk for Fleur, and a bottle for Tim. On a plate she put two thick buttered slices of white bread. After placing the tray on the little night table, she flung open the nursery window, and let down the sides of the cots. Piling the children's sleeping bodies with all the blankets she could find, Grace bent to kiss them for the last time.

In the kitchen, Grace tore a piece of wallpaper from the wall and scribbled Dr Coplin's phone number on it, first checking it against her wall calendar. She stuck the note to the outside of the kitchen door with the last of the packing tape. Then she opened the oven, and knelt on the floor, still sticky with spilled egg. Everything was perfect, ready, complete. She turned the oven's gas jet on to its fullest extent. Taking a clean tea towel from its hook, she folded it into a neat square. She placed her head deep inside the cold oven, resting her cheek on the folded towel. *Let me die*, the voice said again, as she silently, and with relief, succumbed.

❀

CHAPTER 23

Cambridge Crescent, London, February 1963

'Audrey, something too terrible has happened. *Mein Gott*, how can I say it? It's Grace. She's dead!'

'What? What do you mean? I told you, Ben saw her at the PEN meeting only two nights ago. You must be dreaming.'

'Dr Coplin rang me; he had no other way of contacting Larry. I had to tell him the truth about the baby, you see. Luckily he had my number from the first consultation. I tell you, it's true, and the doctor told me to get in touch with Larry straight away. *Scheisse*, I can't. Such terrible news can't come from me. Please, Audrey, could you send Ben around to Larry's flat?'

'But Esther! This is shocking news! I — I suppose I could contact Ben. I'll have to ring him at work. But would he know the address?'

'Larry has rooms in Charing Cross. Tell Ben to call in to see me, here at work, first. I don't dare give his address over the phone. God, Audrey, I can't believe this. What will happen to those children? It's too dreadful to be true.'

'Esther, calm down. Do you know what happened? How did she die?'

'How should I know? Dr Coplin only told me she's dead, that's all. I'm not a family member, so why would he tell me anything? Larry said she had the 'flu quite badly a few weeks ago, but from all reports she'd recovered. Please, please help me Audrey — I don't know what else to do.'

'Of course I'll help you. Now — does Larry have a phone?'

'No, he doesn't — he can't bear to be disturbed when he's writing. Can't Ben go there?'

'Well, I'll see if he can get away. If I can't contact Ben, we'll have to send an urgent telegram.'

Ben was out of the office. With Audrey's help, Esther worded the wire, leaving it unsigned:

PLEASE RING DR G COPLIN URGENTLY STOP ON HAMPSTEAD BX1819 STOP RE GRACE.

❖

Ashen-faced, Larry stared ahead, a look of horror on his face. He was standing, slumped against the mantelpiece, in the front room of the flat. The room was almost bare except for rush matting on the floor, and two raffia chairs. Swathes of red velvet material lay abandoned in the corner. The sight of it made him cringe; Grace was going to make curtains from it, to brighten up the stark white room.

The yellow tape across the doorway of the kitchen was a grim reminder that this was a crime scene. There was a metallic smell coming from the kitchen, which was off limits, while a policewoman and detective completed their inspection.

Larry had just returned from the morgue, where he'd had to identify the body. There lay Grace, white as marble, the light in her brown eyes gone forever, a slight blue tinge around her silent mouth. He'd wept uncontrollably, all the while seeing Grace as if she were the wife of Lot, turned to a pillar of salt for her husband's sins.

'If only she'd believed me when I told her we'd be together again by this summer. I wanted her to come away with me next weekend, but she said she had other plans. In the end she couldn't stay alive without believing in a future for us. I failed her, Aunt; it was up to me to save her, and I failed.'

'Hush, Laurence. You couldn't have saved her. It was she who murdered herself. It's a wicked thing,' said his Aunt Thelma, who'd rushed to the flat in Cambridge Crescent on receiving the news. The long journey from Heptonstall had been interminable, and she'd had to take emergency leave from work, but what else could she do? There were motherless children to be cared for, and a broken-hearted nephew to be supported.

'Nay, Aunt, 'twas I killed her, I and my madness. Grace was my true wife, and I her murderer. If there's a Hell, it's sure I'll be burning in it after this.'

Aunt Thelma shook her head slowly, side to side, wisps of grey hair escaping from her neat bun. She'd had no time to pin it up this morning, when she'd dressed in the darkness and rushed to get the earliest bus to the station. She knew little of her favourite nephew's life in London, gleaning only from her sister Miriam, that there'd been some trouble in the marriage.

'You have your children to think of now, Laurence. You'll be both mother and father to them now. You must be strong for them. Thank goodness that lovely lass was here to tend to them. She's got them off to sleep at last, poor bairns.'

'That's what's so strange, Aunt. I don't believe Grace meant to do it, not after we talked about getting back together, only a month ago. It was Marjorie who found Grace this morning, you know. That's what I can't understand: why would Grace do such a horrendous thing, when she'd arranged for the new nanny to start this morning?'

'I know, dear, I can't understand any of this either. Let's just be grateful that Marjorie's here, and is with the children. But she tells me she can't stay on, not after the terrible shock the poor lass must've had. I suppose I'll have to stay and lend you a hand with Fleur and Tim, at least until you find a suitable nanny for them.'

At that moment the door opened, and Esther burst into the room. Aunt Thelma stared at her, open-mouthed. Who was this imposter, this woman with her dark hair, green eyes blazing? She was wearing a dark blue velvet hood fringed with fur, and looked like some sort of a Russian noblewoman. From the way she looked at Larry with those searching eyes, Aunt Thelma guessed there must be something between them.

Ignoring Thelma, Esther rushed to Larry, and tried to embrace him.

'Larry! Oh Larry, how can this be true? I'm so sorry, my darling. What are we going to do?' she whispered, trying to stroke his face. He pulled back sharply, like a horse about to rear. Glaring back at her, he pushed her away from him with some force. Still looking at Esther, Larry inclined his head towards his aunt.

'Aunt Thelma, this is a friend of mine, Mrs Buchanan. Esther, meet my Aunt Thelma, all the way from Yorkshire.'

Esther glanced haughtily at Aunt Thelma. 'How do you do,' she said frostily, in a voice that could cut glass. Thelma returned the greeting in her soft Yorkshire burr. She felt repugnance for this intruder, and wished her gone. Such a woman did not belong in this house of mourning.

'Where are the children?' Esther said, turning her attention to Larry.

'They're no concern of yours. We have a nanny, Marjorie, from Australia, looking after them. Please leave us, Esther; Aunt Thelma and I need to talk.'

'How can I leave you now? Tell me — what happened? How did she die?'

'She killed herself. Now will you go? '

Esther took a step back and held onto a chair as her knees buckled. She remembered Larry's voice saying, 'It will kill her,' and in that instant knew the child in her womb was doomed.

'No,' she whispered, 'tell me it's not true. She couldn't have done such a thing. Grace never would have left those children. Surely it was an accident?'

'No accident. It was inevitable, only a matter of time. It was always going to be her or me, and I wish to God it'd been me. Now, leave us, please, before you realise what you've done.'

'Me? Whatever do you mean? What have I got to do with this?' Esther faced Larry, her face aflame. 'Look to yourself, why don't you?' With that she turned and walked back through the door she'd entered a few minutes ago, biting her lip so that Larry wouldn't see the gathering tears.

❈

CHAPTER 24

London, February 1963

Esther did not return to work that day. Instead, she took the tube into the city. The streets were still covered in snow, and there was dirty black sludge where it was melting. Her good suede shoes were soaked by the time she reached the station. At first she didn't know where she was going, just that she had to get away from Larry, and the gruesome scene at 23 Cambridge Crescent. Tony would be a comfort to her now, but yesterday he'd been called away urgently to Montreal. His mother was dying of cancer, his sister had wept over the phone, and was calling for Tony, her only son, to be at her bedside.

Esther couldn't bear to go home to the empty flat in Highgate. Without thinking, she found herself at the office building where Rivke worked. Always, Rivke had been there for her in any crisis. She pushed open the door of the building and waited for the shaky old elevator to take her to the fifth floor. Standing in front of the lift she felt darkness descend, and again heard Larry's words: 'It will kill her.' *This will be the end of us*, she thought. *The curtain has fallen.*

Rivke worked as a graphic designer, and had her own private office on the fifth floor of the old building. A polite young woman at the front desk smiled at Esther as she emerged from the elevator. 'How can I help you, Mrs…?'

'Buchanan,' replied Esther in a shaky voice. 'Could you tell Miss Feldmann I'm here?'

'Right away,' said the receptionist, looking nervously at Esther's swollen red eyes and wild expression. She disappeared into the inner sanctum.

Rivke emerged immediately, and enveloped Esther in a boisterous hug. The warmth of it, and its vigour, was like a draught of warm honey.

'Darlink! For me this is a good surprise, but what is wrong that you look like a *meshuggine*? Come in, and we can talk.' She led Esther by the hand into her office, and closed the door behind them.

'Now, sit. Tell Rivke what happened. Is it all right with the baby?'

'God, Rivke. Help me. Grace's killed herself, and Larry's turned against me.'

'What? Killed herself? But how? When?'

'This morning. She gassed herself, leaving those two tiny children without a mother. How could she?' Esther's tears broke forth again, as she collapsed into the proffered chair. Rivke withdrew a crumpled handkerchief from her cardigan sleeve, and handed it to Esther.

'*Oy vey*, that's shocking news. You must be feeling terrible, after all the *tsuris* with you and Larry.'

'Why should I feel terrible? It's nothing to do with me. I wished Grace no harm, although I know she hates me — hated me. I even wanted to be her friend. Are you saying people will blame me?'

'*Schönele*, you know what nasty minds people have. I'd lie low for a while; look after yourself and the little *bübele* inside you. A new life, Essie. Forget Larry, he's no good to you. Go home to your husband, that Tony, who loves you.'

'He's away,' said Esther dully. 'It's his mother — she's dying of bowel cancer. He had to go to Canada. How could he leave me, at a time like this?'

'Tony had to go to his mother, such a *gute mensch*. Essie, you will stay with me tonight, darlink. I'll make you chicken soup just like my own Ima did back in Tel Aviv, whenever I was a bit sick. Jewish penicillin, we call it. Come on, I can finish up early for once, and we'll take a taxi home. Look at your shoes and your jacket, they're soaked. And not even a raincoat in this so bad weather?'

The two women left the office together, Rivke with her ample arm around Esther's shoulders. Once outside the rain lashed their faces, as if the day was weeping, in sympathy with Esther. Rivke hailed a cab with an expert whistle, holding with care onto Esther's limp arm.

In Rivke's tiny bedsitter, Esther tried for her friend's sake to be calm, and to show gratitude for the warm little room, with both bars burning in the radiator. Soon the fragrant smell of chicken soup filled the cosy space. She watched as Rivke cut carrots into chunks, and added onion and bay leaves to the simmering broth. The smell transported her back to her Buba's kitchen long ago in Germany, where her father's mother had cooked for their little family whenever they visited.

That night Esther tossed and turned on the sofa, turned into a makeshift bed by removing the back cushions, and piling the base with all Rivke's spare blankets. It wasn't only discomfort that kept her awake, but the image of Larry in the death flat pushing her away, and the sound of his cruel words echoing in her head, 'leave us before you realise what you've done.'

Her mind balked at the image of Grace, sprawled lifeless with her head in the oven. It was unthinkable, horrific. Instead, Esther's thoughts drifted to her childhood, and the memories of her long friendship with Rivke, the high times and the low ones, made her weep anew.

Esther's thoughts were a confusion of fear and remorse. The memories came flooding in, of danger and pursuit. She was a child again, living in Palestine, remembering the times when all her safeties had been stripped away. But safety, she knew, was an illusion.

❋

Unable to sleep, Esther padded into Rivke's tiny kitchen looking for tea. On the way she tripped over a coffee table, and let out a cry. Instantly a light went on in the next room, and Rivke was stumbling towards her, her auburn hair sprayed round her head like *Struwelpeter's*.

'What happened, Essie? Is it you did hurt something?'

'Hurt? What does it matter, nothing matters now, because Grace is dead. Dead! And now I know I'll never be free of her. I wish it were me in the morgue, instead of Grace. Now Larry will never stop loving her, I know it. God, Rivke, he'll always blame me, everyone will!'

'Shush, *liebling*. Of course they won't. I know it wasn't your fault. Anyone who says so, they will get bad words from me. Come on, we have some tea and talk about the old times.'

'Remember that night we got into trouble at the tea dance?' Esther reminisced. 'And how I borrowed your mother's best choker with that green brooch?'

'You never did give it back. Don't worry, I do forgive you,' said Rivke. 'What about how your Vati came to rescue us, and sweet-talked Miss Tabitha, so we wouldn't be expelled?'

'And how dear Vati promised to treat all of Miss Tabitha's staff for nothing?' added Esther. 'All we got was a firm talking to, and extra homework.'

'I can still hear that old bag, the way she did every day say those words "discretion and dignity, Ladies, that is our motto",' laughed Rivke.

Soon Rivke had lifted Esther's spirits. As long as they kept talking, the fearful images of death and despair were kept at bay.

❖

For once Esther took Rivke's advice, and kept to herself in Tony's flat. It was not in her nature to hide away, but now she had a decision to make, and she could only make it alone. Apart from going out to work each morning, Esther stayed quietly at home.

Tony rang her almost nightly, with reports of his mother's condition. She'd had a major operation for the colon cancer, he told her, and the family was waiting, and praying for her recovery. Esther could hear the desperation in Tony's voice, and wished too that his mother might live, so that at least one woman in his life would be true to him.

From Larry there was no word. Day after day she felt the door closing on their life together.

Grace's funeral was held in Yorkshire on 18 February, delayed because of the coroner's report, which confirmed the cause of death as suicide. There was a small article in the *Times*, with a picture of Grace in which she looked pitifully young. She had just turned thirty, the article said, and was becoming a poet of some repute.

Esther was conflicted whether to attend the funeral in Yorkshire. 'Rivke, what do you think? Should I go? After all, how would it look if I were not there by Larry's side? The world knows we're a couple.'

'Essie, I already told you to leave him alone, let him stay with his children. You don't need him in your life; you have that so good Tony, who loves you and needs you too. Why go *schlepping* all the way up north in this so bad weather, and in your condition, as the English so politely say?'

Again, Esther followed her friend's advice. Rivke, with her large rounded features and capacious bosom, had become a mother figure to her, and made her feel protected. When the phone rang the day after the funeral, and it was Larry, her heart leapt for joy, and she almost dropped the receiver.

'My poor Essie, forgive me. I spoke too harshly to you the other day. It was difficult to talk in front of Aunt Thelma. Everything was in turmoil, still is. I need to talk to you. Can I come around this evening?'

Esther played for time. He'd hurt her terribly, and pride told her to refuse.

She hesitated.

'Hello? Are you there?' Larry sounded impatient.

'No, tonight's no good. I'm expecting a call from Tony tonight. Meet me after work tomorrow, at The Lamb.' She hung up.

❖

CHAPTER 25

London, February 1963

In the dimmest, most secluded corner of the hotel, Larry was waiting for her, staring into a large glass of Guinness. Esther walked towards him through tables of other drinkers. She noticed heads no longer turned as they used to, and felt a moment's pique.

'Esther.' To her surprise he stood up and held out a chair for her. 'We need to talk.'

'Haven't you said enough? Blaming me for your wife's death?'

'Don't do this, Esther. You must know, we can't go through with this.'

'What do you mean?'

'I mean this baby. I told you it would kill Grace, and now it has. You must terminate this pregnancy.'

She stared at him, her pupils unnaturally large, so that her eyes appeared almost black. She clasped her hands protectively over her stomach.

'Whether you believe me or not, this is your child I'm carrying, and nothing or nobody will take it from me. Besides I'm over three months already. It's not safe.'

Larry sank his head into his hands and groaned. 'Why did you let her see you like that? Didn't you know what that would've meant to her? It was the ultimate blow, that and the damned book you had to go and give me.'

'You mean the Shakespeare? As I recall, you were very happy to have it returned to you at the time, after Grace destroyed the original.'

'How can you talk like that, about a woman barely cold in her grave? It's a judgement on both of us. I still can't believe she would take her own life, and leave Fleur and Tim motherless. Yet in another way I can see it as inevitable, written in her stars. It wasn't the first time she'd tried to take her own life, you know.'

'Can't you see? She did it to punish us, of that I'm sure. This is her revenge on me, and on you. Besides, you say everything that happens is determined by fate. So what does your famous horoscope tell you now?'

'Only that everything was leading to this point, and whatever made her do it, we're helpless against the tide of destiny. 'Twas fate pulled Grace to the brink, and now we're in its thrall.'

'Speak for yourself, Sir. You may be content to succumb to your so-called Destiny, but nothing and nobody governs my life. Do you think I'd have survived the war if Vati hadn't had the foresight to leave Germany? Even if we'd been spared from the Holocaust, I'd be a fat *hausfrau* by now, with six snotty-nosed children, if your precious Fate had taken its course.'

'The children! God, what am I to do about the children? Aunt Thelma can't stay. She's been granted only two weeks off her work, so she must get back to Yorkshire by next Monday. Marjorie has found another position; poor lass can't cope with this mess. She's agreed to look after the bairns till the end of the month. What then?'

'Don't look at me. I've no intention of being a nanny to two moth-erless babies. You'll have to advertise, I suppose.'

'But, Essie. I don't want a succession of strangers taking care of them. Erica might be able to come for a while, but how can I expect her to give up her prestige job in Paris for more than a week? Wouldn't you consider helping out, just until Erica arrives?'

'Forget it. Tell your sister that family's more important than career, and she should put you and her niece and nephew first. As for me — aren't you even going to buy me a drink? They say Guinness is excellent for pregnant women, only it's got to be the dark sort.'

Without a word, Larry pushed back his chair and went to the counter. Left alone, Esther's mind was already working on a plan. If Larry truly wanted this of her, she had some bargaining power to keep him in her life. Otherwise, Grace would have won, and destroyed the life she and Larry could have together. Even as Esther determined to take fate into her own hands, she could feel the darkness descending.

❈

CHAPTER 26

Cambridge Crescent, February 1963

Larry sat feeding his son in the kitchen. Death had spread its cold fingers throughout the flat. Timothy was strapped into his high chair. His brown eyes, dull with pain, were darting all over the room. First to the doorway, then the stairwell, back to the doorway, over to the sleeted window, again to the empty doorway. The baby opened his mouth automatically for the spoon of porridge, expecting his father's mouth to open in encouragement, as his mother's always had.

Larry was alone with his son. Aunt Thelma had gone to the shops to replenish milk, bread and baby cereal. She'd taken Fleur, buttoned securely into her little blue Breton coat, to get her out of the morbid atmosphere of the flat. The sound of Tim's wailing on the morning of Grace's suicide, still echoed in his head. Both children had been freezing under the wide open windows, flung open by their mother to protect them from the gas, as one of her last acts.

The black phone on the wall, newly installed only that week, rang insistently.

'Who is it now,' Larry said wearily to Tim's porridge-smeared face. After he could bear the ringing no longer, he picked up the phone.

'Darling, it's me.' Esther's deep voice still sent shivers through him. 'I need to talk to you. When can I come over?'

'Not when Thelma's here; she won't like it. I suppose you could come over now, while she's out, but you'd have to be gone by the time she gets back.'

'Oh, really? So I'm to be slotted in, hidden away like some pariah? Never mind then. A pity, as what I have to say might be in her interests, and yours.'

Before he could reply, the phone on the other end clicked an end to their conversation. He cursed inwardly. What the devil was the woman up to now? All he cared about was getting through each hour of each day, while doing his best to care for his children. He returned to his task of feeding his son. With clumsy fingers he used a tea towel to wipe the baby's tear-streaked face.

❋

Esther banged the phone down on its receiver, frowning with fury. She was alone in the flat in Highgate, which she thought of now as Tony's flat, rather than hers, or theirs. Try as she might to be 'good' and forget Larry, it seemed impossible to break his hold on her, especially now that she carried his child.

It was Saturday, a day to be free, but still too cold to go out. Restlessly, Esther paced her sitting room like a caged animal, fretting for release. She felt ill and a little dizzy. Dr Coplin had told her the nausea should soon pass now that she was well into her fourth month. She longed to speak to Tony, but knew it was the middle of the night over there in Canada.

A sudden pain in her abdomen sent her running to the bathroom. The face that stared back at her from the mirror was white, its eyes huge and burning feverishly under their straight dark brows. She leaned over the basin to vomit, but her spasm produced only a dry retch. She felt wetness between her thighs, and something gushed out of her. Looking down she saw a bright red line of blood streaking its way down her bare leg and onto the cold bathroom tiles.

Instinctively, Esther grabbed herself between her legs, holding her groin with both hands as if to push back whatever was leaking from there. 'No,' she moaned, as a dragging ache pulled at her womb. Grabbing the white hand towel from its rail, she wadded it inside her pants and crawled on all fours to the phone. She dialled Dr Coplin's number.

The phone rang and rang but no one answered. Not on a Saturday afternoon, she realised. Without thinking, she rang Larry's number. 'Please, please, be there,' she prayed. After countless rings she was about to hang up, when a woman's voice answered.

'The Wildes' residence,' said Aunt Thelma in her Northern accent. 'Who is this, please?' she said impatiently, to the silence on the other end. 'If you're from that newspaper, we have nothing more to say to you.'

'It's Mrs Buchanan speaking,' Esther managed at last to gasp, as the wave of pain receded. 'I need to talk to Larry. It's urgent.'

'Well, Mrs — or is it Miss? — I'm afraid Laurence had to go out for a breath of air. The poor lad's exhausted what with looking after these poor bairns and fending off phone calls from the likes of yourself. Look, Mrs Buchanan, I know who you are, and I can't fathom why you'd be bothering my nephew at a time like this, he has enough on his plate, and — '

'Please,' Esther shrieked into the phone 'Tell him to come here as soon as he's back, I beg of you. I'm...'

She dropped the phone as her knees buckled and she sank to the floor. Dragging herself to the bathroom, she heard a low animal moan, and dimly realised it was coming from her own throat. Lying on the cold tiles, she shivered uncontrollably as the pains in her abdomen grew stronger and more frequent. 'Help me,' she wailed as blood began to gush from her womb. She was in a wall of pain, and could only submit.

Dimly, after what seemed hours, she heard a voice close to her. 'I'm here, Sweetling, God, I'm so sorry, we'll get you to the hospital. Thelma could tell something was very wrong; she's not such a bad old stick you know. Here, put your arms around my neck and I'll carry you to the car.' Amongst the great gouts of blood on the floor, Larry saw a tiny foetus, perfectly formed. 'Turn your head away, Esther,' he whispered into her ear, scooping up the bloodied homunculus. Tears gushed from his eyes, as he held it in the palm of his hand for a moment, before wrapping it in toilet paper. He couldn't bring himself to flush it away, not yet.

❦

CHAPTER 27

London, February 1963

Esther woke to whiteness. Walls, ceiling, coverlet, and a white figure leaning over her, wearing a white veil, with a shiny silver watch pinned to a capacious bosom. The watch seemed to advance and recede with a life of its own.

'Mrs Buchanan, can you hear me? We need you to sign some papers.'

Groggily, Esther tried to lift herself by pressing herself up onto her elbows. She fell back, exhausted, onto a heap of white pillows. Thus supported, she tried her voice. It came out with a rasping croak.

'Where am I? What's happened? Is my baby safe?'

'Lie back, dear. You're in Guy's Hospital. I'm afraid you've had a miscarriage, Mrs Buchanan.. It was dangerouly late in your pregnancy. We've had to do a little operation to make sure everything's all right inside you. Here's a nice cup of tea. Can we call your husband to take you home?'

'No! My baby's not gone? Please God, it can't be. Where's Larry? He was here, wasn't he?'

'You mean that kind man who brought you in? He said he's a friend of yours. Now, drink this, dear, and we'll get you ready once you've contacted your hubby. Do you feel strong enough to walk to the phone? Or would you like me to ring him for you?'

Esther stared at the woman's kind open face. How dare she call Larry her 'friend' and tell her the baby's gone? *It's all a dream, a bad dream.* Then it came back to her; the blood, the terrible pains, the mess on the cold tiles of the bathroom floor. It was true, she'd lost the baby, hers and Larry's. She wanted to scream but held it in.

'My husband's overseas, he knows nothing of this. Please ring Mr Laurence Wilde; he's my lover, and he'll have to take me home.'

The nurse's bland face flushed. The brazenness of the woman, talking about her 'lover' like that. Did she have no shame?

'Very well, my dear. Don't you mean he's your next of kin? Just write the number on this form and the office will get in touch.'

The white-veiled figure whisked away on sensible shoes, leaving Esther feeling helpless and betrayed. Her hands went to her stomach, and found it swollen. *Perhaps it's all a mistake, and my baby's still there.* She felt the thick blood-soaked pad between her legs and knew it to be true; the child she'd fought so long and hard to protect had gone. *This is Grace's doing, she's cursed me from the grave.* A terrible emptiness engulfed Esther as she released the tears she'd been holding from the nurse, and wept for her lost child.

An hour later she was dressed and sitting on the side of the hospital bed. 'Mr Wilde says he'll be here as soon as he can, my dear, so let's get you ready,' the nurse had said, bustling about Esther's bedside, not looking her in the eyes. Sister Macleay wondered about this woman, with a face like an angel and a tongue like a devil. *Spitting image of that film star, Elizabeth Taylor, she is, only her eyes are green instead of violet. Scandalous, it is, her calling for her 'lover' when in the same breath she says her husband's away. Who knows what the truth is? Probably a bit crazed, poor woman, losing her baby like that.*

Esther looked up to see Larry looming over her. His unsmiling mouth was a straight line.

'Ah, so here you are, Mr Wilde. Our patient is right to go home, but I just need you to sign here, just a formality you know, in the interests of our patient's safety.' Nurse Macleay chatted on, not knowing how to refer to this strange woman, married to one man and calling this one her 'lover'. She blushed at the thought of it, and kept her eyes down as she handed Larry the release form. He scribbled a black gash of a signature underneath Mrs Buchanan's. When she dared to look at him, Nurse Macleay saw a huge-shouldered man, with a beetling brow and shaggy brown hair, and a chin so prominent it seemed to go on forever.

Tall, dark and handsome, she thought. *No wonder this poor lass let him get her in the family way.*

Ignoring the nurse's curious eyes, Esther stood and threw her arms around Larry's unyielding neck. 'Tell me we can have another baby, straight away, I'll do better next time, I promise you,' she whispered into his cheek.

Larry gently disengaged Esther's arms from his neck, avoiding the nurse's eyes. 'I've got the car waiting downstairs, let's get out of here. Give me your bag.'

In the car, he turned to Esther and said, 'Why make such a spectacle of yourself? This is for the best, you must know that. At least now you can help me with Fleur and Timothy, until I can find a new nanny. Aunt Thelma has to leave tomorrow; she's with the children now, so I'm taking you back to Cambridge Crescent with me. You can rest up there tonight and take over from Thelma in the morning.'

'I'll do no such thing. Take me straight to Highgate Fields, to my own place. You forget I'm still Tony's wife, and he'll have been ringing me there. I must speak to him immediately. I'm sure he'll to come back to London when I tell him this dreadful news. He wouldn't want me to be alone, the dear man.'

'Essie, either Tony must accept that you're with me now, or, if he's deaf and blind, he'll refuse to accept it. The more fool him. You'd think these last six weeks would've changed my feelings for you, but no — they're as strong as ever. And if you go back to Tony now, I don't know what I shall do.'

'Please, I beg you, take me back to Highgate, where I can rest in peace, and I'll see how I feel in the morning.'

Larry shrugged, turned the key in the ignition of the battered old Morris, backed out of the hospital car park, and turned the car around.

❀

'Operator, I need to place a trunk call to Montreal, Canada. Can you tell me what time it is there?'

'It's only six o'clock in the morning, yesterday, madam. Do you still want to go ahead?'

'Yes; put me through to 1-467-5686 special person, Mr Tony Buchanan.'

Esther heard an insistent beep, beep, echoing down the line. A woman's voice, heavy with sleep, answered the operator. 'Hello, who is this so early? My mother's still sleeping, I don't want her disturbed.'

'I have an overseas call waiting, from a Mrs Buchanan, for special person Mr Tony Buchanan. Is Mr Buchanan there?'

'Oh, I see. Just a minute, I'll see if he's awake.' Esther imagined Tony's sister, bleary-eyed, in her dressing gown with an unravelling plait hanging down her back, shuffling off to knock on her brother's door. As the minutes ticked by, and the pennies and pounds mounted up, she began to feel sick with anticipation.

'Hello? Hello, Esther?' It was Tony's voice at last; as soon as she heard it, her love for him came flooding back.

'Darling, I have some awful news. The baby — the baby's gone — I'm so sorry darling.' A sob escaped her, as she imagined the blankness on Tony's early morning face.

A silence, bristling with shock, vibrated down the line. 'Oh, God, Esther,' Tony said at last, 'Darling, are you all right?'

'Except for missing you. Can't you come back home, now that your sister's there, with your Mum?'

'Esther — how can you ask that? And how could this happen to us again? After you told me everything was all right this time? You didn't — you didn't do anything to make it happen? I told you, I didn't care if you thought it could've been Larry's. I'd have given the child my name, treated it as my own.'

'There's something else,' Esther said, conscious of the minutes ticking away. 'Larry's asked me to come and help him with the children for a while, just till he gets a new nanny. If you can't come home, I might as well go to Cambridge Crescent for a while; at least there I won't be alone.'

'Do what you like.' Tony's voice was flat, lifeless. 'In any case, I was going to tell you — my grant's come through, and I've had an offer to go to Spain for six months. I wasn't going to consider it, with the baby coming, but now I ...' There was a click, and the operator's voice came back on the line.' Six minutes are up, madam, do you wish to extend?' Esther thought quickly. 'No, please terminate the call.'

❖

In Cambridge Crescent the next day, Esther made herself at home. Larry had gone to drive Aunt Thelma to the station, leaving the children entirely in Esther's care for the first time. She made a special morning tea of chopped apple and raisins, arrowroot biscuits and milk, sat Tim in his high chair and Fleur at her special little table.

From her Highgate flat, Esther brought colourful rugs and cushions, as well as one or two favourite artefacts from Burma, to try to brighten up Grace's cold white flat. It still seemed to reek of death, and a faint gas smell lingered. Esther felt weak and sick, still bleeding on and off, and when not resting was glad of the small domestic tasks and the constant presence of the two children, who took to her immediately. Tim especially held out his chubby arms to her, and she loved to tickle him under the chin and hear his gurgling laugh. The loss of her own baby hurt a little less each time she held one of Larry's children.

After cleaning up the caked arrowroot biscuit from Tim's face, she lifted him from his high chair and carried him upstairs to his cot. Fleur was absorbed in a game with her pink plastic tea set, giving her dolly pretend cups of tea and talking in a singsong voice. In the nursery Esther cradled Tim in her arms and rocked him gently. The words of the old German lullaby her mother used to sing came back to her, and she crooned softly:

'*Guten Abend, gute Nacht,*
mit Rösen bedacht,
mit Näglein besteckt,

schlupf unter die Deck:

Morgen früh, wenn Gott will,

wirst du wieder geweckt,

Morgen früh, wenn Gott will,

wirst du wieder geweckt.

The baby looked up into her face, searchingly, wonderingly, listening with his whole body. She felt him soften and relax in her arms, and gently laid the boy into his cot. She leaned over and kissed him, inhaling his sweet skin, and drew the coverlet over him.

'Sweet dreams,' she murmured. She pulled the curtains across the window, making sure it was closed tight, and left the room in near darkness.

In the main bedroom, Esther lay on the double bed. *How can I be lying here, on the very bed Grace must have slept in? Did Grace and Larry ever make love on this bed?* Esther's legs were throbbing, and she felt immediate relief as she lifted them on to the bedspread, kicking off her shoes. *I mustn't fall asleep here, Fleur's downstairs by herself.*

Rousing herself with an effort, she bent down to pull on her discarded shoes. From under the mattress she saw the corner of a white envelope sticking out. Intrigued, she extracted it, and there in her hand she held a letter, its envelope stamped, and addressed in crooked blue writing to Mrs Esther Buchanan, care of Mr Laurence Wilde, at his London address. With trembling fingers she tore open the envelope. The shakily written words crawling over the cream embossed stationery made her cry out, and the blood leave her face, as she read the last lines:

With this act I curse you forever. I will always be between you, watching and waiting. The day will come when you and yours will join me in hell.

The note was unsigned. Esther knew only too well who it was from.

❖

CHAPTER 28
Cambridge Crescent, March 1963

I cannot stay here a moment longer, Esther vowed, crumpling Grace's letter into a ball. About to toss it into the wastebasket, she hesitated. *Perhaps she's watching me, I don't want to bring down more curses on my head.* She smoothed the creases from the single sheet of paper, and put it the pocket of her apron; Grace's apron, a gaily coloured floral garment, which Esther had found hanging behind the kitchen door, and which she flung over her smart grey gabardine skirt and cream viyella blouse. She tried not to think of the warm-blooded body this very apron had covered only two months ago.

Esther went down into the kitchen to prepare Fleur's tea, and Tim's bottle. This domesticity was anathema to her, yet she had promised Larry to help with the children until he could find a new nanny. That day could not come soon enough. Where was Larry, why didn't he come to her? She'd fulfilled his wishes, even if by accident. At least now, there would be no baby to explain away.

Seeing that Fleur was still playing quietly with her doll's house, Esther went to the phone, and rang the number for Chalk Farm.

'Where are you?' she said as soon as she heard Larry's voice, although she knew perfectly well where he was: back in the family home, the home he'd made with Grace, no doubt forgetting that he'd left Esther alone with his children for hours. 'I need you here, and so do Fleur and Tim; it's so awful and empty. Larry, I'm frightened; there are ghosts everywhere.' *Will I tell him about the letter, or let it lie? Tread carefully there; keep it to yourself for now.* 'What should I give Fleur for her tea? There's hardly any food here, only breakfast cereal, and half a dozen eggs, and some stale bread.'

'Make toad in the hole, she loves that, and Tim can have some too.'

'What on earth is a toad in the hole? Sounds revolting.'

'It's one of my favourite Yorkshire dishes, that Mam used to make for Erica and me when we were little. You cut a hole in the bread, and fry it up in plenty of dripping — or butter if there's any. Then you drop an egg into the hole till it sets. Delicious. Oh — and don't forget to keep the round bit you cut out for the hole; you fry that up too till it's nice and brown, then stick it on top of the egg, like a lid, don't you see?'

She couldn't help laughing. He'd won her over again, with his voice like warm treacle and his faint North Country brogue. 'Really, Larry, can you see me making such a weird dish? You'd better save that one for when you're back here, which will be soon, yes?'

'As soon as I can, that's if the Crescent's not snowed in. I'm just getting together some of last season's apple crop, to bring to you. There's potatoes too, they've kept well through the winter.'

'I'll give the children scrambled eggs — I do know how to make those — but if you're not back by ten tonight I'll call a babysitter, and take a cab back to Highgate. It's like a mausoleum here.'

'For God's sake, Esther, you can't leave the children alone, with some stranger. Please, it's only for a little while, I promise. I'll see you first thing in the morning. I can't get all the way back to London by ten tonight, and well you know it. Now, Essie, don't be difficult; things are hard enough as it is.'

He hung up before Esther could reply, but in time for her to hear a faint woman's voice in the background.

❀

Winter was turning into spring on The Rose Estate. Each evening grew a little longer and lighter than the previous one, and Esther's spirits lifted a little. Larry had installed her in Grace's flat, so that she could continue the lease until Tony's return, and he could stay at Chalk Farm with the children.

Esther was glad to return to work, where people were being solicitous to her, after her recent loss. Her copywriting sparkled with new and original slogans; it was as if the clever little ditties (*immerse yourself in the softness of Luxe Bouquet for skin as pure as snow*) were an antidote to the pain and confusion she carried inside her. She enjoyed weaving a tissue of lies, or rather half-truths, and she was good at it. Of the new washing powder she wrote: *diamonds of white snowflakes for the gentlest wash of all.* The clever image she'd designed of lipsticks as bullets slung around a model's hips, had won her a raise and another promotion. She loved to add a gloss of elegance to mundane reality, just as she did every day in her dress.

Coming back from work one fine spring night, Esther breathed deeply of the fragrant air, and noticed fresh green sprigs budding on the once bare branches of The Rose Estate. Esther and Larry were secret lovers again, and she looked forward to the clandestine letters, addressed to his secret name for her, *E. Wall, Esq.* Neither of them wanted that busybody downstairs, old Mr Stanford, to intercept correspondence from Mr Wilde, the husband of that unfortunate girl who'd killed herself and almost killed him too. The poor demented woman hadn't realised that the deadly gas would sink; that night there were enough noxious fumes seeping under his door to well and truly knock him out.

As she put the key in the front door, Esther sensed a presence at the top of the stairs. She rushed past Mr Stanford with a quick, 'Good evening,' and ran upstairs, heart pounding. The door opened to her before she reached the top. She took the last stair in one stride, and fell laughing into Larry's arms.

He pushed the door shut behind her. At once his mouth was on hers, and she was enveloped in the aura of him, the strong animal scent that made her wet with desire. He was kissing her face, her neck, her ears, and she sighed and opened to him. Unfastening her blouse, button by button, he buried his head between her breasts, still tender from her recent pregnancy. She pushed him away.

'Wait', she whispered, 'it might not be safe yet, it's only four weeks since…'

'I want you. Now. Here.' He pushed her down onto the brocade sofa and lifted her full skirt, stroking her belly, kissing it. She started to tremble, and reached for him, feeling him hard and pulsing under her fingers. He pushed her hand away, and kneeling, pulled her panties down, burying his head between her legs. She could not help herself, the paroxysm took her, and she cried out as her body jolted and arched to meet his. He pulled away before she could draw him inside her.

Because it was secret, because it was forbidden, their lovemaking was fierce and frequent, whenever Larry could get away from Chalk Farm. He kept his relationship with Esther a secret from his sister and his aunt, and the villagers of Woodberry. To them he presented himself as a young bereaved father, a husband in mourning. Esther enjoyed the secrecy, the delicious surprises of his late night visits. It was like the early days of their passion, yet more tender, now that they knew each other's bodies so intimately. Yet over and over, waking and sleeping, all Esther craved was to feel again the precious infant in her womb. Only another pregnancy could heal the gaping wound left by the loss she'd suffered. This time there would be no doubt whose child it was.

Mr F. Wall, Esq.
c/o Post Office Box 69
Woodberry, UK
30 April '63

Darling Larry,

I had this strange dream last night. You were the key player. We were in a dingy little room, like the back room of that bookshop we both like. You showed me a teapot shaped like a Georgian house, complete with pretty glazed windows, with an attic and a chimney. You were very possessive of it. 'Would you care for a cup of tea?' you asked me, pouring brown milky liquid from the curved spout. 'No thanks, I don't take milk, surely you remember?' I was very cross with you for forgetting, and felt hurt out of all proportion. Your very formality, like a distant friendliness, hurt me. In the dream you said, 'We live in Leeton now. Grace and I have a new life there. That's where I got this teapot. I take it with me everywhere.' Then I woke up and felt terrible.

Larry, what does it mean? You tell me often our dreams can tell us a truth of sorts. Do you remember the dream that first brought us together, the one I had of a giant pike with a foetus floating in its iris? You knew then what it meant far better than I did. And look how it's all come true. I know only that we're meant to be together, that I can give you a love that no one else can. I promise you, I will work things out with Tony when he gets back from Spain; that's if he still wants me. But my dear one, I need to hear from your lips that we will be together, properly together this time, before I break my ties with him. Don't you see? It's not only up to me; we're both prevaricating.

I'm working on the translation you wanted of the short story by Turgenev. It's so sad. The heroine Tatiana is madly in love with Gregor, but it doesn't end well, and she's forced to marry someone else who is 'suitable' but whom she doesn't love — well not the way she loves Gregor. I cried while I was reading it in Russian, and my page of inadequate English words gets covered in inky blue blotches.

Till next time, darling one,

Your Esther

❦

Mrs E. Wall.
c/-23 Cambridge Crescent Rd.

Sweetling,
How could you go on doubting and demanding so, after the night we spent together last Friday? If you mistrust my feelings after that, well, you must be crazy. You keep saying you want surety from me, yet you

yourself are keeping the door open for Tony, and maybe others. Who knows? If your constant prevarication means you're playing cat and mouse with someone else, well, so be it. I won't stand in your way, Essie. But take care, these games of yours are liable to backfire.

I've told you again and again, once the children are settled in the school here in Devon, and Erica's able to go back to her real life in Paris that she's so generously interrupted for me — sisterly love knows no bounds — we, you and I, will find a place of our own, together. In the meantime you must tread as watchfully as a tightrope walker. Take no prisoners, listen to no rumours. The woman's voice you heard on the phone was Erica's. Take no notice of that gossip Audrey, claiming I've been keeping company with that young Australian poetess. As usual, the vile system of Chinese whispers that operates in literary London has it all wildly out of perspective. Angela and I are writing friends, that's all. I couldn't think of her any other way.

You ask if Tony can come back to live with you at Cambridge Crescent. I doubt he'd even want to set foot in the place after what's happened. I think he should find a place of his own, and that you must choose between us. Essie, use the time with him to set things straight, make a clean break, so that you and I can start afresh. It would be kinder to him in the long run.

Your drawing is interesting; I keep it tucked into my journal. Are you still writing yours every day? Show it to no one but me. Keep up the painting and drawing; all art is wonderfully therapeutic.

I liked your translation, or what I've seen of it. I'm working with two friends from the Group to get a book together of all the great poets, Russian, French, German, Israeli — we're calling it 'Poetry in Translation.' You could help us with the German, Russian and Hebrew poetry. You see, you do have a place in my life, even though you doubt me.

Essie, it troubles me that you're keeping my letters; they could do so much damage if they fall into the wrong hands. Let's not give the Greek chorus any more fodder for their evil gossip. I want you to destroy this letter, and all the others of mine in your possession, as I do yours.

Yours, etc. until we meet.

❈

Esther folded Larry's letter, placed it back in its envelope, and added it to the growing pile, which she kept hidden in her underwear drawer. Underneath the stack was the letter from Grace, still creased from where her hand had balled it in a reflex of horror. Esther swore to herself never to burn Larry's letters. They were all precious to her; moreover, they were evidence that she was the mistress of a famous poet.

Esther fell asleep, as she did every night, praying to bear his child. Only then would she be truly in possession, the void within her filled at last.

❈

CHAPTER 29

Cambridge Crescent, London, August 1963

It had not been easy to get pregnant again. Larry's visits to London from Chalk Farm were often brief moments snatched from a legitimate appointment in London. Yet the secrecy of these trysts added a piquancy to their lovemaking.

'Is it all right? You're sure the Dutch cap is in the right place?' Larry would ask. Even at the point of climax, he'd withdraw if he suspected she wasn't wearing her diaphragm.

One morning in early Spring, as soon as Larry had left her bed, Esther went straight to the bathroom; squatting in the empty tub, she hooked her forefinger around the rubber rim of the contraceptive device, and pulled it out of her body. A hot jet of sperm leaked out of her. Esther squeezed her pelvic muscles with all her strength. If only she could keep enough of the precious fluid in her womb. The concave mushroom shaped device snapped back into shape. It was still warm and slimy, slicked with their love juices. Earlier that night she'd felt that strange ache in her abdomen, and knew it to be *mittelschmerz* — the sign that she was ovulating and at her most fertile.

Weeks filled with hope and fear followed. When her period didn't arrive two weeks later, the hope became stronger and was followed by her own private daily prayer. She must have Larry's child, even if, as she was beginning to realise, she would never have the man himself. But his child would be a part of him, would in its very existence be a testament to their love. *Please, please*, she would whisper each morning, before checking for the telltale bloody smear on her panties. It never came. By the time she'd missed a second period, she knew she'd won her desperate gamble.

This time, she told no one. Never again would she be so foolish as to risk others, even Larry — especially Larry — wielding any threat to her precious secret. Nightly she hugged it to herself. She prayed the baby would stay inside her this time, and that it would be a girl, a daughter that perhaps Larry would one day love as much as he did his daughter Fleur.

❈

Spring was turning into summer when a telegram arrived from Spain:

> *ARRIVING BY THE NEXT BOAT ON FRIDAY STOP*
> *CAN'T WAIT FOR US TO BE TOGETHER AGAIN*
> *STOP LOVE TONY*

'What does the poor man think he's going to do? Play happy families, while he knows we've been in each other's beds? How can he leave you alone here, for all these months, and expect you to live like a nun?' Larry said. 'You'd be best to wire back, tell him to go straight to a hotel. Surely he won't want to stay here, in this flat, in the room where you and I make love, in the house where Grace died. Set him free, Essie; it's the kindest thing.'

'Larry, darling, I wish you'd understand. I can't hurt him like that, not yet. He's still my husband, and in a way I do still love him, quite differently to the way I love you. You see, I've always felt it's possible to love two people at the same time. He's been so good to me.'

'For God's sake, Essie, make up your mind. It might be all right with Tony to share you, but it's not all right with me. I need to know you're all mine. Otherwise…'

Esther broke in, her voice firm. 'You're asking too much of me. Let me talk to Tony at least, and see how he really feels. I simply can't tell him to leave now, it would be too cruel. Give me a little more time, do please, darling Larry.' She put her arms around his strong neck, and rested her soft cheek against his rough one, pressing her tender breasts against his chest. 'Come to bed; I want you so much. Let me show you how much.'

Larry pulled away from her, his eyes narrow, his mouth long and hard. 'If you can't see your way clear to releasing Tony, I don't know what I shall do. Now I must go.' Grabbing his greatcoat from the chair where he'd flung it only moments ago, he turned and strode down the steps into the street.

❁

As soon as Tony, golden-haired and tanned, walked in the door, Esther's love for him came flooding back. It was a different love entirely from what she felt for Larry, more a tender protectiveness, and a companionable closeness. How could she ever hurt this man, who'd shown her such patience and forgiveness?

'God, I've missed you, sweetheart. Letters and phone calls come nowhere near to seeing you, smelling you, holding you. Let me look at you — yes, you're as beautiful as I tell everyone you are, and it's good to see you've filled out a little. You were still a little peaky when I left. It suits you, dearest. Now, sit with me and tell me all that you've been doing.'

'Well — the best news is that I've got an interview coming up with that top Agency, Walter Bros. There's a vacancy in their Creative Design Department, so I applied, simply out of boredom, one day. I've been at Prentiss & Son too long, and can't get much further there. Do you think I've got a chance?'

'I'm sure you have. Why, you're the best copywriter Prentiss & Son's ever had; you're much too good for them. When's the interview?'

'On Monday. I'm terribly nervous darling, but, as they say here, nothing ventured nothing gained.' The timeworn cliché comforted her.

Esther and Tony settled back quickly into their easy comradeship. To celebrate his homecoming, Tony took Esther out to a posh French restaurant on The Rose Estate. He was about to order champagne when she stopped him.

'Dearest, I don't feel like drinking tonight. Do you think you can drink a whole bottle by yourself? Perhaps order yourself a glass, and I'll have a little sip. I'd like an orange juice.'

Tony's mouth turned down in disappointment. 'That's not very festive. Are you feeling quite well?'

'I'm fine, just excited to see you, and nervous about the job. Besides, I'm trying to keep my weight down. You don't want me to get fat, do you?'

'Don't be silly, I told you before, a little extra roundness suits you. Oh well,' he turned to the hovering waiter, 'we'll have one glass of the house champagne and one orange juice on ice.'

'Very good, Sir.' The waiter glided off. *Skinflints*, he thought to himself, *won't even fork out for a bottle.*

Tony looked across the white-clothed table at Esther. In the flickering light from the strategically placed candle, her eyes glowed with a silver luminosity, and her skin had that polished sheen he remembered from their first meeting. 'You look younger now than when I left all those months ago,' he said, 'and even more beautiful.'

She smiled and pressed his hand. 'Let's order. I'm starving.'

'I guess I was too busy looking at you to even notice the menu. H-mmm, let's see. I think I'll have the bouillabaisse; it'll remind me of those hearty fish soups I had in Spain, that is when I wasn't eating paella. Oh, Essie, you'd love Spain, the gentle warmth of the sun, the smiling faces of the people, and the shiny black olives you miss so much. One day, we'll go there together, and I'll show you the secret places I discovered.'

Memories of the secret tryst in Spain with Larry flooded Esther, making her stomach flip even more than it had been all night. She almost gave herself away, on both counts. Tony must never know of their tryst, and it was far too early to tell him she might be expecting. Not only superstition stopped her, but also a fierce protectiveness of her secret. She stopped herself in time, changing the subject adroitly.

'Before we can talk about holidays — bit difficult now anyway with a possible new job coming up — what are we going to do about the flat?'

The waiter returned at that moment, placing the tall glass of juice in front of Esther, before presenting the sparkling wine to Tony with undue ceremony. 'Are we ready to order, Monsieur?'

'I'll have the bouillabaisse to start with.'

'And Madame?'

'*Bouillon a l'oignon*' Esther said in her impeccable French accent, meeting the waiter's supercilious smirk boldly. He slid away, admitting to himself that the lady was a looker, too good for the likes of that skinny bloke.

'So — about the flat. Tony, do you really want to live in the place where poor Grace was driven to suicide? It's horrible, I think of her every day. You know I had to let the Highgate place go. I've taken over the lease at Cambridge Crescent to save money, and admittedly it's cheap, but there are too many bad memories. It's not good for us there.'

'You're right, dearest, my thoughts exactly. All I want for us is a clean break with the past. But how can we afford to move? The publishing house said they'll take me back as a manuscript assessor, but they only pay a mere pittance.'

'Darling, you need to concentrate on your writing, perhaps go for another grant. If I get this new position we'll be very comfortable; the salary's twice what I'm getting now.'

'Well ... not sure how I'll feel about being a kept man again, you know. We could look for something cheaper, further from London.'

Her throat constricted. She needed to be where Larry could find her. 'No. I need to be close to Berkeley Square, in the unlikely event that I win them over at this interview on Monday. Fingers crossed. Let's just concentrate on that.'

'Good. We'll find somewhere, away from all the memories. Now, let's drink to your winning this position. Here's to lots of luck on Monday — not that you'll need it, with your talent.' They clinked glasses.

That night Esther made slow careful love to her husband. He was not to know that it was the memory of Larry's touch that fed her passion.

❀

Life in the Buchanan's new abode fell into a comfortable routine. The new flat in St John's Wood was spacious, light, and looked out onto a grove of chestnut trees. Esther's new position as head copywriter of the Creative Department was demanding and absorbing, giving her little time to worry about the fact that she hadn't heard from Larry since his abrupt departure.

Her pregnancy was starting to show. She hid it cleverly by wearing the comfortable new fashion called the Shift, which skimmed the waist and hid bulges. As the weather got cooler she wore strategically draped capes and wraps, managing to look as elegant as always.

She experienced only occasional nausea, so Tony's suspicions weren't aroused until he saw her dressing one morning. That thickening waist, those pendulous breasts weren't those of a woman tending to plumpness; could it be that on one of the few nights she'd taken him to bed, she'd conceived again? He hesitated to speak, until she turned from the mirror, seeing his eyes scan her body.

'I was going to tell you before, but this time I didn't dare tell even you till well past the danger point. It's as you see: I'm four months pregnant.' In fact she was already almost five months, a fact that would entail some explaining. *I'm not ready to tell him it's Larry's, and I'm not ready to make a decision. Just let me keep this baby, and somehow things will work out.* Her thoughts were vague and confused, as if she were living in a dream where the future was out of her hands.

'Darling, that's just wonderful. I didn't dare to think it possible, after our disappointments. I can completely understand why you wouldn't want to tempt fate by telling me too soon, after what happened last time. Are you sure you're over the danger period now? Should you be working so hard? Come, lie down; let me get you some breakfast.'

Esther couldn't help loving him even more, for the comfort he gave her. Forgetting Larry, she rested her cheek in the palm of his hand as they embraced. 'Don't be silly, Tony; I've never felt better in my life. Besides, you know I don't eat much for breakfast. But a cup of tea would be nice.' Along with alcohol, she'd given up coffee and even cigarettes.

She allowed Tony to think the baby was his, although there was no doubt in her mind that the child was Larry's. But where was he? Back in the Chalk Farm, showing no sign of committing himself to his and Esther's life together. What if he'd found someone else by now? The thought terrified her. She remembered the woman's voice she'd heard in the background when they last spoke on the phone. Was it Larry's sister, or someone else? He'd mentioned a neighbour dropping in now and then, to help with a meal or perhaps some other home comforts. She stopped the thought in its tracks; the baby was all that mattered now.

Larry had resumed sending secret letters to a Post Office box in central London. They were mostly filled with the everyday doings at Chalk Farm, and what a sacrifice his sister had made, leaving her life in Paris. There was regret in his letters too, claiming he missed her, wishing he'd made more of their time together in Tony's absence. Esther sensed in him a grudging acceptance, even relief, that she and Tony were back together. She usually went straight to the Post Office before work, and was rewarded one morning with a familiar long blue envelope, addressed in his jagged black handwriting

to Mrs E. Wall.
PO Box 15
Highgate Fields

My lovely one, my little ovenfox, when can I see you again? You say the work keeps you too late to meet after work. What about a lunchtime drink in The Lamb, next Tuesday? I've got Fleur into nursery school two days a week, Tuesdays and Thursdays, so Erica will only have baby Tim to look after. Mind you, he's a handful. I want to hear all your news, and most of all to look at you again, it's been so long — at least five weeks. You see, I'm counting. You must tell me how the Turgenev translation's going, and what your new place is like. Just don't tell me about Tony; I don't need any tales of married bliss.

I'll be in the pub at one fifteen on Tuesday next. Don't reply unless there's an earth-shaking emergency. And please remember to burn this letter.'

As usual, Larry's letter was unsigned.

❖

The following Tuesday, Esther dressed more carefully than usual in a new dress made of the softest blue lambswool, cut on the bias to minimise her expanding girth. Her eyes were highlighted with a pale green shadow and outlined with black eyeliner, her only concession to the latest fashions. She despised the mini-skirt, the thigh-high boots, and the boyish hairstyles sweeping London. Even before her pregnancy, they were highly unflattering, focusing on her wide hips. She retained her allegiance to classic designs, giving Carnaby Street a wide berth.

As soon as Esther entered their old haunt, The Lamb, clasping her fur-trimmed cloak around herself, she felt Larry's eyes on her before she saw him staring and unsmiling. He stood up from the cosy booth where he'd been sitting, and held out a chair in a welcoming gesture quite unlike him. They kissed, and the old flame was alight in her at once.

'I see now what's been going on with Tony,' Larry said, grim faced. 'Why didn't you tell me? You're pregnant again, aren't you?'

'Darling, you weren't supposed to guess so quickly. But yes, it's true. How did you know?'

'Don't you think I know your body by now? One look at you and I saw the change, and knew what it meant. Well, congratulations, you and Tony must be very happy.'

'It's not Tony's. This time I'm absolutely certain it's yours.'

'What? Don't play games with me, Esther. You know perfectly well we took every precaution, unless…'

'Unless what? Diaphragms have been known to fail, you know. I'm five months, and Tony's been back for four. So you see, according to Mother Nature's timing, it can only be your child. But don't worry, Larry.

I'll make no demands on you. I only wanted you to know the truth. Tony thinks he's the father so let's leave it that way.'

Larry's face darkened. 'I can't believe this nonsense. Surely it must be Tony's, whatever you say. I told you not to go back to him, but now that you have, don't expect me to fall for that story.'

He got to his feet and made for the green-tiled bar, without asking Esther her preference. She sat quite still, almost not breathing, until he returned with two glasses of red wine. She pushed hers away. 'I'm not drinking. And I must get back to the office. Please think about what I've said.' Gathering her cloak around her once more, she swiftly left the hotel.

❀

CHAPTER 30

London, March 1964

Through a wall of pain Esther heard the midwife's voice as if it were coming from under the sea. 'Do stop carrying on so, and be a good girl now.'

'I hurt, make it stop! Mutti, where is Mutti? I can't, I can't do this any more.'

'Come now, don't you want to see your baby?'

She heard her own voice, rough and strident, '*Nein, nein, ich kann nicht* — no, no, I cannot, *hilfe mich*, help me...' over and over. Even through her agony, she resented the indignity of having her legs strung up in some sort of stirrup arrangement, as if she were a carcass in the butcher's shop.

Another wave of pain stopped her voice, hoarse from screaming. She felt her whole body tightening, resisting, against the relentless pressure. Then a tremendous surge took her whole body by force, and she screamed as she felt herself splitting apart.

'Ah, well done. I can see the head. Your baby has beautiful long dark hair. Wait — don't push now, dear, you'll damage yourself. Just breathe, Mrs Buchanan, short sharp breaths now.'

There was a second, or maybe a minute, a timeless interval when everything stopped. Esther felt the gathering begin again. With one powerful surge her daughter was born into the light.

The baby was caught mid-air as she hurtled forth in a shower of amniotic fluid, spattering the midwife's glasses as she held the baby aloft. Thus Esther's daughter burst into the world.

❖

Extract from Esther's journal

Guy's Hospital, 3 March 1964

She lies with me, sleeping sweetly. I trace the lovely curve of her cheek with my finger, very gently. I drink her in, her lovely mouth still now, her skin the colour of ivory. I inhale her scent, an indefinable mix, something like cinnamon, delicate yet earthy. Especially I love the surprisingly strong smell of her head, so perfectly formed, the fontanel still pulsing slightly. Her breathing is quick; my heart wants to beat to its rhythm. I wonder if she's dreaming, as her translucent eyelids give a tiny twitch, and her lips open slightly.

As I watch each small movement, listen to each breath, my finger still resting softly on the satiny smoothness of her skin, I feel a love greater than any I've ever known. It floods my soul with wonder, with gratitude. Can this beautiful creature really be mine? She has the same dark hair and white skin of my own mother, who left this world so suddenly. As if my lost mother is returned to me.

Now she wakes and her deep blue eyes stare into mine. I reach out to her as her mouth opens with a little cry. I pull her to me, and she nuzzles at my breast, her tiny mouth searching blindly. I help her find my nipple, put it into her mouth. As she sucks I gentle her head, stroking its dark feathery down. The milk begins to flow and my love for this tiny new being swells to bursting.

She is my miracle, my gift, and my new baby daughter. I will call her Tanya Trudi, in memory of my poor mother, who passed away before I could say goodbye. She will bear Tony's name for decency's sake; but her birth certificate will show the father as Laurence James Wilde.

❧

Larry had ordered a horoscope for this new baby, as a traditional gift from a close friend. The astrologist prophesied that the child would be highly artistic and musical. He did not tell Esther that the horoscope also contained ill omens, predicting severe losses and deaths.

Esther herself was transformed. Gone was the crisp business-like exterior of the advertising executive. Instead she became soft, slow and abundant with maternal love. Her world turned differently. She recalled a poem of Grace's, which she'd read while pregnant with Tanya. It expressed perfectly how Esther had felt in her cow-heavy state. No longer would she be that barren woman mocked and vilified. If only she could write an answering poem, a poem of sisterhood. The miracle of childbirth had surpassed all the bitterness and anger of their rivalry, which had tortured Esther since Grace's death.

To Esther's delight, Yacov paid a visit to see his beloved daughter and new granddaughter. Since his wife Trudi's passing only a few months ago, he'd felt lonely and bereft. A cosmopolitan from way back, Yacov revelled in his daughter's unconventional life, knowing from her letters that she was the secret mistress of a famous poet. Her success in her career did not surprise him; he'd always known his eldest daughter was blessed with brains as well as beauty.

From the train, Yacov went straight to Esther's and Tony's new flat, impressed with its parquet floors and picture windows allowing dappled light to stream in through the budding chestnut trees.

Esther flung her arms around him. 'Dear Vati, how I've missed you. Come and see your new granddaughter.'

'But first, *schönele*, let me look at you.' He held her at arm's length, looking searchingly into those brilliant eyes that had bewitched him from the first time he'd stared into his firstborn's face. '*Ja*, I can see that motherhood is good for you, my little Esther. I see it in your skin, your eyes, even your figure — a little more rounded, yes, but you always were on the too thin side. Now, show me my granddaughter.'

Esther took her father's big warm hand in hers, feeling like a little girl again. She led him into the bedroom, finger on lips, and tiptoed to the bassinet. Lifting the delicate white net decorated with pink and white satin bows, she bent over her sleeping child.

'She's sleeping, Vati, but you can peep for a minute, as long as you don't make any noise. Don't worry, she's due to wake soon, for her next feed. She must have inherited my hearty appetite; the little monkey never misses a feed.'

Yacov gazed at the sleeping infant, taking in her long dark hair and ivory skin. 'Like you were, when you were born. No one could believe you were born with so much hair. In fact the other fathers who came to look at their new babies in the hospital nursery, were drawn to look at you instead when the nurse held you up to the glass. So proud I was.'

'Ssh, Vati. Come and have some tea, or maybe something stronger? I've got your favourite vodka in specially.'

'Ah, a daughter after mine own heart. Come, let us wet the baby's head together, as I believe is the English custom. Tell me her name again.'

'Tanya Gertrude Tatiana — Gertrude is after dear Mutti.'

'A truly Russian name, to honour your daughter's heritage. And a name in memory of your mother also. Did you know that in the Jewish tradition, it is only after one's parent dies, that the child can take the name?'

'No, I didn't; all those customs have passed me by, I'm afraid. Perhaps I knew it deep down. Here, let's drink a toast to Tanya.'

Yacov sipped his vodka, poured straight over ice, appreciatively. Esther clicked her glass, containing fruit juice, against his. 'If only your poor mother could see the child; she worried so about you, my Esther; she always thought that wild streak of yours would get you into trouble. It would have made Trudi so happy to see you now. And your Tony; he must be so proud.'

The room soon filled with the aroma of Yacov's cigar, which had always reminded Esther of cinnamon and vanilla. She found it enormously comforting. Should she tell her father that this baby was a love child? Born to her lover, not her husband? He, of all people, would understand. But something, perhaps her better judgement, perhaps wanting to perpetuate Yacov's ideal vision, stopped her.

'At last you seem settled, married to a good man, and living in comfort. I must admit I was a little worried about my daughter having her first child at such an age. *Elderly primapara*, that's the medical term. Don't look so horrified, my dear. There are higher risks to older mothers, but from what I can see and from what you've told me, you have a perfect child.'

As if on cue, a lusty cry arose from the bedroom; Esther gave Yacov a rueful smile, which said 'what did I tell you?' and went to pick up her baby.

❀

Tony returned home that evening, from his job in the publishing house, to find his father-in-law well ensconced in the only easy chair in the place. It was a wing-backed chair, well worn but comfortable, and Tony felt a twinge of irritation that his favourite resting place had been usurped.

'Welcome, Sir, it's good to see you again, in happier circumstances this time.'

'Ah, so true, my dear boy. So sad about your poor mother. May I wish you long life, as is our custom? Although I am not a religious man, I still adhere to some of the rituals of my background. And please do not address me as 'Sir'; Yacov will do very well.'

'Thank you, Sir — I mean, Yacov. It's great to have you in our home. Especially now. Have you seen our pride and joy?'

'*Mazeltov*, such a beautiful child. May you both have much *nachas* from her.'

'That means pleasure, or joy, in case you haven't guessed,' Esther interrupted, looking at Tony. 'It's an old Yiddish expression. But come, you must both be hungry. Vati, I've made your favourite *sauerbraten*, the only recipe I remember from Mutti. Come, let's eat before Tanya wakes for her feed.'

'M-mm, I can smell it, exactly like Trudi's, may she rest in peace. Now I truly feel at home.' As he spoke, Yacov's voice broke, and his eyes filled with tears. Esther went to him, and leant her head against his chest, inhaling his smell of tobacco and cologne she remembered from childhood.

The taste of Esther's *sauerbraten* matched its aroma, and soon all three were enjoying the rich hearty meal. Esther had not spared the red wine in the dish, and now bent over to fill Yacov's goblet from the same bottle. Tony saw her breasts swelling under her blouse, which strained to contain them. He felt an enormous pride, and a stirring in his loins. To think his dreams of one day being a father had come true at last. And to such an exquisite child, the image of her mother.

Over dinner Yacov regaled them with countless anecdotes; tales of his treating famous dancers from the Bolshoi Ballet, and reminiscences of his own wild youth in Russia, before the revolution had forced the family to Germany.

'*Ach*, I've been running away from something or other all my life, first the Bolsheviks, then the Nazis, even the crazy Zionists in Palestine. Now here I am in England, where perhaps I'll settle to be near my daughter and granddaughter. My poor wife, God rest her soul, always wanted to come to England; too late for that now.'

'But, Vati, you have other grandchildren. Hannah and the boys in Canada would miss you terribly.'

'Nein, they have their own lives, no time for a crazy old man like me. Besides, I can be a help to you both here; I've had plenty of practice babysitting, you know.'

Tony and Esther exchanged glances. Tony said nothing, sipping his water with a faraway expression in his eyes.

'That would be wonderful, Vati. In fact, I do have to go out tomorrow morning, to do a few errands. Perhaps you could be here for Tanya, while she sleeps. I'll make sure to feed her and change her before I leave.'

'*Natürlich*, my dear. Nothing would please me more than to be of some help to you, and to get to know little Tatiana Trudi, I mean Tanya. You have chosen her name well.'

Before they retired for the night, Tony went to the white-netted bassinet where Tanya slept peacefully. He gazed at her in wonder, admiring her long Asiatic eyelids, perfect creamy skin, and full lips. 'A miracle,' he whispered. 'My daughter at last.'

'Shh, come to bed, we only have two hours before she wakes again,' Esther was by his side, drawing him to her. He longed to make love to her, but felt inhibited by the thought of his father-in-law already snoring in the spare room.

'How long does he plan to stay?' Tony whispered, kissing his wife's neck and eyes, as they lay together embracing.

'Come on now, darling. He's only just arrived. But if I know my father, he'll not stay long; he's a born gypsy, like me, always on the move.'

Next morning, after Tony had left for work and Esther had given Tanya her morning feed, Yacov repeated his offer to babysit. 'Are you sure you'd know what to do if she wakes? You mustn't pick her up straight away if she cries; Dr Spock says that will spoil her, and make life chaotic for everyone. She shouldn't need another feed for four hours now, but I'll be back well before then.'

'Go, my dear girl, it will do you good to get some fresh air. Our Tanya will be safe with me, don't worry.'

Esther felt such release when she stepped out into the early spring sunshine, she wanted to dance with joy. The snow had all melted, and green shoots were pushing up in the little park. The chestnut trees had fresh blooms, allowing dappled light to fall in the square. Pulling her coat tightly around her, Esther hurried to the Post Office, straight to the secret box to which only she and Larry had the key. She was rewarded with four fat letters, each one inscribed in his unmistakable hand, to 'Mr F. Wall Esq.' Her heart sang as she put the missives in her carryall, and hurried to the local tea-shop. It was ten o'clock in the morning, too early for the office-workers' tea break, so Esther had no trouble finding an empty booth. There were only two nurses from the local hospital, in starched white uniforms and pert little caps, and a grandmotherly type, at the other tables. Esther sat well away from everyone, and settled down to open her letters, one by one. Her eyes grew moist as she read the first line:

Dear sweet little love sweet Essie sweet love sweetness and sweetest,

I am missing you badly. How does my little chocolate halva? How does the child? I see you've given her a classic Russian name. Why not German, or Hebrew? Well, it's your choice.

How are the translations coming along? Dan very much liked the ones you did from the Italian, and the German. How clever you are, my little ovenfox! Helder is contributing some of his own, translated from the Portuguese.

Thank you for the clever drawings you sent for my birthday. But I was a little alarmed when Erica caught sight of them. You sent them to Chalk Farm although I've expressly asked you not to. It's too dangerous, with all these prying eyes about. Please be careful, and always send them to the new Post Box address I gave you last time.

It hurt Esther that he wouldn't put his name to his letters, as if he wanted to deny his presence in her life. She sipped her tea, gone cold now, and with a clean knife, slid open another envelope. She skimmed the letter, feeling more irritation than delight with each line.

I'm enclosing two more of Amichai's poems, for you to work on. We'll have to get his permission to appoint you as his official translator. You've kept the rhythm of the original Hebrew beautifully. His 'Once a Great Love' could be written about you and me, don't you think?

❄

CHAPTER 31

London, July 1964

'I'm taking Tanya with me today, Vati,' Esther told Yacov, who was scanning the *London Times* from cover to cover. She realised her father was bored, away from his friends and patients. There's nothing for him to do here, she reflected, except jiggle the baby, and smoke his cigars. 'Listen, Vati, why don't you go into town? Visit the British Museum, or maybe a gallery?'

Yacov shook his head. 'It is not for you to worry about me, Essie. It is I who worries about you. What's going on in that so pretty head? Remember, I'm your father. I can always tell when something is not quite right with you. Is it still that poet? The one you told me about in Canada?'

To her surprise, hot tears welled up in Esther's eyes, and she started to sob. 'Oh. Vati. What will I do? He's her — it's his — she's — she's Larry's.'

'You mean — the baby? Tanya? Ah. I am not surprised, my dear. There, now, come to Vati, *schönele*,' He put his arms around his daughter, patting her shoulders gently. She melted into his bear-like embrace.

'I don't know what to do, Vati,' Esther said, wiping her eyes and nose with the clean white handkerchief proffered by Yacov. 'I love Tony, I really do, but it's Larry I want to be with. I've tried so hard to let him go. Now that there's the child — our child — it's impossible.'

'You must follow your heart, daughter,' Yacov said, guiding her to the sofa, where they sat together, her head on his shoulder. 'All I've ever wanted for you is that you be happy, and if you feel such a strong pull — well, you must go wherever it takes you.'

'But, Vati, how is it possible to love two people at the same time? I can't bear to hurt Tony, yet I can't live my life without Larry.'

'Esther, you will hurt Tony less in the end, if you're honest with him. Naturally it will hurt him to lose you, but does he really have you now?'

'Not in the way Larry has me, in my heart and soul. He's been writing me letters, saying if I don't leave Tony, make a clean break, there's no hope for us. I'm afraid this time he means it.'

'You must think carefully. The most important thing is to make a decision, and stick with it, rather than this to-and-fro. Whatever you decide, I will stand by you. Now, go, meet your lover — that's where you're going with Tanya, isn't it?'

'How did you know?'

'Your Vati can read you like a book, my Esther.'

'Dearest Vati. You're right — I'm taking Tanya to meet her father, and to ask him to give me time to decide.'

'Then go, my child. Have courage.'

Tanya, asleep in the wicker pram, stirred and gave a little mewing sound. Esther kissed her father, whispered 'Thank you' and wheeled the baby out into the sun. She hurried, filled with a calm feeling of acceptance, her father's words still echoing in her ears.

Larry had asked her to meet him at the same teashop where she always went to read his letters. He was already waiting for her, hunched in his greatcoat in a dark corner. Esther felt her stomach tighten at the sight of him, and the old desire flood through her body. He looked dishevelled, his hair falling lankly over his brow, his face unshaven. As Esther approached he looked up, stood, and pulled out a chair. He leant to embrace her, but stopped as he caught sight of the perambulator.

'What? You've brought the bairn? Esther, I told you, I need to talk seriously to you, and alone.'

Esther wanted to fall into his arms, inhale him, but she kept her distance.

'Do you really think Tanya will break any of our confidences? She's only four months old, for heaven's sake,' she laughed. 'Just look at her, Larry — have you ever seen a more beautiful child? She's yours, I know it for certain now. See her brow, broad like yours, and that high fore-head? She will have your talent, I can feel it.'

'It's only you I want to look at, Essie. My God, how long is it since we've laid eyes on each other?' Larry kissed her softly on the mouth. He sat her down opposite him, and studied her features. Neither spoke for a long minute. Esther felt a sigh of relief rising through her chest, as she drank in the sight of him.

The child in the pram stirred, and her eyes opened. They had changed from blue to the same greenish grey as her mother's. They stared straight at Larry. The dawn of a smile dimpled the little face. Ten-derly, Esther lifted Tanya into her arms. 'You see? She knows you already. So clever — and her smiles are special, reserved only for those she loves. Don't you want to hold her?'

'Listen to me for a moment, Esther,' Larry said, ignoring the baby. 'Erica's been called back to Paris. I've managed to get Fleur and Tim into a good local day school, and a neighbour can help after school for a few weeks. But the village has turned nasty; it's awash with gossip. Fleur and Tim deserve better. I don't want them to live this fragmented life, motherless as they are. I've had an offer I can't refuse, and if we're …'

Before letting Larry finish his sentence, Esther deposited the little white bundle onto his lap. He looked down at the baby, disarmed in spite of himself, and instinctively lifted her into his arms. 'Ah. I see she has your eyes, and your lovely hair. A sweet child; you are very fortunate to have her.'

'Larry, it's we, you and me, who are fortunate. Why can't you… '

Larry interrupted, 'I've come to tell you that I'm taking a house in Ireland for the summer,' he snapped, as he handed the baby back to Esther. 'My friend in Cleggan has found us a magnificent spot in Con-nemara, and I'm already paying rent just to secure the place. If you and the bairn want to join us there, we could try at last to live together, to see if what we have between us is worth saving. But you will have to break with Tony, a clean break. This is it, Esther; I've waited long enough.'

Esther again heard her father's words. Have courage. Follow your heart. She knew with utter conviction that this was what she wanted: to live with Larry at last under the same roof, to be together day and night, instead of their life of snatched clandestine meetings. She put Tanya back into the pram, covering her tenderly with a soft woollen blanket.

'I promise I'll talk to him tonight,' she said.

❖

Tony felt like a condemned man waiting for the axe to fall. He and Esther were now sleeping separately, ostensibly so that she could more easily get up to feed Tanya in the night. He could feel her withdrawing from him more and more.

When he found the envelope wedged under the sofa where Esther had been sleeping, he knew immediately whose that black jagged writing was. It was enough to see the first word of the letter, "Essie"; he couldn't bear to read on.

At that very moment Tony heard the wheels of Tanya's baby carriage on the front path, and in came Esther, her hair windblown and her eyes shining. She stopped short when she saw him.

'Darling! Why so early? I wasn't expecting you till seven, after your meeting. What's going on?'

'To hell with the meeting. How else will I get time to talk to you alone, with your father always lurking in the background? I'm here because I have to talk to you, without his infernal presence. Thank God he's taken himself off somewhere. Esther, why haven't you told me about this, left where I'd be sure to find it? It's from Larry, isn't it?'

Tony, pale and shaking, waved the letter in front of Esther's face. After all the months of uncertainty, he felt relieved to put an end to this insidious torture.

Esther wheeled Tanya into the sitting room and sat down on the divan opposite Tony. She drew a deep breath. It was confession time.

'Yes, it's a letter from Larry. I'm so sorry, dearest. If you only knew how hard I've tried to forget him.'

'There's no way he'd let that happen, the bastard, with his sneaky letters to 'Essie'. How long has this been going on? For God's sake, tell me: are you in love with him?'

'I don't know what that means. I only know I can't imagine life without him, and at the same time I can't bear to live without you. I love you both, don't you see?'

'You could have fooled me there, the way you've been shut off from me these last months. I thought at first it was because of the baby, that all your love had gone to her. I see now, I was wrong, and I'm not surprised. I think I knew in my bones all along that Larry was still on the scene.'

Esther picked up Tanya and held her close, as if for protection. Her heart thumped against the soft little body. 'I was going to tell you, I really was. I just didn't know how, and now ...'

'You were going to tell me? When? Don't you think I guessed already? We've not slept together, not properly, for weeks. And we're different together; you treat me as if I just happen to live here. Don't take me for a fool, Esther.' His face had reddened now, and his voice grew harsh.

'Tony, I need to get away for a while. With Larry and the children. Please understand, I must do this. There's a house in Ireland, big enough for all of us. I feel I have to go, to give this thing a proper chance.'

'This "thing"? Are you crazy? What about your precious job? They're only holding it for you till June, a month away. I've arranged to take indefinite leave, to care for Tanya while we live on your oh-so-generous salary. Are you forgetting about that too?'

'You'd better tell your editor you've changed your mind. There's no need for you to take leave any more. Tanya is coming with me.'

'Over my dead body. Don't think you can steal Tanya away from me, too.' Tony's face contorted, his voice shaking on the name. 'You're not taking my daughter away, whatever other crazy thing you might do.'

Esther was silent, holding the baby more tightly. *She's not your daughter*, ran through her head, over and over, but she could not say the words.

'Did you hear me, goddam you? I won't let you take her. Go off with that monster if you must, but Tanya stays with me.'

He'd never cursed her before, not even in the terrible days when she'd flaunted her affair with Larry. It spurred her to defiance.

'No one will ever take Tanya from me. Whatever else I may be, I'm her mother. She needs me and you know it. How do you think she'd survive, without me to feed her?' She opened her blouse and put the baby to her breast, where Tanya suckled with little mewing sounds of satisfaction.

Tony sank into the winged chair, and held his head in his hands. A sob escaped from his throat. Esther felt his pain as her own, yet knew she had to keep going. *Have courage.* Her father's words were still giving her strength.

'Forgive me, I beg you. I didn't ask for this to happen, and I never wanted to hurt you. But it has happened, no matter how hard I've tried to put Larry out of my mind. We owe each other the truth, at least.'

'If you leave here, and take Tanya, you can never, ever, come back. Do you understand?'

'So be it. I'll never stop loving you, Tony, but I have to take this chance. Let's face it; we've not been the same together for years, ever since before you went to Canada. We both thought this thing with Larry would end, yet even after what happened to Grace, it's stronger than ever. And all that time you've been so patient,' *too patient*, she thought, *why didn't you fight harder for me?*

The key turned in the lock, and in a moment Yacov was standing in the living room. He looked from one to the other.

'Good evening, how are we tonight?'

Tony didn't greet him, or return his gaze. Esther met her father's eye, and gave a slight nod.

'Ah, I see. Well, I have come to a decision. Much as I love being here, with you, and the *bubele*, it's time I moved on. This is no place for an old man; I need my own space, just as much as you do. So I've taken a room close to the British Museum — magnificent library by the way — and I will move out tomorrow.' With due ceremony he held up the key he'd been holding throughout his speech, and placed it on the little occasional table. 'And now, a vodka to celebrate new directions. I've brought you a bottle as a parting gift.'

❖

CHAPTER 32

Cashel, Ireland, 1965

'Look what we're having for dinner,' Larry's voice boomed, as he strode in through the French doors, after discarding his muddy boots, and getting Tim to do the same.

Esther is here with me and a complete success, Larry wrote to his brother Richard in Australia. He and Esther were ensconced in Cashel House, a sprawling eighteenth century building in the county of Connemara, on the West Coast of Ireland. It stood perched on a ridge, surrounded by wild heathlands, facing the Atlantic. Larry failed to mention that Tanya was with them too, saying only that Fleur and Tim delighted in the place.

Tim's face flushed with excitement. 'Me and Dad, we catched a big one, it tried to get away, but we pulled and pulled on the rod, and I helped, didn't I, Dad?'

'That you did, Son; you'll be a great angler yet,' Larry said, his hand on the boy's shoulder as he threw a look at Esther full of triumph, and longing. Immediately she wanted him, her body cleaving in response.

'Now, Tim, if we're going to eat this beast for dinner, we have to clean and scale it first. Come with me into the scullery, and I'll show you how.'

'What beast are you talking about?' Esther widened her eyes, and put on an alarmed face, which delighted Tim.

'It's a great big sammin, Dad says the biggest fish he's ever catched. Look!' Tim opened the sodden bag at their feet, to reveal a large gleaming fish, its scales glowing pink in the afternoon light. The stink of the river wafted from it. Esther wrinkled her nose.

'Oh — it's magnificent, Tim. I hope you and your dad know how to cook it, because I have no idea.'

'Dad?' Tim looked up at his father, a question in his bright brown eyes.

'Over the open coals, with plenty of lemon juice and some of this wild thyme we have growing here, just for the picking,' Larry's eyes still on Esther, moving from her shining eyes down to her soft white neck, and her breasts pushing at the thin cotton of her floral dress. She felt her nipples jutting erect, wanting his touch.

'We have an hour or so before we need to fetch Fleur from school. Tim, we'll prepare our catch a bit later; I'll just keep it fresh in the icebox, while you can go upstairs and finish making that meccano boat of yours.'

The boy threw his father a disappointed look. 'But Da, I'm starving,' he whined, kicking his bare feet against the skirting board.

'Here, darling, you can have first taste of the *kugelhopf* I made this morning,' Esther called as she moved towards the kitchen, motioning Tim to come with her. There on the rough wooden table stood a freshly baked cake, its fluted sides rippling with alternate stripes of chocolate and a buttery gold. She cut a generous slice, put it on an enamel plate, and handed it to Tim, whose eyes grew rounder by the second.

'Can I have another piece after this one, Aunty?'

'You haven't even tasted it yet, you greedy boy,' Esther laughed, ruffling Tim's thick brown hair. 'We'd better leave some for the others, hadn't we? Tell you what, how about taking your cake upstairs into the playroom — but don't tell Daddy I let you. And please call me Esther, I'm not your aunty.'

Tim ran up the stairs as fast as he could, trying to conceal the cake under his jumper.

'Don't wake the baby,' Larry called after Tim's disappearing back. He turned to Esther.

'At last. Come — there's soft hay in the barn. Tonight's too long to wait.' He pulled her to him, kissed her neck, cheeks, ears, and took her hand in his.

That afternoon, watching Fleur playing happily with Tanya, while Tim proudly showed off his meccano boat to his father, Esther felt a wave of pure happiness. *So this is what it's like, to be a real family, sharing a home with the one you love.* It felt as if she lived in a bubble of golden light, which dimmed only when she remembered Tony. A stab of guilt went through her, and something akin to anger, that anything should be allowed to blight her joy.

'Who wants cake for tea?' she called, shaking away the unwanted memories.

'Me! Me!' Fleur jumped up from the rug where she'd been dressing a doll with Tanya, who jumped up too, echoing 'me, me,' in her baby voice. She was like Fleur's shadow, following her everywhere with a look of adoration in her eyes.

They're sisters, after all, if only Larry could see it, Esther reflected, noticing a subtle resemblance between the two little girls. Fleur, at seven, was bright as a button, with the same deep brown eyes as her mother. Little Tanya had Esther's beautiful grey eyes and dark silky hair. Both children had an indefinable look of Larry about them; she could see the cast of his face, the tilt of his chin, reflected in their faces.

Esther had set the table prettily for tea, with an embroidered linen cloth and a blue and white china tea set. She marvelled at Tanya's delicacy as she lifted the china cup, half-filled with sweetened milk. Not for Esther's daughter the thick enamel crockery; Tanya would become accustomed to elegance from the start.

'Daddy,' said Fleur, through a mouthful of cake, 'we did tables again today, and now I know up to my six-times table. Six ones are six, six twos are twelve, six threes are..'

'Yes, very good, Fleurkin, I believe you. You don't need to say it all over again. Now, what about homework? Did you bring your reader home?'

'I forgot, 'cos I was talking to my bestest friend. Her name's Laura, and she lives in the village. Daddy, can she come to play tomorrow?'

'Daddy, play tomorrow?' Tanya chanted. Larry ignored her, and turned to Esther.

'What do you think? The family might know people in London, and you know how news travels. I couldn't stand more gossip, here of all places.'

'Fleur's entitled to have her friend to play. Why not? You're ashamed of me, is that it? Am I your dirty little secret?'

'Quiet. The children…' Tanya, seeing the change in her mother's face, burst into tears, setting up a mournful whine.

'For God's sake, Esther, can't you keep your daughter quiet?' The afternoon's peace was broken, as Esther glared wordlessly at Larry, cradling Tanya in her arms, soothing her with soft kisses. Fleur and Tim ran off outside, to play hide-and-seek. Tanya set up a loud protest, wriggling out of her mother's arms to follow Fleur.

Within half an hour, harmony was restored. Larry was sitting at his desk, writing furiously. The three children were playing happily outside, the sound of their laughter like birdsong in the air. The strains of a Beethoven symphony filled the sitting room. With a sigh, Esther picked up the translation she'd been working on. She and Larry had already made up, his outburst forgiven after a tender kiss and a murmured apology. *He's a genius*, Esther thought, looking at him bent over his notebook, as the words flowed onto the page. She loved the way an unruly lock of chestnut hair fell over his forehead as he wrote. *A genius is allowed to have his moods. It's all part of who he is; an artist who's above petty worries. I can hardly believe he's chosen me to share his life, here in this magical place.*

❋

The fish supper, cooked over an open fire by Larry, with Tim dancing around in attendance, was a great success. Even Fleur, usually a picky eater, ate some of the sweet flesh. The meal was complemented by Esther's authentic German potato salad, the very same one she'd made for the fateful lunch at Chalk Farm, all those years ago. Esther fed Tanya earlier, and put her to sleep in the little white cot, in the big master bedroom where she and Larry slept. No need for any subterfuge now, or for lies and excuses whenever they'd wanted to meet. Yet their lovemaking was no less exciting for the freedom this place gave them. She'd thought the lack of intrigue might cool Larry's ardour, but the reality was that both felt truly liberated, able to love each other without any boundaries for the first time.

After dinner, they sat together watching the last of the day's light change to deep gold over the waters of Cashel Bay. Still sipping the chilled chablis that had so perfectly accompanied the salmon, they savoured the moment. Larry broke the silence.

'This is perfection, us here together, the children asleep, all of us under one roof at last. I'll be honest, I didn't know at first if this would work, but I had to find out if we could live together. I've come to know you, Essie, really understand you for the person you are, underneath all that façade of glamour and haughtiness. You're really a loveable kitten underneath it all, not the prowling leopard of Ein-Gedi. And the children have really taken to you. Tell me, do you miss your work, and London, very much?'

'I thought I would, especially since my success with the Sea-Witch commercial. It was all my idea to parody a Greek myth, the sirens enticing the Gods, tossing their long dark tresses. Did you know it's been shown in lots of cinemas? I'm told it got a standing ovation in the Oxford movie house. All that fuss over an ad for hair dye! So I suppose I can always go back to the Agency. Officially I'm on sick leave, an extension of the minuscule allowance one gets here for having a baby. But I know they'd welcome me back with open arms. Not that I have the remotest intention of leaving here. I love this place.'

'Ay, it's the closeness to nature, and these magnificent surroundings, and the peace and quiet, all working their magic. It's working for me, too, in another way, freeing my mind up. After such a long drought, the poems are pouring out of me like never before. This new work is a saga; I'm calling it *Fox*. And I'm dedicating it to you, my Esther.'

'Not to Grace?' The words were out before she could stop them.

Larry's smile faded, his eyes darkened. She couldn't bear to see the pain in them, and to know that she'd caused it. He looked away from her.

'Everything in my life is a dedication to Grace, and nothing or nobody can ever change that.' He stood up from the sofa they'd been sharing, and walked back to his desk.

❖

Esther didn't feel at all like writing. In spite of Larry having installed her at the very desk he'd made for Grace (solid wood, thick, fashioned with love by him from an old oak door which he'd found in the workshop at Chalk Farm), her hand felt limp and the page stayed blank.

On the first page of the open volume, a poem lay before her.

She'd rather gaze out of the open window at the wild North Atlantic pounding the shores of Cashel Bay, and lean out to inhale the fragrant spring air. She'd rather make love to Larry out there in the open, in the shade of the great mountain range. Her body stirred at the thought of him. Once again she doubted her ability to fill that page, and to fulfil his expectations. What did he really want from her?

Larry had taken Cashel House on a six-month lease, although both he and Esther would have liked a longer one. After four years lived mostly by letter and stolen visitations, she and Larry could at last be under the same roof together. But was six months long enough to test the resilience of their relationship? To Esther, it sometimes felt too long, especially if Larry was in one of his black moods, when she was sure he was thinking of Grace. At other times, she felt like his true wife, the mother of his child. There was no doubting Larry's passion when they made love, here in the splendid isolation this gracious old house afforded them.

Esther closed the book of poems with a sigh, put down her pen, and moved from the desk to the big picture window. For a long moment she stood looking out at the stormy Atlantic, and the wild heath. In the distance she saw Larry coming towards the house, along the rocky track. Timothy trotted by his side, both of them carrying fishing rods.

Esther's heart flipped at the sight of Larry in his rough country clothes, as if she were seeing him for the first time. He was in his element, she could see that, surrounded by the sheer natural beauty of this corner of Ireland. She saw him suddenly as a little boy in Mytholmroyd, trotting alongside his big brother Richard. Only now it was Tim who was the young boy, and Larry who was like the big brother, teaching him the wonders of fish, bird and beast. Her heart swelled with a different love, and pride that Larry had allowed her into his inner world.

As the months at Cashel passed, Esther felt her life entwine more closely with Larry's than with any man before him. Not once did she regret her decision to give up the life she'd known, the husband who loved her, the career she'd prospered in. If she could support Larry, inspire him, her life would never be in vain. She loved Tony still, in an entirely different way to the animal closeness she had with Larry. She and Tony still wrote to each other, but he was becoming more and more distant.

It was full summer now in Ireland, and the children loved playing on the shores of the Bay, collecting shells and sea-creatures. Little Tanya still followed Fleur around like a faithful puppy, but was becoming more her own person. The child showed a talent for music, swaying and dancing to the classic recordings Larry played on the gramophone.

'Just look at her, Larry,' Esther exclaimed one day, watching her daughter's rhythmic movements with pride. 'She must have some of your poetry in her, don't you think so?'

'Tony's a poet too,' Larry replied tersely, glancing at the little girl.

'Why do you insist on denying Tanya's your daughter? A mother knows who's fathered her child, and besides the fact that she looks so much like you and Fleur, there's no doubt in my mind that she's yours. Can't you see how she loves you?'

Tanya, as if on cue, came out of her musical trance, and ran to Larry, pulling at his hand. 'Daddy, come show me the fishes in the water, like you show Fleur.'

'Oh, all right then, you clever little one, I'll show you now, but you must be quiet till Fleur's home from school, and Tim from kindy.' Larry picked Tanya up and set her on his shoulders, where she perched like a life-sized porcelain doll, her face shining with excitement.

'By the way, I'm going to ask for an extension on the lease tomorrow,' Larry called over his shoulder to Esther, as he carried Tanya outside.

❀

CHAPTER 33

Cashel, Ireland, 1966

The letter was postmarked Woodberry, Devon. Larry opened the envelope and read the single page with a frown. 'It's Ma,' he said, without looking up, ' she's poorly again, and this time the doctor says she can't be moved. Pa can't look after her on his own. We'll have to go back.'

'We?' Esther's voice was shrill with alarm. 'Can't you go over there for a few days, and arrange a nurse or something? You know your parents don't like me. Let me stay here, and look after the children, while you go and sort it out.'

'There's something else. I wasn't going to tell you yet, but the landlord can't extend our lease on this place. It's tourist season and they have other tenants waiting. So we'd have to be gone in another month anyway.'

'No! It's perfect here, we can't just leave. Surely we can find another place to rent nearby. And what about the children? Fleur's doing so well at the village school, and Tim's made friends at the kindergarten. Let's not uproot them again.'

'Esther, it's my mother's health we're talking about. The children will be fine, they're more resilient than you think. And we've proved we can live together here, so why not at Chalk Farm?'

'With your parents, who hate me? With Tanya, who they ignore? With all those busybody neighbours?' *With Grace, who haunts me?* She thought but did not say. 'Larry, how can you ask this of me?'

Esther felt tears gathering, and brushed them away angrily.

'All right then. I'll go back tomorrow to see how the land lies, and to get the best care for Ma. You stay here with the three bairns. You could even make enquiries at the local realtor, although now it's summer there's probably nought to be had. I have no choice but to go, if they both need me. After all, there's no one else.'

'What about Erica? Doesn't she have some responsibility for her parents too? She says she's her own boss over there in Paris, so she could get away any time. Larry, if we leave here, we may never find such bliss again. And your work — you can't stop working on *Fox* now that it's going so well. Please, Larry.'

'I'll do what I can, but I can't promise anything. Erica's already had to abandon her post in Paris once, to come to the rescue; I can't ask her again.'

Esther felt anger rise to choke her. She didn't trust herself to speak. Turning away without a word, she went to pick up Tanya, who'd just woken from her afternoon nap. *How can he throw all this away,* she thought, as she held her daughter close. *In the end it will be just me and Tanya against the world.*

By the time Larry returned to Cashel from Chalk Farm, Esther felt like a rag doll that had been mauled by a puppy. All week Tim and Fleur had been fractious and disobedient, no doubt because they'd missed their father. Tanya trailed after them, grizzling at being ignored by her big sister.

As soon as Larry walked in the door, it was as if the sun had come out. 'Daddy! Dad's home,' the children shouted. Tanya did her best to join in, chanting 'Dada, Dada 'ome,' in her lilting voice. Larry swept Fleur up first, and swung her around in the kitchen, nearly knocking Tim and Tanya over in the process. Tanya began to cry, while Tim just stood there, biting his lip. Larry put Fleur down and knelt in front of his son, taking his hand in his and giving it a manly shake.

'How's my fishing mate, eh? Did you catch any more salmon while I was away?' Tim shook his head. 'No, Dad, 'cos you weren't here,' and he burst into tears.

'Come, boy, that's no way to greet me, after I've been off to see your folks. Nana and Grandpop send their love, to both of you.'

Esther felt the omission like a sting. Obviously, Tanya didn't count as far as Larry's parents were concerned. She scooped up her daughter, thankful that Tanya was oblivious to the slight, and confronted Larry with the little girl in her arms.

'Tanya missed you too. Have you nothing to say to her?'

'Come on, Esther, you're far too sensitive on that issue,' Larry replied, absent-mindedly stroking Tanya's silken head. 'Can't we all settle down and have some tea, while I tell you the news?'

'But Da, can we go catch sammin' now?' Tim shrilled, jumping from one foot to the other, his tears dried and a look of bright expectation on his face.

'Tomorrow, son. I promise. Now, how about you and Fleur go and find me the biggest shells you can, while I talk to Aunt Esther.'

The two children ran off to the little sandy bay, not far from the French doors, and well within sight of their watchful father. Esther settled Tanya into her high chair.

'I do wish you'd stop them calling me "Aunty".' Esther was warming up milk in the little enamel pot. 'After looking after your children all week, I think I'm much more to them than an aunt.'

'Fleur and Tim have only one mother,' said Larry, his face clouding over, as it always did at any reminder of Grace.

Yes, thought Esther, *and you will only ever have one wife.*

'Let them call me just "Esther", or "Essie," if they like. But no more "Aunt", please. Now, tell me what happened in Devon?'

'It's not good. Ma can't get out of bed; the doctor says it's her arthritis making it too hard to move, and on top of that she's got bronchitis. He's worried about her heart, too. Pa's like a lost soul, doing his best to tend her, but anyone can see he's beside himself. Thank goodness for good neighbours, they'd be lost without them.'

'So — where does this leave us? Can't you get the neighbours to help, perhaps pay them something? If we leave here now, things will never ever be the same.'

'What on earth are you talking about? Beverley and Trevor have their own two children to care for. They've already done far more than any neighbour should. How can you suggest such a thing? Pay them, indeed ...'

'Beverley? You never mentioned her before,' Esther said, feeling a coldness in the pit of her stomach. 'Are they new to the village?'

'That they are, and luckily for us, Beverley used to be a nurse. But they've both done quite enough. We absolutely have to go back. But listen,' Larry moved towards Esther and took her tenderly in his arms, 'it's not forever. We know now we can live together, if not here, then anywhere. Chalk Farm must be our home for the next few months, or until Ma's well enough to move back to Yorkshire.'

Esther shuddered at the thought of living in Grace's house, surrounded by constant reminders of her. 'But Larry, Ireland's where we can be happiest, I know it. And we still have a month to go on the lease.' She'd pinned her hopes on a return to Ireland, and had found that although most accommodation in Connemara was booked out for the tourist season, there'd be plenty of options at the end of summer. Her heart sank with disappointment as she saw their blissful days drawing to a close.

Tanya watched them both from the vantage of her high chair, her expression serious, nibbling on bits of apple and pear her mother had cut up for her. Larry sneaked her a jellybean when Esther wasn't looking, and smiled at the child as if they had a pact between them.

'Tanya is becoming a very beautiful, precocious, little girl,' Larry had written to Richard, always stopping short of calling her 'my daughter'.

'The landlord's agreeable to us cutting the lease short, because he's got another family waiting to come in. Don't worry, we'll get our bond back,' Larry said in his matter-of-fact voice, pouring the strong tea into thick china cups. 'Here, love, sit yourself down.'

Esther complied, happy to be close to Larry again, feeling the warmth from his body warming hers.

'Well,' she said, snuggling up to him, ' while you were away I managed to canvass some property agents, and I've put our names on a waiting list for a sweet little cottage in Cashel. It'll be available around the end of September. What do you think?'

Larry frowned. 'You put our names on a list? What names might that be?'

'Mr and Mrs L. Wilde, what else?' She stood up again, steeling herself for an impending storm.

'Are you crazy? I've told you again and again, here in Ireland I'm incognito. That's the whole point of us being here. How could you give some village idiot my name? It'll be all over the place now. Don't ever, ever, do that again.'

Esther was silent. *So he's ashamed of me, doesn't want anyone to think I'm his wife. It's not his so-called fame he's escaping, it's any commitment to me and Tanya.*

She remained standing, and began slicing a loaf of fresh white bread, its convex crust shiny and black. *He's planned all this behind my back; he's determined to go back to the life he had with Grace. Between her and his mother he'll have no time for me.* The knife passed through the soft dough viciously, and nicked her left thumb. Drops of blood fell with the thick slices onto the breadboard, marked with its many scars.

❊

CHAPTER 34

Chalk Farm, 1967

At first all was peaceful at Chalk Farm. Esther tried to continue their life as they'd lived it at Cashel, planting the same vegetables in the fertile garden, playing the same classical music on the gramophone. She made every effort to turn this house into another love nest.

Sleeping again in the bedroom she'd once pretended to admire, Esther felt the ghost of Grace in the air. Her first act was to remove the scarlet curtains from the bedroom. She replaced the liberty print bedspread with a pure white European eiderdown. Next she went hunting through antique shops in neighbouring villages, for a second-hand bed to replace the one, which she sensed still bore the imprint of Grace's body. She wanted the room filled with light, and instead of heavy curtains, purchased pale cream roman blinds for the casement windows. It was no use; all her attempts at exorcism were in vain.

Over the next few months, Esther tried to make Chalk Farm more her own, being careful not to make too many changes to Grace's former décor. She knew that Edward and Miriam, Larry's parents, would object to anything that might tarnish the memory of their beloved daughter-in-law. Perhaps in time, she hoped, they would gradually accept her, and also come to love their little granddaughter.

In the village, heads turned away, nodding to one another. *That's the one he left her for. They say she's a Jewess. Shameless, showing herself in public, not even wearing decent stockings. Did you see that blouse? If 'twere any lower, it'd show all the bits that lured the poor man away.*

One bleak autumn day, Esther visited the local chemist, in search of a hair dye to conceal the grey streaks at her temples. There she spied a package of Sea Witch Permanent Hair Colour. Her heart skipped a beat. Its colourful outer package, which she'd designed in her glory days, was like a talisman of her former self. The finished product seemed to mock her: *see how far you've fallen*, it said. Now she was reduced to a domestic slattern, in need of the very product she'd promoted as restoring a woman's youthful allure.

'Did you know I created the artwork for this product, and all the ads that go with it?' Esther said to Mr Grant the chemist, a surly man, his own thinning grey hair revealing a circle of pink scalp. She handed over a pound note. 'Really, it's too bad I have to pay for it, don't you think?' She stopped short of demanding a reduction, knowing it would reinforce the stereotype of her race.

'Well, I wouldn't know about that, Miss.' said Mr Grant, licking his dry lips. 'All well with you lot down at the big house, is it? Saw the master looking a bit glum the other day. Lucky he got his poor bairns into our little school; still, it must be hard for him with his wife gone. Lovely woman, she was.' His expression was bland, as he handed over the correct change.

It was the 'Miss' that hurt Esther most, another sign that she'd never be accepted in this village as Larry's wife, or mother to his children. For the most part she ignored the taunts and stares of the villagers, contemptuous of those she regarded as ignorant peasants.

Winter was already approaching when, while browsing in an antique shop in a neighbouring village, Esther bumped into a friend of Larry's. He was a local gentleman, who sometimes joined Larry and his father for cards in the evenings, and had been kind and courteous to her.

'Frank,' she said, when she spied him contemplating an ornate vase, 'Fancy seeing you here. I didn't know you were interested in antiques.'

'Oh, indeed,' Frank replied, his moustache twitching with the pleasure of seeing a friend, 'not only am I interested, I'm also thinking of setting up my own little business in Woodberry, so that folk won't need to come all the way to this village to buy their wares.'

'Really?' Esther's eyes widened under their straight black brows, and she automatically went into flirtation mode, fixing those eyes on his, and moving imperceptibly closer. Most men responded to her with an answering twinkle, but not Frank. The spark of sexual energy Esther usually ignited in the opposite sex just wasn't there. *Am I losing my touch?* she worried, then comforted herself with the thought that Frank was perhaps one of those men who were not interested in women, and with whom she could feel safe. He was shorter than her, with a ruddy face and brilliantined hair, which she suspected was dyed dark brown. His eyes twinkled bright blue, and Esther immediately warmed to him.

'What a coincidence,' she continued. 'I was thinking to myself just now, what fun it would be to buy and sell antiques. I did a little of that when I lived in Canada, you know, and also collected some marvellous artefacts from my time in Burma.'

'Capital,' replied Frank. 'I've been looking for someone who might be interested in going into business with me — fifty-fifty you understand — and I reckon you might just fit the bill; why don't we talk about this over lunch?' So saying, they adjourned to the nearby teashop, and over an indulgent Devonshire tea, chatted amicably.

Frank was the only friend Esther made in the village. With his worldly taste and enterprising nature, they had much in common. Esther's natural artistic flair, and her eye for a bargain, made her the ideal business partner. She did the foraging, and even supplied some of her own treasures, while Frank handled financial matters. He and Esther split the profits fifty-fifty, as Frank had promised.

Larry was delighted that Esther had found an outlet for her talents, and was even bringing in a little money, although he and Esther always held separate accounts. He liked and trusted Frank, and they continued to play cards with Larry's dad.

Esther rarely joined the card-players, partly because she had no interest in card games. The other reason for Esther's absence was obvious: Edward's dislike of her was palpable. Larry was confronted with it daily; at mealtimes his father refused to sit at the same table as Esther. When she served food to the family, Edward would push his plate away, never meeting her eyes. His sheer rudeness was an affront to Larry, as well as to Esther. Feeling torn between his lover and his father, Larry tried to remonstrate with Edward.

'It's the fake accent I can't abide,' said Larry's father, 'gives herself all those airs and graces, when anyone can see she's not English. Delusions of grandeur, I'd call it.'

'Pa, Esther's way of speaking's not fake at all. She was educated at an all-British school, studied our history, learned all the British poets, and was taught by Oxford-educated teachers. Hence her accent; I know she sometimes seems more English than the English, but to her it's entirely natural to speak as she does. And she does have a name, Pa; you've never once addressed her as "Esther".'

This was one of the few occasions when Larry had defended Esther to either of his parents; usually, to keep the peace, he said nothing. It was clear to him that Edward and Miriam saw Esther as the Jezebel who'd seduced their son, and who dared to live with him in sin, under their very roof.

❖

'I say it again, it doesn't fall to many men to murder a genius,' Larry said to Esther one day, after reading a particularly nasty article by a well-known American feminist, all but accusing him of the crime he was admitting to. Esther hadn't been quick enough to tear the offending article from the page and throw it in the fire.

Grace's poetry collection had been published to great acclaim, and her novel followed soon after, both published posthumously. Esther was sick of hearing Grace's praises being sung on the BBC radio programs, and of reading rave reviews in the *Observer* or the *London Times*. Larry, as Grace's executor, was at first thrilled with his wife's posthumous success. But soon the adulation was tempered with more critical reviews, accusing Larry of changing the original order of Grace's poems.

Although Grace's old study was off limits to everyone in the house except Larry, Esther managed to sneak into the attic room one day, when Larry had forgotten to lock it. Tiptoeing inside, her hand still on the door handle, she felt faint from the musty odour of old paper, dusty books, and something else: could it be that some of Grace's body smell still lingered?

Terrified, Esther felt a presence in the room. Her skin prickling, she went over to the desk, the same heavy board of oak that Larry had fashioned for Grace, and that he'd even had shipped to be with them in Ireland. She snatched three or four sheets which lay loosely inside a manila folder, without looking at their content. It was enough to know that the handwriting was the very same as that of the menacing letter she'd found from Grace years ago.

❖

Old Mr Wilde was sitting in his favourite chair in the breakfast room, in a sunny spot next to the window, when Esther walked in cradling a cup of tea between her cold hands.

'Oh,' she said, still shaky, 'can I get you anything? A cup of tea, perhaps?' She never knew what to call him; 'Edward' seemed too familiar, and 'Mr Wilde' ridiculously formal.

The old man folded his paper, and with a slow deliberation, lifted himself from the chair without once looking at Esther. She stood in front of him, seething with anger. He looked right through her and left the room. Suddenly it was all too much for her.

'I was talking to you, good sir, but you must have left your manners back in Yorkshire,' she called after his retreating back. He gave no sign of having heard her.

The tension in the house was becoming unbearable to Larry; his mother pining in bed, her silence a reprimand in itself, his father outright hostile. Even the children, sensing conflict, had begun to squabble among themselves. Tanya was unhappy, crying whenever Esther was out of her sight. Neither of Larry's parents had taken to the girl, regarding her as Esther's daughter, and as such, clearly not of their family.

As a means of escape, Larry locked himself in his study all day, when he wasn't tending to Miriam, or playing pool with his father. His work on *Fox* had come to a standstill, and he craved the inspiration that Cashel House had given him. Esther had told him she'd put their names down for a house to rent in Cashel, for the summer, but that was months away.

At times, Larry sought relief from the chaos in the house, by working in the garden, which had been much neglected during their sojourn in Ireland. Esther would observe his broad shoulders, the muscles rippling under his skin as he toiled over spade or shovel. To her he was still a being of pure beauty in both body and spirit, and she thought it miraculous that he'd chosen to share his life with her. She felt worthless, inferior, and the feeling of impending loss came more and more often. No longer dressed in her elegant city clothes, Esther wore drab loose skirts or *dirndl* dresses, which concealed her thickening waist and thighs.

In late May, just as Larry was about to arrange the family's return to Ireland for the summer, Miriam deteriorated. In spite of the warmer weather, Miriam's asthma increased, and soon the doctor was coming daily.

'She can't be moved,' Dr Stewart said to Larry, just outside the bedroom door, and out of his mother's earshot. 'She's not only weak in her body; there's something else worrying the poor woman, and I'm afraid this melancholy of hers won't help things along.'

Larry was desperate. He knew how much his father hated Esther, but hadn't realised her unwanted presence might be playing on Miriam's mind. He'd noticed his mother's silence whenever Esther's name was mentioned, and her quick change of subject. He knew Miriam wasn't one to speak ill of anyone, yet her unspoken disapproval was adding to the household tensions. He suspected that while Esther lived in this house, his mother would never recover.

Sometimes Larry's neighbour, Beverley, would join the card-players in the long evenings at Chalk Farm, while her husband, Trevor, minded the children. Beverley got on famously with Larry's father, which irritated Esther. Worse, Esther sensed a definite attraction between Beverley and Larry, noticing how his eyes lit up whenever she appeared, seemingly at any time she liked.

Edward made no secret of enjoying Beverley's company, and treated her with all the deference and courtesy he denied Esther. Beverley was slim and attractive, with curly blonde hair and a vivacious face. Esther hated her on sight; it seemed to her that Larry was flirting with Beverley, just the way he'd first flirted with herself in this very house.

❀

'We'll have to let the Ireland place go for good,' Larry said after Dr Stewart had left. 'Mother can't be moved now; it's out of the question for her and Pa to go back to Yorkshire. Believe me, that's all they want to do, while things are as they are here. Esther, I think it's time we talked about you and Tanya finding a place in London.'

'What do you mean? Are you banishing me, just because your father hasn't the manners to treat me like a human being, and your mother pretends I don't exist? Tanya's their granddaughter, but you'd never know it. So now you want me to disappear as well?' Esther felt her face grow hot, her stomach clench into a knot.

'Darling, don't carry on so. You must see that this whole arrangement just isn't working. I can't even write any more, torn as I am between you, my parents, and the children. I'm only talking about a temporary move, until Mam's better, and we can find a place of our own again.'

'So you're getting rid of me — us — how convenient for everyone. Especially that upstart, Beverley. Just who does she think she is, waltzing in here as if she owns the place? I'll consider going to London on one condition: that you stop Beverley and that oafish husband of hers dropping in whenever they feel like it.'

'Don't be so ridiculous; they're good neighbours, that's all; where would we have been last summer, when they tended to Mam, while we were sunning ourselves back in Cashel?'

'Yes, that's right, back in Cashel, when we were happy together, as we'll never be again. Now you're throwing me out, like an old rag. Why don't we end this charade, stop the pretence?' Larry tried to embrace her, but she pushed him away with such force, he staggered.

'If it's conditions you want,' Larry said, ' you can read this; I wasn't going to show it to you yet, but now….'

The heading on the typed page read:

<u>Draft constitution for Ovenfox of Chalk farm</u>

1. She should not loll around in her silk robe in the mornings.
2. She should invent a new recipe on the Sunday of each week, and teach it to Fleur.
3. She will teach her native language, German, to the young foxes three hours a week.
4. She should supervise their meals and homework.
5. She should emerge from her sleeping hole no later than 8am each morning.
6. Ovenfox should remember her true origins, and stop pretending to be English.

There were more orders, like tidying her clothes, and baking fresh cakes for the children's tea, and never cooking the same recipe twice. Esther didn't bother to read on. She threw the page in Larry's face.

'Is this your idea of a joke? Don't try to cover up your stupid demands with clever words. Just leave me alone!' Esther cried, and fled to the bedroom she'd failed to make hers. Flinging herself onto the bed, she'd soon soaked the snowy white eiderdown with her tears. She heard again Grace's words, cursing her, and felt the ghostly beckoning.

There's only one solution. If I follow Grace to the grave, Larry might come to love me, as much as he still does her. What a trick that witch played; there's no way I'll ever be good enough for him, or his hateful parents. If it weren't for my Tanya, I'd finish it now.

Esther's thoughts were jumbled, incoherent, as she lay there sobbing. She reached under the mattress and extracted the pages she'd stolen from Grace's study.

As she read the words scrawled over the first page, she caught her breath in shock. This was no poem, but a page from a novel, full of bile and malice. Its content shocked Esther. The barren, haughty woman in

Grace's story was clearly Esther, and her incompetent husband was a cruel sketch of Tony.

How she must have hated us. And now she's making sure I suffer for it. Fury and despair fought inside her, and she had to stop herself from tearing the page to shreds. Instead, spurred to action by sheer anger, Esther reached for pen and paper.

Chalk Farm
Woodberry
3 May 1967

Liebste Hannah,

I can't tell you how dreadful it is here, since Larry and I moved back to Chalk Farm. His parents are in residence, and seem to permeate the very atmosphere. The mother languishes in bed all day, putting emotional pressure on Larry who feels constantly guilty that he can't do more for her. As for Larry's father, he's a total nightmare. He leaves the table whenever I come near it, and refuses to speak to me or even make eye contact. Larry excuses his behaviour, saying his father saw terrible things in the trenches, in the First World War; I wonder if the old man knows of the horrendous slaughter of our people in the Second World War, the unspeakable atrocities against the Jews, which are only now coming to light.

Do you ever think, Hannah, that if our Vati hadn't had the foresight to get us out of Germany when the troubles started, we'd have gone up the chimneys too, burnt alive like our Buba and Zaida and the rest of his family? I think of that often, and shudder each time I hear another horror story about the camps.

*Hannah, I'm writing to tell you things are not good with me and
Tanya; I feel so ill, in my spirit at least, and sometimes I fear for my
Tanya. What will happen to her if I were to die, either from illness
or accident? I couldn't bear to leave her to the mercies of some strange
nanny, or whatever woman is next in line to share Larry's bed. Dear
Hannah, do you think you could come here, just for a week or two? I
want little Tanya to get to know you, because I'm appointing you as
her guardian if the worst happens. I know you have your own little
ones to care for, and your family needs you. But Tanya and I are your
family too, and it would mean the world to me just now to see your
face. Please, please, come to us, dearest Hannah,*

Alles Liebe,

Deine Esther.

❖

2 June 1967

Liebste Esther,

*I was terribly distressed to get your last letter. I tried to get through
to you long distance, but the stupid operator said there was no Mrs
Buchanan listed at that number, even though I gave Larry's name
too. Darling, please see a doctor for whatever ails you, and get some
rest. You should ignore unkind people, show them you're above all
that small-mindedness. Remember who you are, Esther: my beautiful,
talented, sister, who can achieve anything she sets her mind to. Larry
is so lucky to have you.*

*As for your idea of my coming to London, I'd love nothing better than
to see you and little Tanya, but it's impossible for me to get away at
the moment. I haven't weaned the baby yet, and she's come down
with a cold in the last few days. The boys have just started the new*

school term, and they need me here. I feel so torn, but I simply can't come just now.

Why don't you and Tanya come over here, for a holiday? Vati would be overjoyed to see you both, and so would we all. Think of Tanya being able to play with her cousins at last. And it seems a break is just what you need right now.

Liebling, remember you are never alone; we will always be your family. I'm sure if you can put some distance between yourself and the situation there, you'll see things in the right perspective.

Bitte, Komme!
Grüsse und Küsse
Deine Hannah

❀

Chalk Farm
5 July 1967

Liebste Hannah,

I cannot leave here now. You don't understand how delicate my situation is with Larry. He needs me, and if I'm not here for him, he'll find someone else. I can't let that happen.

I'm sending you a trunk by sea-mail (it's cheaper than air.) In it are some of Tanya's favourite books and toys, some clothes for when she's a little older, and a copy of her birth certificate, and immunisation record. I've included a legal document appointing you as Tanya's guardian. There is also a cheque to cover her airfare, if and when the time comes.

The other documents are very precious. They are from an unpublished novel by Grace, which came into my hands by chance. As you can imagine, with all the fuss surrounding her name of late, they'll be worth a fortune one day. I'm sending them to you as Tanya's legacy, so there'll be enough for her education if she needs it.

Guard the manuscript with your life, and show no one.
Alles Liebe,
Esther

❖

CHAPTER 35

St John's Wood, London, August 1967

The move from Chalk Farm to London was like being in a time warp, exchanging the staid old ways of the country for this psyche-delic new world. London had changed years since Esther had lived and worked there. Gone was the drab garb of the office-workers, the tired floral dresses of the housewives, and the padded shoulders and flowing skirts that had suited Esther so well. Young girls were wear-ing mini-skirts, not only baring their knees but a goodly area of thigh above, sometimes allowing a glimpse of knickers to peep from below the truncated hemline. Some of the young men had succumbed to fashion, wearing tight bright shirts, flared trousers, and wide-lapelled jackets. The streets were bright with colour, women of all ages wearing the geomet-ric prints of the popular designer, Mary Quant. Words Esther hadn't heard before, such as 'mini-skirt', 'swinging sixties', or 'flower-power', were bandied about.

'Lucky you,' Larry had said, on the eve of Esther's departure from Chalk Farm, 'to be getting out of this mayhem, back to a space of sanity.'

'Lucky?' Esther had turned on him. 'You must be joking. Lucky to be a woman alone in a big city, with our child without her sister and brother? To say nothing of her father.'

Esther's first few days back in London were a whirlwind of job interviews, as well as house hunting for an apartment. A nanny for Tanya was topmost on her agenda, provided she'd have the salary to pay for one. Presentation was a vital factor in securing a position; should she conform to the current fashion, or maintain a dignified distance?

Avoiding the outrageous fashions of the King's Road, she shopped in her old favourite, Harrods, and discrete little boutiques, which dressed the more discerning citizens. She continued to wear her well-cut jackets and classic suits, as well as full-skirted dresses well below the knee, her waist cleverly minimised with a wide belt. The ultimate effect was of soft femininity, a classic elegance that surpassed the fickle fashions of the day. Her one concession to fashion was to visit the famous salon of Vidal Sassoon, where she allowed her straight raven hair to be trimmed into a shoulder-length bob.

After three gruelling days of interviews, Esther felt like giving up. As a last ditch attempt, she decided to personally hand in her resumé to Mathers & Sons, the most prestigious advertising Agency in town. Walking into the shiny glass and chrome foyer, she drew a deep breath, conscious that her new turquoise suit showed her figure to perfection.

'Yes, Madam. Can I help you?' The receptionist, a plump girl wearing one of those impossibly short mini-dresses in hues that shouted the brazenness of youth, looked at Esther with faint interest, her bright red nails continuing to tap on the sleek Olivetti. Through the open door behind the reception desk, Esther glimpsed a trousered leg and polished shoe.

'I'm here to present my resumé,' Esther said, pitching her voice slightly higher than necessary.

'Applications closed on Friday for the new position, I'm afraid, dearie.' The young receptionist, her hair cut in the latest geometric style, spoke with a cheeky Cockney accent. She barely looked up at Esther, continuing to type at a frightening speed. The shiny red phone on her desk rang.

'Yes, Sir ... Oh ... but I told her that application was closed.' There was a long pause while she listened, her face turning a mottled pink. 'Whatever you say, Sir.' The young woman put the receiver down. Standing to her full height of five feet nothing, she motioned Esther to follow her. 'Mr Horvath will see you now,' she said, in a sulky voice.

'Good morning — or is it afternoon?' The owner of the sharply creased trouser leg and polished shoes was a florid-faced man of around fifty, his double chin flowing over his spotless white collar and broad tie, its geometric print echoing the colours of his secretary's mini-dress.

'I'm Bill Horvath, Human Resources Manager, which is a fancy new name for the person who hires and fires.' The manager extended a well-manicured hand, and pressed Esther's warmly. 'You, Mrs Buchanan, need no introduction; you may not remember, but we were at a conference together a couple of years ago. I've long been an admirer of your work, particularly the Lux commercial. Excellent. So, where have you been hiding that talent of yours, all this time?'

'Thank you for the compliment,' Esther said, fixing the manager with her shining eyes, enhanced by the latest black eyeliner and mascara. She knew she had him. 'I've been freelancing, working on my own projects, and heard you had an opening for creative director. Here's my resumé.'

'No need.' He waved the typed sheets away. 'Only problem is, we've closed the file, but no one's been appointed yet. I'm sure we can get around that small technicality. I was about to go out for lunch. How about joining me for a bite to eat, while we talk business?' Without waiting for an answer, he ushered Esther ahead of him, and they went down in the elevator together.

Finding a home in London for herself and Tanya was the next challenge. There was hardly time to think about what it all meant, this separation from Larry and his family. Whenever her mind dared go there, Esther felt a coldness around her heart, and a voice in her head, mocking her. *He couldn't wait to get rid of you, and Tanya too*, it whispered. She countered the voice — Grace's voice — with her own defiant optimism. She would make him love her recklessly, the way she loved him.

❀

'Darling, I got the job!' Esther crowed over the phone to Larry that night. 'You won't believe the salary — more than twice as much as Walter Bros Agency paid me. And I've found a perfect apartment in St John's Wood; it's top floor, big and airy, right near where Tom and Vivien Eliot used to live. We could be so happy there, darling. There's room for all of us, three good bedrooms, and even a study where you can work on *Fox* in peace. I never thought I could afford to live in such a place …'

'For heaven's sake, Esther, calm down,' Larry said. 'You're getting ahead of yourself. You know I have to stay here with Mam so ill, and what about Fleur's new school? I can't disrupt her again.'

'What's happened to the idea of us living together again, away from the strain of your parents? You said this separation was supposed to be temporary. It's all hot air, isn't it? Tanya's distraught, by the way, calling out for Fleur all day, and her Daddy all night. It's cruel for her to be torn away from her family like this. You don't give a damn about your own daughter.'

'Don't start that again. Look, I really have to go, Tim's waiting for his story, and Fleur's light's still on.' As Larry's voice receded, Esther was sure she heard Beverley's trill laugh in the background.

'Is that Beverley I can hear? You promised ...'

Larry cut her off. 'Don't be ridiculous, it's only the radio, Pa's favourite comedy show, *Hancock's Half Hour*. Now I really do have to go.' The phone clicked dead, and Esther felt as if something inside her was dying too.

Esther checked her watch; it was 6pm. The evening edition of the *London Times* was lying on the coffee table. She turned the pages to the entertainment section, and looked up the radio programs listed for between 6 and 7pm. There was *News of the World* on the BBC, a soap opera on another station, but no mention of any comedy program. The title *Hancock's Half Hour* sprang out at her; it was scheduled for three hours away, at nine pm. 'Liar!' she screamed into the empty room. She threw the paper aside, shaking with fury.

In the morning Esther woke to hope again. *It was just a silly mistake on Larry's part*, she told herself. *He got confused, that's all, or maybe they play programmes at different times down in Devon.* Like the seasons, Esther's moods kept changing from the storms of winter, to the promises of spring. Her inner life was all peaks and troughs, shaking her this way and that like the April winds.

❂

CHAPTER 36

Festival Hall, London, August 1967

'Just look at this invitation: Mr Larry and Mrs Esther Wilde are invited, as guests of honour, to a cocktail party to launch the Festival of Spoken Poetry.' She read out the words in a proud voice, with an extra flourish on the 'Mrs'. 'So that's how others see me — everyone except for you, that is.'

'Come off it, Essie. It's mere protocol, words to comply with outdated convention.'

To Esther, the wording on the invitation meant more than mere protocol. They were at last an acknowledgement of her rightful place beside Larry. Forgotten were her awards from the advertising world, her talents as a miniaturist, her legendary wit and generosity.

Larry moved towards her, and took her in his arms. They seemed to Esther like a puppet's arms, limp and lifeless. Her body shrank from him, and there was a bitter taste in her mouth. Behind her, she sensed the ghost of Grace pulling the strings. *She will always be here, wherever I am. I can't fight her any longer.* Esther shuddered when his lips brushed hers. There was no fire in his kiss.

'I'm relying on you, Essie. There's so much at stake for this festival. Have you organised the speakers' accommodation?' At once Esther felt the burden of responsibility, knowing Larry had invested his reputation in this international festival. 'Please don't let me down, now; I need to be sure everything's in place. Did you contact the Palace Hotel?'

'It's all arranged. As you very well know, anything I organise will be perfect. More importantly,' Esther said, 'what on earth should I wear?'

Larry looked at Esther appraisingly. 'Anything would look good on you, as long as you don't attract too much attention. You're not twenty any more,' he bent over and kissed her lightly on the brow, 'but you're still a beauty.' Esther moved away.

'Don't worry, I won't disgrace you. Look to yourself, why don't you? That jacket's years old, and you badly need a haircut.' She knew he'd ignore her, on both counts, and felt a sudden disconnection from him. *Let him wear that shabby old jacket, leave his hair unkempt. Why should I care?*

'Off you go, then,' Esther said. 'I've got work to do on the programme design you left for me to fix. As if I don't have enough on my plate. Oh, and you can go and wake Tanya from her nap before you go. She's been asking for you incessantly.'

'Can't stay, sorry. Give her a kiss from me when she wakes. I'll be back this evening.'

❀

Heads turned when Larry and Esther entered the Festival Hall on the opening night. She was strikingly beautiful, resplendent in shimmering white satin, her skin glowing pale gold. Larry towered next to her, seeming immense against her delicacy, wearing his signature corduroy jacket, his thick hair unruly, looking every inch the romantic poet.

In keeping with the cosmopolitan theme of this star-studded occasion, Esther's Semitic beauty was the perfect foil to the English gentility of the guests on their home ground. There were suppressed 'oohs' and 'ahhs', especially from some of the younger women. Esther moved with an easy grace, ignoring stares, some of admiration, others mocking.

Amongst the luminaries, Larry Wilde and Esther Goldberg Buchanan reigned as the royal couple. To Esther, this night was a fulfilment of all her fantasies, enhanced by the bridal theme of her gown.

The visiting speakers included Pablo Neruda from Chile, Miroslav Holub from Czechoslovakia, and Allen Ginsberg from New York. For Larry and Esther the most important guest was Yehuda Amichai, from Israel. They both knew and loved his poetry. A leonine presence, Yehuda arrived escorting his young wife, Sharon. It was rumoured that Yehuda and Sharon once had a clandestine affair, and that he had left his wife for her. Esther couldn't help seeing the obvious parallels between their relationship, and hers with Larry. The thought gave her hope that she, too, would one day walk at Larry's side with dignity and respect from the world outside.

Larry discovered Yehuda's work when researching for his book of translations, and Esther had worked on them in Ireland. The two poets became close friends, sending letters back and forth over the sea. Larry was full of admiration for Yehuda's honesty and courage. Like Esther, Yehuda Amichai had fled the Nazis in Germany as a child, but unlike her, he had made Israel his permanent home.

'My — er — wife grew up in Israel too,' Larry told Yehuda, as they sipped cocktails at the reception. 'I can highly recommend her as a translator, if you'd consider a joint project on your poetry. We worked on the translations together when we lived in Ireland last year.' Esther knew that Larry was trying to ingratiate himself with the great poet, who'd become like a touchstone of genius for him. Still, a small thrill of pleasure had gone through her, hearing Larry say the words 'my wife.' And to think he'd trusted her with this important work!

'We'll work on Yehuda's poems together,' Larry told Esther later, after the Israeli poet had enthusiastically agreed to appoint Esther as his translator. 'You can do the technical part, finding the roughly equivalent words, while I'll fashion the language into poetry.'

Esther felt affronted; wasn't she attuned to the nuances of Hebrew, able to turn Amichai's powerful poetry into the equivalent in English? Besides, Larry knew hardly a word of Hebrew, that ancient language with its spidery backwards script. He'd been studying the Kabbalah scriptures recently, but only in their English translation. She assumed he knew, however, that the art of translation is not just a matter of nuance of language and powerful images, but of many other dimensions and metaphors existing in the lines. *Give me some credit*, she'd thought, but hadn't said.

Finding English words to replace Yehuda's evocative imagery, the nuances of his Hebrew metaphors, was complex and challenging. Esther knew she was the right person for this task, with her fluency in both

English and modern Hebrew. She determined to replicate the music of his language, so that her translations would resonate with Larry's readers.

❀

Esther emerged from a long soak in a perfumed bath, and changed into the silk skirt with the swirly blue pattern, just in case Larry would be true to his word, and visit her tonight. When she heard the key in the door, her heart jumped.

Larry let himself in, his hair awry from the cold wind outside. For a moment she regretted giving him the key to her flat. It was an unreciprocal arrangement, with Chalk Farm now barred to her. As always, her anger dissipated as soon as she saw him and caught his male scent.

'Darling, you'll never guess,' Esther said, greeting Larry with a perfunctory kiss. 'Tanya's already learned two songs in German, and now talks to Maria in German, and to me in English. She'll be bilingual, you know. It'll be such an advantage to her in the future. Aren't you proud of our daughter?'

'Esther, Tanya's your daughter, and just like the rabbis say, that's all we, or anyone for that matter, can be sure of. It's written in the Torah. We can only know who a child's mother is, because the father could be anyone. Such down to earth common sense in those old texts.'

'Oh, how very convenient, calling on those ancient superstitions to wriggle out of your paternal responsibility. So, you're suddenly the expert in Judaism now? Where's all this religious knowledge coming from?' she said. She was sitting close to him on her new sofa, upholstered in the latest shade of mushroom. When her arm accidentally brushed his she instinctively drew away.

'From you, Essie. You know I've always been fascinated by your religion, whether you follow it or not. In any case, I've been studying the Kabbalah for years, long before I met you. There's so much wisdom in those ancient writings, such richness there, and — well — they damn well inspire me.'

'For heaven's sake, Larry, don't keep talking to me about religion. Since the Holocaust, and what happened to my father's family — murdered, every one of them — I've no time for a God who'd allow such monstrous acts. I want to leave all that behind me. This sudden interest of yours wouldn't have anything to do with your hero, Yehuda, would it?'

Larry shook his head. 'It's the great suffering of your race that's inspired the works of such writers as Amichai. Esther, stop pretending to be a bourgeoise English woman; that's one of the things that most irritated Pa, and Ma as well. What I first loved about you was your 'many-blooded beauty', coming from the race you do, the same one as Amichai. Speaking of Yehuda, when will you have that last poem of his ready for our new book? We have a publishing deadline, you know.'

Esther had found little time to put her own linguistic skills to work on the translations she'd promised Larry. The prospect of being published, her name alongside Larry's on the title page, thrilled her. Yet finding the time to write was an almost insurmountable challenge.

Late at night, she started to translate one of Yehuda's poems, *Small Change,* one of her favourites. Its Hebrew letters stood stark and black, their angular shapes like stick insects. No, she did not feel like writing, transforming those sharp aggressive shapes into safe round English letters. How dare she take another's thoughts from their original language and attempt to put English words to them? Some words just did not translate.

It all seemed much too hard. She sighed, foreseeing another sleepless night ahead. Having to keep on top of her colleagues in the highly competitive world of advertising, and coming up with new, fresh ideas constantly, was exhausting: working all hours, often till ten at night or later, meant falling into bed at midnight, after tucking in Tanya, who was always asleep. She thanked the fates for bringing her Maria, the German au pair who spent far more time with Tanya than Esther did herself.

'I finished translating Yehuda's 'Small Change' this morning. I hope he'll like it.'

'Better show it to me first,' Larry said. Esther felt rebellion rising in her chest. *Why should I show it to him. What would he know about translating?*

'They make me work like the devil at the Agency,' she said, changing to a safer subject. 'It's a jungle at Mathers; I've seen copywriters sacked for not being super-productive. By the way, you never said anything about my landing such a high-powered job. Did I tell you there were dozens of other applicants, better qualified than me? I think I deserve a *mazeltov*, at least.'

'Fate works in strange ways, Essie. It seems your reputation precedes you, and you've had a stroke of luck; probably the right place at the right time. At least you won't be so strapped for cash. Perhaps now you can see your way clear to repaying that loan I made you, for the move. I'm expecting a new grant from the Arts Council soon, but till then, I'm broke.'

Without a word, Esther rose from the sofa and went to the bedroom. Shaking with anger, she took her chequebook from her handbag. In the sitting room, she stood at the buffet and wrote out a cheque for far more than she owed.

'Here you are. Does this discharge my so-called debt to you? I would've thought that being your children's nanny for two years, and slaving away as unpaid housekeeper while your parents treated me like dirt, would more than make up for any cash you'd lent me. So how will you discharge your debt to me? Money won't do it. Unless we can all live together again, like we did in Ireland, it's over between us.'

She wanted to strike out at him, but held herself back, as she tossed the hastily scrawled cheque at his feet. Larry stooped to pick it up, and pocketing it, stood up as if to leave.

'Essie, listen to me. We can work out an ideal life: four days a week you and Tanya could stay in London, and you'll both come to Chalk Farm at weekends. I'll come to stay here in this new place of yours, whenever I can get away. It's not easy being both mother and father to Tim and Fleur, you know, and Ma needs me too. You wait, it'll be like old times, only we won't have to sneak around, hiding from everyone. Remember old Mr Stanford, and my Fly on the Wall? '

Esther felt the joy leaking out of her. Larry's voice, once like sweetest honey to her soul, grated on her ears.

'Yes, like old times, just a slinky affair,' she said.

❖

Extract from Esther's Journal, November 1967

The hot flame of jealousy searing me again. Last night I dreamed Larry was in bed with another woman. She was a large-breasted, athletically built blonde, the type who always makes me feel insignificant. In the dream, Larry and I were promised to each other in an arranged marriage. Yet he declared his love for Miss Bosom Queen quite openly. He seemed as obsessed with her as I've been with him. I kept glimpsing this woman in crowds, in cafés, always elusive, leading him a merry chase. I realised the woman was Grace, grown older and sexier. She isn't dead at all. To see him pursuing her, fixated on her, with her wild blonde hair and animal smell, was unbearable. I want to escape this hell, the only possible way. I woke up sobbing.

Esther hid the journal in amongst her lingerie, along with the pile of Larry's letters. He'd instructed her to burn them, and to stop keeping a journal. She'd assured him she'd do so, all the while fearing that one day he'd find the precious papers, before she had time to make sure they were safe. They were evidence that Larry had once loved her, and would be Tanya's inheritance when the time came.

❖

November, 1967

Meine Liebste Hannah,

Remember how I used to get sometimes, when the whole world seemed black, and even you couldn't cheer me up? Hannah, I think I'm very ill. Nothing will shake this grey shadow of fear from me, no one can make me smile any more, except my darling Tanya who I love more than anything or anyone in the world. Larry has abandoned us, yet keeps up a pretense that he and I are still together in what he calls a 'civilised' relationship. That means we live separately, so that he can do as he pleases, and seduce as many women as he likes, while I stay incarcerated in this flat.

'Leave him,' I hear you say, over and over. Hannah, believe me, I've tried many times, and failed as many. Even if I had the time or the energy, I could never find another man to match him. I tell myself that a genius such as Larry must be allowed his little peccadillos. If only I could believe it. In spite of all his neglect, his seeming indifference to our daughter, he's the only one for me. No man has ever had this effect on me. I am caught in his thrall, and always will be, as long as I'm alive.

Remember how dear Mutti used to put cream on her face, right up till the day she died? I can understand her now, her fear of growing old and ugly (which she never did). I have more lines on my face at forty than she did at seventy, and I cry when I look in the mirror. I always said I wanted to die at forty-two, before the signs of age set in. Life just wouldn't be worth living with slack skin and grey hair. If it weren't for my Tanya, I'd end it now.

(Don't worry, darling, I'm not serious, but that's the extent of my misery.)

On the bright side, Tanya's now happily talking away in both languages, and can sing 'Röslein, Röslein' with perfect pronunciation. She has a sweet voice, and is naturally musical. I wish you and Vati could see her. But I don't dare leave London now; besides the demands of my job. (Did I tell you I'm already in line for promotion?) I need Tanya to be near her father. My dear sister, I've made provision for you and for Tanya in my will, and will send you a copy as soon as I've seen a lawyer to ratify it. I'm bequeathing all my possessions to you, to be passed on to Tanya. You must take great care of my netsuke collection — it's exquisite. The letters and manuscripts I have of Larry's will be valuable one day, and I'll keep them in a bank vault with the will, and Mutti's jewellery, which she left me. I know I can trust you to be good to Tanya, but I shudder to think what might become of her without me. She and I are so close to each other, you see; I call her my little self, almost as if we were one and the same soul.

Viele Liebe, deine Esther.

❀

CHAPTER 37

St John's Wood, London, December 1967

'Stunning' read the review of Amichai's poems in the *London Observer*. 'Such depth of feeling, the vivid mages of displacement and survival, are the works of two brilliant minds. These poems, translated from the original Hebrew by Esther Goldberg Buchanan, are so eloquent, they don't read like translations. In fact, they are fresh and immediate. Edited by no less than England's leading poet, Larry Wilde, this small volume belongs on every poetry-lover's shelf.'

'Larry, have you seen today's paper?' Esther trilled over the phone, her heart so full of pride she could hardly get the words out. No one answered on the other end, and her heart fell with each unanswered ring. About to hang up, she heard Larry's voice, thick with sleep.

'For God's sake, Esther, do you know what time it is? Barely eight o'clock on a Saturday morning, and the phone's woken Ma. Tim's still asleep. What's this about the paper?'

Like air releasing from a balloon, her soul deflated. In a small voice, she said,

'Our book's reviewed in today's *Observer*. I thought you'd want to know what it says, but never mind. So sorry to disturb you, and whoever else might be sharing your bed.' She hung up before he'd hear the sob in her voice. She knew that post-coital tone in Larry's voice, and had a vision of Aunty Beverley, as Fleur called the neighbour, stretched languorously in his tangled sheets, her body replete with his loving.

Esther read the review again. It seemed silly, insincere, this time. Was the reviewer trying to ingratiate herself with Larry? Hot tears of anger ran unchecked down her cheeks. Why didn't the world see her as Larry's partner, 'Esther Wilde', as she'd started to call herself?

The phone rang, and instantly she grabbed for it. This'll be Larry, ringing to apologise. *Of course he's not in bed with anyone, how could I be so stupid?* 'Hello, Larry?' she said into the receiver, wiping away tears.

'Darling, it's Rivke, I just wanted to say *Mazeltov*. I'm so proud of you. Champagne tonight?'

'Oh. So you've read the review?'

What, you think I would miss any word about my best friend? There's another mention of your translation in the *Times*, calling the book 'superb'. *Ach*, Essie, I always knew you'd be famous.'

'Come on, Rivke, don't exaggerate; it's such a flimsy volume. Anyway, most of the credit should go to Larry, for making it all happen.'

'How can you sell yourself so short? If I got a review like that, I'd be ecstatic. I see I've chosen the right person to translate my play. Have your fees gone up, by the way? They really should, now that you're a famous translator.'

'Nonsense, darling. Now, I really must go, I'm expecting another call.'

But the phone stayed silent. Esther went to wake up Tanya, and dress her for the day. They'd go out, she decided, in spite of the cold outside. Coffee in the King's Road, and the flea markets with their colourful wares, would prove a distraction for them both. With Christmas so close, they might pick up some decorations and delicacies, in preparation for the lunch she planned to host.

At almost four years old, Tanya was a serious, wide-eyed child with an extraordinarily deep voice. No matter how miserable Esther felt, she was impelled to get up for her child each and every morning. Esther loved to pick her up, feel her softness, inhale her sweet smell. Whitest skin, finer than silk. Eyes so luminous and deep Esther wanted to enter them, to pass into her child's world. *How can I ever let her go?*

❖

You are cordially invited to Christmas Lunch, at 51 Marlborough Place, St John's Wood, at twelve noon for twelve-thirty. Esther and Tanya Wilde would be delighted if you can join them at this festive time.

The wording on her hand-drawn invitations was deliberately formal. Esther had illustrated each invitation with vivid miniatures of Christmas bells and mistletoe, and had Tanya sign her childish scrawl, a squiggle faintly resembling an 'T'.

As well as Larry, Fleur and Tim, she'd invited Larry's sister Erica who'd returned to London from Paris, and her close friends Rivke and Audrey, and Audrey's family. On Christmas Day Esther decorated the flat with red and green streamers, and a small green tree in its pot of earth, glittering with silver and gold baubles. On the very top of the tree, she placed a figurine of an angel in a frosty white gown, as she remembered her mother Trudi doing every Christmas.

Esther loved entertaining, and the lunch was suitably lavish. On the day itself, snow began to fall softly, and guests arrived bundled into overcoats and various forms of headgear. She greeted each visitor at the door, her new crimson dress covered with a Christmassy apron.

Rivke burst in, her rosy face bringing warmth to the gathering, full of smiles and hugs. She ran to little Tanya, and bent to cuddle her.

'Here's your present, *schönele,*' she gushed. 'A dolly for a dolly.'

Tanya, wide-eyed and serious, unwrapped the cellophane to reveal a pretty girl-doll, almost as big as she was, with what looked like real golden hair curling around its pink porcelain face. '*Danke* — thank you,' she whispered, enraptured, and ran off hugging the doll to her chest.

Soon Audrey and Ben, and their two boys arrived, No sign of Larry. *Where is he?* ran through her head as a constant refrain.

❀

It was already twelve-thirty before Esther served pre-lunch cocktails. She kept running to the kitchen to check the turkey and trimmings, frequently giving it an extra baste. The whole flat was filled with delicious aromas of roasting vegetables, onion and garlic, and a sweet cinnamon smell — a mélange of fragrances.

Just as Esther had given up hope, and was about to serve the lunch, the bell rang. There stood Larry on the doorstep, his head bare and looking as if he'd just got out of bed, with Erica in her elegant fur-trimmed coat, and the two children, their rosy faces peeping out of beanies and hooded jackets.

'At last,' said Esther, hugging the children, shaking Erica by the hand, and kissing Larry's cheek. 'Come in out of the cold. We're about to sit down, so you're just in time.'

'We were held up at home,' said Larry, 'the neighbours dropped in for a drop of Christmas cheer.'

Esther froze. *So Beverley's on the scene again. Damn the woman.*

Tanya, hearing her father's voice, ran up to him, jumping up and down.

'Daddy, we got a tree inside our house, and there's presents under it, one for you too.' Her voice was high with excitement. Larry didn't bend to pick her up, although she held her little arms out to him.

'Daddy, is Aunty Beverley coming for lunch too?' asked Fleur.

'Be quiet, Fleur. Of course she's not. Don't you remember they've all gone away for the holidays?'

'So who — who were your visitors?' asked Esther, before she could stop herself.

''Twas only that nosy neighbour Regina, busybody that she is, wanting to snoop I'll wager. Nothing's private any more in Woodberry.'

'I see. What exactly do you need privacy for — or should I say "who"?'

'Come on, Esther. Let's not argue today, not at Christmas. The children are starving. Is lunch ready?'

Pressing her lips together, Esther led her guests into the dining room, where she'd laid her best silver and crystal on a snowy white linen tablecloth. There were sprigs of mistletoe at every place. The entrées of pâté garnished with parsley were already on the table, along with freshly baked bread rolls. Jugs of fruit punch added colour to the festive board.

'But darlink! You've gone to too much trouble,' Rivke trilled, kissing Esther's cheek. The other guests murmured their agreement. The adults took their seats around the big dining table, while the children — five of them including Audrey's two — were on special chairs at a square folding table. Esther had prepared a different entrée for them, of crispy croutons, which Tanya especially loved, dipped into a creamy cheese fondue.

'Who's going to carve the turkey?' asked Esther. They all looked at Larry, as if he were the man of the house. He shrugged, and stood up to move to the head of the table.

When everyone was full to bursting with turkey, sauce, and salads, followed by a Christmas pudding and brandy sauce, the group retreated to Esther's warmly lit living room. A small gas fire warmed the space.

'There's a present for everyone, but you have to find your own,' said Esther, her rancour of the morning forgotten. There was a general dive on the brightly wrapped gifts under the tree, followed by shrieks of joy when present and recipient were matched. There were a few glum faces too, when the hoped-for cricket bat or necklace didn't appear.

'I have a treat for you all, come gather round. Choose a seat or a cushion, ready for the show. Tanya's been practicing all week, ' Esther addressed her guests with a note of pride in her voice.

Tanya, needing no encouragement, took centre floor, pausing for a moment to make sure she had all the adults' attention. She was already in her fairy dress, a pale pink tutu of stiff net, with a silk chemise top. Looking gravely around the room for a moment, she held out her skirt and curtseyed, then began to whirl and twirl in a dance of grace and gaiety. The room went silent, watching the sweet-faced three-year-old.

When Tanya sang the popular old song her mother had taught her, 'In my Sweet Little Alice Blue Gown', everyone smiled and clapped, and tried not to laugh at the contralto tones coming from the tiny throat. As an encore, Tanya sang the first few lines of 'Röslein, Röslein, in der Heide', in almost flawless German.

The guests spontaneously clapped again as Tanya gave her final bow. Esther whirled her daughter around, holding the tiny soft hands in her own, till the little girl's feet left the ground and she spun out in a circle. Tanya laughed aloud with delight, seeing her mother's rare happiness.

'She's so talented,' Audrey whispered to Larry, 'aren't you proud of her?' His answer was lost in the general shouts of 'Bravo!' and 'Encore!'. Erica, her face impassive, said nothing as she watched her niece take another bow.

Tim stood up, not to be outdone, and recited the only poem he knew by heart: *Now We Are Six* by A.A. Milne. His Aunt Erica, who had given him a signed copy of the book for his sixth birthday, applauded the loudest. The other children all wanted to perform as well; Fleur, and Audrey's daughter of the same age, did handstands and various athletic poses.

'Stop, there's not enough room here, I'm afraid,' said Esther, laughing a little, moving a precious vase to the top of her netsuke vitrine.

As the guests were leaving, Esther gave each adult a copy of the newly published book, *Yehuda Amichai in Translation*, by Laurence Wilde, translated by Esther Buchanan.

'Signed copies,' she told them, not adding that only her own signature graced the flyleaf.

'*Oi*, didn't I always say you'd be famous? So clever you are, darlink,' said Rivke, her loud guttural voice drowning out the others' polite thank-yous.

'Come on, children, we must be off,' Larry said, holding out Fleur's thick blue coat. Erica was already shrugging herself into her fur coat.

'But — but surely you're staying? I was hoping Fleur and Tim could sleep over. Tanya would be thrilled.'

'Afraid not,' said Larry. 'I've got to get back.'

'Oh, goody, is Aunty Beverley coming for tea, with Pip and Julie?' said Tim.

'Quiet, will you,' Larry said in a low voice.

Tanya began to cry, big fat tears of misery coursing down her cheeks, as she watched her father and Aunt Erica leaving, taking Fleur and Tim away from her.

Left with the wreckage of her party, Esther felt the old black demon descending. She went to the bathroom cabinet where she kept the tablets Dr Coplin had prescribed. 'Take a half tablet at night for three weeks, then one tablet daily. Only to be taken under strict medical supervision,' said the typed label. She tipped three tablets into her cupped hand, and swallowed them with a gulp of water from the tap in the hand basin.

Tanya was still crying pitifully. It was only four o'clock, but already almost dark outside.

'Come, *schönele*, we'll get ready for bed, and clean up this mess in the morning. ;Your dancing was wonderful, my darling. Mummy felt so proud of you. Let's take your fairy dress off and put on some warm 'jamas.'

But Tanya shook her head violently, running away from Esther and banging on the front door.

'I want Dada and Fleurie.' She sobbed, mucous and tears running from her nose and eyes. Esther picked her daughter up and cuddled Tanya's hot, shaking body. She longed for the oblivion of sleep, and comfort of bed. Holding Tanya close, she kissed her wet face until the crying stopped. The two of them slipped into Esther's bed, under the heavy white eiderdown, and were soon asleep.

❃

CHAPTER 38

St John's Wood, London, January 1968

Esther resolved that this was the year when all would be settled, once and for all. She and Larry had been house hunting together; didn't that prove he must be serious? They'd already seen one place that might be perfect, Green Farm at Hexham. The farmhouse was almost a replica of Cashel, the Irish cottage where, only two years ago, she and Larry and the three children had lived as a real family.

New Years' Eve had come and gone. That night Esther and Tanya spent a lonely night at home, while Larry was entertaining his brother and sister-in-law at Chalk Farm. *That's what you think*, the voice, always in her head, taunted her. It was Grace's voice, harsh and bitter. *Don't you know he was with that Beverley woman, in her bed, no doubt climaxing together as midnight struck?*

Larry had agreed to a belated New Years' celebration with her tonight. Why would he have agreed to a dinner date, if he'd been involved with another woman? And dinner might lead to — who knows? The old animal magic between them would work again, she was sure of it.

Esther felt again the thrill of those first heady days of their courtship. *If you could call it that*, scoffed the voice in her head. *Shut up*, she hissed at Grace. While Tanya was having her afternoon nap, Esther ran herself a hot bath, scented with fragrant lily-of-the-valley bath salts. The rich smell of *sauerbraten*, simmering on the kitchen stove, wafted through the flat. Esther closed her eyes and let the steam soften her skin, trying to empty her mind of the voice always there.

Dressing slowly, she surveyed herself in the mirror. She'd chosen the dark green sheath dress, her final choice after she'd tried on three other outfits, each one scrutinised intensely for any unflattering bulges. Sucking in her rounded stomach, she noted with satisfaction how the well-cut straight skirt of the green dress slimmed her widening hips, while the bodice, agreeably low cut, showed just a hint of cleavage. She added the sheer black stockings Larry had always liked, twisting her body around awkwardly to fasten the back suspenders, and bending down to straighten the seams.

She felt happier tonight, more hopeful. She and Larry would talk about the house over dinner; the house where at last their long-postponed happiness would be granted them, their past vicissitudes all forgotten. It would be a home where, finally, their life together could begin again, far enough away from Chalk Farm to make it a fading memory. They'd be safe in this new place, removed from the angry stares of Larry's parents. Perhaps they'd work on other projects together, with Esther using her considerable artistic skills to illustrate a book he had in mind, based on a pack of playing cards. Perhaps their friends from London would come to visit for a weekend. They could even hold literary soirées, or hold poetry readings for the intelligentsia of London.

Spraying Larry's favourite Chanel No. 5 a little more liberally than usual, Esther examined her face in the bathroom mirror. She searched it for spots and blotches, applying just a little makeup. Turning her head to examine herself, she noticed an unwanted hair on her chin, and had to hunt through cluttered bathroom drawers to find tweezers. One more adjustment to her hairstyle, back-combed just a little to hide the creeping grey strands, and she was ready. She gazed again into her own eyes in the bathroom mirror.

As Esther looked at her reflection, her eyes became unfocused. The mirror seemed to dissolve in soft waves. She let herself imagine the house she and Larry planned to inspect tomorrow; it was in Tyneside, near Newcastle, overlooking the sea. For a moment she thought how it would be when they moved: Larry and Esther their faces soft, gazing down at their child.

'Daddy's going to tell you another story tonight, my darling' Esther would whisper, bending down to the little girl, kissing her softly. She envisaged herself turning to quietly leave the room. She would be going to prepare the evening meal, a small supper just for the two of them.

Tanya would have her meal earlier, in the nursery in front of the fire. But where were Fleur and Timothy? Ah yes — Larry had decided to send them away to boarding school mid-week. They would come to visit at weekends, and Tanya's cries of excitement when she saw her half-siblings would ring like a bell through the house.

Esther saw herself inside that big old house, the very centre of her future. She would be standing at a big bay window, with Larry looming protectively at her side. She does not need to look at him. The bulky warmth of his presence, its solidity, is enough. They look out together in silence at the grey sea beneath them. "Tanya's waiting for you to read to her. What'll it be tonight?" she would say to him. "Time for another made-up story — she loves those best," Larry whispers, as they turn and leave the room together.

Gazing still at the vision of her future, Esther sees the puffiness around her chin and jaw gone, her strong cheekbones again emerging, the frown-marks between her eyes fading. Her hair shines black and glossy, all traces of grey vanished. Her eyes are clear, their grey-green irises shining under thick black lashes. She has a waist again, and the skin above her breasts is smooth and silky. She's the Esther Larry had fallen in love with all those years ago.

A cry from Tanya broke the fantasy. The child was tucked up in her little white cot.

'Ima's coming, my *liebling*, in just a minute,' she called through the door to Tanya's room. A final check in the mirror, a slick of lipstick, which she hoped would be kissed away, and she was ready.

Before Esther reached Tanya's room, the phone rang. *Scheisse! Who's this? Maybe Larry to say he'd be late.* She snatched up the receiver.

'*Shalom*, darling,' Rivke's voice brought Esther back to the present. 'Esther, I want to talk to you about the play. There's one line in it no good, maybe you fix it before we get it typed, and...'

'Rivke, can't we talk later? Tanya's just woken up, and I'm expecting Larry any minute.'

'For sure, darling. But can I just tell you which is the line I want to change? While it's still in my head?'

'For God's sake, leave it, Rivke. I must go, he'll be here soon.'

Esther had no sooner hung up, when the phone sprang to life again, the still air vibrating with its insistent ring. Esther stared at the squat black machine with fury. Rivke never stopped pestering her about translating her play from Hebrew to English. *Don't tell me she's ringing again. I'm not going to answer it. That Rivke just won't give up.*

She went to pick up Tanya, nuzzling her sweet, slightly sweaty hair for the comfort it always gave her. The smell reminded her of vanilla, and fresh bread.

The phone kept ringing until she could stand it no longer. Holding Tanya in her arms, she picked up the receiver with an angry 'What?'

It was Larry. His deep voice resonated through her body. It still had the power to thrill her. 'Something's come up just now, so I can't make it tonight.' No *dear*, no *darling*, no apology.

Tanya began to wriggle, trying to climb down to the floor. Esther put her down, automatically giving the child a wooden jigsaw from the toys scattered around the room.

'But — I've cooked dinner for us, *sauerbraten*, your favourite. Can't you come on later?' she hated the sound of her voice, wheedling, demeaning.

'Well, it'll be much later. Don't wait up.'

Esther felt a cold fury building up, her stomach clenching with it. 'So — are you seeing your little blonde slut? Is that it? Is Saturday night reserved for her? You're sleeping with her aren't you? Rivke's right, I can't trust you.'

'Trust? That's a joke, coming from you. You can talk, with your three husbands, each one cuckolded by you.'

'At least I've always been open and honest with them, not sneaking around and lying. Tony knew about us from the start.' Her voice started to shake, and she fought to keep it controlled.

'Poor wretch, you rubbed his nose in it, didn't you? For God's sake, stop screaming like a fishwife. I've had enough. Don't try to put me on a leash; I'm sick to death of this whole business. Just remember, I'm a free agent, and that's the only way we can be with each other.'

'If you're a free agent, as you put it, why don't you forget about me and Tanya? But oh no — you want it both ways, a little wifey at home and one or two good time girls on the side.'

Tanya, hearing her name, looked up from her game, and gazed questioningly at her mother.

'You're just not capable of being with one woman.' Esther was trembling now, her voice choking on the words.

There was a silence on the line before Larry said, 'There'll only ever be one true marriage for me. Birds in the wild mate for life, and so do I.'

'How touching. Easy to be faithful to a dead woman. I can never replace Grace, can I?'

'No one can. But if you stop this hysteria we can talk about it later, like adults.'

'*Schweinhund!* I hate you! you're not half the man Tony is, my true husband. How I wish I'd never left him!'

'I've had enough. I'm going.'

'Go for good, then!' She screamed into the phone and smashed it down. Her mascara, mixed with tears, ran in dark rivulets down her cheeks. Tanya began to cry too, big tears wetting her flushed face. Esther scooped her up, and sat by the phone, rocking Tanya back and forth, stroking her hair.

For what seemed like hours, she sat rigid and seething. Her stomach knotted with cold anger, but underneath that, there was always the hope, the longing. *I'll kill myself,* she thought, *but that would only make him happy. No doubt that's what he wants. One woman's already taken her life, for love, or hate, of him.*

The doorbell rang. Esther walked downstairs, majestic in her dark green dress. Her earrings glittered in the light from the foyer, as she opened the door. It was Rivke, clutching her manuscript.

'*Shalom*, darling; I just had to drop this in to you, so you've got my new copy to work with. *Gott im Himmel*, what's wrong? Is it ? Essie, you look a sight.'

'Come in,' Esther said wearily, 'let's have a drink.'

❖

The air in the flat smelled stale. It was as if no life could exist in this dreary place. Only six months ago it had seemed such a cheerful place, when Esther had taken over the lease from a former colleague. True, it was on the wrong side of London — but the rent was lower, in keeping with her reduced salary since she'd been demoted at work.

The long Sunday stretched ahead. Tanya had gone to play with Audrey's children, and for the first time, had been allowed to sleep over, a decision Esther regretted. The child's absence felt like a huge hole in her chest.

In the emptiness only the phone, squatting like a black toad, seemed alive. Esther reached for it and dialled Larry's number. Ten insistent rings, unanswered, mocked her. She put the phone down with a mixture of relief and anger. Maybe he was telling the truth about the fishing trip after all. *Or maybe — he just doesn't answer the phone because he somehow knows it's me.*

Outside the weather was bleak, the sky white, but at least there was movement in the few trees still bearing leaves. Larry had left her his car for the weekend, while he was on his fishing trip with Richard, who was on a long overdue visit from Australia. Esther snatched up the car keys from the front hallstand, and walked out just as she was, still wearing her old grey skirt and green woollen sweater.

The car was a few blocks away, where Larry always parked it. Walking across the nearby Common invigorated her, and sharpened her purpose.

There was the battered old Morris, right where Larry had promised it would be. Even that small token of trust lifted Esther's spirits. She inserted the key in the door, and breathed a sigh of relief when it opened.

Settling herself in the driver's seat, Esther turned the key in the ignition, and edged the car out of its tight parking spot.

Half an hour later she was breathing the fresher air of The Rose Estate, to her mind the prettiest place in London. Oblivious to the cold, she made her way through the little park, past the zoo where she'd first heard the lions roar, and found herself in Eliot Court, the very place where she'd first laid eyes on Larry, six long years ago. Looking up to the top floor, she remembered the day she and Tony had rung the door-bell of Flat 6, unaware that their lives would change forever, once that door opened.

A block further took her to 23 Cambridge Crescent, the death flat. It bore a blue plaque outside, proclaiming 'Edward Butler Yeats lived here'. Grace had lived here too, and she'd died here. Grace was still a little-known poetess, and a young housewife and mother, for whom this cruel winter had proved too much. Perhaps one day she'd be famous, and there'd be a plaque to Grace, too.

Esther looked up and said aloud, 'Why won't you leave me alone?' A young mother walking past, pushing a pram, crossed to the other side of the street when she saw that strange dishevelled woman talking to herself, looking wild-eyed at the sky. With an enormous effort Esther shook herself free. Grace was dead, and surely couldn't stand in her way, unless she, Esther, allowed her to live on inside her mind. With one last look up at the window, the same window Grace had flung open to save her children from the gas fumes, Esther turned and made her way back to the car, away from The Rose Estate. *How could Grace have done such a thing; I would never leave my Tanya alone, like Grace left her own poor children.*

❀

On Monday, Esther sat opposite Rivke in the teashop. She'd rung her without thinking about it, knowing only that she'd have to talk to some-body, anybody, or else go completely crazy.

'This is such a good surprise!' Rivke crowed. 'I did not think you have the time to see me, so soon. So — how is little Tanya?'

'She's adorable. I sent her off with the nanny today. They've gone to the zoo. Now, let's order. I'm starving.'

Rivke looked into Esther's eyes for a long moment, seeing the pain there.

'Ah, now I see. Don't tell me, you are always waiting in for that man to ring. God, Essie, he makes me so angry. No use waiting for such a man. That Larry Wilde makes the laws for him only — you should know that by now — and he doesn't want just one woman.'

'Don't be ridiculous darling. He adores me. One can't expect any great artist to abide by the common man's rules. You know what he said the other day? "Every work of art stems from a wound in the soul of the artist." Isn't that brilliant?'

The waitress hovered to take their order. She'd been slow to come to their table, seeing the two foreign-looking women together. The tip of her nose was red and moist, as she sniffed away her incipient cold.

'This is disgraceful!' Esther snapped. 'We've been waiting half an hour; I expect better service from a place like this. Now — we'll have two minestrone soups, and a glass of your best red each. And make it snappy.' Esther felt the ball of fury inside her erupt, and saw the young girl flinch.

'S-sorry, ma'am, we're very busy today, after the holidays 'n all. I'll be right back. Is there anythin' else I c'n get youse?'

Esther waved the waitress away without answering.

'You see, I understand Larry, Rivke. We're both unconventional people, unlike the rather boring set — what do they call them these days? — straight? — that you mostly mix with.'

Rivke looked hurt. It wasn't fashionable in these days of the swinging sixties to be called 'straight'.

'I'm so sorry, it's *meshugge* of me to mix in your affairs,' Rivke said, her voice disappointed. 'Have you had a good holiday from work, after such a grand party you made?'

'It might turn into a permanent holiday, darling. The boss has given me warning, and taken some big clients away. Not productive enough, he said. How can I do more? Rivke, I'm so tired these days.

'And your trip up north with Larry? How did it go, Essie? Did you find a good house yet?'

'Too short, only four days. I'm still exhausted. My clothes were all wrong, and I ruined my shoes in all that mud.' There'd been no trip north, but Esther had fabricated an elaborate tale, to preserve the fiction for her friends that she and Larry were a couple.

At least she and Rivke could talk about clothes together. Fashion had been their common interest, ever since their teenage years in Tel Aviv. Esther still cared excessively about what she wore, although she could no longer afford the elegant fashions she loved, now that she had another mouth to feed. Meanwhile she had bills to pay. All the trivia of life, the washing and the shopping, kept her mind from slipping further into despair. She tried to concentrate on the present, to stop obsessing about Larry and the future.

'So — let's talk about your play. I thought it quite good, although these days it's all kitchen sink dramas, and yours is — dare I say it — old-fashioned. Actually, Rivke, you're right. I really will have to put my fees up. But for you, darling — you always get my best rate.' Esther felt her mind wandering, heard herself raving, and called for the bill. Her bowl of minestrone sat untouched before her.

❊

CHAPTER 39

St John's Wood, London, March 1968

Esther woke in her cold flat, with the sound of wailing in her ears. Her mouth felt dry, her throat parched; no doubt the result of one glass too many of cheap wine last night. Her eyes were stuck together with the gluey detritus of sleep. Even before she forced them open, she reached over for Larry, forgetting that he was rarely there. The empty space mocked her.

Vestiges of a nightmare haunted her. Had she been cursed by a bad fairy in her cradle? Her dream came back to her: images of bodies on train lines, and the wild bear of Larry's poem. It had sprung at her, ready to disfigure her face, tearing her delicate skin from the raw flesh, clawing at her eyes, blinding her. Again she heard her own cry of pain.

Swimming up through the currents of her dream, Esther felt her face with trembling fingers, expecting to find her skin ripped from the bone, her cheeks a bloody mess. Thank God, she was intact, as if by magic. It must be those tablets Dr Coplin had given her, causing these nightmares every night. *'Gott im Himmel! It's five am; too early, still dark I need time to remember...*

Her dream had ended in a long queue at Heathrow Airport; she was waiting to go home. But where was home? Berlin, Tel Aviv, Vancouver? London had failed her. She had nowhere else to run.

Where was Larry? *He's most likely warming another woman's bed.* Yet he commanded her total allegiance. It was unthinkable to contemplate even a dalliance with another man. None could ever attract her again, so great was Larry's hold over her. And none had ever caused her such pain.

Depression paralysed her. Her limbs felt too heavy to move out of her lonely bed. A poem she'd scribbled last night lay on the bedside table. Tanya was still sleeping. This was the perfect time to write, to prove to herself that she was not a failure, to produce something that Larry could be proud of one day, as he was of Grace's poems. Then perhaps he would acknowledge her, even admire her again.

How she missed Tony now, his kindness to her, his constancy, his forgiveness. Always she'd believed that Tony and she were soul mates, destined to be together. Tony had loved Tanya as his own, told her they could have another child, if she'd so desired. She remembered those once romantic words of Larry's, 'in spite of all marriages'. Now they were cruelly ironic. *I am a perverse, ungrateful creature,* she thought, as she dragged her leaden self from the bed. *I deserve to die.*

A cry came from the nursery. 'Ima, sicky!' Tanya's voice was slurred and thick.

'I'm coming, *liebchen,*' Esther answered, instantly wide awake. *This is why I stay alive, this is my reason to get out of bed.* Cow-heavy in her long white nightgown, she hurried to the nursery. There was Tanya, standing up and holding the bars of her cot, face flushed with sleep. Esther picked her up and held her close. Despite the vomit clogging Tanya's hair, she kissed her tear-streaked face over and over again.

She carried her whimpering daughter into the cold bathroom. Turning on the rusted taps, she ran tepid water into the big white bath, waiting for it to become warm, then gently lowered Tanya into the tub. She soaped the child's tender skin, still as silky and soft as a baby's, and cleaned the traces of vomit from around her face and mouth. As the warm water loosened Tanya's matted hair, Esther sang the age-old lullaby, '*Guten abend, gute nacht, mit röslein bedacht…*' in a low sweet voice, until the crying gradually stopped. When the water began to cool, Esther lifted Tanya's slippery little body into a fluffy pink towel, and carried her back to the nursery, kissing her face all the while.

'There — you'll be all better now,' she whispered into the child's ear, where tendrils of her dark hair still drying. 'What about a sip of water, to take the nasty taste away?'

'No, Ima, me want more Wed Widing Hood,' Tanya lisped. It was her favourite fairy tale, although the wolf dressed as an old woman always frightened her.

'Not now, *liebchen*. Ima has some work to do. Here's the picture book for you to look at, and here's your water bottle. It's much too early to get up.'

Tanya looked at her mother defiantly for a brief moment, then gave up, and settled back into her freshly made cot, turning the pages full of brightly coloured pictures. Her compliance always amazed Esther. *How could I be cursed when I've been given this treasure? Perhaps there's a good fairy in my life after all.* She crept with a lighter step back to her bedroom.

There was her notebook and pen, as if waiting for her return. At first she couldn't make sense of her scribbled poem. Slowly she spoke the words aloud:

> *To see again and no more*
> *The black northern pond,*
> *Its autumn spent*

Esther picked up her pen, and wrote the next line.

❀

An hour or more passed. Tanya had gone back to sleep, her book still splayed open on the coverlet of her cot. Esther stirred and stretched. *Time to get breakfast.* She was pleased with her poem. With the satisfaction of a job well done, her earlier despondency lifted.

The phone rang in the hallway. Esther sprang up to answer it, her heart aflame. Is it Larry? *Please let it be him, but for sure it won't be.* She picked up the phone, to hear the familiar, deep voice, and her heart almost stopped.

'I've rung to tell you Yehuda's in town,' Larry said, 'and he wants to meet us. I've arranged a morning tea at the Queen Victoria tearoom on Paddington Station. Can you be there in an hour?'

'But — but Larry, I'm — I'm not ready, and Tanya's still sleeping, she hasn't even had breakfast yet. It's Maria's day off, so I'll have to bring her with me.'

'I really don't think that's a good idea. Is there no one you can leave her with?'

'Even if there were, I can hardly ask someone at the last minute, can I? Besides, she's been asking for you. So of course I'll bring her.'

'If you must,' said Larry, and hung up before any more could be said.

Esther forgave his coldness, her heart lightening with the thought of seeing him again. At once she felt beautiful, svelte, and alive. She almost danced to the kitchen, and stirred oatmeal into a saucepan for Tanya's breakfast. Setting out the Beatrix Potter bowl and spoon, a Christmas present from Audrey & Ben, she felt her mood lighten even more. Moving the pot from the burner to where it could keep warm on the stove, she went to wake her daughter.

'*Guten morgen, meine liebling,*' she crooned, lifting the side of the cot from its safety catch, and sliding it down. Tanya immediately sat up, her face still rosy from sleep, and smiled her wide smile at her mother. 'We're going on an outing this morning, to see your Daddy, and another nice man, who's our friend.'

'Daddy, I want to see Daddy,' Tanya said in a singsong voice.

'And you will see him, you will, my darling. Breakfast first, then we'll dress you in something special.' Tanya ran ahead into the warm kitchen, excited to see her new bowl and spoon, still novelties. The oatmeal porridge was already steaming in her Peter Rabbit bowl.

'Can I have some honey on it, Ima? And some milk to drink?'

'Is your tummy all better now? Maybe no milk today, just in case.'

Esther drizzled honey onto the creamy oatmeal, while she herself sipped black coffee from the Italian pot always on the stove.

They dressed quickly. Tanya wore a soft woollen white dress, which Rivke had knitted for her, and a matching white headscarf. This morning her little black leather shoes, the ones with buckles, were too small for her chubby feet. It made Esther unaccountably sad.

A simple white blouse and blue skirt, the colours of the Israeli flag, was Esther's chosen outfit for the day. *I wonder if Yehuda will even notice what I'm wearing?* Anticipation fuelled her energy as, grabbing their coats, she and Tanya hurried out the door.

❈

Esther felt proud and excited to be showing off her lively daughter to Yehuda. It was more than a week after Tanya's fourth birthday. Larry had made some excuse on the day. *Would he remember to bring her a gift? Would he at least show some pride in their daughter?*

On the tube to Paddington Station, Tanya kept up a constant chatter. 'When I see my daddy I can show him my bestest Christmas present?' She'd brought a little straw bag with her, from which a golden-haired doll's face peeked. 'When will my daddy give me my present? Will he give it to me today?'

'Your daddy's a very, very busy man. Maybe he hasn't had time to go shopping yet, but he will, my darling, I'm sure he will. Perhaps he's waiting to give it to you when we're all together.'

Arriving at Paddington, they found Larry waiting impatiently at the station. 'Daddy!' Tanya cried, and ran to him, hugging his knees. Larry bent down and absent-mindedly patted the little girl's straight dark hair, which had escaped from beneath her white scarf.

'Hurry up,' he said in greeting to Esther, 'Yehuda's due to meet us at ten-thirty, and it's already ten.'

'I know, and we're early,' Esther smiled, longing to touch Larry's face, but not daring. 'This is such good timing. We left home at half-past eight, and just made the nine o'clock to town.' She filled the emptiness between them with more inconsequential chatter; anything to erase Larry's grim silence.

Esther asked for a high chair for Tanya, which a sulky waitress reluctantly brought, as if it were a huge imposition on her time. She positioned their daughter between them. Tanya began talking to Larry in a high, excited voice, her little face alight.

'See my dolly?' Tanya said, tenderly extracting her doll from its wicker basket, and holding it up in front of Larry's face, 'Look, she's got blue eyes, and they open and shut, like this.' She rocked the doll back and forth, its vacant eyes alternately staring and disappearing behind thickly lashed lids. Larry managed a smile.

'Tell me, does she walk and talk too, as cleverly as you do?' he said, his face close to Tanya's, looking into her wide grey eyes.

'Well-ll, I'm teaching her some words, and I can help her to walk, like this.' She moved the doll's jointed limbs back and forth. 'Her name's Arabella, it's out of a story book Mummy reads me.' Tanya chattered on, oblivious to her mother's sudden restlessness.

'Larry,' Esther interrupted,' I saw an ad for a place in Devon, it might be just the right place for us, well away from the village, but close enough to — '

But Larry was standing up, drawing himself up to his full height, and holding out his large hand in welcome. A middle-aged man, with handsome, swarthy features and silvering hair, had entered the coffee shop. He threw both arms around Larry in a warm embrace.

'Yehuda — so good to see you again,' Larry said with the old grace Esther remembered, but which was rarely exhibited to her any more.

'Esther is here too, with her daughter,' Larry said, almost apologetically. He turned to indicate mother and child.

Esther rose, and hugged Yehuda, before saying, 'this is our daughter, Tanya. Say hello to Uncle Yehuda, sweetheart.'

'How do you do, my dear, it is indeed a pleasure to meet you,' said the visitor with gravity. 'Ah — what's this you have here? Is it a monkey?'

'No, silly!' Tanya's high voice pealed with laughter, 'It's my dolly! Here, you want to hold her?'

Esther tried to catch Larry's eye, to share a moment of pride in their daughter's precocity. But he was looking irritable, and lifted a hand to summon the waitress.

'Three cream teas, and a lemonade for the little one,' Larry said to the young girl in her frilly white cap and apron, pencil poised over her notebook.

'Yes, Sir,' she simpered, 'will there be anything else, Sir? An ice cream for the little girl, p'raps? Or', she winked at Tanya, 'we have some freshly made gingerbread men.'

'Yes, me have ginger-ginger men,' Tanya called out, delighted with the bountiful offer of treats.

'Hush, dear, a lemonade will be enough for you, ' Esther said softly.

'That'll be all,' Larry snapped at the waitress.

Tanya's face fell, and tears threatened. Larry glared at Esther for a moment. He turned to find the visitor's seat was empty. In a moment, Yehuda returned, after a quick word with the waitress.

'Now, Larry, how've you been since the Festival? How's *Fox* progressing? Judging from those excerpts you've sent me, it's going brilliantly.'

'Ah, thank you, Yehuda, praise from you is praise indeed. Actually I brought you here to talk about starting a new book together.'

'So why don't we talk business later? For now, should we not enjoy each other's company after so long? Since that lunch at your home during the Festival, we haven't laid eyes on each other. I seem to remember, the little one here was but a baby when we last met.'

Tanya was still quietly crying. Esther took a lacy handkerchief from her handbag, and gently wiped away the tears.

'Come now, what would Arabella think of her mother crying like a baby?' she said softly to Tanya, who stifled a sob and stroked her doll's stiff golden hair.

A moment later, their waitress returned, and unloaded her tray, placing a large plate bearing six fluffy scones, a bowl of whipped cream and a side dish of strawberry jam in the middle of the table. There was a blue and white china teapot, three matching cups and saucers, and a frosted glass of lemonade. Lastly, and with a ceremonial gesture, she set a plate in front of Tanya, containing a golden brown gingerbread man, complete with a mouth and eyes made of white icing, and red and green jubes for buttons, all the way down its oval torso. Tanya's eyes lit up, and she squealed in delight, clapping her little hands together.

'Look, Arabella, it's the ginger man! Do you want to eat his arms or his legs first? Let's leave his buttons till last.'

Larry's face darkened. Yehuda put a hand on his arm, and said to Esther, 'It's my small treat for your daughter. I can't bear to see any child deprived, especially one of us, after the horrors some of our people went through.'

'Thank you; thank you so much,' Esther whispered the words to Yehuda, turning her face up to him. *A face like a flower*, he thought, a poem already forming in his mind.

After morning tea, they walked back together to Paddington Station. Esther had given copies of her own poems to Yehuda, and he'd promised to discuss them with her in a day or two.

Suddenly, without a word, Larry shook Yehuda's hand, muttered something in his ear, and strode away towards the waiting train without a backward glance.

'DADDY! MY DADDY!' Tanya screamed. She dropped her basket, and started to run after Larry. Esther pulled her back. 'I want Daddy! Come back here, my Daddy!' she called hysterically, while Esther, even as she tried to soothe her daughter, burst into tears herself.

'How can he do that to a little girl? What sort of a *mensch* is he?' Yehuda said, angry now, and trying his best to comfort both mother and daughter.

'It's — it's not his fault, Yehuda, please understand. He has such pressures, two other children, a farm to run, sick elderly parents, and publishers breathing down his neck; you know how it is,' said Esther, composing herself. But her heart was like a stone again, as she bent down to enfold the crying child in her arms.

❈

CHAPTER 40

Manchester, March 1968

Larry, Esther, and the three children, had a compartment all to themselves on the well-appointed Northern Express. The train ride from Manchester, where Larry had given a poetry reading, had been a rare chance for them all to be together. Esther felt almost happy, lulled by the rhythmic chuffing of the train, and the feeling of being a family again.

Fleur and Timothy sat with their father along one hard leather seat, opposite Esther and Tanya. The children were getting fractious, especially Tim, who kept whining that he was hungry. Larry took the remains of an Eccles cake from the pocket of his baggy tweed jacket. He broke it in two, giving half to Tim and the other half to Fleur. As usual he ignored Tanya, who crept closer to her mother. Fleur broke off a piece of her half, and passed it across to her little sister.

Just then the train gave a great jolt. Fleur, who'd been leaning forward, was catapulted into Esther's lap. Larry braced himself and held on to Tim's shirt tail. A squeal of brakes followed and the train groaned to a shuddering stop. From somewhere in another compartment they heard a woman's scream. Tanya began to cry, still clutching her morsel of cake. Esther held her close with one arm while protecting Fleur with her other.

'What's happening?' she asked the world in general, starting to shake. A memory flashed into her mind, of another train ride years ago, and the sound of heavy boots sending her childhood self, terrified, to hide under the seat.

'You stay here with the children,' Larry said, 'I'll try to find out. And for God's sake, can't you stop your daughter snivelling?'

Esther turned her face away, smoothing Tanya's hair tenderly. 'It's all right, *liebchen*. Soon we'll all be home.' To Larry she said coldly, 'you seem to forget that *our* daughter has just turned four. Just like you 'forgot' to come to her birthday party. This trip's a great deal harder for her than it is for Fleur and Tim.'

Before Larry could answer, a man's voice boomed over the loud-speaker: 'this train will terminate at Birmingham. There will be a delay of thirty minutes while the track is cleared. All passengers may use their existing tickets for transfer onto the next train to London. Passengers must not attempt to leave the train before it reaches Birmingham.'

Timothy, staring out of the window, called out, 'There's two police-men — they've got proper helmets on, and they came in a big black car. Is there really a dead body? With real blood coming out? Can I go outside and look?'

'Back in a minute,' said Larry. He stood up and walked out of the carriage towards the guard's van. Tim ran after him. The other three sat in silence except for Tanya's whimpering.

'Can you wait till your father comes back, and then I'll take you?'

Fleur shrugged. 'I just want to go home. It's school on Monday, and I have homework. I'm cold. And I want to go to the loo.'

'Say "lavatory", dear, it's more polite,' Esther said, recovering herself by concentrating on the children.

'I come too, Ima.' Tanya always followed Fleur around like a little lamb.

Larry pushed through the carriage door and sat down heavily opposite Esther. 'Some bloke's jumped off the train. Bloody inconven-ient time to top yourself.'

'You mean he's…?'

'They're just waiting for the ambulance from Manchester. Rather pointless, I should think — he's made a good job of it.'

Esther shuddered. She picked up Tanya and motioned to Fleur. 'Come on, Fleur dear. There's a lavatory at the end of this carriage.' She held Fleur's hand as they both made their rocky way to the only latrine in the carriage. It was smelly, and dirty, but at least they were out of earshot of Larry's graphic description.

It amused Esther that Tim seemed to revel in the bloody account. *Like father, like son, she thought.* Yet she knew Larry was protective of his children. *After all, he hasn't yet told them the truth about how their mother had died.*

As Esther and the two little girls returned to the carriage, Larry pulled a dog-eared train timetable from his other pocket and studied it for a few minutes.

'There's a train back to London in an hour's time. You and Tanya had best catch it and go back to London. I'm taking the children back to Chalk Farm.'

'What on earth are you talking about?' Esther tried to keep the panic out of her voice. 'We're all exhausted, and the children need a meal, and somewhere warm to spend the night. I know the best place, a little hotel where I stayed last time, after I saw that house in Hexham. We could ...'

Larry cut her off. 'No. It won't work. I have to get them back for school. Fleur's got homework.'

'Then we'll come with you. After all, we've spent two days walking around Manchester looking for a house where we can all live together. We might as well start now.'

'It won't work, I tell you. Not when Mam's staying with us at Chalk Farm, and still poorly. She's far too ill to go back to their cold old place in Yorkshire. Besides, It'll only upset her, to see you again. You and the girl had better go back to the flat, and I'll ring you tomorrow.'

'Are we going to see Aunty Beverley tonight, Dad? I want to play with Harriet.'

'So that's it. You're seeing *her* again. I should have guessed.'

Larry got up and pulled the door to their compartment closed. 'Let's not have one of your scenes here, of all places. I've had enough for one weekend.'

'And the house in Tyneside? The home we're going to make together? Our new life? What about that?' Esther's choked back tears of anger. The last thing she wanted was to go back to that cold, empty flat with Tanya, where only misery awaited them. But she was too proud to plead.

She thought of the body on the tracks. It was *Anna Karenina* all over again, the final solution. *A fitting end*, she thought, *for a half-Russian misfit like me.*

The five of them sat in silence as the train started with another jolt and slowly chugged the last two miles into Birmingham.

❁

It was already dark when the train carrying Esther and Tanya left for London. Both of them felt keenly the absence of Larry, Fleur and Tim, who were already halfway back to Chalk Farm.

There'd been an interminable wait while railway officials and police interviewed the driver and passengers, about the accident. Tanya, curled up on Esther's lap, fell into a fitful sleep. Esther sat, cold and rigid, going over and over in her head the pros and cons of the house at Tyneside. It was her last hope.

On the other hand, there were disadvantages to the move: the house was too far from London to commute, so work would be difficult, even if she could find another job. How would they manage for money? Larry was alternately lavish and frugal, full of grand schemes one minute and penny-pinching the next. Without her salary they'd have no steady income except for the occasional grants, which seemed to come Larry's way whenever he was at his most impecunious.

Still, she reasoned, the rent was cheaper than London, and she would enjoy making do. Recipes for economical one-pot meals ran through her mind, and she saw herself as the true country wife, wearing a dirndl with a ribbon in her hair. Just as Grace had been when she'd first met her, she realised with a jolt. *I have become a wife, taken for granted as she was. No wonder Larry's seeking amusement elsewhere.*

By the time they reached London four hours later, Esther's mood had turned from hope to despair. She thought of the body on the tracks and wished again it had been hers. But what would become of her precious Tanya? How could her little daughter survive in England, where she had no family, except for Esther? Larry wouldn't take her — he found even two children difficult. The memory of Larry's absence at Tanya's birthday party still rankled, yet Esther was careful never to pass on her doubts and fears to their daughter.

Esther entered the dark flat with the sleeping child in her arms, and went straight to the nursery, where she laid Tanya gently in her cot. The little girl whimpered and turned to Esther in her sleep as if seeking comfort. Esther sang the German lullaby her own mother had sung to her, while she gently stroked Tanya's forehead. It was a nightly ritual, which comforted them both. Just as Esther stood up from where she was kneeling beside Tanya, the doorbell rang.

It was Rivke, carrying her manuscript and standing patiently on the landing. Instantly Esther went into hostess mode.

'Come in, darling. I hadn't forgotten you.' It was a white lie, for Esther had no memory of an arrangement with Rivke. 'I was just making tea — your timing is excellent. Or would you like something stronger? I can only offer you whisky, I'm afraid,' she gushed while ushering her friend into the dimly lit living room.

'Tea would be lovely, *danke schön*,' replied Rivke in her rich Israeli accent, still overlaid with the harsher sounds of her native German.

'I've brought the last Act of my play for you, just like I promised. I nearly went *meshugge* trying to get the finish. Darlink, you think you could do translation on it by Monday? It's just that the publisher...'

'Don't worry, Rivke dear, *natürlich* I'll do it for you. Back in a minute — make yourself comfortable,' she called as she hurried into the kitchen to put the kettle on. Quickly she hid a bottle of pills inside a drawer, and got two cups and saucers from her china cabinet. 'No milk, I'm sorry — we'll have to drink our tea Russian style, black, while we suck sugar cubes.'

Esther lit the gas ring, put the kettle on it, and went back into the living room where Rivke had settled herself on the old Victorian sofa. 'Are those your drawings?' Rivke asked, pointing at some charcoal sketches on the opposite wall.

'Yes, they're my poor attempts,' Esther laughed. 'I'm such a dilettante — what is it they say in English —"jack of all trades, master of none"?'

'But Esther, how can you say that? You're so talented — everyone thinks so. I wouldn't have anyone else touch my work.' Even as Rivke spoke, she noticed a change in Esther. The light had gone from her eyes, which were puffy, as if she'd been crying. 'But what's wrong, *liebchen*? Are you not well?'

'It's Larry. He doesn't want me any more — it's no good, and it never will be…' To Rivke's horror, Esther began to weep, not noisily but with big tears welling up and spilling down her cheeks. She didn't try to wipe them away, but let them roll down her face unchecked. The kettle started its loud whistle, and Esther turned to the kitchen.

Rivke followed her, saying, 'Essie darlink, you can have any man you want, with your looks and talent. Forget Larry, a typical selfish man he is, a *nebbisch*, not worthy for you and Tanya.'

'Rivke, it's impossible. There is no other man for me. He is Tanya's father after all, although one would never know it, seeing them together. And anyway, we've been house hunting — we saw a perfect house in Tyneside. It had a fabulous study for Larry, looking over the ocean. The children loved it too.' Esther composed herself, reverting to her bright, breezy persona.

'Larry did not even come to Tanya's birthday party, Esther. His own daughter, for shame! I know you will find another man. This Larry, he's not good enough for you, with his lying and secrets. And how would you survive outside London?'

'Don't you mean how would I survive without Larry? I couldn't. I'd kill myself first.'

'Don't be such — how they say — drama queen. You think you live in a Russian novel, like that poor Anna Karenina?'

Esther saw again the body on the tracks. *No, not that.* She would have to find another way.

❈

CHAPTER 41

London, Saturday 22 March 1968

Esther was too ashamed to tell anyone what happened at work. It felt as if everything that had built up her life to this point was being stripped away. Everything except Tanya, her one last treasure.

She'd returned to work a week ago, after taking yet another two days off to go house hunting. Mr Horvath called her in to his office the minute she arrived, late as usual. He cleared his throat, and stayed sitting behind his large polished desk; it felt like a barricade between them. Esther was suddenly aware of her hair greying at the temples, and her dark brown mid-length skirt, so unfashionable in this age of the mini-skirt. How different she must look from that first day, when she'd wooed this man into giving her a job just by looking at him.

'Ahem — er — Mrs Buchanan, we need to have a serious talk. You've put me in a most awkward position. As you must realise, this Agency runs on the goodwill of our clients, and the number of contracts we take out. Your own input, which I must say was excellent when you first started here with us, has declined considerably. In fact, your productivity for the last quarter was below even the minimum for new starters. I've managed to turn a blind eye to all that, but the loss of one of our biggest clients last week, one who would have signed up with you had you been here, was, I'm afraid, the last straw.'

He paused, stretching out a well-clad leg and examining the point of his polished tan shoe with intense focus, before going on.

'So I have no alternative, Mrs Buchanan, but to let you go. Naturally, you'll have severance pay, and your exit won't take effect for a fortnight, as the regulations state.'

Esther's voice was steady, her face calm. 'That won't be necessary, Bill. I've been planning for some time to give my notice, but didn't want to let you down. I feel my skills and experience are wasted here, with the ridiculous demands of this organisation, which would stultify anyone's creativity. So you've made it easier for me. My letter of resignation will be on your desk by five o'clock today.'

Replaying the conversation in her head, Esther felt some small satisfaction that at least she'd had the last word. At the same time, the thought of losing her daily escape into work filled her with terror. There'd be no money to pay the rent, or food, or clothes and toys for Tanya. Nothing. There was nothing left, only the shreds of her pride. She might even have to let Maria go. Esther thought she heard Grace's laugh, staccato and bitter, and shook her head to free herself.

❦

'Maria, could you get that? Please remember, I'm at home to no one, except Mr Wilde.' The telephone in the front hallway kept ringing. Esther held her breath.

It seemed an eternity until she heard Maria's soft voice announcing, 'Mrs Buchanan's residence.' Her words changed from English to German, and Esther knew it wasn't Larry on the phone.

'Well? Who was it?' Esther hadn't meant to snap, but her tension was wire tight.

'*Ach*, Mrs Buchanan, Olga it was, she would like for me to stay with her tomorrow evening. I will feed Tanya and put her to bed first, *natürlich*.'

'No, don't bother. Tomorrow's Sunday, your day off, remember? I put her to bed myself at weekends. And yes, you may stay with your friend. By the way, you needn't call me Mrs Buchanan any more. I thought one day you might call me Mrs Wilde, but that will never be. Mr Wilde doesn't want me any more, Maria.' Her voice grated on her own ears. *Why am I saying this?*

'But, for sure he must, Mrs B — how do I call you?'

'Esther will do, my dear, for the moment. Would you be a darling, and put the coffee on? I'm dying for it. Such a bleak, cold day –,' she broke off suddenly, the voice in her head drowning all else out.

'*Aber* what is wrong, Mrs Buchanan? *Entschuldige*, I mean to say "Esther"? So white you are — are you ill?'

'No, no, dear. Just tired, and in need of that coffee. I'll go and dress Tanya; she'll need her woollen leggings today, it's so cold.'

Esther looked again at the official-looking brown envelope, which had been lying in wait for her just inside the front door last night. Tired and broken from the train trip, she hadn't opened it straight away; her first priority was to put Tanya in her cot. *She can sleep in her clothes tonight, poor little mite.* Esther removed Tanya's little white shoes, and covered her with an extra warm blanket.

This morning, the letter glared at her, daring her to open it. *Probably another parking fine.* She noticed a second envelope, caught up with the brown one. It was a plain white envelope, with her address written on it in a big loopy hand, which she didn't recognise. She opened the white envelope, pulled out a sheet of fine writing paper, and began to read:

Dear Mrs Buchanan,

I managed to find your address from your employer, a Mr Horvath of Mathers in London. We met a couple of years ago, in the village of Woodberry. I'm the local midwife and nurse there. At the time we met you were living at Chalk Farm, along with Mr Wilde, and the elder Mr and Mrs Wilde. I often came to tend to Mrs Wilde, so sickly she was, poor soul.

I thought you should know that young Mr Wilde plans to marry again. Since his dear wife died he's never been the same; such a kind, helpful young man he was, back then. It was me delivered Mrs Wilde's second child, young Timothy. It breaks my heart to see those two sweet bairns without a mother.

Over the last few months, Mr Wilde has been keeping company with a lovely young woman from a nearby village; I won't name her, as I don't think it's right, but I can say she's a pretty thing. Fleur and

Timothy seem very fond of her. No one could replace Grace, but like I said, they need a mother.

Some say in the village that you and Mr Wilde separated when you went back to London. Others seem to think there is still some sort of understanding between you. It's a hard thing to say, but knowing you're still married to Mr Buchanan, and you have a dear little girl to take care of, I think it'd be for best for everyone if Mr Wilde settled down at last.

I'm telling you this for your own sake, my dear. Perhaps now you can get on with your life, make a fresh start. I wish you all the very best, and hope life treats you and your daughter kindly,

Yours sincerely,

Daphne O'Leary.

Esther sat quite still on the hard kitchen chair, reading the words over and over again. She gave a short laugh, screwed the letter into a ball, and tossed it into the waste-paper basket in the corner. *Nasty bitch*, she thought. *No wonder Larry couldn't stand her. Who does she think she is, meddlesome old cow, telling me how to live my life? It's not true, anyway. Beverley's not all that young, and anyway, she's already married.*

She took a kitchen knife and slit the other envelope open. It was as she feared; there it was in black and white, the typed letters mocking her. The *Decree Nisi*, stating that she, Esther Goldberg, was no longer the wife of Mr Anthony Buchanan, and therefore was free to marry again. What hurt most was seeing Tony's own signature scrawled at the bottom of the official document, a vivid reminder of the man himself. All that he'd meant to her came surging back, and she wept for her lost true love.

❀

Esther looked around her sitting room that she'd furnished with such high hopes, and with such care. There on the wall were the framed miniatures she'd painted for Larry, and behind the glass of her tall vitrine, gleamed the tiny figurines of her precious netsuke collection. *I'll make sure Audrey will have those, she's always admired them, and she's been kind to me and Tanya, inviting us to share meals with her family. But I can't go on taking charity from friends.*

'Maria,' she called, 'it's time for Tanya's nap. Make sure she's been to the lavatory, and had her milk. I'll come and settle her down in a few minutes.'

In the nursery Esther tucked Tanya into her cot, and whispered, "sweet dreams." The child smiled up at her, and Esther's heart almost broke. *No, I won't, I can't do it, there must be another way.* Tears of desperation welled in her eyes, and she turned from the room quickly, so that Tanya wouldn't see her crying.

❀

CHAPTER 42

St John's Wood, London, Sunday 23 March 1968

Sunday was so cold, they all three stayed indoors. Maria and Tanya played with the doll's house, while Esther had letters to write. There were only a few hours left. The first letter was to her father in Canada. How she missed him, would always miss him. She addressed him by the pet name she and Hannah sometimes used.

Dear Vatinka,

I write to tell you that I must go away, far, far away, where no one will ever find me. The life I'm living now is too painful, as a single parent with no job, and no prospects of marriage. I can find no joy in staying, except for my darling Tanya, my little self. There is no one in this world who could love her as much as I do. I have thought long and hard, and although it breaks my heart, I know I must take her with me.

I had pinned my hopes on a life with Larry, but all that has gone kaput. He doesn't want me any more. And Tony and I are finally divorced. So I'm quite alone, you see.

Forgive me, dearest Vatinka, and don't be sad for me. It's the only way out for me and Tanya. You wouldn't wish this hell of a life on me for another thirty years, would you?

Alles liebe, Esther.

She sealed the letter, and wrote 'Vati' on the envelope.

❧

Esther determined to give Larry one last chance. She started to shake, and cold dread ran in her blood. No use waiting for him to ring; there wasn't time. She lit a cigarette to calm her nerves, picked up the phone in the hallway, and dialled Larry's number. All would be decided by this phone call; it would make or break her.

'Hello, who's this?' Larry sounded annoyed. Thank God it was Larry who'd answered the phone, not some woman. Esther was breaking the rules by ringing him at Chalk Farm, but she couldn't care less.

'It's me, your Essie, remember me? We have some unfinished business to discuss.'

'Don't give me that. I've no patience for any more of your games.'

'No? What about your promise that you'd ring me about the house in Devon? Or have you forgotten?'

His voice was slow, its tone world-weary. 'I did check the address you gave me, as a matter of fact. It's an ugly little house, utterly devoid of charm, built over a swamp. Do you really want to live in a damp, foul-smelling place?'

'The house looked pretty in the ad. And I thought you'd gone off the place we saw in Tyneside, even though I thought it perfect.'

'Be practical for once, Esther. That house had a huge garden to look after, and was nowhere near a train station. How would you get to work?'

Should I tell him I've lost my job? Throw myself on his mercy? No — too demeaning. If he wants to be with me, it must be for myself, not out of pity.

Larry broke the silence. 'Look, I have to go,' he snapped. 'The children leave for the States tomorrow, to spend the Spring break with their grandmother. I'm stretched to the limit, working to the publisher's deadline. We can discuss all this later this week, if you must.'

Something exploded in Esther's chest. 'There's not going to be any later!' She screamed into the phone, and smashed it down. The room swam in front of her eyes, and she put her head down between her legs, about to throw up, or black out. Rage filled her, its energy forcing her to act. Without thinking, she dialled Larry's number again.

' I hadn't finished what I need to tell you.' Esther knew her voice sounded ugly, rasping, choked with unshed tears.

'I told you, don't ring me here. It interferes with my work,' Larry barked. 'It's a crucial time for me now, just as 'Selected Poems' is finally starting to take shape. Just give me time before we talk again.'

'There *is* no more time. Don't worry, you won't have to put up with me any longer.' She spat the words out. 'It's over, Larry, and I mean it this time. I'm leaving, and taking Tanya with me.'

'What are you talking about? Where the hell are you going? Don't mess me around like this, Esther. I can't take much more.'

'So go and cry on Beverley's shoulder, why don't you? Is it true what I've heard, that you're going to marry her?'

'Are you crazy? She's a married woman with two children. For God's sake, calm down.'

'I rang to tell you I'm no longer married, by the way. My divorce from Tony came through yesterday, so I'm a free woman. Aren't you going to make me an offer?' She laughed into the phone, a harsh broken sound.

'Esther, stop this. I'm not marrying anyone, you know why. I've told you many times: like the greylag goose, I have only one true mate, and I mate for life.'

'It's Grace, isn't it? It's she who's always been between us. It's cruel of you, not to let her rest in her grave.'

Larry gave a short laugh. 'That's rich, coming from you, with all your talk of ghosts and visitations. Leave it alone, Esther. Sentimentality doesn't suit you, neither does superstition. Now I've really got to go.'

'So do I,' Esther said, her voice under control, 'I'm going for good. I'll never see you again. Never. Please don't try to contact me.'

'For God's sake, Essie, not that again ...'

Esther hung up, cutting off Larry's voice as she closed the door on their future. She took the receiver off the hook, and called the nanny.

'Maria, isn't it time you left for Olga's?'

'Oh, Mrs — I mean Esther — don't you want me to prepare your lunch first?'

'No. I'm not hungry. Go, now, or you'll be late.'

Maria's eyes grew round and a crease appeared between her fair eyebrows. Her brown curls bobbed as she shook her head. 'I don't like to leave you, I think it is not well you are. And Tanya — she will soon wake, I must help you with her.'

'Nonsense, Maria, I told you, I'll take care of her myself tonight. You go, and enjoy yourself. Quickly now, or you'll miss your train.'

Maria shrugged herself into her coat, and with a worried backward glance, let herself out the front door. 'I'm back tomorrow,' she called as the door shut behind her.

There was fire in Esther's veins now; so much to do, and so little time. She hurried to her bedroom. There was one more thing she had to do. On a fresh sheet of paper, she scrawled a new note:

> *Finally, you have what you've wanted from me these long six years. Poetic justice, don't you think? Grace and I can rejoice in our escape from you, for all eternity. I'm taking Tanya with me, so she'll never have to suffer the life of an exile, as I have. There is no way I'd leave our daughter amongst my enemies. In that I include you, Tanya's father. You are not worthy of that role. You have rubbished my life, and dragged me down. I leave you with nothing.*

There was no signature; none was necessary. She folded the note, and propped it against the phone, the receiver dangling by its twisted cord towards the floor.

Throwing the sheets and blankets from her bed, Esther pulled the double mattress free from its base, and using all her strength, dragged it into the kitchen. She laid the mattress in front of the oven, shifting the table out of the way to do so. It was as if there was someone else inside her, lending her superhuman strength. Next she pulled the feather-filled eiderdown, white and fluffy, from the bed and took it to the kitchen, and laid it on top of the mattress. Two white pillows completed the resting place. She closed all the windows, and laid towels in the gap under the doors.

Back in her bedroom, she pulled open the top drawer of her bureau, scrabbling for the bottle of pills, which she'd talked the kindly doctor into prescribing. Insomnia, she'd told him, and general exhaustion. Could he give her something to help her sleep, just for those really bad nights? She wasn't depressed, she'd assured him; just overtired. The label on the bottle said: 'Seconal: take one to two tablets, half an hour before bedtime.'

There were twenty- five white pills in the little brown glass bottle. Taking it with her, Esther went into the kitchen and reached into the top cupboard for the full bottle of Scotch whisky; full because she kept it only for guests, and there'd been none to drink it. She herself hated the taste, but she poured a measure into one of her precious crystal shot glasses, and swallowed two tablets with it.

'Ugh,' she said, as the fiery liquid slid down her throat, burning her empty stomach. She poured another tot, larger this time, and swallowed another three Seconal pills with it. Three more times she poured herself a whisky, each dose a little more than the last. She swallowed five tablets with each glass, until at last there were only five left in the little brown bottle.

She heard a voice calling her, '*Ima, Ima*, I want pee-pee.' She weaved her way unsteadily into Tanya's room. The little girl was standing up in the cot, small for her, trying to get one pyjama-clad leg over the rail. With all her strength, Esther scooped Tanya up and staggered with her to the bathroom. She sat the child on her little pink potty, and smiled as she heard the little tinkle.

Tanya looked up at her, suddenly anxious. 'Where's Mawea?' she lisped. 'We play shops now?'

'Maria had to go out, my darling. But we're going to play another game. It's called "In the Snow". '

Enfolding sleepy Tanya in her arms, Esther carried her into the kitchen. She dissolved two Seconal tablets in a glass of milk, flavoured with Tanya's favourite strawberry powder.

'First we drink this magic potion, to make us sleep well in the snow,' she said, putting the mug of milk to Tanya's lips, and pouring a final tot of whisky for herself. With it she swallowed the last three tablets, dropping the empty bottle to the floor.

Tanya looked at her mother questioningly. 'What other things can we do in our game, Ima?' Esther smoothed the child's dark hair away from her pale face.

'We pretend we're in the snow, but we're quite safe, because Ima's going to turn on a pretend fire to keep us warm. See, here's the pretend snow.'

She showed her little girl the bed she'd made on the kitchen floor, all soft and white. Tanya's little head was nodding, her beautiful grey eyes heavy with sleep, their pupils dilated. Esther laid her daughter gently onto the mattress, under the fluffy white eiderdown. With her last waking strength, she turned on all the jets on the stove. She opened the oven door, so that the full stench of gas hit her. She breathed it in. Her knees buckled as she collapsed onto the mattress. She enfolded Tanya back into her body. Esther's last vision was of her daughter's sleeping face, turned peacefully towards her.

❖

CODA

"Execute yourself and your little self efficiently," Assia wrote in her diary, several days before she took her own life, and tragically that of her daughter. She and Ted were on a house-hunting trip in Manchester, and had argued bitterly. She added the postscript: "It's Sylvia – it's because of her."

Assia had clearly planned her suicide some months earlier. Her letter to her father, which is fictionalised in this novel, was written two months earlier, in January 1969. In the actual letter, she pleaded with him not to wish "another thirty years of hell" on her, and assured him she was quite sane in making the decision to end her life. She added that she couldn't possibly leave little Shura alone and motherless in a hostile world.

Throughout Shura's short life, Ted Hughes rarely referred to her as his daughter. Yet we are told that he was overcome with grief at the loss of the child. In the recently published *Letters of Ted Hughes*, a friend of Hughes recalls that, at the funeral of Assia and Shura, "Ted stood like a pillar of salt, tears streaming down his cheeks and nose." Some months later, Hughes wrote of his children to his friend, Leonard Baskin: "I had a third, a little marvel, but she died with her mother." To Celia Chaikin, Assia's sister, he wrote: "Little Shura was the most wonderful little girl, full of fire. And really beautiful."

Over the next twenty years, Assia's life seemed to have been forgotten in Hughes's poetry. Then, in 1990, Hughes's *Capriccio* appeared, in an extremely limited edition. The book was designed to be rare, almost as if Hughes did not want to share his memories of Assia with his readers.

There is evidence in the *Letters of Ted Hughes*, edited by Christopher Reid, that Ted Hughes blamed himself for the deaths of Assia and Shura. In a letter to Assia's sister, Celia Chaikin, he wrote: "Assia was my true wife, and the best friend I ever had."

The Death of A.G.

Half an hour ago...
My crying stopped...
I can't understand your death in London
In the mist
As I can't understand
My life, here, in the bright light.

– Yehuda Amichai, from

Songs of Jerusalem and Myself, NY, Harper & Row, 1973

The Lost Poems of Ted Hughes

Capriccio, Ted Hughes's series of twenty poems about his relationship with Assia Gutmann Wevill, was first produced in 1990 as a luxurious leather-covered volume, with grotesque illustrations by Leonard Baskin. At approximately US$4000 a copy, and printed on hand-made paper, this small sequence of poems was designed to be rare. The publisher was Gehenna Press. Perhaps significantly in this case, 'Gehenna' is the Hebrew word for 'Hell'.

In the many biographies, reviews, and scholarly works on Ted Hughes and his poetry, the sequence *Capriccio* barely gets a mention. It is seen as a minor work compared to such better-known collections as *The Hawk in the Rain*, *Lupercal*, *Gaudette*, *Birthday Letters* or *Crow*. Not until 2003 was *Capriccio* published again in its entirety, in *The Collected Poems of Ted Hughes*, edited by Paul Keegan. Thus, the *Capriccio* sequence was virtually lost to the public for many years.

Why did Hughes wait thirty years to publish *Capriccio*? Why did he tell Negev and Koren that 'these poems were perhaps not the ones I should have written'? Was this work an apologia for Hughes's role in the death of Assia and their daughter Shura? Was it intended to show destiny as the culprit? There is considerable dissension among literary critics on this question.

Some critics see the tenor of *Capriccio* as bitter and accusatory towards Assia Gutmann Wevill, the woman who came between Ted Hughes and Sylvia Plath. In *The Death and Life of Sylvia Plath*, Ronald Hayman describes these poems as 'a relentless assault' on Assia, who, he writes, was 'harshly anatomised' by Hughes in *Capriccio*. Throughout the sequence, Hughes enters a plea of 'not guilty', seeming to exonerate himself from the responsibility of three deaths.[1]

Other biographers and reviewers interpret the *Capriccio* poems differently, that is, as a recognition of Assia's connection to the Holocaust, which she narrowly escaped as a child. Assia is portrayed as the victim of historical and political circumstances. Hughes writes as if her death was predestined, blaming her for 'consciously burning herself on Sylvia's funeral pyre' and disassociating himself from Assia's suicide. He describes it in *The Locket* as a *fait accompli*, as if Assia were doomed, unable to escape the Fate of her fellow Jews in spite of her having escaped Nazi Germany with her family as a six-year-old child in 1933.

Next to Hughes's award-winning *Birthday Letters*, the autobiographical nature of *Capriccio* went barely noticed for many years. In 1990, when the book was first published, few people knew of the affair between Ted Hughes and Assia Wevill. Five years later, eight of the twenty poems were reprinted in *New Selected Poems, 1957-1994*; yet there was still no revelation that Assia was the woman addressed in *Capriccio*. Hughes himself wrote in a letter to Seamus Heaney in 1998, that his poems about Assia were 'written very differently' to those about Sylvia. Indeed, Hughes told Assia's biographers, Eilat Negev and Yehuda Koren, that he felt the poems were so obscure, most people wouldn't realise he'd 'given his secret away'.[2]

Diane Middlebrook, in *Her Husband: Hughes and Plath, A Marriage*, devotes a whole chapter to Hughes's *Birthday Letters*, yet she gives only a few lines to *Capriccio*.[3] Referring to Hughes's theme of the power of destiny, 'this [destiny] is the idea signified in the unsettling title, *Capriccio*, that Hughes gave to the book [of poems] he addressed to Assia Wevill.' In the *Capriccio* sequence, reminders of Fate in all its capriciousness combine with horrific images of mass murder, suicide, and infanticide.

The title *Capriccio* has several interpretations. Hughes's version of the word comes from seventeenth century Italian, and is made up of '*capo*' (meaning 'head') and '*riccio*, (meaning 'hedgehog'). Hence, '*capo-riccio*' means hedgehog-headed, and describes a head with the hair standing on end. Indeed, the original illustrations by Baskin foreshadow shock or horror. The word also indicates caprice or whim, from the Latin '*capra*' – the goat.

'None of these definitions of the title *Capriccio* is appropriate,' writes Ann Skea, 'either for Ted's opening poem [*Capriccios*] or for the whole sequence, both of which are carefully structured, and serious in mood and theme.'[4] Overall, the title of Hughes's *Capriccio* suggests unmotivated, purposeless acts, as well as horror, and helplessness in the face of destiny. The basic idea throughout the sequence is that no-one is free to deviate from the script Fate has written. *Capriccio*, like *Birthday Letters*, is Hughes's defence against the accusations that he was responsible for the deaths of three victims of Fate: Sylvia Plath, Assia Wevill, and Shura Hughes Wevill.

Nathaniel Tarn, a close friend of Assia and David Wevill, writes in his diary: 'It is not true that Assia took Hughes from Sylvia. [People] pushed the guilt onto Assia.' He gives a first-hand account of this mysterious woman, describing her as 'a peasant, very unsure of herself. She seems fantastically isolated, always on the outside, and inadequate to cope.'[5]

Critics have detected a strain of anti-Semitism from Hughes towards Assia; Ronald Hayman writes that *Shibboleth* and several other poems in *Capriccio* display considerable revulsion against her Jewishness. 'Her Jewishness is made to seem like an avoidable error. 'However, Hughes's fascination with ancient Jewish texts, and his biting contempt for the bigots at the party, give the lie to accusations of anti-Semitism. Indeed, his closing line in *Shibboleth*, 'lick of the tar-brush?' is a sneer at the prejudice he detects in England's upper classes. [6]The exotic stranger at the party, whom Hughes describes in a letter (and in the poem *Shibboleth*) is clearly Assia, although Hughes does not name her.

He writes that the 'stranger' had no defenses against the veiled bigotry, 'being a jew [sic] born in Hitler's Germany.'[7] Assia was a displaced person, having been born in a country which was shortly afterwards at war with Britain. In the common English parlance of the time, she came from the 'other side,' although the polished British accent she had acquired since leaving Germany disguised this. Hence the veiled hostility by the English upper classes towards her, described by Hughes in *Shibboleth*.

In a letter to his translators written in November 1997, Hughes refers to the 'fringe-aristocracy' guests, who were disturbed by a very beautiful foreigner who spoke 'an elocutioner's English more lofty than the élite English who sat around her'. The other guests at the English country house tended to affect 'violently racist and often quite anti-Semitic attitudes', Hughes writes, thus disassociating himself from their sentiments. His words certainly don't sound like one who is himself anti-Semitic and racist; rather, they express his disgust at those very attitudes evinced by his countrymen. In this letter by Hughes, we detect far more compassion and affection for Assia than is shown in any of the more vituperative poems of the *Capriccio* sequence, such as *The Locket*, and *The Mythographers*.

There is little mention in *Capriccio* of Hughes's own destructive influences. Hughes appears to argue that he's biologically predetermined to be Assia's prey, and that the winds of Fate brought them together (*The fate she carried sniffed us out*).[8] The fact that it was he who pursued her, and persuaded her to leave her husband, David Wevill, as evidenced in the *Letters*, somewhat weakens his case for attributing the relationship, and its tragic outcome, to Fate.

Some take a kinder view of Hughes's motives in writing the *Capriccio poems*. Elaine Feinstein writes that 'In [Hughes's] memory, her beauty has not diminished, nor has she lost the power to arouse his desire.' 'Her saliva: instant amnesia', Hughes writes in *The Mythographers*. In his recently published *Letters*, he wrote: 'I've concentrated all my life now on these two children & on what you and I might do… and if now you stay with David I don't know what I shall do.' Unlike his other letters to Assia, this one is actually signed: '*Ted.*'

Feinstein writes that in *Capriccio*, Hughes still remembers Assia's beauty, and her power to arouse his desire, as in *The Locket*: 'Your beauty, a folktale wager/ was a quarter-century posthumous.' There is further evidence that Hughes loved Assia in his letters: 'Assia was my true wife and the best friend I ever had,' he wrote to Assia's sister, Celia Chaikin, after the two tragic deaths of 1969.

In writing the *Capriccio* sequence, Hughes called on his vast knowledge of mythology, in particular the ancient Hebrew texts of the Kabbalah. The incorporation of these ancient myths throughout these poems could be seen as a distancing strategy, making them less personal, and also less confessional, than *Birthday Letters*.

Ann Skea describes *Capriccio* as the first stage of Ted Hughes's journey through the Kabbalah. Notes found in Ted Hughes's note-book in the British Library summarise the story of a Jewish Talmudist, Rabbah bar Hannah, who set down his life story of perilous adventures, etching them onto a rock. Throughout *Capriccio*, Hughes references the thirteenth century Kabbalistic text, the *Zohar*, particularly in such poems as *Shibboleth* and *The Mythographers*.

Carol Bere, in her article *Complicated with Old Ghosts* (a line taken from Hughes's letter to Celia Chaikin) calls *Capriccio* 'a mosaic of ancient myths and historical events'.[9] Bere describes these poems as a re-working of myths, a device which serves to distance the writer from emotional involvement, and perhaps allows a way for Hughes to come to terms with his affair with Assia. In keeping with Hughes's reluctance to name Assia in his letters, this interpretation suggests either that he felt some shame about the relationship, or that, even after all those years, he needed to keep their affair a secret.

In his article *Sorrow in a Black Coat*, Jonathon Bate describes Hughes as a man torn between confessional biography, and one who draws on ancient texts to create characters of mythic power. Bate calls *Capriccio* 'the short book of dark poems inspired by Assia Wevill.' He describes the poem *Opus 131 as* a 'bitter little poem...pronouncing on the unimportance of the menopause' and typical of the tenor of *Capriccio*. [10]

Whether or not Ted and Assia were the pawns of capricious gods, as Hughes suggests in these poems, the fact is that he and Assia did fall passionately in love, even though that love is often portrayed as a nightmare. Ted reveals, in his letter to Assia's sister, that he had argued with Assia in their last phone call on the day she died, and that he wished he could have given her more assurance. 'If I had only moved, only given her hope in a more emphatic way', he writes in his *Letters*, clearly blaming himself for the tragedy.

The poems in *Capriccio* are a cleverly constructed sequence, in which religious and symbolic imagery serve to distance Ted Hughes from painful memories of the past. Intense and mordant as they may be, the poems are also love songs hiding behind mythological metaphors. Readers are encouraged to access the twenty poems of the *Capriccio* sequence, and to decide for themselves whether they are malicious or apologetic, accusatory or defensive.

At the time of the deaths of Assia and Shura, Hughes was writing *Crow*, a major work, which he had frequently discussed with Assia. Indeed, he penned the final verses on the train leaving Manchester, on their last trip to search for a house where they could live together. After their deaths, Hughes found himself unable to continue work on *Crow*. The tragedy had effectively blocked Hughes's creative output. He wrote to his friends that all his writing had ceased over the next two years. When *Crow* was finally published in late 1970, the dedication reads: 'In memory of Assia and Shura.'

Capriccio can be seen as a eulogy to Assia's memory. In these poems Hughes displays a deep understanding of Assia's fractured background. By portraying her as the mythical force, Lilith, the dark side of the feminine in the Kabbalah, he is trying to come to terms with the relationship between himself and the woman he both loved and feared.

❖

1   Hayman, Ronald, *The Death and Life of Sylvia Plath* 2nd ed. Sutton, UK,   2003.

2   Yehuda Koren and Eilat Negev, *Lover of Unreason,* NY, Carroll & Graf,   2007.

3   Middlebrook, Diane, *Her Husband: Hughes and Plath, A Marriage,* Little, Brown, 2004.

4   Ann Skea, *Capriccio: The Path of the Sword,* in *Ted Hughes: Alternative   Horizons,* Moulin, J. (Ed.), Routledge, London, 2004.

5. Tarn, Nathaniel, *Collected Papers*, Courtesy of the Department of Special Collections, Stanford University Libraries.

6   *Ted Hughes, Collected Poems*, ed. edited by Paul Keegan, Faber and Faber,   2003.

7   *Letters of Ted Hughes*, selected and edited by Christopher Reid, NY, Farrar Strauss and Giroux, 2007.

8   Ted Hughes, *Dreamers*, from his *Birthday Letters*, Faber and Faber, 1998.

9   Carol Bere, *Complicated with old Ghosts* in *Ted Hughes: Alternative Horizons*, Moulin, J. (Ed.), Routledge, London, 2004.

10 Jonathon Bate, *Sorrow in a Black Coat,* Times Literary Supplement, February 7, 2014.

Appendix II

The Capriccio poems by Ted Hughes as they appear in *Collected poems of Ted Hughes*, edited by Paul Keegan, 2003

Capriccios

The Locket

The Mythographers

Systole Diastole

Descent

Folktale

Fanaticism

Snow

The Other

Possession

The Coat

Smell of Burning

The Pit and the Stones

Shibboleth

The Roof

The Error

Opus 131

Familiar

Flame

Chlorophyll

BIBLIOGRAPHY

The following sources were used in the development of this book, and may be of interest to the reader:

ALEXANDER, Paul, *Ariel Ascending: Writings About Sylvia Plath*, NY, Harper & Row, 1985.

ALEXANDER, Paul, *Rough Magic*, 2nd ed. NY, Da Capo, 1999.

ALVAREZ, Alfred, *The Savage God: a Study in Suicide*, London, Weidenfeld & Nicolson, 1971.

ALVAREZ, Alfred, *Where Did It All Go Right?* London, Bloomsbury, 1999.

AMICHAI, Yehuda, *Selected Poems, trans. Assia Wevill*, London, Faber and Faber, 1971.

AMICHAI, Yehuda, So*ngs of Jerusalem and Myself,* NY, Harper & Row, 1973.

BATE, Jonathan, *Ted Hughes: The Unauthorised Life*, London, Fourth Estate, 2015.

BECKER, Jillian, *Giving Up: The Last Days of Sylvia Plath*, London, Ferrington, 2002.

BERE, Carol, *Complicated with Old Ghosts: The Assia Poems*, in *Alternative Horizons*, ed. Jenny Moulin, Routledge, 2004.

BRAIN, Tracey,   *The Other Sylvia Plath*, NY, Longman, 2001.

BUTSCHER, Edward, *Sylvia Plath: Method and Madness*, 2nd ed., Tucson, Schaffner Press, 2003.

BUNDTZEN, Lynda K, *The Other Ariel*, Amherst, Uni of Massachusetts Press, 2001.

FAAS, Ekbert, *Ted Hughes: The Unaccommodated Universe*, Santa Barbara, Black Sparrow, 1980.

FEINSTEIN, Elaine, *Ted Hughes: The Life of a Poet*, London, Weidenfeld & Nicolson, 2001.

HAMMERMESH, Mira, T*he River of Angry Dogs – A Memoir*, Pluto Press, 2004.

HAYMAN, Ronald, *The Death and Life of Sylvia Plath*, NY, Sutton Publishing, 2003.

HUGHES, Ted, *Birthday Letters*, London, Faber and Faber, 1998.

HUGHES, Ted, *Capriccio*, London, Gehenna Press, 1990.

HUGHES, Ted, *Collected Poems*, ed. Paul Keegan, London, Faber and Faber, 2003.

KOREN, Yehuda & NEGEV, Eilat, *Lover of Unreason: Assia Wevill, Sylvia Plath's Rival and Ted Hughes's Doomed Love*, NY, Carrol & Graf, 2006.

KROLL, Judith,   *Chapters in a Mythology: The Poetry of Sylvia Plath*, NY, Harper Colophon, 1976.

MALCOLM, Janet, *The Silent Woman: Sylvia Plath and Ted Hughes*, Knopf, 1994.

MIDDLEBROOK, Diane, *Her Husband: Hughes and Plath, a Marriage*, London, Little, Brown, 2003.

MORGAN, Robyn, *Monster*, Random House, 1970.

MOSES, Kate, *Wintering: A Novel of Sylvia Plath*, NY, St Martin's, 2003.

MURPHY, Richard, *The Kick, a Memoir*, London, Granta Books, 2002.

MYERS, Lucas, *Crows Steered, Bergs Appeared*, Sewanee, Tennessee, Proctor's Hall Press, 2001.

NEGEV, Eilat, *Haunted by the Ghosts of Love*, The Guardian, April 10, 1999.

NEWMAN, Charles, *The Art of Sylvia Plath: A Symposium*, Bloomington, Indiana University Press, 1971.

PERLOFF, Marjone, *The Two Ariels: The (Re)making of the Sylvia Plath Canon*, American Poetry Review, Nov-Dec 1984.

PLATH, Sylvia, *Ariel, The Restored Edition*, London, Faber and Faber, 2004.

PLATH, Sylvia, Collected Poems, London, Faber and Faber, 1981.

PLATH, Sylvia, *Letters of Sylvia Plath Volume II, 1956 – 1963*, ed. Peter K. Steinberg and Karen V. Kulkil. London, Faber & Faber, 2018.

PLATH, Aurelia (ed.), *Sylvia Plath's Letters Home*, London, Faber and Faber, 1975.

PORTER, Max, *Grief is the Thing with Feathers*, London, Faber and Faber, 2016.

PORTER, Peter, *Ted Hughes and Sylvia Plath: A Bystander's Recollections*, Australian Book Review, August 2001.

REID, Christopher, ed. *The Letters of Ted Hughes*, NY, Farrar, Straus and Giroux, 2008.

ROLLYSON, Carl, *American Isis: The Life and Art of Sylvia Plath*, NY, Picador, 2013.

ROSE, Jacqueline, *The Haunting of Sylvia Plath*, London, Virago Press, 1991.

ROSE, Jacqueline, *This is Not a Biography*, London Review of Books 24, no. 16, August 22, 2002.

SAGAR, Keith, *The Art of Ted Hughes*, Cambridge, CUP, 1975.

SEXTON, Anne, *The Barfly Ought to Sing*, in *The Art of Sylvia Plath: A Symposium*. ed. Charles Newman, Bloomington, Indiana University Press, 1971.

SIGMUND, Elizabeth, and CROWTHER, Gail, *Sylvia in Devon: A Year's Turning*, London, Fonthill Media, 2014.

SKEA, Anne, *Ted Hughes: The Poetic Quest*, Armidale, NSW, UNE Press, 1994,

THE TED HUGHES ARCHIVE, *Various papers*, London, The British Library, Dept of Manuscripts.

STEINER, Nancy Hunter, *A Closer Look at Ariel: A Memory of Sylvia Plath*. NY, Popular Library, 1973.

SONNENBERG, Ben, *Lost Property: Memoirs & Confessions of a Bad Boy*, NY, Summit Books, 1991.

STEVENSON, Anne, *Bitter Fame: A Life of Sylvia Plath*, Boston, Houghton & Mifflin, 1989.

TARN, Nathaniel, *Selected Poems 1950-2000*, Middletown, Wesleyan University Press, 2002.

TARN, Nathaniel, *Papers, 1939 -2014*, Stanford University, Green Library, 2014.

TENNANT, Emma, *Burnt Diaries*, Edinburgh, Canongate Books, 1999.

TENNANT, Emma, *Sylvia and Ted, A Novel*, NY, Henry Holt, 2001.

VAN DYNE, Susan R., *Revising Life: Sylvia Plath's Ariel Poems*, Chapel Hill, University of California Press, 1993.

WAGNER, Erica, *Ariel's Gift*, London, Faber and Faber, 2000.

WAGNER-MARTIN, Linda, *Sylvia Plath: A Biography*, NY Simon & Schuster, 1987.

WALKER, Ian, *Poetic Justice*, Adelaide SA, The Advertiser, May 1987.

WELDON, Fay, *Down Among the Women*, London, Head of Zeus, 2014.

WEVILL, David, *Birth of a Shark*, Toronto, Macmillan, 1964.

WEVILL, David, *To Build My Shadow a Fire*, Missouri, Truman State University Press, 2010.

WURTZEL, Elizabeth, *Bitch: In Praise of Difficult Women*, NY, Rando House, 2012.

ZORITTE-MEGGED, Eda, *Last Game*, (playscript). trans. Assia Wevill, London, Purcell Room, 1970.

ACKNOWLEDGEMENTS

After a long gestation and a protracted labour, 'Capriccio' is finally delivered to you by Cilento Publishing. My heartfelt thanks go to Leone Sperling, fellow writer and supreme editor, Evan Shapiro, and all at Cilento Publishing for their patience, understanding, and skill.

Special appreciation is due to Eilat Negev and Yehuda Koren, authors of 'Lover of Unreason', a biography of Assia Wevill. Their well-researched book became my bible for its sensitive portrayal of a woman who would otherwise be written out of history.

I would also like to thank the Randwick Writers Group for their constant support and encouragement, the Waverley Writers Group, and the former Darwin Authors Group for critiqueing early chapters. I appreciate Professor Mark Onslow's assistance with the technical aspects of writing this novel. Thanks also to Dr Catherine Heath for her structural edit of the first version of 'Capriccio'. To Angela Bowne, Barrister, my appreciation for her legal advice regarding my disclaimer, and copyright issues.

Many texts contributed to my novel, in particular 'The Collected Poems of Ted Hughes', 'Birthday Letters' by Ted Hughes, 'The Letters of Ted Hughes' by Christopher Reid, 'Collected Poems of Sylvia Plath', 'Colossus' by Sylvia Plath, 'Ariel: the Restored Edition', by Frieda Hughes, 'Burnt Diaries', by Emma Tennant, 'Giving Up' by Jillian Becker, 'Wintering' by Kate Moses, and 'The Early Poems of Yehuda Amichai' translated by Harold Schimmel, Ted Hughes and Assia Gutmann. Other texts which fed my imagination are too numerous to mention here. I am grateful to the British Library in London for allowing me access to the unpublished manuscripts of Ted Hughes.

Heartfelt thanks to my friend and mentor, Thomas Keneally, for his kindness and generosity. 'Capriccio' would not have reached completion without his genuine interest and constant encouragement.

Thanks to Justine Davis for a final proofread, to Anna Davis and David Steinberg for their help with cover design, and to Bella Davis for the photography

To my early readers, Kit Edwards, Richard Davis, Anne Skyvington, Penelope Nelson and Leone Sperling, goes my appreciation for their valuable feedback. The 'Capriccio' they reviewed was a very different volume from the one you hold in your hands today. In the present version, I have removed all quotations from Hughes's poetry, and changed names and places, which would too closely identify the protagonists of this tale.

I would like to thank Celia Chaikin for her permission to quote 'Winter's End, Hertfordshire' by Assia Gutmann Wevill.

The lyrics for *Wiegenlied: Guten Abend, Gute Nacht*, also known as "Brahm's Lullaby" quoted several times in this novel, come from a book of German folk poems, *Des Knaben Wunderhorn* (1805).

To my children, Justine, Joshua and Anna: you will always have my love and admiration. I hope to make you three as proud of me, as I have always been of you. Finally to Kit, my long-suffering spouse, I give my love and appreciation. You have been my 'doula' and protector during this long and often painful labour. Few would have lasted the distance.

❖

AUTHOR PROFILE

Dina Davis decided to be an author at the age of eight. Since then she has been a 'closet writer', secretly filling journals with stories, poems, memories and dreams. Dina is a member of the Northern Territory Writers' Centre, Writing NSW and the Australian Society of Authors.

In 2015 Dina was shortlisted for the NT Literary Awards with her essay 'Capriccio: the Lost Poems of Ted Hughes'. In 2018 she was a finalist for the fiction award with her short story, 'Edge'.

Dina lives in the Top End of Australia and the Eastern seaboard of New South Wales. When not writing, she practices yoga and attends Film Festivals. She holds an MA in English and Linguistics from the University of Sydney.

More about this author can be found on her Blog, Dina Davis on *Writing Matters* at www.dinadavis2015.wordpress.com or on her website www.capricciothenovel.com